WICKED NIGHTS

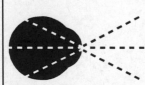

This Large Print Book carries the
Seal of Approval of N.A.V.H.

WICKED NIGHTS

GENA SHOWALTER

THORNDIKE PRESS

A part of Gale, Cengage Learning

GALE
CENGAGE Learning·

Detroit • New York • San Francisco • New Haven, Conn • Waterville, Maine • London

GALE
CENGAGE Learning®

Thorndike Press® Large Print Romance.
The text of this Large Print edition is unabridged.
Other aspects of the book may vary from the original edition.
Set in 16 pt. Plantin.

LIBRARY OF CONGRESS CATALOGING-IN-PUBLICATION DATA

Showalter, Gena.
    Wicked nights : angels of the dark / by Gena Showalter. — Large print ed.
        p. cm. — (Thorndike Press large print romance) (Angels of the Dark series ; #1)
    ISBN 978-1-4104-5035-7 (hardcover) — ISBN 1-4104-5035-X (hardcover)
    1. Large type books. I. Title.
PS3619.H77W53 2012
813'.6—dc23   2012018210

Published in 2012 by arrangement with Harlequin Books S.A.

Printed in the United States of America
1 2 3 4 5 6 7 16 15 14 13 12

To Jill Monroe,
for encouraging phone calls
and emails, and the laughs!
(And I want it forever noted
that you are listed first.)

To Sheila Fields and Betty Sanders,
for the friendship, the brainstorming,
and the laughs!

To Joyce and Emmett Harrison,
Leigh Heldermon, and Sony Harrison,
for the support, the love,
and the laughs! (Yes, I'm
big on laughs.)

To Mickey Dowling and Anita Baldwin,
fantastic ladies I adore!

To Kresley Cole and Beth Kendrick —
a thousand thank-yous, ladies.

Actually that's not enough.
A million thank-yous, ladies!

And to Kathleen Oudit
and Tara Scarcello,
for seriously knocking this
one out of the park!
So gorgeous!

PROLOGUE

The morning of her eighteenth birthday, Annabelle Miller woke from the most amazing dream feeling as if her eyes had been ripped out, dipped in acid and shoved back into their sockets. She became aware of the sensation gradually, her mind still fogged from sleep. When full awareness finally struck, her entire body tensed and bowed, a scream ripping free of her throat.

She pried her swollen eyelids apart, but . . . there was no dawning light. Only darkness greeted her.

The pain spread, riding the too-swift tides in her veins and threatening to burst through her skin. She rubbed at her face, even clawed, hoping to remove whatever was causing the problem, but there was nothing out of the ordinary. No bumps, no scratches. No . . . wait. There *was* something. A warm liquid now coated her hands.

Blood?

Another scream left her, followed by another and another, each like a serrated piece of glass scraping her throat raw. In seconds, panic chewed her up and spit her out. She was blind, bleeding — and dying?

The whine of hinges, the clack of high heels against the hardwood floor. "Annabelle? Are you all right?" A pause, then a hiss of breath. "Oh, baby, your eyes. What happened to your eyes? Rick! Rick! Hurry!"

A curse was followed by the pound of hard, fast footsteps. A second later, a horrified gasp filled her bedroom. "What happened to her face?" her father bellowed.

"I don't know, I don't know. She was like this when I came in."

"Annabelle, sweetheart." Her dad, now so tender and concerned. "Can you hear me? Can you tell me what happened to you?"

Annabelle tried to speak — *Daddy, help me, please, help me* — but the words became diamond hard and too jagged to swallow. And oh, dear heaven, the burn migrated to her chest, flames sparking every time her heart beat.

Strong arms slid under her, one at her shoulders, the other at her knees, and lifted her. The movement, temperate though it was, jostled her, magnifying the pain and she moaned.

8

"I've got you, sweetheart," her dad assured her. "We'll get you to the hospital and everything will be okay. I promise."

The sharpest edges of her panic ebbed. How could she not believe him? He'd never made a promise he couldn't keep, and if he thought everything would be okay, everything would be okay.

Her dad carried her to the SUV in the garage and laid her across the backseat as her mother's sobs echoed. Her dad didn't bother with a buckle, just shut the door and sealed Annabelle inside. She expected his door to open next, then her mom's. She expected her parents to climb inside and drive her to the hospital, as promised, but . . . nothing.

Annabelle waited . . . and waited . . . seconds ticking by with excruciating slowness, the raggedness of her inhalations becoming laced with the taint of rotten eggs, fetid and sharp enough to nip at her nostrils. She cringed, confused and frightened by the change in the air.

"Daddy?" she said. Her ears twitched as she listened intently for his reply, but all she heard was . . .

Muffled voices through the glass.

The shrill grind of metal being scratched.

Eerie laughter . . .

. . . a grunt of agony.

"Go inside, Saki," her father shouted in a terrified tone Annabelle had never before heard him use. "Now!"

Saki, her now-shrieking mother.

Grimacing through the pain, Annabelle managed to struggle into a sitting position. Miraculously, the unbearable blaze in her eyes at last faded. As she wiped away the blood, tiny rays of light pierced her line of vision. One second passed, two, then the light spread, colors appearing, blue here, yellow there, until she was taking in the full scope of the garage.

"I'm not blind!" she cried, but her relief was short-lived.

She spotted her father, shielding her mother against the far wall, his gaze darting this way and that but never landing on anything specific. Grisly cuts marred his cheeks, blood drip . . . dripping from each.

Shock and horror blended, becoming an unstoppable avalanche tumbling through every inch of her. What had happened to him? There was no one else in the small enclosure and —

A man materialized in front of her parents.

No, not a man, but a . . . a . . . What *was* that?

Annabelle scrambled backward, hitting

10

the other side of the car. The newcomer wasn't a man but a creature plucked from the depths of her worst nightmare. Another scream formed, this one lodging in her desiccated throat. Suddenly she couldn't breathe, could only stare in revulsion.

The . . . thing was freakishly tall, the top of its head brushing against a ceiling she couldn't reach with a stepladder. It possessed a barbarian's oversize bones and fangs she'd only ever read about in vampire novels, with skin the darkest shade of crimson and as smooth as glass. Claw-tipped fingers dripped with blood. Gnarled wings of pitted black stretched from its back, and small horns protruded along the length of its spine. A long, thin tail curled from the base, ending in a blood-soaked metal spike that clanged against the concrete floor as it swished back and forth, back and forth.

Whatever it was, she suspected it had caused her father's injuries — and it would only cause more.

Fear overcame every other emotion inside her, yet still she lurched forward, banged her fist against the window and forced her voice to work. "Leave my parents alone!"

The beast looked back at her with shockingly lovely eyes that reminded her of newly cut rubies. It flashed those razored fangs in a parody of a grin — before slashing its claws across her father's throat.

In an instant, flesh tore and blood sprayed a thin line over the car window. Her father fell . . . hit the ground . . . his hands wrapped around his weeping throat, his mouth open as he gasped for air he couldn't, wouldn't, find.

A sob left her, formed from incredulity but sharpened by rage.

Her mother shrieked, scanning the garage with wide eyes as her father had done, as if she had no idea where the threat had come from. Her hands tented over her mouth and tears tracked down her cheeks, smearing the blood already splattered there.

"D-don't hurt us," she stuttered. "Please, don't."

A forked tongue flicked out, as though tasting her fear. "I like the way you beg, female."

"Stop!" Annabelle shouted. *Have to help her, have to help her.* She wrenched open the car door and flew out, only to slip in a pool of her father's — no. No, no, no. Gagging, she fought to stay upright. "You have to stop!"

"Run, Annabelle. Run!"

More eerie laughter — before those claws

struck, silencing her mother. Her mother, who collapsed.

Shocked, Annabelle stopped fighting. She toppled to the floor, uncaring as oxygen burst from her lungs. Her mother . . . on top of her father . . . twitching . . . stilling.

"This can't be happening," she babbled. "This *isn't* happening."

"Oh, yes," the creature said in a deep, rasping voice. She caught the undertone of amusement, as if her parents' murder was nothing but a game.

Murder.

Mur. Der.

No. Not murder. She could not accept that word. They had been assaulted, but they would pull through. They had to pull through. Her heart slammed against her ribs, bile searing a path up her chest and past her larynx. "Th-the cops are on the way," she lied. Wasn't that what all the experts on all the reality shows about survival said you should do to save yourself? Claim help was on the way? "Go. Leave. You don't want to get in any more t-trouble, do y-you?"

"Hmm, I love the sound of more trouble." The monster turned, facing her fully, its grin expanding. "I'll prove it." It began to swipe . . . swipe . . . swipe at the bodies . . .

13

clothes and skin ripping, bones cracking, pulp and tissue flying.

Can't process.

Can't . . . But oh, she really could. She knew. If her parents had had any chance of survival, that chance had now withered to ash.

Get up! You let that thing *mutilate the people you love. Are you going to allow it to mutilate you, too? And what about your brother, upstairs, alone, probably asleep and unprepared for a slaughter?*

No. NO! With a roar that sprang from a soul soon to be shredded by grief, Annabelle launched herself into that massive, boxy chest and punched at that ugly face. The monster fell back, but swiftly recovered, rolling her over and pinning her down. Wings outstretched, curtaining the rest of the world so that only the two of them existed.

Still she punched and punched and punched. For some reason, the creature never tried to claw her. In fact, it batted her hands away and tried to . . . kiss her? Laughing, laughing, never stopping with the laughing, it pressed its lips against hers, blew fetid breath into her mouth and shivered with sublime pleasure.

"Stop," she cried, and it thrust its tongue

so horribly deep she gagged all over again.

When it lifted its head, it left a white-hot slime behind, the disgusting substance coating the lower half of her face. Ecstasy shone in its eyes. "Now, this is going to be fun," it said, and then it was gone, vanishing in a puff of putrid smoke.

For a long while, Annabelle felt paralyzed in mind and body. Only her emotions were on the move, and they were escalating at an alarming rate. The fear . . . the shock . . . the grief . . . each pressing against her chest, nearly suffocating her.

Do something! Finally, the flicker of a thought. *It could return at any moment.*

The realization gave her the strength to free herself from the prison. Slipping and sliding, she made her way to her parents' bodies. Bodies she could not put back together, no matter what she tried.

Though everything inside her rebelled at the thought, she had to leave them behind if she hoped to save her brother. "Brax!" she screamed. "Brax!" She tripped her way into the house and called 911. After a hasty explanation, she dropped the phone and ran upstairs, again shouting for her brother. She found him in his bedroom, sleeping peacefully.

"Brax. Wake up. You have to wake up." No

matter how hard she shook him, he merely muttered about wanting a few minutes more.

She remained with him, protecting him, until the first responders arrived. She showed them to the garage, but they could not put her parents back together, either.

The cops arrived soon afterward — and within the hour, Annabelle was blamed for the murders.

CHAPTER ONE

Four years later

"How does that make you feel, Annabelle?" The male voice lingered over the word *feel*, adding a disgusting layer of sleaze.

Keeping the other patients in the "trust circle" in her periphery, Annabelle tilted her head to the side and met the gaze of Dr. Fitzherbert, otherwise known as Fitzpervert. In his early forties, the doctor had thinning salt-and-pepper hair, dark brown eyes and perfectly tanned, though slightly lined, skin. He was on the thin side, and at five-ten, only an inch taller than she was.

Overall, he was moderately attractive. *If you ignored the blackness of his soul, of course.*

The longer she stared at him, rebelliously silent, the more his lips curled with amusement. Oh, how that grated — not that she'd ever let him know it. She would never willingly do anything to please him, but she would also never cower in his presence. Yes, he was the worst kind of monster, power hungry, selfish and unacquainted with the truth, and yes, he could hurt her. And would.

He already had.

Last night he'd drugged her. Well, he'd drugged her every day of his two-month employment at the Moffat County Institution for the Criminally Insane. But last night he had sedated her with the express purpose of stripping her, touching her in ways he shouldn't and taking pictures.

Such a pretty girl, he'd said. *Out there in the real world, a stunner like you would make me work for something as simple as a dinner date. Here, you're completely at my mercy. You're mine to do with as I please . . . and I please plenty.*

Humiliation still burned hot and deep, a fire in her blood, but she would not betray a moment of weakness. She knew better.

Over the last four years, the doctors and nurses in charge of her care had changed more times than her roommates, some of them shining stars of their profession, others simply going through the motions, doing what needed doing, while a select few were worse than the convicted criminals they were supposed to treat. The more she

18

caved, the more those employees abused her. So, she always remained on the defensive.

One thing she'd learned during her incarceration was that she could rely only on herself. Her complaints of abominable treatment went unheeded, because most higher-ups believed she deserved what she got — if they believed her at all.

"Annabelle," Fitzpervert chided. "Silence isn't to be tolerated."

Well, then. "I feel like I'm one hundred percent cured. You should probably let me go."

At least the amusement drained. He frowned with exasperation. "You know better than to answer my questions so flippantly. That doesn't help you deal with your emotions or problems. That doesn't help anyone here deal with *their* emotions or problems."

"Ah, so I'm a lot like you then." As if he cared about helping anyone but himself.

Several patients snickered. A couple merely drooled, foamy bubbles falling from babbling lips and catching on the shoulders of their gowns.

Fitzpervert's frown morphed into a scowl, the pretense of being here to help vanishing. "That smart mouth will get you into trouble."

Not a threat. A vow. *Doesn't matter,* she told herself. She lived in constant fear of creaking doors, shadows and footsteps. Of drugs and people and . . . things. Of herself. What was one more concern? Although . . . at this rate, her emotions would be the thing to finally bury her.

"I'd love to tell you how I feel, Dr. Fitzherbert," the man beside her said.

Fitzpervert ran his tongue over his teeth before switching his attention to the serial arsonist who'd torched an entire apartment building, along with the men, women and children living inside of it.

As the group discussed feelings and urges and ways to control them both, Annabelle distracted herself with a study of her surroundings. The room was as dreary as her circumstances. There were ugly yellow water stains on the paneled ceiling, the walls were a peeling gray and the floor carpeted with frayed brown shag. The uncomfortable metal chairs the occupants sat upon were the only furniture. Of course, Fitzpervert luxuriated on a special cushion.

Meanwhile, Annabelle had her hands cuffed behind her back. Considering the amount of sedatives pumping through her system, being cuffed was overkill. But hey, four weeks ago she'd brutally fought a group of her fellow patients, and two weeks ago one of her nurses, so of course she was too menacing to leave unrestrained, no matter that she'd sought only to defend herself.

For the past thirteen days, she'd been kept in the hole, a dark, padded room where deprivation of the senses slowly drove her (genuinely) insane. She had been starved for contact, and had thought any interaction would do — until Fitzpervert drugged and photographed her.

This morning, he arranged her release from solitary confinement, followed by this outing. She wasn't stupid; she knew he hoped to bribe her into accepting his mistreatment.

If Mom and Dad could see me now. . . . She bit back a sudden, choking sob. The young, sweet girl they'd loved was dead, the ghost somehow alive inside her, haunting her. At the worst times, she would remember things she had no business remembering.

Taste this, honey. It'll be the best thing you've ever eaten!

A terrible cook, her mother. Saki had enjoyed tweaking recipes to "improve" them.

Did you see that? Another touchdown for the Sooners!

A die-hard football fan, her dad. He had attended O.U. in Oklahoma for three semesters, and had never cut those ties.

She could not allow herself to think about them, about her mother and father and how wonderful they'd been . . . and . . . oh, she couldn't stop it from happening. . . . Her mother's image formed, taking center stage in her mind. She saw a fall of hair so black the strands appeared blue, much like Annabelle's own. Eyes uptilted and golden, much like Annabelle's *used* to be. Skin a rich, creamy mix of honey and cinnamon and without a single flaw. Saki Miller — once Saki Tanaka — had been born in Japan but raised in Georgetown, Colorado.

Saki's traditional parents had freaked when she and the white-as-can-be Rick Miller had fallen hopelessly in love and married. He'd come home from college on holiday, met her and moved back to be with her.

Both Annabelle and her brother were a combination of their parents' heritages. They shared their mother's hair and skin, the shape of her face, yet had their father's height and slender build.

Although Annabelle's eyes no longer belonged to either Saki or Rick.

After that horrible morning in her garage,

after her arrest for their murders, after her conviction, her lifelong sentencing to this institution for the criminally insane, she'd finally found the courage to look at herself in a mirror. What she'd seen had startled her. Eyes the color of winter ice, deep in the heart of an Arctic snowstorm, eerie and crystalline, barely blue with no hint of humanity. Worse, she could see things with these eyes, things no one should ever have to see.

And oh, no, no, no. As the trust circle yammered on, two creatures walked through the far wall, pausing to orient themselves. Heart rate spiraling, Annabelle looked at her fellow patients, expecting to see expressions of terror. No one else seemed to notice the visitors.

How could they not? One creature had the body of a horse and the torso of a man. Rather than skin, he was covered by glimmering silver . . . metal? His hooves were rust-colored and possibly some kind of metal as well, sharpened into deadly points.

His companion was shorter, with stooped shoulders weighed down by sharp, protruding horns, and legs twisted in the wrong direction. He wore a loincloth and nothing else, his chest furred, muscled and scarred.

The scent of rotten eggs filled the room,

as familiar as it was horrifying. The first flood of panic and anger burned through her, a toxic mix she could not allow to control her. It would wreck her concentration and slow her reflexes — her only weapons.

She needed weapons.

The creatures came in all shapes and sizes, all colors, both sexes — and maybe something in between — but they had one thing in common: they always came for her.

Every doctor who'd ever treated her had tried to convince her that the beings were merely figments of her imagination. Complex hallucinations, they said. Despite the wounds the creatures always left behind — wounds the doctors claimed she managed to inflict upon herself — she sometimes believed them. That didn't stop her from fighting, though. Nothing could.

Glowing red gazes at last settled on her. Both males smiled, their sharp, dripping fangs revealed.

"Mine," Horsey said.

"No. Mine!" Horns snapped.

"Only one way to settle this." Horsey licked his lips in anticipation. "The fun way."

"Fun," Horns agreed.

Fun, the code word for "beat the crap out

of Annabelle." At least they wouldn't try to rape her.

Don't you see, Miss Miller? one of the doctors had once told her. *The fact that these creatures will not rape you proves they are nothing more than hallucinations. Your mind stops them from doing something you can't handle.*

As if she could handle any of the rest. *How do you explain the injuries I receive while bound?*

We found the tools you hid in your room. Shanks, a hammer we're still trying to figure out how you got, glass shards. Shall I go on?

Yeah, but those had been for her protection, not her mutilation.

"Who goes first?" Horsey asked, drawing her out of the depressing memory.

"Me."

"No, me."

They continued to argue, but the reprieve wouldn't last long. It never did. Adrenaline surged through her, making her limbs shake. *Don't worry. You've got this.*

Though no other patients were aware of what was going on, they were all sensitive to her shift in mood. Grunts and groans erupted around her. Both men and women, young and old, writhed in their seats, wanting to run away.

The guards posted at the only exit stiffened, going on alert but unsure who was to blame.

Fitzpervert knew, pegging Annabelle with his patented king-of-the-world frown. "You look troubled, Annabelle. Why don't you tell us what's bothering you, hmm? Are you regretting your earlier outburst?"

"Screw you, Fitzpervert." Her gaze returned to her targets. They were the bigger threat. "Your turn will come."

He sucked in a breath. "You are not allowed to speak to me that way."

"You're right. Sorry. I meant, screw you, *Dr.* Fitzpervert." Unarmed did not mean helpless, she told herself, and neither did bound; today, she would prove it to the creatures *and* Fitzpervert.

"Feisty," Horsey said with a gleeful nod.

"So amusing to break," Horns cackled.

"As long as I'm the one to break her!"

And so began another round of arguing.

From the corner of her eye, she saw the good doctor motion one of the guards forward, and she knew the guy would take her jaw in an inexorable grip and shove her cheek against his stomach to hold her in place. A degrading and suggestive position that humiliated even as it cowed, preventing her from biting so that Fitzherbert could inject her with another sedative.

Have to act now. Can't wait. Not allowing herself to stop and think, she jumped up, pulling her knees to her chest, sliding her bound arms underneath her butt and over her feet. Gymnastics classes hadn't failed her. Hands now in front of her, she twisted, grabbed and folded the chair, and positioned the metal like a shield.

Perfect timing. The guard reached her.

She swung to the left, slamming her shield into his stomach. Air gushed from his mouth as he hunched over. Another swing and she nailed the side of his head, sending him to the floor in an unconscious heap.

A few patients shouted with distress, and a few others cheered her on. The droolers continued leaking. Fitzpervert rushed to the door to force the remaining guard to act as his buffer, as well as summon more guards with the single press of a button. An alarm screeched to life, tossing the already disconcerted patients into more of a frenzy.

No longer content to bicker on the sidelines, the creatures stalked toward her, slow and steady, taunting her.

"Oh, the things I'll do to you, little girl."

"Oh, how you'll scream!"

Closer . . . closer . . . almost within striking distance . . . totally within striking distance . . . She swung. Missed. The pair laughed, separated and in unison reached for her.

She used the chair to bat one set of hands away, but couldn't track both of her adversaries at the same time and the other managed to scratch her shoulder. She winced but otherwise ignored the pain, spinning around to — hit air, only air.

Laughter growing in volume, the creatures ran circles around her, constantly swinging at her.

I can handle this. When Horsey was in front of her, she rammed the top of the chair under his chin, knocking his teeth together and his brain, if he had one, into the back of his skull. At the same time, she kicked out a leg, punting Horns, who was behind her, in the stomach. Both creatures stumbled away from her, their grins finally vanishing.

"That all you got, girls?" she goaded. Two more minutes, that's all she had, and then the summoned guards would rush inside and tackle her, pinning her down, Fitzpervert and his needle taking charge. She wanted these creatures finished.

"Let's find out," Horsey hissed. He opened his mouth and roared, his awful breath somehow creating a strong, unstop-

28

pable wind that pushed the arsonist at Annabelle.

To everyone else, it probably seemed like the guy was leaping at her of his own volition, intending to restrain her. Another swing, and the chair sent him flying through Horsey's body and to his butt, as if the creature were nothing more substantial than mist. To Fire Boy, he wasn't. The creatures were only ever tangible to her and whatever she held.

Sometime during the exchange, Horns had moved beyond her periphery. Now he managed to sneak up behind her and rake his claws against her already bleeding shoulder. As she turned, he turned with her, once again raking her with those claws.

The pain . . . oh, the pain. No longer ignorable.

Stars winked in her line of vision. She heard laughter behind her, and knew Horns was there, ready to claw her again. She darted forward, out of the way, and tripped.

Horsey caught her by the forearms, preventing her from falling. He let her go — only to punch her in the face. More pain, more stars, but when he lifted his hand for a second blow, she was ready. She jerked the chair up and nailed him under the jaw, then spun so that he broke his knuckles on

29

the seat of the chair rather than her cheek-bone. His howl rent the air.

Footsteps behind her. She kicked backward, connecting with Horns. Before her leg landed, she spun and kicked out with the other, scissoring her ankles to double tap his gut. When he collapsed, wheezing for air, she flipped the chair upside down and finished him off, slamming the metal rim into his trachea.

Black blood pooled and bubbled around him, frothing and sizzling as it seared the tiled floor. Steam rose, curling through the air.

One minute to go.

Maximum damage, she thought.

Horsey called her a very rude name, his entire body shaking with his wrathful intent. He closed the distance with stomping steps and lashed out with those clublike arms. No claws, just fists. Playtime was over, she supposed. She blocked, ducked and bowed her back to ensure those meaty hammers only ever swiped the chair. All the while she punched at him with the dented metal, landing multiple blows.

"Why did you come for me?" she demanded. "Why?"

A flash of bloodstained fangs. "Just for the fun. Why else?"

Always she asked, and always she received the same reply, no matter that each of her opponents was different. The creatures came once, only once, and after raining havoc, creating chaos, they disappeared forevermore. *If* they survived.

She'd cried after her first kill — and her second and her third — despite the fact that the creatures had only ever wanted to hurt her. There was just something so terrible about taking a life, no matter the reason for doing so. Hearing the last breath rattle . . . watching the light dim in someone's eyes . . . and knowing you were responsible . . . She always thought of her parents. Somewhere along the way, her heart had hardened into a block of stone and she'd stopped crying.

The backup guards finally arrived, three hard bodies slamming into her from behind and knocking her to the ground. When she crashed, she crashed hard, cracking her already injured cheek on the tile. She experienced a sharp lance of pain as the taste of old pennies filled her mouth, coated her tongue. More of those too-bright stars winked through her vision, corrosive things that grew . . . grew . . . blinding her.

That blindness panicked her, reminding her of that terrible, fateful morning so long ago. "Let me go! I mean it!"

31

Inflexible knees dug into her bleeding shoulders, her back and her legs, and rough fingers pressed all the way to bone. "Be still."

"I said let me go!"

Horsey must have fled because the scent of rot was suddenly replaced by the scent of bacon and aftershave, warm breath caressing her cheek. She didn't allow herself to cringe, didn't allow herself to reveal her abhorrence for the doctor now looming over her.

"That's enough out of you, Annabelle," Fitzpervert said in a chiding tone.

"Never enough," she replied, forcing herself to calm on her own. Deep breath in, deep breath out. The more emotion she displayed, the more sedative he would have to use.

"Tsk, tsk. You should have played nice. I could have helped you. Sleep now," he crooned.

"Don't you dare —" Her jaw went slack a second after the expected pinch in her neck. In a blink of time, there was white lightning in her vein, spreading just as swiftly as the stars.

Though she despised this feeling of helplessness and knew Fitzpervert would be paying her a visit later, though she fought with

every bit of her remaining strength, Annabelle slipped into the waiting darkness.

CHAPTER TWO

"Look at me, Zacharel! Look how high I'm flying."

"You're doing so well, Hadrenial. I'm proud of you."

"Think I can flip without falling to the ground?"

"Of course you can. You can do anything."

A laugh as sweet as tolling bells, echoing through the sky. "But I've already fallen three times."

"Which means you now know what not to do."

"Sir? Your Great and Mighty Highness? Are you listening to me?"

The masculine voice drew Zacharel from the past and the only bright light in an otherwise dark life, jerking him straight into the present. He glanced at Thane, the self-appointed second in command of his angelic army. A promotion he had not disputed, despite the warrior's attitude. The fact was,

Thane was the best of the lot — which wasn't actually saying much.

Every angel in his army had pushed the Deity, their king, past the limit of his patience. Each had broken so many rules, skirted so many laws, it was a miracle they still had their wings . . . and an even greater miracle that Zacharel had tolerated the warriors as long as he had.

He cleared his throat. "I'm listening, yes." Now.

"My humblest apologies if I bored you before" was Thane's flippant reply.

"Accepted."

A crack of the angel's jaw as he realized Zacharel had taken no insult. "I asked if you were ready for us to attack."

"Not yet."

Thane hovered beside him, the great length of their wings outstretched but not touching. Neither of them liked to be touched. Of course, Thane always made allowances for the females he bedded, but Zacharel made no such exceptions for anyone.

"I'm eager to fight, Majesty. We all are."

"I've told you before not to call me by that title. As for your request, you will wait as ordered. All of you." To disobey was to be punished — a concept Zacharel himself was now intimately acquainted with.

It had begun a few short months ago, when he was summoned to the Deity's temple, that sacred sanctuary so few angels were privileged to visit. During that unprecedented encounter, snowflakes had begun to fall from the feathers of Zacharel's wings, a constant storm and a sign of his Deity's cold displeasure. And the Deity's words, though softly spoken, had been just as biting as the snowfall.

Apparently, Zacharel's "severe detachment from emotion" had caused him to ignore "collateral damage" during his battles with demons. On multiple occasions, the Deity had charged, Zacharel had chosen to slay his enemy at the expense of innocent human life. Of course, such behavior was "unacceptable."

He'd apologized, even though he wasn't sorry for his actions, only that he had angered the one being with the power to destroy him. In truth, he did not understand the appeal — or usefulness — of the humans. They were weak and frail, claiming all they did was for love.

Love. Zacharel sneered. As if mere mortals knew anything about unselfish, life-giving love. Not even Zacharel knew. *Hadrenial* had — but Zacharel wasn't thinking about him anymore.

His apology meant nothing, his Deity had told him. Actually, less than nothing, for his Deity could see into the dark mire of his chest, where his heart should beat with emotion — but didn't.

I should take your wings and immortality and banish you to the earth, where you will not be able to see the demons living among us. If you cannot see them, you cannot fight them as you are used to doing. If you cannot fight them, you cannot kill the humans around them. Is that what you want, Zacharel? To live among the fallen and mourn the life you once had?

No, he wanted nothing of the sort. Zacharel lived for killing demons. If he could not see and fight them, he was better off dead. Again he'd voiced his contrition.

You have apologized to the Heavenly High Council for this very crime many times in the past, Zacharel, yet you have never changed your ways. Even still, my trusted advisors have long recommended leniency. After everything you've suffered, they hoped that in time you would find your path. But time and again you've failed to do as the Council has asked, and no longer can they turn a blind eye to your transgressions. Now I must intervene, for I, too, am answerable to a higher power — and your deeds reflect poorly on me.

In that moment Zacharel had known there would be no talking his way out of his sentence. And he'd been right.

Words are so easily spoken, as you've proven, the Deity had continued, *but so rarely are they backed up with action. Now you will carry the physical expression of my unhappiness, so that you never forget this day.*

As you wish, he'd replied.

But, Zacharel . . . do not doubt that worse awaits you should you disobey me again.

He'd thanked his Deity for the chance to do better and he *had* meant it — until his very next battle. He had hurt and killed multiple humans without thought or mercy, because they had hurt and killed Ivar, one of the Deity's Elite Seven. A warrior of unimaginable strength and ability.

The fact that Zacharel's actions had been in the name of vengeance hadn't mattered — had actually harmed his cause. The Most High was to decide how to handle such a situation, and as He was the higher power Zacharel's Deity answered to, His word was law. Zacharel should have displayed patience.

The following day, the Deity had again summoned him.

He'd hoped that, despite what he'd done, he would be chosen as the next Elite, but instead he learned he had earned another punishment. "Worse," he discovered, was exactly that.

For one year, Zacharel would lead an army of angels just like him. The ones no one else wanted under their command. The rebellious ones. The tortured ones. His assignment: to teach them the respect that he himself had yet to demonstrate — for the Deity, for the sanctity of human life. And to ensure that he took his responsibility seriously, he alone would bear the consequences of his warriors' actions.

If any of his angels killed a human, *he* would suffer a whipping.

He'd already suffered eight.

At the end of the year, if Zacharel's good deeds outweighed the bad, he and all of his angels would be allowed to stay in the heavens. If the bad outweighed the good, he and all of his angels would lose their wings and their place in the sky.

Clearly, Zacharel had mused, the Deity was cleaning house. This way, he could rid the heavens of every thorn in his side in one fell swoop, and none on his Council could call him cruel or unfair, for he'd given them a year's worth of chances to redeem themselves.

So here Zacharel and his army were,

tasked with handling chores far beneath their skill level. For the most part, that meant finding a way to free demon-possessed humans, aiding those who were immorally influenced and participating in the occasional insignificant battle.

Tonight marked his army's nineteenth assignment — though only their third round of combat — and each one had ended worse than the last. No matter what he threatened, the angels seemed to enjoy disregarding his orders. They flipped him off. They cussed at him. They laughed in his face.

He did not understand them. This year was their last chance, too. They had just as much to lose. Shouldn't they seek his favor?

"Now?" Thane asked eagerly, his voice more smoke than substance. Once upon a time, his throat had been slit . . . and slit and slit until scars had become a permanent necklace.

"Not yet. I mean it."

"If you fail to sound the battle cry soon . . ."

They would act anyway.

"Does no one care that they will suffer my wrath?" he groused. He peered down at the Moffat County Institution for the Criminally Insane, which was hidden in the mountains of Colorado. The building was

40

tall and wide, with a barbed, electric fence, and armed guards walking both the parapet and grounds. Halogens shone bright light into every corner, chasing away the shadows.

What the guards couldn't see, no matter how intense their lighting, were the demon minions crawling all over the walls, desperate to slink inside.

But like the guards, the demons could not see the threat surrounding them. The twenty soldiers under Zacharel's command remained hidden. Their wings, usually white threaded with gold, were now a star-pricked onyx, a mirror of the heavens. The effortless change was made with only a single mental command. More than that, their angelic robes were now shirts and pants fitted to their muscular bodies, black and combat ready.

"Why would demons choose to overtake this place?" Zacharel asked. And they had attempted to do so for years, apparently. Other armies had been sent, but none had made any real progress. As soon as one set of minions was taken care of, a new crop would arrive.

There were only two reasons no other army had thought to find out why. One, they had not cared to aid the humans inside the building. Or two, their job had ended with the battle. Either way, Zacharel would not make the same mistake. He couldn't.

Golden hair curling innocently around a face somehow more devilish than saintly, Thane cast a wicked sapphire gaze his way. The contrast between innocent and carnal could be mesmerizing, or so Zacharel had heard. Human and immortal females alike threw themselves at Thane — who made no secret of his sexual desires when he revealed himself to those who were not supposed to know he was there. Especially since his desires skirted the edge of dangerous . . . of acceptable.

Most angels belonging to their Deity, whether they were of the warrior class or among the joy-bringers, were as immune to the passions of the flesh as Zacharel. But then, most had not been captured by a horde of demons, trapped and tortured for weeks, as Thane had been.

When you lived as long as they did, he supposed, especially when those years were spent at war, you were more likely to learn the true meaning of pain and to seek refuge in whatever pleasure you could find.

Xerxes and Bjorn, Thane's equals in terms of strength and cunning, had been trapped and tortured, as well. The three were now inseparable, the trauma and horror of the experience bonding them. Warping them — yes, that, too, as proven by their place within his army's ranks, but bonding them nonetheless.

"Evil craves the company of other evil, desperate to destroy anything worth saving," Thane said, wisdom replacing his earlier irreverence. "Perhaps someone inside summoned them."

Perhaps. If so, the battle had just become a dilemma. The summoning of demons was strictly forbidden, a crime punishable only through death. Death that would not be collateral damage but intentional, and yet, Zacharel was not sure how the Deity would react to such a slaying.

Humans, he thought, shaking his head with disgust. Nothing but trouble. They had no idea the dark power they danced with. A power that might seem exciting at first, but one that would merely eat away at their humanity.

"None of the demons have actually entered the building," he said. "I'm curious as to why."

Thane's head tilted to the side, his study of the demons intensifying. "I hadn't noticed, but I see now that you are correct. *Majesty.*"

No reaction. "Capture one of the demons, and cart it to my cloud for questioning."

"That will be my pleasure." As much as Thane enjoyed debauching his lovers, he enjoyed torturing demons more. "Anything else, Lord of Us?"

No. Reaction. "Yes. On my signal, the army may attack, but I want Bjorn to bring the most feral demon he can find to the roof of the institution. Quickly." Zacharel could have — should have — spoken the orders inside the minds of his soldiers, as all commanders could do, but doing so would have invited *their* voices into *his* mind, and that was an intimacy he would not allow.

A smile of relish flashed, straight white teeth revealed. "Consider it done."

Before Thane could whisk himself away, Zacharel added, "I'm sure I don't need to remind you that no humans are to be harmed during the battle. If you must forgo a demon kill to save a human life, do so. Make sure the others know."

At first, he hadn't minded when his men opted to destroy a human to get to a demon. After his third whipping for a crime he had not committed himself, he'd begun to mind.

One beat of silence, two. Then, "Yes, of course, Leader of the Supremely Unworthy." With that parting shot, Thane dis-

44

appeared in a burst of motion to alert the others even now circling the building.

A scant minute later, swords of fire appeared in every angel's hand, the flames more intense, far purer, than any found in hell. Menacing shards of amber light licked over determined expressions and hard-won muscle . . . and those lights began to arc down in swift succession, screams of pain — and final gasps of breath — soon echoing. Scaled, gnarled and now-headless bodies rained from the walls.

So much for waiting for Zacharel's signal. That would have to be dealt with later.

Though he would have enjoyed slaying the demons alongside his men, he waited, for he sought bigger prey this night. A path eventually cleared, and he glided down . . . down . . . and landed gracefully on the flat edge of the roof. He tucked his wings into his back.

"The feral demon, as requested, Magnificent King," a familiar voice said from beside him. "Quickly."

A huge beast thumped lifelessly at Zacharel's feet. Poison beaded at the end of its claws. Large horns protruded from its shoulders, and patches of fur and scales formed a double helix pattern on its legs.

Slight problem. The demon had no head.

"This demon is deceased," he said.

Only the barest of pauses before Bjorn responded, "Thane relayed your order verbatim. In this, you were not wise enough to specify a preference."

"True." He absolutely should have known better.

Bjorn, hovering at the side of the building, said, "Shall I bring you another or do you think to reprimand me for your mistake, Glorious King?" The words held a bitter edge.

Bjorn was a brute of a man with bronzed skin veined in gold and glittering, multi-hued eyes of purple, pink, blue and green. A startling contrast.

Soon after his rescue from the demons' brutal clutches — and his subsequent rampage of death through the heavens, where none had been safe from his indiscriminate wrath — the Heavenly High Council had ruled Bjorn unstable and unfit for duty. Falling was too lenient a punishment, they'd said, and so he had been sentenced to a true death, his spirit, the power that fueled his life, his soul, the embodiment of his emotions, and his physical body to be wiped from existence entirely.

Thane and Xerxes had protested, demanding the warrior be reinstated and promising they would be responsible were any other problems to arise. They'd also vowed to ensure they died the true death as well if separated from their friend.

The Council had reluctantly given in. With the amount of demon activity plaguing the world, warriors of their caliber were in high demand. Still, Zacharel doubted such a threat would ever work again.

"There will be no reprimand," he said, and Bjorn blinked in surprise.

Zacharel's gaze caught on the serpe demon even then slithering over the railing in an attempt to escape notice. Serpes possessed the head and torso of a human but the lower body of a snake, and were more temperamental than the two combined.

Leaning over, Zacharel grabbed the thick, rattling tail and jerked. The serpe twisted, fangs bared, arms raised to attack whoever had dared stop him. Zacharel maintained a tight hold, winding its length along his forearm while using his free hand to latch on to the demon's neck. He squeezed.

Crimson eyes widened with alarm as talon-tipped fingers slashed at him. "Not Zacharel, anyone but Zacharel! I go back, I go back, I ssswear."

Finally, respect for his authority.

"This one will do," he told Bjorn. "You

may continue with your duties."

The angel inclined his head even as his eyes glazed with bafflement. But he said nothing more, instead springing back into battle.

"Pleassse! I go!"

The demons might have been unable to enter the building for whatever reason, but Zacharel had no such problem. He commanded his body, as well as the serpe's, to mist, and the two of them sank through the stone. Seconds later, Zacharel stood on the building's bottom floor.

Forgetting who held him, the serpe sighed with bliss and reached up toward the ceiling. "Time for my fun . . ."

Zacharel tossed the demon across the lobby's freshly polished floor. Multiple security guards patrolled the area and several human females manned the desk, but not a single one noticed the intruders in their midst.

Up the walls the serpe slinked, ghosting through the ceiling and disappearing from view. Following him proved easy. Zacharel moved from floor to floor, a mere step behind. Finally the serpe ceased climbing, shooting into one of the rooms on level fourteen.

Inside, the walls were covered with black

padding. There were no windows. A single vent in the ceiling provided the only breeze, and a frigid one at that. The room was barren except for one lone piece of furniture. A hospital gurney, with . . . a young woman strapped to the top.

Every muscle in his body knotted. For a moment, the past threatened to rise up and swallow him whole.

Kill me, Zacharel. You have to kill me. Please.

Long ago he'd built a dam to hold back his memories of the past, a barrier he'd desperately needed. Would always need, it seemed. He refortified that dam now, blanking his mind of anything but the present.

At first glance, the woman appeared to be asleep. But then her head lolled to the side, her attention seemingly ensnared by the demon she shouldn't be able to see. Horror, anger and fear suddenly pulsed from her.

Had she, a mere human, somehow sensed the serpe?

Zacharel considered her. She wore a paper-thin gown, dirty and torn, her slender frame shivering. Long hair tangled around a delicate face, the strands so black they appeared to be a breathtaking midnight-blue. Dark circles marred the fragile skin under her eyes, and her cheeks were more hollowed than they should have been, not to mention terribly bruised and scratched. Her lips were red, chapped. Her eyes were ice-blue, and in their depths he saw a never-ending storm of pain no human was equipped to bear.

No, those eyes did not belong to a mortal, he realized. They belonged to a demon's consort.

Somewhere out there was a demon high lord — the most dangerous of all hell's fiends — who considered this human his exclusive property. His to possess, his to torture . . . his to enjoy in whatever fashion he desired. The demon had poisoned her eyes, marking her, ensuring she could see into the spiritual world that coexisted alongside the mortal one. *His* world. In doing so, he had brought her to the attention of other demons, as well.

She had to have been a willing participant in her marking, for humans could not be forced. Seduced, yes. Tricked, absolutely. Eager to dabble in the dark arts, beyond a doubt. But never forced.

Had the high lord grown tired of her? Was that why she was here without him? No, Zacharel decided a second later. A demon never grew tired of his human. He stuck around until the bitter, bloody end — or until the human wised up and forced him to leave.

So . . . why not kill her and try to hide his crime? Demon and mortal pairings were forbidden, the act carrying a sentence of death. The demon's *and* the human's. Not that Zacharel or any of his men would kill this one. That still was not on today's menu. There would be no collateral damage.

"Stay away from me," she said, drawing Zacharel out of his mind. Her voice was raspy, either from drugs or strain. Or was that her natural tone? "I'm a terrible enemy to have."

For someone who had agreed to bond her life to a demon's, she did not sound happy with the results. He was willing to bet she had been seduced or tricked, and now regretted it.

Humans so rarely learned until too late, yet it didn't have to be that way.

"I'll hurt you if you come any closer." She clearly possessed Japanese ancestry, yet her voice held no hint of an accent. Odd in a way, but all the more exotic because of the lack. Soft and lilting, and the perfect contrast to her bold features.

"Hurt me, female. Pleassse . . ." Tail rattling a fatal rhythm, the serpe slithered

51

around the bed. His forked tongue darted between his fangs. "That'sss what I like — before every sssnack."

The minion wanted her, not because of *her* but because creatures of the underworld loved nothing more than one-upping their brethren. Bragging rights were as valuable as gold, as was the accompanying sense of superiority. Well, that, and the thrill of ruining someone who was supposed to be under the protection of the heavens.

Tensing, the female said, "Touch me once, just once, and I'll find a way out of these restraints. I'll remove your head. I've decapitated your kind before, you know. Maybe even friends of yours, eh?"

An interesting response, going deeper than mere regret.

The brave words earned a hiss of anticipation. "You lie, you lie, you delight me asss you lie. Ssso deliciousss."

"I'm serious! If you think a little thing like shackles will stop me, you're more brain damaged than I thought. And news flash — I thought your IQ was in the single digits."

She gazed left, right, as though searching for someone to help her. While the female could see the serpe, she could not see Zacharel. That wasn't exactly a revelation — if he did not wish to be sensed, he would not be sensed; not by a demon, or a demon's consort, or even by other angels.

Curious about her reaction to him, Zacharel materialized in his natural form, at the same time creating a sword of fire from nothing but the air. His gaze never leaving the female, he slashed, decapitating the demon and ending its miserable existence. Yes, killing was that easy for him. He dismissed the flames.

"What — How —" Crystalline eyes found him and widened. Her teeth began chattering. "A-am I dreaming? The drugs . . . I have to be tripping. Or dreaming, maybe. Yes, that makes sense."

"It does not, for you are not."

"Are you sure? You look like the prince I once . . . uh, never mind."

She once . . . what? "I am positive."

"Then wh-who are you? *What* are you? How did you get in here?"

Despite her questions, she seemed to know that he was not like the creature he had just defeated. Demons did their best to evoke fear. Angels did their best to evoke a sense of calm. Or rather, they were supposed to.

"What are you?" the female asked again. "Are you here to kill me?"

Kill me, Zacharel. You have to kill me.

Please. I can't live like this anymore. It's too much, too hard. Please!

Again the past threatened to rise up and consume him. Again he blanked his mind. Though he owed the female no explanation, though she was a demon's consort and couldn't be trusted, he found himself saying, "I will not kill you. I am an angel."

As with all the Deity's angels, Zacharel's voice held an undeniable ring of truth. Typical of her kind, she flinched at its purity — but she could not doubt him.

Blinking rapidly, she said, "An angel. As in, an angel from heaven, defender of all that's good and right?"

Perhaps she *could* doubt him. Her tone had been sneering. But he found it interesting that she did not spew the same hate at him that she had spewed at the demon. As the mate of a high lord, she should despise Zacharel above all others. That she didn't . . . *Definitely tricked.*

"Well?"

"Yes, I am from the heavens, though I am probably not the race of angel you are familiar with." He stretched his wings. Snowflakes continued to fall from him. His feathers were once again pearlescent, the gold threaded between each one shimmering. He frowned when he noticed the gold was thicker than ever before.

Thousands of years had passed, and his feathers had never changed color, for such a change usually indicated that an elevation of status was in the works. For those under the Deity's charge, only the Elite Seven were blessed with wings of solid gold. Joy-bringers were characterized by wings of solid white. Warriors such as Zacharel possessed the white with mere traces of the gold. But what he had now was more than a trace.

There had to be some other explanation. Much as he'd hoped otherwise, his Deity had said nothing to him about rising to the level of the Elite. And he was hardly in a position to be considered for an advancement, anyway, when he was fighting so staunchly to keep the title he did have.

"There's more than one race?" she asked after looking him over. "Never mind. Don't take this the wrong way, but . . . you're not a nice-looking man. And I'm not talking about your sexiness factor."

"No. I'm not nice." Humans often pictured angels as soft, cuddly beings who frolicked in the sunshine, made roses bloom and painted rainbows in the sky. He knew that. And some angels were, but so many were not.

"What can I do for you, Mr. Mean?"

He should not have allowed curiosity to get the better of him. Should not have opened this line of conversation.

That ended now. "Enough, human. You have picked up more trouble than you can currently carry. I do not suggest you seek any more."

"Well, what do you know?" she said with a laugh devoid of amusement. The pink tip of her tongue swiped over her lips. "The doctors finally got something right. I'm hallucinating. Only in my mind would an angel treat someone so poorly."

"I have not treated you poorly, and you are not hallucinating."

"The drugs are affecting my brain, then," she insisted.

"They are not."

"But . . . you *can't* be an angel. Only evil comes here."

"Wrong again." At least today.

"I . . . I . . . Okay, I can roll with this. I mean, why not. Let's say you're actually real —"

"I am."

"— and that you're one of the good guys, since you're not here to kill me. Are you here to . . . release me?"

She had asked the question with such

56

sweet hesitation, he knew she dared not hope he would rescue her, yet with every ounce of her being she wanted to believe escape was imminent.

Perhaps another man would have been moved by her plight, but not Zacharel. He'd seen suffering in all its forms. He'd *caused* suffering in all its forms. Had watched his friends, immortals who should have lived forever, die.

Had watched his twin brother die.

Hadrenial, his twin, his only treasure, now resting in an urn on his nightstand. He'd been identical to Zacharel in appearance, with the same black hair and green eyes, the same sculpted face and strong body. Yet, emotionally they'd been complete opposites. Though only minutes younger, Hadrenial had seemed *years* younger. So innocent and sweet, so kind and caring, beloved by all.

"I cannot stand to see the humans cry, Zacharel. We must help them. Somehow, someway."

"That is not our purpose, brother. We are warriors, not joy-bringers."

"Why can't we be both?"

Zacharel's hands curled into fists. *You must stop thinking of him.* Pondering what had happened would not change a single detail. It was what it was. Beautiful and ugly.

Wonderful and terrible.

He forced his mind onto the female and her plight — but he decided not to answer the question about her release. "Do you know the name of the demon who marked you?"

Disappointment mixed with bitter acceptance flashed in her eyes. "Maybe you are real," she said. "It would require a dark side I don't have to create someone like you."

"You forgot to say 'no offense' before making that statement."

"No, I didn't. I meant offense."

Bold little human, wasn't she? "Shall I repeat *my* question?" he asked, in case she'd missed it the first time.

"No. I remember. You want to know if I know the name of the —" Her eyes widened, the disappointment and acceptance changing to shock. She whispered, "Demon," the revelation seeming to affect her far more potently than when she'd learned of *his* origins. "As in, a demon that belongs in hell?"

"Yes."

"A vile being whose only purpose is to ruin human lives?"

"Yes."

"A hideous creature without an ounce of

light, only darkness and evil?"

"Exactly."

"I should have known," she breathed. "Demons. All this time I've been fighting demons, and I never realized it." Relief joined the shock, both dripping from her words. "I'm not crazy, and we're not alone. I told them, but the only two people who ever believed me were the schizophrenic abducted by aliens and his invisible friend. I told them!"

"Human, you will answer me now."

"I told them," she continued blithely. "I just had no idea I was fighting demons. I should have guessed, though, but I got stuck on vampires and mythological monsters, and then hallucinations, so I —"

"Human!" *Do not raise your voice to her.* There would be no way to explain to his Deity that he hadn't *meant* to scare her to death.

She shook her head, pulling herself from her clearly whirling thoughts with the same determination he had used. To her credit, she appeared far from cowed by him. "I can't answer you because I have no idea what you're talking about. A demon *marked* me? How? Why?"

Genuine confusion. He knew it was, for the lies others told always tasted bitter on his tongue, and just then the only thing he tasted was . . . the sweetness of her scent? A subtle hint of rose and bergamot seeping from her skin, that smooth expanse of bronzed cream.

That he'd noticed such an unimportant detail irritated him. "You do not recall agreeing to mate with a demon, by fair means or foul?" he asked.

"Never!" The long length of her black lashes fused together, her gaze lancing at him. "And now it's my turn for an answer. Are you here to save me or not?"

If she was strong enough to insist on an answer, when she had already guessed at the truth, she was strong enough to hear the response. "No. I am not." But he would have liked to remain with her long enough to solve the mystery of her marking. When had it happened? Who had done it? How had she been tricked?

The details do not matter. The end result matters.

She choked out a laugh as bitter as her earlier acceptance. "Of course you're not. Why should I ever have hoped otherwise?"

Hinges creaked as the steel door was suddenly thrown open. Zacharel shielded himself from prying eyes, and the female tensed. A baton-wielding guard stepped aside to allow a human male to stride into the room, a thick folder in hand. He was of average height for a human, missing quite a bit of hair and bearing a falsely sympathetic expression. A white coat draped his thin build, the material stained by small spots of dried blood.

"She puts up a good fight," the man said, "but she's restrained and she can't hurt me. Pay no attention to what you hear. Also, this therapy session will take some time, so don't come back in until I signal you."

The guard cast the female a sympathetic glance, but in the end, he nodded. "Whatever you say, Doc." He closed the door, shutting the newcomer inside.

Zacharel told himself to leave. Not even joy-bringers, who were the most actively involved with the humans, were to interfere with free will. Plus, the most important aspects of tonight's mystery had been solved. The demons had come for the girl, inexorably drawn to her, delighting in hurting what belonged to another of their kind.

As for her, she would find freedom only in death.

Yes, I really should leave. And yet, he found himself lingering. Fear and revulsion now wafted from her, creating the . . . Surely not. But yes, there was no denying its presence. Creating the tiniest of fissures in the ice and darkness that lived inside his chest. Creating a flicker of . . . guilt?

He did not understand. Why here? Why now?

Why her?

Instantly the answer slid into place, and though he wanted to shy away from it as he had earlier, he couldn't. She reminded him of Hadrenial. Not in demeanor — she was too full of fire — but in circumstance.

Hadrenial had died while tied to his bed.

Doesn't matter. You must walk away. Emotions were nothing more than a waste. Zacharel had mourned his brother for centuries. He had wept and he had raged and he had sought death himself, but nothing he'd done had eased his guilt or his shame. Only when he'd cut himself off from *all* emotions had he experienced any relief.

And now . . .

Now, the frigid crystals weighing him down and dripping from his wings proved to be a blessing, reminding him of his status — commander — his duty — defending heavenly laws — and his goal — victory against the demons without any collateral damage. The girl could not, would not, matter.

"So predictable, Fitzpervert," she taunted.

"I knew you'd come for me."

"As if I could stay away from my sweet little geisha. After all, we need to discuss your behavior today." Lust glazed the man's eyes as he perused her slender body, lingering over her very feminine curves.

Her gaze darted between the human and Zacharel. He knew she could no longer see him, that she was simply trying to reason out whether or not he was still there. And he knew the moment she decided that yes, he was still there, for quivers of humiliation overtook her.

"Why don't we discuss your behavior instead?" A tinge of desperation belied her bravado. "You're supposed to help your patients, not hurt them further."

A lecherous grin met her words. "What we do together doesn't have to hurt. If you make me feel good, I'll make you feel *very* good." He tossed the folder to the floor, removed his jacket. "I'll prove it."

"Don't do this." Her nostrils flared with the force of her breathing. "You'll get caught, lose your job."

"Darling, when are you going to learn? It's your word against mine." Withdrawing a syringe from his pant pocket, he walked forward. "I'm a highly respected medical professional. You're a girl who sees monsters."

"And I'm seeing one now!"

He chuckled. "I'll change your mind."

"I despise you," she said, and Zacharel watched as she rallied her wits one more time. "Do you not realize this will come back to haunt you? If you plant seeds of destruction, you will have to live with the crop you grow, thorns and all."

"How cute. A life lesson from one of the institution's most violent inmates. But until my harvest comes in . . ."

She looked away from the human, from where Zacharel stood, and stared somewhere far away. Tears shone in those otherworldly eyes before she blinked them away. She would not break this eve; and really, this man would not break her for many months or even years. But she *would* hurt this eve. Badly.

CHAPTER THREE

The moment Zacharel flew out of the room, the fissure inside his chest elongated, and he would have sworn he heard ice cracking. Would a few words with the doctor truly be considered interfering? he wondered, slowing down. Afterward, he could return to his cloud, forget the female and continue on the way he had always continued on, alone, unaffected and unconcerned. The way he liked it. The way his Deity probably preferred it.

Very well. He was decided.

Zacharel returned to the room and materialized in front of the human male. A male who deserved to die for his crimes. But Zacharel would not be the one to harm him. He could only content himself with the knowledge that the doctor would one day reap a harvest of all the evil he had sown. Everyone always did.

Before the man could panic, Zacharel

peered deeply into his eyes and said coldly, "You have something better to do."

The doctor flinched and, snared by the ring of truth in Zacharel's tone, replied, "Something better. Yes. I do."

See? Zacharel wasn't interfering as much as helping the doctor rediscover . . . whatever he considered better than harming one of his patients. "You will leave this room. You will not come back. You will not remember this night."

A nod, and the man turned on his heel, rapped on the door.

Zacharel shielded himself inside a pocket of air as a surprised guard stepped into the room and looked the girl over. "All done, Dr. Fitzherbert? I thought you said you'd take a while."

"Yes, I'm all done" was the monotone reply. "I will leave now. I have something better to do."

"O-kay."

Once again Zacharel found himself alone with the girl. He stepped from his shelter.

"I thought you weren't going to save me," she whispered, still looking somewhere outside the room. What did she see with those eyes?

Beautiful eyes, if he cared about that kind of thing — which he did not. "You asked if

I had come to save you, and I had not. I came for another reason."

"Oh." She cleared her throat, swallowed. "Well, thank you anyway. For sending him away, I mean."

Huh. Zacharel liked hearing *thank-you* from her lips. As rusty as her tone had been, he suspected she had not uttered those words very often. Perhaps she simply hadn't had reason to — and why was his chest aching again? "What would he have done to you?"

Silence.

"Hurt you, then." That, Zacharel had already guessed. "Has he hurt you before?"

More silence.

"That's a yes." Killing humans wasn't something Zacharel usually enjoyed, but it wasn't something he detested, either. He would do anything to anyone and never experience a moment of remorse. However, ripping the doctor's heart out of his chest might have given him a small thrill. "Correct?"

And even more silence.

I'm being purposely ignored. Never before had he been disregarded. Not even by his men! Feral as they were, even they listened to him — before blatantly disobeying him. And his former leader, Lysander, had taken his every word under advisement. What's more, the only beings outside of his race that he counted as . . . what? Not friends, but not potential targets for elimination, either. The demon-possessed immortals known as the Lords of the Underworld had fought beside him and earned his respect for resisting the evil of their demons so forcefully. They had always watched him with rapt fascination. The few humans to see him throughout the centuries had been utterly mesmerized.

That this tiny fluff of nothing so easily dismissed him was baffling.

Before he could decide how best to handle this, Thane walked through the far wall. Fury crackled over his expression the moment he spotted the girl. He did not question Zacharel, however. A small blessing.

"The demons have been eliminated, Majesty, and the one you requested has been taken to your cloud. Alive." His smoky voice contained the same treacherous crackles.

Slowly the female turned her head, hunks of that tangled hair falling over her forehead and shielding her eyes. She blew the strands away and studied Thane.

"I'm certainly popular tonight. Are you an angel, too?" she asked, her gaze stroking over the man's still-black wings.

Zacharel noticed Thane did not elicit the doubt that he had. Why?

"Yes." Thane sniffed the air, frowned and whipped his gaze to Zacharel. "You plan to free her?"

"No." Why would he think that?

The frown deepened. "But why . . . Never mind. If you have changed your mind about her, I will take her with me."

When they did not know why she was here or what she had done? "No," he repeated.

Thane bowed, as though he were a slave humbled by his master. "Of course not, Majesty. How dare I entertain such a silly desire. No one in such a place as this deserves compassion, correct?"

Would his men ever simply obey him without question? "Were any humans harmed during the battle?" he asked. The girl was not the only one whose queries he would disregard.

Head held high, Thane replied through clenched teeth, "One of the guards. A sword of fire sliced through his middle."

Zacharel found his hands tightening into fists for the second time that day. Direct disobedience — again. "A sword of fire does not slice through a human by accident." While angels operated on the spiritual plane, not even their weapons could be sensed — or felt — by the humans. Therefore, the angel who'd done this deed had deliberately entered the mortal realm.

"The guard was demon possessed and needed to die," Thane said.

"And yet he was still human. Who disobeyed my orders?"

Thane ran his tongue over his teeth. "Perhaps it was I."

Familiar with the tricks that could be used to circumvent the ring of truth, Zacharel knew Thane was not the culprit. "Who? You will tell me or you will watch me penalize Bjorn and Xerxes." Truth. He would do it without a single qualm.

Another pause, this one several beats longer. "Jamila."

Jamila. One of four females in his army, but the one he had trusted most. She was the only one who had never challenged his authority. Yet now, because of her, he would receive another whipping.

"You," the female on the bed said, her timbre shaded with irritation. "New guy. Angel Boy. Colonel Curls, or whatever you want to be called. I'm done asking, so now I'm commanding. Free me."

Zacharel actually had to fight an urge not to smile. Him. Smile. The absurdity was staggering. But she'd just called his warrior by several insulting names, the same way that warrior often called Zacharel by insulting names.

Thane relaxed, a soft chuckle escaping him. "Colonel Curls. I like that. But, my beautiful human, you asked me to save you, not to free you."

"Same thing," she said, exasperated.

"They are quite different, I assure you. But what will you do if I fail to heed your command, hmm?"

She uttered a silky, "Believe me, you don't want to know."

Zacharel pursed his lips, no longer amused. Was this flirting? This had better not be flirting. He and Thane were on a mission.

"Because knowing will not deter me?" Thane asked just as silkily.

"Because it's so horrible even hearing it will make you puke."

Thane coughed — or covered up a snort. It was too difficult to tell. "Did you hear that?" he asked Zacharel, speaking to him as if they were friends for the first time in their acquaintance, as if they were sharing a moment of understanding. "She just ordered me to obey her will, then threatened to hurt me if I failed to comply."

"I have ears," he replied drily. "I heard."

But why hadn't she done the same to Zacharel?

"And she actually believes in her success," Thane continued, bewildered.

"You do not have to sound so impressed," Zacharel said, not liking the idea on any level. Impressed, Thane would desire the female . . . perhaps stop at nothing to have her.

Thane frowned at him. "I'm simply curious. And, very well, I will ask what is not my business. Why have you claimed her as your own if you plan to leave her here?"

"I have not claimed her." Zacharel could not get the words out fast enough.

"Then why have you spread your essentia all over her?"

"I have not touched her."

"And yet her skin bears your tinge."

"Not mine." Essentia, a substance that swirled inside each of their bodies, sometimes seeping through the pores of their hands to become a fine powder, allowing them to claim any object they considered their exclusive property. Demons produced a similar substance, only theirs was tainted.

Zacharel's attention whipped to the female. "I have never claimed a human." He'd never had so much as a yearning to do so. "She does not glow." He saw nothing out of

72

the ordinary about her skin.

She watched him unabashedly, and he nearly shifted on his feet. Him. Shifting. Inconceivable!

"I promise you," Thane said, "the gleam is very dull but there, and it's a definite warning to other males not to touch what belongs to you."

Him? Impossible. "You are mistaken, that's all."

"Argh!" the girl interrupted. "I'm done listening to this meaningless jabber. Team Winger sucks! Just forget that I'm here. Oh, wait. You already have. So here's an idea — leave."

She had more mettle than even Zacharel had realized, and he was trying not to be impressed, or baffled, himself. "Go," he said to his warrior. "I want you and my other advisors —" which included Jamila "— waiting in my cloud. No, strike that. Not you. Go and find every detail about this human that you can." A need to learn more about her kept pricking at him. Better to heed it than to regret not doing it.

"Whatever you say, glorious leader." Thane stalked from the room. Just before he vanished, he cast the girl one final glance, causing Zacharel's hands to clench into fists. How many times would the action happen in a single day, when before he'd gone years without doing it once?

"If you want to know about me," she snapped the moment she was alone with Zacharel, "you could have just asked me."

"And give you the chance to lie?"

Hurt cascaded over her features, but only for a second. Pride took its place, and remained. "You're right. I'm a no-good liar, and you're Mr. Truth. So why are you here, Mr. Truth? I'm pretty clear on the fact that it's not to save or free me."

There was no reason not to tell her. "I was told to destroy the horde of demons trying to get inside the building."

A beat of panic. "Horde, as in army?"

"Yes, but they are no longer any type of threat. *My* army was successful against them."

Slowly she exhaled. "They wanted me, right?"

"Yes."

Another beat of panic before she sagged against the bed. "But why me?"

She had no idea what had been done to her. None at all. Yet she would have remembered being tricked . . . or seduced. So *how* had the demon managed to mark her?

"Well?" she demanded.

Ignoring her, Zacharel claimed the folder

still lying on the floor, the one the doctor had dropped, and riffled through the pages.

She banged her head against her pillow once, twice. "Fine. Pretend I'm not speaking. Whatever. I'm used to it. But please, *glorious leader,* allow me to save you the trouble of digging through the little details, since even a liar like me would have no need to fudge those." Without pausing to allow him to respond, she added, "To start, my name is Annabelle Miller."

The truth, confirmed in the notes. Annabelle. Latin for *loveable.* "I am called Zacharel." Not that it mattered.

"Well, Zachie, I —"

"Glorious leader," he rushed out. "You may call me glorious leader."

"There's no way I'm calling you that," she said, despite the fact that she had already done so, "but enough about your exalted opinion of yourself. I'm here because I killed my parents. I stabbed them to death, or so I'm told."

He glanced up, watched another of those tremors rock her. Perhaps he should fetch her a blanket.

Fetch her a blanket? Seriously? His frown returned. Her comfort did not concern him. "So you were told? You do not remember?" he asked, remaining in place.

75

"Oh, I remember." The bitterness returned to her voice, thicker now. "I watched a creature . . . a demon do it, tried to stop him, tried to save them, and when I told the authorities what had really happened, I was deemed criminally insane and locked here for the rest of my life."

Again, he knew she spoke truthfully. Not just because the details she mentioned were typed, scribbled and repeated throughout the pages in the folder — though none of her doctors had believed her — but because he tasted only the rose and bergamot, both fragile, delicate flavors he liked. Odd. He'd never cared for scents or tastes before. They were what they were, and he'd had no preference.

"Why have these demons targeted me?" she asked again. "Why? And just so you know, telling me is the only way to stop me from pestering you about it."

"That's not exactly true. I could leave, and then you would not be able to pester me about anything." Rather than ignore her yet again, however, he decided there was no reason not to give her this information, either. Her reaction interested him.

Fires of hell, but something must be wrong with him. *Nothing* interested him.

"Sometime before your parents were

killed," he stated, "you invited a demon into your life."

"No. No way." Violently she shook her head, tangling those blue-black strands around her temples. "I would never invite one of those things *anywhere*. Except, maybe, a house-burning party."

How was she expressing such undeniable doubt about something he had said, with the ring of truth as ripe as ever in his tone? Yes, there were humans who possessed doubts more powerful than that ring, but Annabelle did not fit the type.

"Humans fail to realize how easy demons are to welcome. The negative words you speak, the detestable things you do. Utter a lie, meditate on hate, entertain the urge to commit violence, and you might as well sound the dinner bell."

"I don't care what you say. I never welcomed a demon."

How could he make her understand? "Demons are the equivalent of spiritual deliverymen. Your words and actions can be a request for a package. In other words, a curse. They come to your door, knock. It's your choice whether or not you open that door and accept. You did."

"No," she insisted.

"Have you ever played the Ouija?" he

asked, trying to reach her stubborn core from a different angle.

"No."

"Visited a psychic?"

"No."

"Cast a spell? Any spell?"

"No, okay? No!"

"Lied, cheated or stolen from a neighbor? Hated someone, anyone? Feared something, anything?"

The next tremor to slide the length of her body proved stronger than the others, locking her jaw, silencing her and rattling the entire bed. By the time she stilled, her anger had drained and she radiated a bleakness that somehow widened the fissure in his chest by the minutest degree.

"I'm done talking to you," she said quietly.

Meaning yes, she had. He had seen proof of hatred and fear already. "But I am not done talking to you. Spiritually, all of the things I mentioned grant your enemy permission to attack you."

"But how can a person stop feeling fear?"

"It is not what you feel that truly matters but what you say and how you act while feeling that way."

A moment passed as she absorbed his words. Ultimately, she sighed. "Okay, look. I'm tired, and you were kind enough to

78

ensure Fitzpervert wouldn't be coming back. This will be my only chance to rest without someone sneaking up on me. Will you just go already?"

If you cannot do what I need, then leave me here. I hate that you're seeing me like this. Go, please. For once, listen to me and obey. Go!

He gritted his teeth. No more thinking about his brother.

"I will go, yes," he said, "but you? What will you do?"

"The same as always." Her tone was as emotionless as his own, and he wasn't sure he liked that. He much preferred her mettle. "I'll survive."

But for how much longer?

For several minutes, Zacharel debated what to do with her — and reeled over the fact that a debate was needed at all. Were he to take her with him, she would cause problems. Of that, there was no doubt. He would have interfered in a human's life, many human lives, and he would surely be chastised. Right now, he already had one whipping looming over his head. Jamila's. But were he to leave Annabelle behind, she *would* eventually break. The thought of her crying and begging as his brother had done disturbed him.

79

He could visit her once a week, he supposed. Check on her, guard her. Unless he was called to battle, of course. Or injured. And in the meantime, while he was gone? What would happen to her?

A counterargument sparked to life. If he aided her, he would not be interfering. Not really. He would be protecting her fully, and that's why he was here, after all. That's what his Deity wanted him to do: protect the humans at any cost. Zacharel would be rewarded, not reprimanded. Surely.

Well, then, decision made.

When he closed the distance between them, he . . . at last discerned the glow Thane had mentioned. A soft, gentle light the same shade as Zacharel's eyes seeped from her, washing over her, bathing her with a subtle radiance.

But . . . he had not touched her. Not once.

"Have you been in contact with another angel?" he asked, though no two angels produced the same shade of essentia. But a demon could not have done it. There was no way the epitome of evil could have produced such a magnificent color.

"No."

Truth. There had to be an explanation. Perhaps . . . perhaps the glow was all her own, natural. Just because he had never

80

heard of such a thing did not mean it was impossible.

"What are you planning to do to me?" She met his gaze, surprising him with the ferocity banked there, daring him to do . . . something.

"We will find out together." He reached out, intending to undo one of the cuffs, and she flinched.

"Don't!" she said.

Realization dawned. She had been abused, and she expected the same treatment from him.

To promise never to harm her in any way was, perhaps, to lie to her, and he could not lie to her. Humans were sensitive beings, their feelings and bodies easily hurt. Accidents happened. No telling what she would find fault with in their dealings together.

Just how long do you plan to be with her?

"Right now, I plan only to free you and escort you from this place," he said. "All right?"

Hope flickered in those crystal eyes. "But you said —"

"I changed my mind."

"Really?"

"Really."

"Thank you," she rushed out. "Thank

81

you, thank you, thank you, a thousand times, thank you. You won't regret this, I promise. I'm not a danger to anyone. I just want to go somewhere and be by myself. I won't cause any trouble. I promise! And seriously, thank you!"

He undid the first cuff, walked to her other side and repeated the entire process.

Tears filled her eyes as she pulled her hands tight to her chest and rubbed at her wrists. Not from pain, he didn't think, but from joy. "Where will you escort me?"

"To my cloud, where you will be safe from the demons."

A shake of her head, as if she wasn't sure she'd heard him correctly. "Your . . . cloud? As in, a cloud in the sky?"

"Yes. You may bathe, change clothes, eat. Whatever you wish." And then . . . still he had no idea.

"But — and stop me if this sounds crazy — I want to stay on solid ground, where I won't plunge through mist and fall a bazillion feet only to go splat."

He loosened one ankle cuff. "Were I to take you anywhere on land, you would be hunted by your own people . . . not to mention other demons. You'll be safe in my cloud, I promise you." He loosened the other cuff.

The moment she was free, she jerked upright, threw her legs over the bed and stood. Though she swayed, she managed to remain on her feet. "Just get me out of the building, and we can go our separate ways. You'll have done a good deed, and I will remain hidden forever."

Refusal to obey him, when he'd finally decided to aid her. Was she *trying* to twist him into knots? "I cannot liberate you without supervision, for I would be blamed for any damage you caused."

"I won't —"

"Mean to, I know. But you will."

"Just give me a chance!"

That's what he was trying to do. "You have two choices, Annabelle. Stay here, or go to my cloud. Nothing else will be considered."

Her chin lifted, painting her the very picture of stubbornness. "Can I stay with the other angel, then? The blond."

Thane? "Why?" he demanded.

"Don't take this the wrong way, but I like him better than I like you."

There was a *right* way to take that statement?

Honesty was to be commended, and yet Zacharel suddenly battled an inexplicable need to shake her. "You cannot know who

83

you like better. You only spent a few seconds in his company."

"Sometimes a few seconds is all it takes."

The fissure in his chest widened. No guilt this time, but a measure of . . . anger? Oh, yes. Anger. *Zacharel* was the one who had prevented the doctor from violating her. *Zacharel* was the one who had freed her. She should like him best. "I am just as fierce a warrior as he is. Fiercer, even."

A tremor shook her.

Such a reaction . . . "Perhaps you do not want fierce," he said, more to himself than to her. Perhaps she craved what she clearly had not encountered in this place. Kindness.

"Look, Winged Wonder. Get me out of here, *then* we'll hammer out the details about where I'm staying. Okay?"

"Winged Wonder," he said, nodding. "I find that I do not mind that one. It fits."

"Captain Modesty fits better," she muttered.

"I disagree. Winged Wonder is clearly the better choice for a man such as me, and we will discuss the details now." He could hardly believe he was having a conversation such as this one. "I will not have you acting out later because there was a misunderstanding between us. I'm dealing with

84

enough of that already." His gaze pinned her in place. "Tell me why you wish to stay with Thane."

She gulped but said, "I feel safer with him, that's all. And besides, snow wasn't falling from his wings. Why is it falling from yours?"

"The answer does not pertain to you. As for your safety, I have already promised you will be unharmed in my cloud. Therefore, your requirement is met and the details are hammered out. You will stay with me. Come. I will waste no more time with arguments."

She could not fly, could not flash from one location to another with only a thought, which meant he would have to touch her. He would dislike every second of the contact, he was sure, but he would endure it nonetheless. He extended his hand, motioned with his fingers. "Last chance. Do you stay or do you go?"

I'll soon be free of this hellhole, Annabelle thought, wanting to laugh and cry at the same time. She wanted to dance with relief, then hide under the covers from panic. Escape . . . finally . . . but would it be the heaven she'd craved — or another version of hell?

Does it matter? You'll be free of Fitzpervert,

85

free of this cage, free of the drugs and the other patients and the orderlies . . . free from the demons.

All this time she had been fighting evil beings from hell. Neither of her parents had believed in an afterlife. They had raised her to be skeptical, too. Well, they had been wrong, and she had been wrong, and now she had a lot to learn.

"Annabelle," Zacharel prompted, again motioning with his fingers.

This man could teach her, she thought. This heavenly man who appeared so devilish, like a dark, seductive dream meant to lure a female straight into midnight temptations.

Dangerous . . . Yes, this man is dangerous. . . .

The words were a soft, erotic whisper against her flesh. A whisper she'd heard and felt since the moment he'd entered the room.

Still she said, "I . . . choose to go." Staying with him any longer than necessary was another story, however. He might remind her of the dark fairy-tale prince she'd dreamed about so long ago, the night before her birthday, but this man was no charmer.

Trembling, she wrapped her fingers around his. At the moment of contact, he sucked in a breath as if she'd somehow burned him and she nearly jerked away. *Steady.*

Zacharel called himself an angel, but she had no idea what that meant or what it entailed other than the standard "good and right" stuff. More, she had no idea where he was taking her — a cloud? really? — or what he planned to do with her when he got her there.

"Are you okay?"

"I . . . need a moment to adjust," he said, a strain in his voice.

Good, because she needed a moment, too. "Take all the time you need, Captain Modesty."

"I am Winged Wonder, and I will. Do not move."

"Uh, that might be a problem." As cold as she was, his skin proved to be colder. Soon the shivers would overtake her.

He offered no reply. Just peered down at her through narrowed lids, as if he blamed her for something catastrophic.

Could she trust him? Maybe, maybe not. But she wanted her freedom and he could give her that. And yeah, she also wanted to be on her own, relying only on herself. One day, she would be. For right now, escape would suffice.

If he tried to hurt her when they got to . . . wherever he was taking her, she would fight the way she'd always fought — dirty — whether he was an angel or not.

"This contact," Zacharel said. He frowned, the downward curve of his lips surely a default expression he couldn't control. Not once had she seen him smile.

Was there anything that would amuse him, or even rattle him?

"What about it?" she forced herself to ask.

"I expected certain sensations to fade, but they still have not." His grip tightened on her hand, as if he sensed she verged on pulling away. He tugged her closer, closer, until her body was flush against his. "This is not what I imagined."

As he wrapped his free arm around her waist, he peered down at her with those eyes the color of emeralds. Her birthstone. Once her favorite stone, in fact, but her birthday had become synonymous with death and destruction and, well, she'd decided emeralds sucked.

But she couldn't deny his eyes were gorgeous. Long, thick lashes framed those jewel-toned irises that lacked any hint of emotion, softening his features from impossibly cruel to maybe-I'll-only-make-you-scream-a-little-before-I-slay-you.

He had silky hair that reminded her of a starless night. And oh, how long since she'd stared up at the sky? His forehead was neither too long nor too wide, his cheek-bones hollowed as though chiseled by a master sculptor. His lips so lush and red a woman needed only a single glance to fantasize for the rest of eternity.

If only he'd been short. But, no. He was tall, at least six foot five, with wide shoulders and the most superb muscle mass she'd ever seen. And his wings? A-maz-ing. They arched over his shoulders and cascaded all the way to the floor. Feathers of the purest white glistened with the essence of the purest rainbow, thick threads of gold forming a hypnotic pattern that led into patches of down.

The other guy, the blond, had been visually delicious as well, but despite the depraved gleam in his cerulean eyes, she'd thought she could handle him. At least better than she could handle this one.

Too late for that. And maybe that was for the best, she decided then. She was filled with so much hate, anger, desperation and helplessness — each, apparently, an aphrodisiac for the demons — Zacharel's coldness would be a refreshing change.

"So, uh, what did you imagine?" she

finally asked.

"Nothing I will tell you. Now, put your arms around my neck," Zacharel commanded, his voice rough with expectation.

Had anyone ever told him no? she wondered as she linked her fingers at his nape.

"Good. Now close your eyes."

"Why?"

"You and your questions." He sighed. "I plan to whisk you through the walls and into the sky. The view might disconcert you."

"I'll be fine." Closing her eyes would make her far more vulnerable than she already was.

If he was impressed by her bravery, he didn't show it. His lips, those gorgeous red lips, pursed, even as his wings burst from his back to glide up and down, slow and easy. Mesmerizing. "Also," he added, "I do not wish to look into your eyes and see the taint of the demon."

She had a demon's eyes? *That's* why her irises had turned blue? "But I can't be a demon," she gasped out. "I just can't be."

"You are not. You are tainted by one. As I said."

Gradually she calmed — despite the fact that his tone shouted, *If you had listened, you would have realized that.* "What's the difference?"

"Humans can be influenced, claimed or possessed by demons, but they cannot become one. You have been claimed."

"By who?" The one who had killed her parents? If so, she would . . . what? What could she really do?

"I do not know."

If he didn't know, there was no hope for her. "Well, I don't care if you find my eyes repellant." She so cared. She disliked the fact that a part of her appeared demonic. "You can deal."

Several seconds passed in silence. Then, he nodded and said, "Very well. You have only yourself to blame."

A strange sensation coursed through her, chilling her blood another degree and icing over her skin. The tile beneath her vanished. Suddenly she was in the air, seeing room after room whiz past her, then the roof of the building, then the sky, pinpricks of light scattered in every direction.

Oh, my. Tears of happiness welled in her eyes. She had been liberated from what had seemed to be a life of endless torture. She was truly free. And for the first time in years, she had something to look forward to rather than something to dread. A joy like she'd never known flooded her, consumed her. This was . . . this was . . . too much.

The sheer splendor of the night over-whelmed her, and the tears splashed onto her cheeks. The most amazing perfumes fragranced the air. Wildflowers and mint, dew and freshly cut grass. Milk and honey, chocolate and cinnamon. The subtlest hint of smoke, curling on a gentle breeze.

"I had forgotten," she whispered, hair whipping against her cheeks. But even that was a delight. She was free, she was free, she was finally free.

"Forgotten what?" Zacharel asked, and there was something strange about his voice. The first hint of emotion, perhaps.

"How beautiful the world is." A world her parents had left far too soon. A world her parents would never again enjoy.

Sadness threaded through the joy.

She'd gone from helpless victim to murder suspect to tormented convict far too quickly to mourn the passing of her mother and father. She couldn't help but wonder how they would have reacted to this moment. No question, Zacharel would have flab-bergasted them both. Not just because of what he was, but because they had been an emotional, volatile couple, and had fought as passionately as they'd loved. They would not have known what to make of his cold-ness. But this . . . this they would have welcomed. A flight through the glittering stars, breathing air that dripped with emancipation as she glided toward a future now brightened with hope.

Forget the sadness. She would deal with that later. Right now, she would simply enjoy. For the first time in four years, Annabelle threw back her head and laughed.

CHAPTER FOUR

Zacharel released the girl the moment he was able, depositing her in the center of an empty room and stepping away from her tempting warmth, the sweetness of her scent and the gentle caress of her hair against his skin. He'd liked touching her. He shouldn't have liked it on any level, but no matter how many lectures he'd given himself, the like had only intensified.

During the flight, the changes in her expressive face had entranced him. He'd watched her go from rapture to sorrow, then back to rapture again. He, who had long-ago battled back his emotions until he no longer experienced them, had actually found himself envious of her willingness to reveal all she thought and felt.

She had looked so uninhibited, utterly caught up in the moment. And when she'd laughed . . . oh, sweet heavens. Her voice had washed over him, enveloping him, embracing him.

She had intrigued him, perplexed him, transfixed him, and he'd marveled about what had brought about those quicksilver changes, but he'd had too much pride to ask.

She was the consort of a demon, his enemy. Not by choice, no, but a consort nonetheless. She was also a human and therefore beneath him; her emotions could not matter to him.

He should not have brought her here, he realized. He should not have accepted the pleasure of having her in his arms.

He should not be looking at her now, wondering if the delight she'd found in the midnight sky would extend to his home. He should not *want* her delight.

"Why did you laugh?" he asked. So much for his pride. He had to know the reason.

"I'm free, I'm free, I'm finally free," she replied, with a twirl.

The tumbling length of her hair flew around her, slapping him in the face. He barely curbed the urge to grab on to the strands and rub them between his fingers, just to remind himself of how soft they could be.

Her head tilted to the side as she looked at him. "What?"

"What do you mean, what?"

"You're frowning at me."

"I frown at everyone."

"Good to know. So this is your cloud, huh?" Her brows scrunched in confusion. She studied the walls that looked no more substantial than mist. The floor was as thick as morning fog, clinging to her ankles, and seemingly just as flimsy.

"This is my home, yes."

"I gotta say, it's exactly as I predicted."

Was that derision in her tone? "What do you mean?" he asked, trying not to reveal how insulted he was. Another reaction, now? When they weren't touching? Truly?

"Mist, mist and more mist. I'm only surprised the foundation is solid."

"The entire enclosure is solid."

She extended her arm to the side. Awe consumed her features when her fingers disappeared inside the mist. "Solid . . . but not. Fascinating."

You *are fascinating.*

No. No! She wasn't.

He'd had females here before. Fellow warriors, and even joy-bringers he considered friends, as well as the once human, now immortal named Sienna, who just happened to be the new queen of the Titan gods — immortals who considered themselves rulers of the entire world. She liked to stop by unannounced, and he liked to kick her out.

Then there was Lysander's wife, Bianka, a Harpy no one dared deny. She held their leader's heart in her hands, and her happiness was his, but still Zacharel could never get rid of her fast enough. And yet, seeing Annabelle here affected Zacharel strangely. She was here, surrounded by *his* walls, ensconced in *his* world, safe because he had made it so. He, and no other.

The thought should not have filled him with satisfaction, but it did.

Time to leave her, he decided. For real. Distance would do him some good. Put him back on his game and numb him out, the way he preferred.

"I want you to be at ease, Annabelle," he said. "Demons would not dare try to enter."

Her relief was tangible. "Good."

"I have business I must attend to, but I will not be far. Only a few rooms over." He hadn't meant to snap, hadn't known he was capable of doing so, but snap he had. "However, you will remain inside this one."

Just like that, her countenance changed. Her eyes narrowed, and her lips pursed. "Are you saying I'm your prisoner? Did I trade one cell for another?"

Forced to tell the truth for thousands of

years, he had found ways to misdirect. "How can you consider yourself a prisoner when your every wish will be granted while you are here?"

"That's not an answer."

Suspicious, prickly human. She was annoyingly perceptive. "And yet it addressed some of your concerns, I'm sure."

She stomped her foot, every inch the willful child — but that didn't annoy him as it should have. "I won't be held captive. Not ever again."

Her words, on the other hand . . . A glint of anger formed inside the fissure, burning in the center of his chest. Too many people had questioned his authority lately, and he'd reached the end of his tolerance. "You would rather die, Annabelle?"

"Yes!"

She blinked at her own vehemence, and so did he.

"Yes," she said softly.

The claim was false, even though he could not taste a lie. Surely. "You do realize I could crush you in seconds, yes?"

"Believe me, at this point, death would be a mercy. So crush me if you can't tolerate being told off, because I will never be a cooperative prisoner. I will fight you forever if necessary."

Death would be a mercy. One other person had uttered those words to him, and death had indeed been a mercy then. For Hadrenial, but not for Zacharel. He would suffer eternally for what had transpired that terrible night.

You must stop comparing Annabelle to your brother.

Right now, he had two choices. Convince the female she was not a prisoner, which would take time he did not have, or let her go. Neither appealed to him. Perhaps there was a third option, though. One he'd never before attempted. Courtesy.

It was worth a shot, he supposed. "I humbly request that you remain here. Whatever you desire, you have only to ask for it, and it will be yours." The moment he spoke he recalled her liking for Thane. The small flame of anger intensified, and he would have sworn he heard a *drip, drip.* "Except for a male. You may not summon a male."

Zacharel had saved her. Zacharel would see to her care.

The light in the room hit her at a different angle, and he saw the bruises marring the soft skin under her eyes, the deep hollows of her cheeks. So breakable, this human. "I don't understand. Do you have servants

99

who will bring me what I want?"

"No servants. I will show you how it works. What is something you desire? Besides a male," he hurried to add.

"A shower." Offered with no hesitation. "Without anyone watching me."

"A private shower," he said, then motioned behind her.

Expression set in disbelief, she spun. Mist began to thicken and take shape, until a shower stall stood tall and proud. It was encased by smoked glass, and had multiple knobs and a drain in the floor.

She gasped with equal parts pleasure and disbelief. "Food," she said next, immeasurable relish in her tone.

Drip, drip. Except . . . no longer was anger at the center of the flame. He wasn't sure what was.

A pout curved her mouth downward. "Nothing happened."

"You must be specific," he instructed.

Her tongue emerged, swiping over her lips. "I want lobster mac-and-cheese, biscuits and gravy, asparagus risotto, beef enchiladas, chicken-fried steak, brownies with frosting, brownies without frosting, blackberry cobbler with vanilla ice cream, turkey and dressing, and . . . and . . . and . . ."

Beside him appeared a large, round table, wings intricately carved into its legs. Next came an elegant white tablecloth that perfectly conformed to its size. The requested dishes appeared next, one at a time, until the surface was covered with steaming bowls and perfectly arranged plates.

Shaky limbs brought her forward. She gripped the table's edge, closed her eyes and breathed deeply, rapture consuming her lovely features. "I don't know where to start," she admitted.

"Start at one side and work your way to the other."

She licked her lips. "Are you hungry? Do you want anything? If so, I'll need to summon more."

More? "No, thank you. I will eat on the morrow." He never ate before battle, and he wasn't quite done with his assignment. But he would have enjoyed watching her, he thought. Witnessing her delight, her passion and — *what are you doing?* "No one will disturb you."

She gave no reply, was reaching for the ice cream.

He turned on his heel and stepped through the mist. When he turned back, that mist blocked her from his view — but as insubstantial as it seemed, it would hold her inside.

He held out his hand and commanded the seams of the door to seal. Only he would be able to unseal them. Only he would be able to enter — or leave. What's more, Annabelle would hear nothing that happened outside her room.

That done, he stalked down the hall, the floor extending before him with every step. Past his bedroom, his private sanctuary, and into the holding bay, where the five most trusted warriors of his army awaited him. *Trusted* being a relative term, of course.

Thane, Bjorn and Xerxes stood off to the side, together as always and somehow separate from the others. Unlike most other angels, Xerxes lacked physical perfection. He had long white hair he kept pulled back in a jeweled torque. His skin was without color, as though death had settled beneath the surface, with tiny scars forming patterns of three. Three lines, gap, three lines, gap, three lines. Red eyes watched the world with an intelligence — and anger — matched by few.

Just then, those demonlike eyes were glaring at the minion even now bound by tendrils of cloud that clung to her gnarled wrists and ankles like ivy, holding her in place with no hope of escape.

Beside her stood the equally bound fallen angel Zacharel had brought here months ago. The male refused to behave, causing trouble for the new queen of the Titans, and so Zacharel, who had been told to curry her favor, had to restrain him.

Zacharel's attention moved to the other angels. In the far corner, Koldo cleaned his hooked sword, seemingly oblivious to the rest of the world. He had sun-drenched skin and black eyes as deep and fathomless as a pit of despair. He also possessed a thick black beard and long black hair that hung down his back in multiple braids.

As a child, demons had ripped out his wings. And because of his young age, his regenerative powers had not yet taken hold, so those wings had never grown back and never would. Instead his shoulders, back and legs were tattooed with crimson feathers depicting the wings he must miss with every ounce of his being. Not that he ever complained. Koldo was a man of few words, and those he did utter were deep, hoarse and soul chilling.

Jamila paced in front of the demon. With her dark skin and the long black ringlets cascading down her back and eyes of the sweetest honey, she was one of the original joy-bringers, promoted to warrior only after she had ventured into hell, alone, to rescue one of her pet humans.

Weeks had passed before she'd emerged, and though she'd saved the human's spirit, she had not saved herself. Something down there had changed her. No longer did she laugh easily or flitter through life without a care. No one looked over her shoulder more than Jamila, as if expecting evil to be waiting in every corner.

Until tonight's battle, though, Zacharel hadn't understood why she had been given to his care. Now he knew. Clearly, she had a problem following orders . . . not to mention the fact that she no longer prized human life.

She would have to be punished. She would probably cry.

I should have chosen Axel as my fifth. The male was irreverent, always laughing, obsessed with wreaking havoc, but he would not shed a single tear when Zacharel pronounced his sentence.

Xerxes noticed him first and straightened. The others followed suit.

"The human girl," Thane said. "I would like to return for her."

Still thinking of her, was he? "No need. She's here with me," he replied with an unexpected edge to his tone. "You may tell me what you learned about her once we finish with the demon."

A satisfied gleam entered Thane's eyes, and that, more than anything else that day, angered Zacharel. Did he hope to win her? "I've yet to learn anything. There hasn't been time."

Another order unheeded. "You will make time when you leave."

Something in his tone must have gotten through to Thane. Rather than issuing one of his customary retorts, he nodded. "I will."

"What human girl are we discussing?" Jamila asked.

Zacharel waved the question away. "The only human that should matter to you is the one you killed during the battle."

"Yeah. So? So what if I killed one?" she shot back, and he heard the unspoken, *So have you. So have they.*

His eyes narrowed on her, lances of resolve. "How many times in the past three months have I told you that you are not to make a demon kill if it causes you to harm a human?" He could have pulled her aside, could have chastised her in private, but she had committed her sin in front of others and she would now deal with the consequences in front of others.

Red suffused her cheeks. She gazed at her peers before refocusing on Zacharel. "There are approximately thirty days in a month, and you have mentioned it at least once a day. So my guess is ninety."

The number was not an exaggeration. "And yet you made the kill anyway."

She raised her chin in haughty defiance, eyes nearly black in the shadows cast by her lashes. Eyes completely dry. "I did. He taunted me through the human."

Too many females had raised their chins at him today. Actually, one was too many. Annabelle had been allowed because she was human and knew no better, and had no other way of expressing her displeasure with him. And he'd been oddly . . . charmed by her. That was not the case in this instance.

"A good soldier knows to ignore the insults hurled at him. Your rebellion has earned me another whipping. Not you. *Me*." And perhaps that was the problem. Jamila gave no thoughts to reprisal. None of them did.

"I'm sorry," she gritted out.

Exactly what he'd said to his Deity, but surely not in that same irritating manner. "You aren't sorry for your actions, only that I found fault with you." The moment his words registered inside his mind, he scowled.

Was his Deity laughing right now? He had said those very words to Zacharel.

What a turn of events. Zacharel had gone from rebellious to exemplary, simply to continue fighting the beings responsible for his brother's torture. Well, his soldiers would find he'd do a lot worse to them than the Deity had done to him.

Jamila's lips pressed into a mulish line, no response forthcoming.

"If this happens again, Jamila, I will make you suffer in ways you cannot yet imagine, for whatever punishment I am issued, I will return to you a hundredfold." After this next whipping, he still might. As for now, an example had to be made. "Tonight you will visit every member of my army and apologize for your actions. You will beg for their forgiveness — for you are the reason they will spend tomorrow morning in human form —" their wings hidden from mortal eyes "— cleaning every alleyway and street in Moffat County, Colorado." The scene of the crime.

Humiliating for her, infuriating for them. Everyone would learn.

She inclined her head, but she did not cry.

Good. "Anyone who refuses to obey this order will be held in my cloud, my prisoner until the end of the year. I will not tolerate your disrespect any longer." He met each warrior's gaze.

He received reluctant nods. Reluctant, yes, but a nod was a nod.

"Now, let us speak no more of this," he said.

Xerxes jerked a thumb toward the fallen angel. "Who is he, and why is he here?" A pause. "If I may ask," he added.

The change of subject was welcome. "His name is McCadden, and he is now your responsibility." McCadden had committed crimes against his fellow angels, as well as humans, to be with a woman who had not even wanted him.

But why he had been deemed unfit for the heavens, stripped of his wings and kicked to the earth, while Zacharel and these five had not, was a mystery. On the surface, McCadden looked no different from any of Zacharel's other men. He'd dyed his pale hair pink, had tattooed bloody teardrops under his eyes and added silver piercings to his brows. Underneath all that, he must be a cesspool of darkness.

"When we finish here, you will take him from my cloud and keep him locked in your home at all times," Zacharel said. He didn't want the former angel in the same location as Annabelle. "And now, I will not be blamed for any crimes *he* commits. You will."

Xerxes gnashed his teeth, but offered no complaint.

Thane snickered, and Bjorn drilled his knuckles into Xerxes' biceps. "Lucky."

"Now, for the captured demon," Zacharel said.

Relish glimmered from every angelic body, including his own. In unison, the six of them turned and faced the being in question. She writhed against her bonds, mist stretching over her forehead and inside her mouth, holding her still, keeping her silent. Mist also plugged her ears, blocking the sound of their voices.

She was a minion of Disease. Her skin sagged, was paper-thin and covered in sores. Her skeletal body lacked muscle and any hint of fat. What few teeth she had were yellow, as pitted as her skin, and as pointed and curling as her claws.

"Allow her to hear us," Zacharel commanded the cloud. The plugs thinned, dissipated completely. "Allow her to speak." Just as quickly the mist covering her mouth thinned and dissipated.

She hissed out a terrible curse.

"In case you are unaware of how this

works," he said, ignoring her insult for the ineffectual lash-out it was, "I will instruct you."

"Not Zacharel," she moaned. "Anyone but Zacharel." A scent of rot wafted from her, evidence of her sudden burst of fear.

His penchant for torturing his enemy was well known. "You will die this day, minion. That outcome will not change. The method of your execution is the only variable you can control." Demons, he knew, were more susceptible to the ring of truth than humans; this one flinched every time he finished a sentence. "I have questions for you, and you will answer each one honestly."

"You know we will taste your lies," Thane said.

"Taste and rebuke," Bjorn added.

"Why did you remain outside the Moffat County Institution this night?" Details were more than important; they were necessary. Without quantifiers, demons could infer anything they wished and answer accordingly.

Her thin lips lifted at the corners. "For the same reasonsss the other demonsss did so, I ssswear it."

Truth without enough context to be helpful. Cute.

"For what reason did the other demons

remain outside the Moffat County Institution?" he asked. "You will not receive another chance to answer this question."

"I'm happy to anssswer. They ssstayed outside for the sssame reassson I ssstayed outsssside. That'sss the truth, you have my word."

Zacharel reached into an air pocket and withdrew his vial of water from the River of Life. To even set foot near the river's shoreline hidden inside the temple given to the Deity by the Most High, an angel had to sacrifice the skin off his back — literally. To capture a single vial of the precious, life-saving liquid? The angel had to sacrifice much, much more.

Zacharel had only a few drops left, but he considered a demon's torment worth the loss.

"I find that your truth does not satisfy my curiosity, so I am forced to take my satisfaction another way. You will receive a castigation from each of us, as warned." From his nod, his soldiers knew what he wanted them to do. They might have worked together only a short time, but in this instance, they desired the same thing.

Koldo moved behind the demon and pinned her head against his massive chest, his long, thick fingers applying pressure to her brow. Xerxes and Thane stepped forward, both summoning metal blades. In unison, they stabbed her in the gut. As black blood sprang from both wounds, she released an unholy scream of agony. The wounds wouldn't be fatal, but they would hurt and weaken her.

While humans were to be protected, demons were never extended the same courtesy.

Bjorn and Jamila replaced Xerxes and Thane in front of her. After Bjorn pried open her mouth, Jamila produced a thin scalpel to remove all of the demon's remaining teeth.

By the time the five were finished, the demon could only plead for mercy. Mercy she had never shown her own victims. Mercy Zacharel did not have. Minions of Disease purposely infected human bodies with sickness, feeding off their growing frailty and despair, their pain, their panic, and loving every moment of it.

He was the next to move in front of her. "I warned you," he said.

"I didn't lie, told only the truth," the minion slurred, thanks to Jamila's impromptu root canal.

"You played with the truth. With me."

She stopped writhing, another eerie smile

112

lifting the corners of her mouth, black blood dripping from her lips. "And you don't like being played with, angel? I doubt that. You reek of human female right now. Did you play with *her?*" The words were even more garbled than before, but Zacharel was able to decipher her meaning.

He motioned to Thane.

The warrior returned his blade to her gut — and left it there.

A grunt. A gurgle of blood from her mouth. Through panting breaths, she said, "All right, all right. You don't like to play. Perhapsss I can change your mind. Give me five minutes, and I will do thingsss to your body . . . thingsss you'll dream about for yearsssss."

As she spoke, he upended the vial he held, allowing a single droplet of the water to catch on his fingertip. "Ah, but in five minutes I believe you will have more pressing matters on your mind. For the time has come for me to have my turn." He reached out and shoved his finger into her mouth, forcing the droplet down her throat.

The shrill, broken scream that followed made a mockery of the one that had come before, the water attacking the disease she perpetually carried, spreading health and vitality. She bucked against Koldo with so

113

much force, several of her bones snapped out of place.

When at last she quieted, tears sliding down her pitted cheeks, the putrid scent of her rot fading, Zacharel said calmly, "I have decided to be benevolent and give you one last chance. Why did you remain outside the institution this night?"

There was the barest of pauses before she offered faintly, "Wasssn't . . . my time . . . to enter." Her words were punctuated by gasps of residual pain.

"According to whom?"

A longer pause as she considered what more Zacharel could do to her. In the end, she decided an evasion was not worth it. "Burden."

Burden. A demon who had once been second in command to the high lord of Greed, and widely regarded as one of hell's fiercer warriors. Currently he was without a master.

Was *he* the one who had marked Annabelle? "Where is Burden right now?"

"Don't . . . know."

He detected no lie this time, either. "How did Burden contact you?"

"Disseassse too busssy . . . with humansss . . . I had to align myself . . . with sssomeone. Burden wasss . . . the mossst

114

powerful . . . of my optionsss."

"What were his orders?"

"What do you . . . think . . . they were?"

He nodded to Thane.

Thane twisted the knife.

The minion grunted through the renewed pain. "We were . . . to have fun . . . with a human female. The one currently . . . ssscenting your . . . robe."

"Why?"

"Did . . . not ask. Did . . . not care."

Truth. "You have earned your death, minion. She's all yours," he told his soldiers.

Thane removed the blade, and she sagged against her bonds. A second later, five fiery swords appeared, and in the next blink of time, the minion was missing her head and all her limbs. Demons liked fire, yes, and could withstand the flames. But the fires in hell were fires of damnation. The soldiers' swords possessed the fire of justice, and that the demons could *not* withstand.

His warriors held the tips of their swords against each piece of the minion, until flesh and bone caught flame, charred to ash and swirled away in a sudden breeze.

Zacharel had the answers he'd sought. The question now was what to do with them.

CHAPTER FIVE

So much for enjoying her change of scenery, Annabelle thought.

Well, that wasn't exactly true. She had. At first.

After she had devoured all her favorite foods, her stomach so full she could have burst, she had showered, feeling cleaner than she had in four years. If only she'd felt cleaner than *ever,* but no. There was a film of dirt under her skin, in her blood, that she had been unable to wipe away.

Wah, wah, whatever. No whining. Not now. She dressed in the tank and soft flowing pants she had requested. Then she stood there. Just stood there, exhaustion completely overwhelming her. She asked the cloud — the cloud! — for a bed. A king-size monstrosity with gorgeous silk sheets appeared, and she crawled on top gratefully. But . . . she was unable to sleep, too afraid of being vulnerable, too worried about the nightmares that would plague her — too caught up in thoughts of Zacharel.

Where had he gone? Who was he with? What was he doing?

Why did it matter to her?

By morning, little aches and pains in her body made their presence known and she forgot all about her curiosity. Soon after that, she began to shiver and sweat from withdrawal. So many years of continuous drug use and now, quitting cold . . . probably not the wisest course of action. And yes, she could have asked the cloud for a sedative, but she resisted the idea with every fiber of her being. Never would she do to herself what the doctors had done to her.

The second day, she vomited over and over again, until there was nothing left inside her stomach except — surely — glass shards and rusty nails. And maybe a herd of stampeding buffalo.

The third day, she returned to the trembling and the sweating, so weak she could barely lift her head or even open her eyes.

Eventually, sleep battered past every wall of resistance she had erected, and she slipped into the land of dreams. Her parents hugged and kissed her, telling her how much they loved her. Her older brother, Brax, rubbed his knuckles into her hair. Oh, how she had missed him. Since her incarceration, he'd made his dislike of her very clear.

Once upon a time, he had threatened any boy who'd wanted to date her. He had smiled at her every morning as he'd fixed her breakfast, her parents having already rushed off to work. On the drive to school, he had lectured her about studying harder and keeping her grades up so that she could get into a good college and have the best possible future.

That wasn't possible now. The man Brax had become did not believe Annabelle's recollection of that fateful morning. He did not trust her, and he certainly did not adore her and want the best for her.

Best? What was the best for someone like her? Despite the euphoria she'd felt upon first leaving the institution, despite her desire to live on her own, happy and carefree, the truth was now unavoidable. The only future she had was one on the run from the law.

The dream morphed, her parents and Brax pushed to the back of her mind and replaced by the demons she'd fought throughout the years. She saw blood-soaked floors no one else could see, her feet slipping and sliding in the puddles as she cried for help she would never receive.

Thankfully, that dream morphed, as well. She lay beside Zacharel, and he placed his cold hands on her, gently brushing her hair from her face as he mumbled about troublesome humans. He stuffed sweet, juicy clumps of fruit down her throat, and she somehow found the energy to slap him for being such a turd about it.

The fourth day, everything changed. Her sleep calmed, her mind blanking. The aches and pains faded. Finally, blessedly, even the trembling and the sweating eased, and strength returned to her limbs. She stretched and struggled to a sitting position, dizziness waiting at the fringes of her mind, ready to devour her entire being.

She looked at her surroundings — she was still inside the cloud — then at herself. She was dressed in a white robe as soft as cashmere and scrubbed clean from head to toe, despite the length of time that had passed. Who had changed her? Bathed her?

Zacharel?

Her cheeks flushed with heat. Yeah, Zacharel. His part hadn't been a dream, after all, but straight-up reality.

How . . . nice of him.

Zacharel didn't seem like the type to concern himself with the suffering of others, especially at the expense of his own comfort, but he'd risked a few slaps from a whacked-out female just to ensure she ate.

Poor guy. He probably regretted releasing her.

She threw her legs over the side of the bed and stood, swayed. It was time to hunt Zacharel down, thank him and figure out her next move.

"Pesky human," Zacharel muttered as he paced the center of his cloud. He had never before taken care of a sick human, or even a sick angel, for that matter. Clearly. Under his care, Annabelle had only gotten worse.

And she'd slapped him! On multiple occasions! Not even his Deity had ever dared such a thing. Whip him, yes. Zacharel was still recovering from his latest round with the leather strap, but slap him? Never. Not that the puny actions had hurt. It was the principle of the thing. He'd taken time out of his day to care for her, precious time he should be devoting to his new army and their various missions, and she couldn't thank him?

"Typical mortal," he grumbled now. His anger with her did not stem from worry, he was certain of it. He rubbed the heel of his palm up and down the center of his chest and smacked his lips, cringing at the sour taste in his mouth.

He wouldn't voice a lie, but he would certainly entertain one in his own mind.

Annabelle would live or she would die, and Zacharel wasn't going to concern himself one way or the other any longer. He just wasn't.

He grimaced as that sour taste intensified. Enough of this! He would do what any other man would have done in this situation. He would summon a female to take over. Jamila. Yes, Jamila would ensure Annabelle's safety.

"Inform Jamila I require her presence," he told the cloud.

How long would it take her to fly here? It would take him less than a minute to thrust Annabelle into her arms and kick them both out of his home. He was tired of thinking about Annabelle, tired of wondering how badly she hurt, if she would survive whatever sickness had struck her. Tired of reaching inside the air pocket containing his vial of water from the River of Life, only to catch himself before he made contact with it. To even consider giving her the remaining drop was ludicrous.

"More threats?" Jamila asked the moment she arrived.

At last. He whirled to meet her head-on. "You're late."

Golden eyes glittered with . . . anger? Couldn't be. There was heat there, but nothing irate. "How can I be late? You didn't give me a time frame." Her wings tucked into her sides, and dark curls settled over her shoulders, falling down the smooth expanse of her arms. "Besides, I didn't feel a need to rush to another scolding."

"I have no intention of scolding you further. You disobeyed the night of the battle, and I proclaimed your punishment. That subject is now closed."

She twirled one of her ringlets around her finger. "Then why am I here?"

"You are female."

A slight quirk of her mouth. "Nice of you to notice."

"I want you to . . . I need you to . . ." He pursed his lips, massaged his tongue against the roof of his mouth. He tried to speak again. Failed. The words refused to leave him.

If he placed Annabelle in Jamila's care, he would not be able to see her without begging an invitation to the angel's home. He would never know what happened to her. And Jamila was so impulsive, so often controlled by her emotions. What if Annabelle angered her? Annabelle possessed a bit of a temper, and did not always mind her words. How would Jamila react to a callous retort from a lowly human? Not well, that much he knew.

I can't place Annabelle in her care.

A strange sort of relief crashed over him, lifting a debilitating weight from his shoulders and shining something light and bright into his heart. No, not relief. Couldn't be. He felt irritated by this turn of events, surely. He was back to where he'd started, to where he had no desire to be.

The angel was staring at him expectantly.

"What do females require?" he asked, refusing to change his mind yet again. Annabelle stayed, and that was that.

Jamila shifted to the side, her robe rippling with the motion. "Require for what?"

"For the meeting of needs."

Her eyes widened, her pupils flaring and gulping down all that gold. Rosy pink flushed her cheeks, her lips softening, parting. "I had no idea you had begun to experience desire, Zacharel. You should have said something sooner. I could have told you that I require only your cooperation."

As he tried to process her words, she stepped into the line of his body, wound her arms around his neck and lifted to her tiptoes. Then she meshed her mouth into his, and forced her tongue past his teeth.

O-kay. The ultracold Zacharel *was* capable of emotion. Desire. But that didn't make him any less of a jerk.

Annabelle had wanted to know where he was, not because she cared about the man — she didn't — but because he'd done something to the cloud to prevent her from leaving her room. Enraged, she'd demanded that the cloud show her where he was and what he was doing, and it — he? she? — had.

A TV-like screen had appeared just in front of her, comprised of nothing but air. She'd watched, her hands fisting, her eyes narrowing, as a stunner with curling dark hair wrapped herself around Zacharel, molding the two of them together and feeding him a decadent kiss. The rise in her temper wasn't about jealousy, but about her circumstances. She was trapped, and he was making out.

Now she watched as Zacharel jerked away from the girl. He growled, "What are you doing?"

Again the stunner conquered the distance, trying to refit her mouth over his. "I'm kissing you. Now kiss me back."

"No." Frowning, he set her away from him, and this time, he held her in place. His wings were tucked into his sides, though they arced backward, away from the female. Snowflakes rained from their tips, tiny crystals that formed little piles on the floor. "*Why* are you kissing me?"

The girl's sensual confidence died a slow, torturous death. "Because you hunger for me as I have hungered for you these past few months?" A question when she'd probably meant it to be a statement.

"I do not hunger for you, Jamila."

Ouch. There was such brutal honesty in his tone, even Annabelle flinched.

"But you said . . ." Jamila floundered. "I thought . . ."

Oh, honey. Just walk away before he does more than trample on your pride, Annabelle thought, sympathy for the girl momentarily superseding her anger with Zacharel.

"I said nothing to make you think I desired you," he stated with the same coldness that always infused his words. "You simply assumed. Therefore, now I will tell you plainly. I do not want you. I have never wanted you, and I will never want you."

Okay, so, wrong again. The man had no feelings.

A sob parted the woman's lips, and she

spun on her heel, her wings expanding in a burst of movement. Hers possessed far less gold than Zacharel's, but they were lovely nonetheless. She shot into the air and out of the cloud.

He faced the screen Annabelle still watched, and she knew he was headed into her room. Not wanting to be caught spying, she waved the TV screen away. "Go!"

The air thinned, until only the cloud wall remained.

A second later, Zacharel stepped through that wall, seeming to appear out of a forbidden midnight dream far better than the ones she'd entertained. Thick, silken black hair tumbled down a flawless forehead and into a gaze that studied her with unwavering intensity. Though his features had been painted with a brush of youth, he appeared beyond ancient, the wintry green of his eyes seeing everything, missing nothing.

A long, white robe draped him, somehow displaying his incredible strength, and oh, oh, oh, but he had brought the chill of the Arctic with him. She drew her arms around her middle for warmth.

He looked her over. Something passed over his expression, something she couldn't read, before he carefully blanked his features. "You are well."

I will not be intimidated, and I absolutely will not be awed by his appearance. Annabelle forced herself to unleash the ire she'd been nursing. "And *you* are a douche. You made me a prisoner, after I told you I'd rather die!"

Far from intimidated, he said, "That is no way to speak to me, Annabelle. I am in a dangerous mood."

Like she wasn't? "Well, well, the mighty Zacharel actually feels something," she said snippily. "It's a Christmas miracle."

"It is not Christmas, and I suggest you sweeten your tone. Otherwise, I might take you at your word and kill you. How about that?"

She gasped, stepped back until she hit the edge of the bed and almost fell. "You wouldn't dare. Not after you went to so much trouble to save me."

Stark self-loathing darkened his eyes. "I killed my own brother, Annabelle. There is no one I will not take down."

Wait, wait, wait. He'd done what? "You're lying." He had to be lying.

He snapped his teeth at her, reminding her of an injured animal in too much pain to accept aid from anyone. "I do not lie. There is no need. People lie because they worry over the consequences of admitting

127

the truth. I worry over nothing. People lie because they wish to impress those around them. I seek to impress no one. You would be wise to remember that."

How was this the same man who had cared for her so sweetly? "Why did you kill your brother?"

"That is none of your concern."

She persisted. "*How* did you kill your brother?"

Silence.

"An accident?"

"Annabelle!"

A chastisement if ever she'd heard one. Fine. She'd drop the subject for now. The wounded-animal thing made sense, though. Whatever he'd done, he suffered for it.

"Why are you letting me stay in your cloud," she said, "when I so clearly frighten you? And I do frighten you, no matter what you say. Why else would you lock me up?"

A heartbeat of quiet, his anger seeming to drain from him. "You mean to bait me with that question, I think. You hope to embarrass me into apologizing, into vowing never to lock you up again."

"No." Well, maybe a little.

"Did you wish to leave my cloud?"

"I wished to leave the room."

"And failed in your attempt."

"Your cloud was the failure, not me."

He rolled his eyes. "Why did you wish to leave?"

Rather than lie — or slap him again as he so richly deserved — she tossed his earlier words back at him. "That is none of your concern."

Were the corners of his lips twitching? "Did you want to see me? Speak to me?"

Every word caused heat to deepen in her cheeks. "I will not answer those questions, either."

"Smart girl. You have realized it is better to refuse me than to lie to me. But with your nonanswers, you have told me what I wanted to know. Yes, you wished to see me, to speak to me. But about what?"

Irritating angel. "Look. Either you promise never to lock me up again, or I bail sooner rather than later. And I realize that's not really a deterrent for you, but those are the only options I'm willing to entertain."

"Fine. I will never again lock you in this room."

He offered the vow so easily, she was momentarily taken aback. "Well, okay, then."

"You will stay?"

"Yes." For a little while longer, because she wasn't sure where else to go . . . or how to return to earth without spilling her guts. "But enough about me," she said, not wanting him to change his mind. "Did you have to be so mean to that woman?" So much for hiding the fact that she'd been spying.

His gaze flicked to the empty space beside her, narrowed and returned to her. "You watched me." The words were velvet, soft in a way he probably hadn't intended. All the while, vapor puffed in front of his face, adding to the erotic-dream factor.

This isn't your business, Miller. And yet she nodded to encourage him to continue. "I did," she said, and the scent of him . . . suddenly clinging to every inch of her . . . nearly sent her to her knees. How had she missed its allure before this moment?

One of his brows arched, slipping under that fall of hair. "How was I mean to her? I simply told her the truth."

"You told her the truth, sure, but you did it with no concern for her feelings." *Do not reach out and brush that hair away.*

"Yes, and she kissed me with no certainty of *my* feelings."

All right. Okay. That changed everything. Annabelle had been forcibly kissed before, and she had hated every moment of it. She had lashed out at the culprit, too. His reaction was understandable.

"Actually," he added, "if I *was* mean to her, and I'm not admitting that I was, it was to *spare* her feelings in the future. Now she knows my thoughts on the matter, without any doubt. She will not make the same mistake twice. Furthermore, the truth might hurt but when used properly, it's never purposely cruel."

What kind of woman would take this man on? she mused. A brave one, certainly. And why was she even entertaining such thoughts? His stupid scent must be affecting her brain.

"Are you married?" The notion shouldn't bother her, but it did. But only because she would feel guilty about finding him so attractive when he belonged to another woman, surely.

"No, I am not married," he said.

"Dating anyone?" Though the word *date* seemed way too mundane to be applied to the celestial being in front of her.

"No."

"Wanting to date anyone?"

"No. Enough questions."

"Have you *ever* dated anyone?"

He worked his jaw in irritation. "I have never dated anyone, nor have I ever wanted to date anyone."

Her eyes widened. "But that would

131

mean . . ."

"That Jamila's kiss was my first, yes."

No way. No way that had been this beautiful man's first kiss. Despite his standoffishness, someone would have tried to seduce him before now. "Did you like it?" Oh, no, no, no. She had *not* just asked him that.

"Clearly not." He moved around her, fingered the silk of the sheets draped over the bed. Very casually, he asked, "Have *you* ever been kissed?"

She sighed as memories assailed her. The good, the bad and the wretchedly ugly. Before the institution, the kisses she'd experienced had been with a boy of her choosing. Some had been sweet, some had been passionate, but all had been welcome. After the institution . . . She shuddered with revulsion. "Yes." Would Zacharel think less of her now?

"Did you like it?"

There'd been no condemnation in his voice, which was the only reason she responded with, "Depends on which kiss we're talking about."

He released the fabric and faced her, flattening one of his hands on the bedpost. "More than one person has kissed you?"

Still no judgment, and yet, there *was* something in his tone. Something hot. So hot, in fact, the snow stopped falling from his wings, the cold somehow suddenly sucked away.

Well, crap. She changed her mind a third time. He couldn't be emotionless. Raw fury blended with sensuality, radiating from those heavy eyelids to his lush lips, already plump and glistening, to the pulse hammering in his neck, to the slow curl of his fingers. "Yes," she said. "But only one actually counts. Before my confinement, I had a boyfriend. We were together for over a year and did things together. Those kisses I liked." Or thought she had at the time. "After my parents' murder, he broke up with me and never came to visit." She shrugged, as if she hadn't cared.

Truth was, she'd more than cared. She'd needed someone who knew her to believe her, to believe *in* her, to show her a measure of support or understanding. Heath's defection had cut deeper than her brother's, leaving her hollowed out and disheartened. She'd trusted him, and yet he'd so easily walked away from her. Now she had to live with the fact that he'd seen her naked.

"Who else?" Zacharel asked.

"A few times, while in lockup, a patient or a doctor . . ." Another shrug, this one stiff, jerky.

133

As she spoke, he lost that hint of sensual-ity, the coldness returning to him. She took comfort in that. Like her, he hated the thought of others being forced.

"What made the kisses with your boy-friend so nice?"

"We loved each other. Well, I loved him. Turns out he was just using me for what I'd give him. I wonder if that's a teenage boy thing, or just a Heath thing." She chewed on her bottom lip, her mind still caught on Zacharel's confession of total and complete abstinence. "How old are you, anyway?"

"Older than you can possibly imagine."

Please. "One hundred? Two hundred?"

He shook his head.

Her jaw dropped. "Five hundred? A . . . thousand." When he gave another shake, she said, "No way. Just no way. You can't be older than a thousand."

He arched a brow.

"You are," she gasped out. "You really are."

"I am thousands of years old."

Thousands, as in more than one. She flat-tened her hands over her twisting stomach. "And you've really never kissed anyone? Of your own free will, I mean."

He stepped into her personal space, say-ing softly, "This doubt you express toward my confessions is as offensive as it is baf-fling." Cold breath trekked over her face, clean and sweet. "I have never, in all my centuries, spoken a lie."

I will not inch away. I will not show weakness. "Sorry, it's just, you've been around a long time, have probably seen humans do everything." She paused, waiting for his confirmation. Confirmation he gave with a single nod. "I'm just surprised."

He gathered a lock of her hair between his fingers, rubbing the strands together. The contrast between the blue-black of the lock and the sun-kissed sweetness of his skin was magnificent, almost magical.

If she wasn't careful, *she* would throw herself at him. And she would find herself rejected and embarrassed, just like the other girl.

She had to remind herself that she wasn't interested in a romantic entanglement right now. After everything she'd been through, she wasn't sure how she would even react to a man's advances.

While rape had never happened, plenty of other things had. Hands, wandering. Fingers, massaging. Tongues, licking. Her utter helplessness had disgusted and sickened her. And the fact that Fitzpervert had pictures of her . . .

Might vomit. Had he shown anyone? Did he sometimes laugh about the pain he had caused her?

"What's wrong?" Zacharel asked.

She forced her mind to return to the cloud and the angel still towering in front of her. He had released her hair, had backed away from her. Snow once again rained from the tips of his wings, the air now so frigid little goose bumps were popping up all over her body.

"Nothing's wrong," she muttered.

He smacked his lips as if he tasted something foul. "You lie."

"So?" See? Already dark memories were affecting her dealings with a man, tainting everything.

"So? I tell you the truth, yet you lie to me. That is intolerable, Annabelle, and I will not allow it."

And how did he plan to stop it? "Let's just say that if something's wrong, it's none of your business." Just then, only one thing mattered. Answers. "Before, you told me I had been marked by a demon."

He accepted the change of subject with a soft "Yes."

"And he did this to claim me as his property?" She remembered waking up with burning eyes. She remembered the creature

136

in her garage, clawing her parents to death. She remembered the way he'd kissed her — the worst kiss of her life.

"Yes. He must have seen you, desired you and decided to keep you, even if he couldn't take you with him. Did he say anything to you?"

"Only classic B movie stuff. You know, *I love the sound of trouble.* And *this is gonna be fun.*"

"He didn't ask you to belong to him, and you didn't say yes?"

"Hardly. But he will come back for me, won't he?" She'd always wondered. She'd always feared. And, according to Zacharel, fear was a draw for all kinds of evil.

A more hesitant yes was offered this time.

She wasn't going to fear anymore. She was going to prepare. "Well, I plan to kill him when he finds me. So, on that note, I have one more question for you. Will you give me one of those fire swords?"

Zacharel peered down at the human woman who had made him feel more in the span of five minutes than anyone had in the centuries since his brother's death. He did not understand this, or her, or what was happening to him.

Those otherworldly blue eyes were filled

with so many secrets, haunting secrets. He wanted to plumb her depths and discover everything she tried to hide. And he wanted to . . . touch her. Was her skin as soft and smooth as it appeared? He'd held her, but her clothes had prevented him from knowing the texture of her skin. Would her warmth seep past the layers of cold encasing him and consume him?

He wanted to kiss her, to discover if her taste would match her succulent scent. Wanted to know if her kiss would differ from Jamila's. Wanted to know if she would enjoy his kiss as much as she had enjoyed the former boyfriend's. And he hated that others had touched and kissed her without permission, the knowledge fanning to sparkling life an urge to maim and kill the culprits.

He had not wondered about these things before, had not cared who did what with whom. He, who had seen humans engage in every sexual act imaginable, had never even contemplated a female in an erotic way. Had never cared enough about anyone to experience any type of jealousy.

Until now. Until Annabelle. This girl was brave when she should cower, vulnerable when she should be hardened, kind when she should be cold. Exactly as Hadrenial had been.

But others had been brave, vulnerable and kind, as well, yet Zacharel had never reacted this way to any of them. And the fact that she kept reminding him of his *brother* should have doused any flames of arousal.

However, the flames were not doused.

Though he'd never preferred a physical "type" before, he clearly did so now. At the top of his What I Find Irresistible list? Blue-black hair, crystalline eyes and soft pink lips. Oh, and skin that appeared to be dipped in bronze and dusted with diamond powder.

Zacharel's attraction to her was driving his thoughts, he knew that, but he had no weapons to combat it. He was too inexperienced, had never come against anything like this. Somehow, though, he had to find a way to resist her. He also knew that once a man feasted at the table of temptation, he would not leave it, would glut himself again and again.

But . . . she wasn't a temptation he had to resist to remain in the heavens, was she? And what would be so bad about feasting on her, learning what it felt like to have her softer body pressed against his harder one? She was not expressly forbidden to his faction.

He gritted his teeth. Already he was a step closer.

He studied her more intently. Colors were not something he'd ever cared about unless they pertained to camouflage, yet the pink she now wore complemented her Asian ancestry perfectly. He knew what waited underneath those clothes, had stripped her during her sickness. But he had paid no attention to her feminine curves. Now he wondered . . .

Another step.

"What are you thinking about?" she asked, suspicious. "I'm guessing it's not about the weapon I requested."

His cheeks heated with embarrassment and he spun away from her. He couldn't lie, but he wouldn't tell her the truth, either. Therefore, he would ignore her.

"Zacharel?"

Even her voice appealed to him. Soft, lyrical, firm yet beseeching. He'd noticed before, but now . . . yes, now everything had changed. Yet another step.

"The sword," he said. "You say you want one, but could you really take a life?"

"Yes," she replied, the assertion offered without any hesitation. "I have before. Demon life, that is, not human, just so we're clear."

140

Surprising that she'd found the strength to defeat an enemy most of her kind couldn't see and often denied. "Even still, I will not give you a sword of fire. I cannot, for only my kind may carry them."

"Oh," she said, disappointed.

"But there are other ways."

Immediately she brightened. "Will you teach me?"

He did not have time. He had an army to train, battles of his own to fight. And he did not like the thought of her fighting a race of creatures without any limits to their depravity. But whoever had marked her *would* want her back, whether he'd left her willingly or not — especially when he learned that Zacharel had her. More than one-upping each other, demons lived for one-upping angels. And this demon would not hesitate to hurt Annabelle in the vilest of ways to do so. No demon would.

How she had survived even this long, Zacharel wasn't sure.

"Yes," he found himself saying. "I will teach you how to kill demons."

CHAPTER SIX

Thane returned to Zacharel's cloud with a dossier about Annabelle Miller's very short, very miserable life. The new leader of the Army of Disgrace, as so many of their peers had begun to call them, accepted it with his customary politeness. Meaning, none at all. Zacharel was as cold as always, offering no murmurs of thanks but giving a curt nod of dismissal.

More and more, Thane actually liked the warrior's directness. Liked Zacharel, too, and that was a fact that shocked him to the marrow of his bones. He hadn't been part of an actual army for more than a hundred years, and he never would have joined another if his Deity had not commanded him to follow Zacharel . . . or else.

At first, Thane had seethed. How dare anyone tell him how to spend his time? If he wanted to laze in bed, seduce any female that caught his eye and fight every demon he encountered, he would. But what he decided, his boys decided. They were one for all and all for one, or however the humans said it. That's how things worked with the three of them. He, Bjorn and Xerxes were in this together, whatever *this* happened to be, and he could not allow them to rebel because he could not allow them to suffer the consequences. Thane could endure anything but that.

Now, three months into their new arrangement, he was suddenly glad he had not rebelled. Well, he *had* rebelled against Zacharel with little insults here and there, but he had also joined the army rather than fall. He realized the lack of leadership and structure had rubbed him raw, that his life had been nothing but a chaotic mess and he'd needed order *somewhere.*

Thane flew to The Downfall, a pleasure house in the Deity's section of the heavens. Over the centuries, more and more of the Deity's angels had succumbed to temptations of the flesh. They had needed a place to indulge without judgment from anyone but themselves, and so Thane had given them one.

The Downfall belonged to him. He, Bjorn and Xerxes lived there, as did the immortal lovers they kept. Lovers that never lasted long, for each male preferred new and different.

Despite this proclivity, they had not yet warranted the ultimate fall, though Thane knew they teetered on the brink.

Angels in the Deity's faction fell from grace because they welcomed evil into their hearts, because they habitually cheated, stole, lied — yes, it was possible — or committed cold-blooded murder. Because they succumbed to the follies of hatred, envy, fear or pride, or because they refused to turn away from some sort of depravity.

They were not to aid a demon, or seek revenge against another angel for a perceived offense. They were to bring their grievances before the Heavenly High Council.

Since Thane's escape from a demon prison those hundred years ago, he and his boys had done everything but aid a creature of the dark. He wasn't sure why they had been given this chance.

If they failed to correct their behavior, their sins *would* eventually catch up to them. He knew that. But still Thane could not bring himself to change. He was what the demons had made him.

Stars twinkled all around him as he landed on the roof of the towering building. He'd chosen brick-and-mortar rather than a cloud, for he'd suspected too many patrons would have taken advantage, commanding the cloud to produce all manner of illicit things. Plus, clouds were expensive. While he could afford one, and could have chosen to live separately from the club, he knew himself well enough to know that he, too, would have taken advantage.

Two doorways were accessible from the roof. One led to the club itself, and the other to his private chambers. Two angelic guards stood at attention on either side of both. He nodded to the pair in front of his personal entrance, and they moved aside. A mental command caused the wide double doors to glide open.

The slow bump and grind of music echoed from below as he strode down the empty hallway to his sitting room, where Bjorn and Xerxes waited. Both reclined in plush velvet chairs and sipped at their drinks of choice.

Thane stopped at the wet bar and poured himself a tumbler of absinthe. He turned, leaned against the marble counter. This sanctuary was a study of indulgence, he thought as he scanned the room. Everywhere he looked he saw treasures given to him by kings, queens, immortals and even humans. Intricately carved tables, polished to a glossy shine. Couches and chairs draped in luxurious fabrics, each a different jewel tone. The rarest of rugs, chandeliers dripping with precious gems rather than crystals.

"Has Zacharel begun shagging the human yet?" Bjorn asked. He was, perhaps, one of the most beautiful angels ever created, his skin gilded with all that gold, his eyes like a mosaic of the most expensive of amethysts, sapphires, emeralds and tourmaline.

But Thane remembered a time when the warrior had not looked so pretty. Their captors had chained Thane to the filthy floor of their cell and strung Bjorn up above him. Over the ensuing days, those same demons had peeled the skin from Bjorn's body, careful, so careful not to damage the flesh. Blood had rained upon Thane in a continuous flow, soaking him.

Oh, how the warrior had screamed . . . at first. By the end, his lungs had deflated and his throat had been nothing but pulp. The demons had then taken turns wearing the skin as a coat, laughing, pretending to be Bjorn while performing all kinds of lewd acts.

Xerxes had been chained to the wall across from them, his stomach pressed into the stone, his arms shackled over his head, his legs pried apart. He was forced to listen to everything that was done to his friends, but unable to see it. And maybe that was worse. He'd never known what happened around him as he was whipped and . . . other things were done to him.

The horror of his time in that cell had wiped all color from his once auburn hair and peach-tinted skin, leaving him as white as milk. Blood vessels had burst in his once amber eyes, turning the irises red.

None of them ever spoke of their incarceration and torture, but Thane knew just how his friends really were. After every fight, Bjorn spiraled out of control. After every sexual encounter, Xerxes vomited. But neither one would stop the fighting or the bedding.

Thane had learned to embrace this side of himself.

"Someone's lost in his thoughts," Bjorn said. The spiral from this last battle hadn't yet hit him . . . but it would. It always did.

"Feed him his teeth," Xerxes suggested. "He'll respond, I promise."

They'd asked him a question, hadn't they . . . about Zacharel and the human, he recalled. "What do you think?" he at last replied. "Zacharel was in his office, writing a report about something. Our performance,

147

most likely."

"Think he'll ever thaw?" Bjorn asked.

Thane shuddered. "Let's hope not."

Xerxes rubbed the scars on his neck. Everyone assumed his immortality had failed him and he'd somehow ended up looking like a poorly put together puzzle, but the truth was, his body was simply always in the process of healing from the damage he constantly inflicted.

"I killed sixteen demons at the institution," he said. This was one of the only topics of conversation he enjoyed.

"Twenty-three," Bjorn said, a thread of darkness in his tone.

Thane added his tally in his head — he never forgot a kill. "Only nineteen for me."

Bjorn grinned, but there was no light in his expression. "I win."

Xerxes flipped him off.

"Such a sore loser." Thane *tsk*ed. "And now a babysitter, too. So where is the fallen you've been tasked with guarding? You haven't mentioned him once since taking over his care and feeding."

He saw a flare of panic in those crimson eyes, quickly masked. "He's chained in my room."

The panic nearly broke Thane's heart, for he knew Xerxes would never willingly hold anyone but a demon prisoner. "What are you going to do with him?"

"I . . . don't . . . Buy a cloud, I suppose. Keep him locked there."

"I do not recommend that, my friend. If you think he's able to care for himself, you'll never check on him." His guilt wouldn't let him.

"And the problem with that?"

"The fallen are practically mortal. He could decide to starve himself, waste away." *And you would only blame yourself.*

Xerxes confronted Thane dead-on, determination radiating from him. "You're right."

"Aren't I always?"

"I'll leave him here for now. Check on him once a day. Force him to eat if necessary."

"While you're at it, talk to him," Bjorn suggested. "Find out why he fell."

Both of his boys knew it was just a matter of time before they, too, lost their wings and immortality. They would delay the inevitable for as long as they could, hence their cooperation now, but like Thane, they would never veer from the path they were on.

The demons had made sure of that.

Thane drained the rest of his drink, poured himself another and drained it, too. The potent alcohol burned going down, but by the time it reached his stomach, it cooled to a sweet, drugging warmth. And yet, the pleasant sensation did nothing to lessen the tension inside him.

"Did you find us girls for the evening?" he asked no one in particular.

"I did," Bjorn answered. "They await us now."

"What is mine? Vampire? Shifter?" Not that he cared. A female was a female was a female.

"She's a Phoenix."

All right, perhaps he did care. Excitement joined the tension that always hummed inside him, lighting him up from the inside out. So many immortal races walked the earth and several realms of the heavens. The Harpies, the Fae, the elves, the Gorgons, the sirens, the shifters and the Greek and Titan gods and goddesses — or so they liked to call themselves, when in truth they were nothing more than kings and queens who had allowed pride to exalt their opinions of themselves — and countless others. The Phoenix were the second-most dangerous.

Snake-shifters were the first.

Still, the Phoenix were blood-hungry and cruel, deriving glee from destruction. They lived and thrived in fire, and they could force the dead to rise from their graves —

and those that rose were then bound to serve them, enslaved for the rest of eternity.

Thane set his empty glass on the bar and straightened. "I don't want to leave her waiting any longer."

Bjorn and Xerxes stood. Six long steps and he stood between them. They stalked forward, then branched apart, heading to three separate bedrooms. Only silence emanated from his. His hands were surprisingly steady as hc shoved open the double doors. Closed them.

He heard the soft click of his friends' doors as he considered his soon-to-be conquest.

The female reclined on the bed, a mound of pillows at her back. She was gloriously naked, hair of gold and scarlet like crackling flames and tumbling over one shoulder. Even at this distance, Thane could feel the heat of her, the warmth licking at him. Thin chains forged by an immortal blacksmith circled her wrists and ankles, rendering her a slave to her captor's commands, the metal somehow compelling her to obey orders.

Bjorn must have purchased her in the sex market. "Do you want this?" he demanded. "Want me? Speak true."

She licked her lips. "Oh, yes."

"You do not feel forced?" There was only

one line Thane would not cross in the bedroom, and that was forcing himself on another. "No matter what happens between us, you will be free to leave this place."

"No, I'm not being forced. I was told I'd be paid."

Ah. She wanted money, not him. He was utterly okay with that, had had to go this route before. "You will be."

"Then why would I leave when wealth awaits me if I stay?" she asked, hooking a lock of hair behind her ear.

An ear that pointed at the end. "Excellent question."

She grinned, and he saw that her teeth were fanged like a vampire's. Her body was a study of beauty, a wealth of sensuality. Though he couldn't see the back of her, he knew she would be covered in tattoos that bore the mark of her tribe.

"You were told what would be required of you?" he asked.

"Yes, which means all this talking is merely wasting my time and your money."

"We don't want that." With a single tug, his robe fell away from his body, leaving him bare. The material was so light, it made no sound as it landed on the floor.

Thane crawled onto the mattress, the edge dipping with his muscled weight. A moment later, the female was on him. For a long while, he knew nothing but the burn of her nails and the scrape of her teeth. Then little beads of fire began to seep from her pores, blistering him just right and wringing exquisite groan after exquisite groan from him. He loved it as much as he hated it.

She performed every terrible act he required without hesitation, and he toyed with the idea of keeping her far longer than he'd ever kept another. Usually he was done after two or three beddings, not wanting to see revulsion smoldering in eyes that should be filled with desire. Because, after a while, the females always gave way to revulsion. They thought about what they'd done, what he'd done, and they regretted it all. But this female laughed with genuine pleasure as she performed, and he would be willing to bet she always would. Her greed for money would allow nothing less.

When it was over, Thane lay still, trying to catch his breath, enjoying the sensation of burning from the inside out.

Through the wall at his left — purposely thin so that he and his boys would hear if they were needed — he caught the heartbreaking echo of Xerxes retching into the toilet, just as he always did after sex.

He wanted more for his friend. Better. But

he had no idea how to help.

He dressed and left the Phoenix exhausted on the bed. Bjorn was already in the sitting room, alone and peering blankly into a fresh glass of vodka.

Thane fell into a chair. Bjorn never glanced up, too lost in his head, in the darkness that had finally come for him.

Xerxes stepped out of his room, pale and shaky, and avoided Thane's gaze. He, too, fell into a chair.

Thane loved these men. He did. He would happily die for them — but he would not let them die. Not like this. Not in misery.

They'd crawled out of that dungeon together, and somehow, someway, he would drag them out of their self-imposed hell.

CHAPTER SEVEN

The next morning, a naked Zacharel sat at the edge of his bed and rolled his brother's urn in his hands. It was a clear, hourglass-shaped jar, the substance inside a thick liquid as transparent as the urn, with only the tiniest of rainbow flecks glittering in the light.

This urn was Zacharel's greatest treasure. His only treasure. Now and forever, he would protect this urn as he had not protected his brother.

"I love you, Zacharel."

"I love you, too, Hadrenial. So much."

"Do you?"

"You know I do."

"And you would do anything for me?"

"Anything."

"Kill me, then. A true death. Please. You can't leave me like this."

"Like this" had been broken, bloody and violated in unspeakable ways. *"Anything but that. You'll recover. One day you will even be happy again."*

"I don't want to recover. I want to cease to exist, now and forever. That's the only way to end my torment."

"We'll make the demons pay for what they did to you. Together. Then we can talk about this again." And Zacharel would once again deny him.

"If you don't kill me, I'll kill myself. You know what will happen to me then."

Yes, he'd known. You could not render the true death upon yourself. Hadrenial would have been able to slay his own body, but his spirit, dark as it had currently been, would have lived on and been cast into hell. That hadn't swayed Zacharel. Still he'd said no. But in the end, Hadrenial had stayed true to his promise. He had tried to end himself over and over again. Always Zacharel had brought him back with the Water of Life.

Those years, his entire existence had been spent chasing after his brother, saving his brother and, finally, killing his brother to at last end his pain. It was a decision Zacharel regretted to this day, for this urn contained all that was left of Hadrenial.

Zacharel had mined from deep inside his brother's chest the essence of all the love he'd ever felt, then poisoned him with the

Water of Death, taken from the stream that flowed beside the Deity's River of Life. That water was the only way to kill an immortal once and for all.

To obtain the smallest of vials, an angel had to go through the same process as for the Water of Life: a whipping to prove his determination, followed by a meeting with the Heavenly High Council, where permission was granted or denied. If granted, a sacrifice of the Council's choosing had to be made.

Zacharel had gone through all of that — after his brother had been denied — but he had hesitated inside the temple. The two rivers ran side by side, life and death, happiness and sorrow. The choice had belonged to him. He could have taken from Life. He *should* have taken from Life. But all that would have done was heal his brother's body, not his mind.

Spending time in the presence of the Most High would have been needed to save his mind, for the Most High could soothe and save *anyone,* but Hadrenial had refused to try. Still he'd wanted an end.

"How could you ask that of me?" he demanded. "How could I do it?"

Of course, there was no response. There never was.

Zacharel had poured Death down his brother's throat. Had watched the life drain from him, the light dim in his eyes. Had then burned his body with a sword of fire. Had watched his brother turn to ash and float away.

He'd followed pieces of that ash for days.

Now he gazed down at the black smudge growing on his chest. The day of his brother's death, Zacharel had removed his own sense of love, a portion far smaller than Hadrenial's had been, placing it inside the urn, and glorying as it mingled with all that was left of his brother. There, at least, they were still together.

A week later, a tiny black dot had appeared on the exact spot he'd taken that portion from, and over the years that dot had slowly but steadily increased in size. However, after Zacharel's appointment with the Deity, when the snow began to drip from his wings, the rate of increasing had quadrupled.

He knew what it meant, what the end result would be, but he wasn't concerned. Was actually glad. If he failed in his mission this year and was kicked from the heavens, he wouldn't have to suffer long.

"I wonder if Annabelle would have fascinated you, too."

He paused, picturing the two together. Yes, Annabelle's courage would have delighted the gentle Hadrenial. Would they have fought for her?

No, he decided. Because Zacharel would have given her up. Planned to do so now, in fact, after his obligation was fulfilled.

Very carefully Zacharel set the urn on his nightstand and stood. He could have hidden the thing in a pocket of air, dragging it with him wherever he went. But other angels would have scented his brother and asked questions he had no wish to answer. Demons would have scented him, as well, and tried to destroy him all over again.

He tugged on a robe before stalking to Annabelle's door. There he paused, unsure whether or not he should enter. Yesterday he had been angry with himself for agreeing to help her learn to fight demons, and had left her to her own devices.

As promised, he had not locked her in the room. He had expected her to hunt him down, but she had stayed put — and that had made him angrier.

What was she doing to him? Usually he was a man without a temper. For centuries he had been known for his coldness both inside and out, yet around her he felt as though he were teetering at a very sharp ledge of danger. Even now he was tense, his jaw aching from the constant grinding of his teeth.

All night he'd imagined kissing her. Kissing her deeper, harder, *better* than the man who had come before him, finally giving into temptation that he kept trying to convince himself wasn't truly temptation. Why? She wasn't special. She was a nuisance, a burden, existing for only a brief span of time. There were thousands like her.

Were there really?

Yesterday he'd peered down at those lush pink lips and craved. He'd never before craved. Maybe because he'd had another woman's taste in his mouth, his interest in the act had been pricked, a desire kindling to compare what was forced with what was given. Maybe not.

The report Thane brought him had made Zacharel want Annabelle a thousand times more. She had endured multiple beatings from humans and demons alike, yet they hadn't diminished her audacity. She had an older brother who'd written her terribly hurtful letters, lashing out at her for her actions, yet she had responded with only kindness and understanding. Doctors had locked her up, overmedicated her, harmed her irrevocably, but she had fought back with

160

every bit of her strength.

No, there weren't thousands like her.

He should walk away from her now, before he decided to nix his plan, abandon common sense and keep her — and later lose her. Before he caused collateral damage on purpose, simply to avenge her.

Zacharel had only to stay with her a little while longer. A few weeks, perhaps a few months — no longer than a year — and she would be able to fight the evil that hunted her. He would make sure of it. They could then part, and he would never again have to think about her . . . though he had no idea where he would take her or how he would absolve himself of her responsibility in the Deity's eyes, but those were details for another day.

Determined, he entered the room.

She sat at the edge of the bed. When she spotted him, she hopped to her feet, her blue-black ponytail swinging back and forth. "I think it will be best if we end our association now" were the first words out of her mouth.

Then you should have worn something else, he thought, dazed as he drank her in. Gone were the tank and soft, flowing pants. Instead, she wore a black leather bustier that revealed more cleavage than it concealed, and scuffed black leather pants that molded to the lithe strength of her.

Suddenly self-conscious, she shifted from one booted foot to the other. "I asked the cloud for battle-ready clothing, and this is what I got. There are slits all over the pants, for easy access to the weapons, I'm guessing. But the bustier has me stumped. Unless, of course, the cloud thinks my cleavage will stun my opponents into stupidity." Frowning, she anchored her hands on her hips, shook her head. "My outfit doesn't matter. Take me back to Colorado."

"No, it doesn't matter and no, I won't. I thought we had come to an arrangement."

"Yes, but . . ." Her gaze dropped to her feet, only to snap back up and narrow.

"What?"

"You are beyond frustrating," she grumbled. "Why can't you do what I ask you to do without issuing a million questions first?"

"I could say the same to you."

"I don't — Argh." She raised a fist at him. "So maybe I do ask a lot of questions. So what. Anyone in my position would do the same. Besides, I'm a girl and that's my job. You're a boy. You're supposed to pound your chest with your fists and grunt, then do everything in your power to please me."

"Hardly. The man you just described is more likely to knock you over the head with a club and drag you away by the hair."

With his every word, amusement had grown in that blue, blue gaze.

The show of her temper, and the subsequent humor, delighted him. But only a little, he assured himself, and only because he could not guess what she would do or say next. "How are you feeling?" he asked, studying her once more. She still had bruises under her eyes, her lips were chapped from being chewed and her limbs shook. "You are unwell again?"

"I'm still suffering from withdrawal, that's all."

Zacharel recalled the long list of medications she had been prescribed. Such withdrawals would be substantial. He could give her the remaining drop of water from the River of Life, but — His jaw clenched. Considering such an option before, while she'd been bedbound, he could justify. He hadn't known whether she would live or die and that's exactly what the water was for. Life and death. It was not for relieving a few aches and pains.

"I'll be fine," she added, probably to fill the sudden silence. "Now. Will you please take me back? *Without* asking me any more

163

questions."

"I might be beyond frustrating —" in fact, he was pretty sure the name Zacharel meant *bastard* in several languages "— but you are safer with me than with anyone else."

"Safer with the guy who threatened to kill me?"

Ah. Now he understood. After a good night's sleep, her head finally clear, she had recalled what he'd said to her — *I could kill you now* — and wanted to escape him. "I did not threaten you." Truth. He had merely stated a fact. He could kill her at any moment.

"But you said —"

"I know what I said. But I tell you now, again, that you are safer with me than with anyone else." Even if he hurt her, even if he did decide to slay her, she was still safer with him. Everyone else would do far worse.

For once taking him at his word, she drew in a deep breath and nodded. "All right, I'll stay. For now."

He felt an odd urge to say thank-you but managed to bite the words back. "You are simply too good to me."

She crossed her arms over her middle. "Is that sarcasm? I think I detect sarcasm."

"Are you sure I even know what that word means?"

She *tsk*ed under her tongue. "Another question from your end." Her head tilted to the side and she studied him for the first time since he'd entered, the visual perusal a whispering touch over his entire body. "Your wings . . ."

"Yes?" He stretched out one, then the other, examining their lengths. Snow still trickled from each, but the glistening crystals were smaller than usual.

"They're more gold than white. Yesterday the opposite was true."

She was right. The amount of gold had increased yet again. That could only mean . . . he *was* evolving into one of the Elite, whether his Deity had spoken to him about it or not.

But . . . but . . . *that* could only mean his Deity was pleased with him and that Zacharel had been chosen to replace Ivar. There was no other explanation that made sense.

But why?

Because Zacharel had saved a human, despite the risk to himself? Because he had finally taken charge of his army, was finally earning the respect of his men? If so, that would mean his Deity had never wanted him to fail, that the promotion was to be his prize.

"Well?" Annabelle prompted. "And don't think I was complaining. Your wings are very pretty."

Pretty? The word should not have offended him, but it did. They were magnificent, thank you.

He owed her no explanation about this, and had to stop offering details so freely. When they parted, and they would, she could be captured, could give the information to his enemy. But still he did it. Still he told her. His training would ensure she was never captured. Surely.

"A p-promotion. H-how cool," she said through suddenly chattering teeth. Mist swirled in front of her face. "Not to change the subject, but, uh, is it cold in here to you?"

Reminded of when he'd first found her, of how frozen she'd been, Zacharel decided he was no longer accepting or grateful for the chill he carried with him. Annabelle suffered, and that he did not like. He would have to ask his Deity for leniency in this matter. And perhaps he would receive it, now that he knew there was a way back into his leader's good graces.

"A coat," he said now, and Annabelle's eyes gleamed with anticipation.

"I should have thought of that."

"I'm sure you would have." He held out his hand and a white faux-fur coat appeared.

"Thanks," she said. "You know, you are one huge contradiction. You're mean one moment, then nice the next. Threatening one moment, then protective the next."

"You mean for me to take offense, like before at the institution?"

"Not this time."

"But you do not sound pleased by the knowledge."

"Well, I'm not. It's too hard to get a read on you."

"I am not a book," he said.

She nodded. "Exactly."

"But —"

"Just stick with the meanness and the threatening," she interjected. "I don't want to like you."

A more confusing conversation he'd never had. "Why?"

"I plead the fifth."

He no longer liked this evasive strategy of hers. "You cannot refuse to respond to all of my queries."

"Uh, not true. I totally can."

As she'd just proven. "Then we must work out some sort of reward for when you do answer." Though that smacked of bribery

— because it was — and implied that he cared — which he did. There could be no more denying that, he supposed. Not that the admission would change anything.

One of her brows arched in a parody of an expression he'd given her more than once. "And a spanking for when I don't?"

"Do not be silly. I would never spank you for such a minor offense, Annabelle." He liked her name on his lips. Liked the sound of it, the feel of it. "For something major . . . maybe. But I would never do anything that would cause lasting damage. You are not one of my soldiers. More than that, you are human. You could not withstand much."

"You might be surprised by my fortitude."

He meant to respond, he truly did, but he was suddenly snagged by a desire to trace his fingertips over her cheeks, her lips, to know if she would burn him, if her pulse would hammer out of control as he suspected his own would do. He wanted to know if she would inch closer to him or turn away.

You are not a slave to such mortal desires. He would not touch her, and he would not consider her response. But while he could fight the physical — and win — he found he could not fight the mental. His curiosity about her was too great and he found himself saying, "Your mother was Japanese, yet your name is not."

Annabelle accepted the change of subject with a relieved squaring of her shoulders. "She spent most of her life in the States. And I was named after my father's mother, Anna Bella." She drew the lapels of the coat tighter and gave in to her own curiosity. "I've been wondering. Are you like the angels in the Bible? I, uh, had the cloud provide me with one last night. I read a few passages, and . . . well . . ."

"You see differences between me and the angels you read about," he finished for her.

"Exactly. And I do remember you saying you were part of a different race . . . or something."

He couldn't help pointing out, "I could refuse to answer, as you have done to me."

"But that would be the equivalent of a spanking," she pointed out, "and you, who never lie, won't do that to me."

A very smart girl, his Annabelle. Wait. *His* Annabelle? "What you read is true. In human terms, my Deity is a king. He rules only a certain portion of the heavens and serves under the Most High, who rules *every* inch of the heavens, even what the Greeks and Titans claim to own — but that is another story. And we are not like the Most

169

High's angels because we were not created for the same purposes."

She tossed up her hands. "Then why are you called angels?"

"We are winged, and we fight evil. It's a label, and it stuck."

"Argh! But if you both fight evil, how are you different?"

He had so rarely interacted with humans, and he had never had to explain this kind of thing. "All humans are living beings, yes, and share many similarities, but not all have the same purpose. Some build. Some entertain. Some teach."

No sooner had he finished speaking than the walls of the cloud darkened, thickened, lightning strikes sparking from within, small at first, but growing in length and intensity. Confused, he searched for other differences, found none.

Annabelle reached out, intending to stroke her fingertips over the lightning. He grabbed her wrist and stilled her.

"Cloud?" he said. "What's the problem?"

Demons . . . A whisper inside his head. *Attacking* . . .

Impossible. Right? But . . . what if it wasn't? Zacharel summoned his sword of fire. Demons rarely ventured into the heavens, much less to an angel's residence, but it *could* be done.

All the color drained from Annabelle's face. "What's wrong? What's happening?"

"We're under attack." Either the demons had no idea who owned this cloud, or their desire to obtain Annabelle was too great, their ability to track her far better than he had anticipated.

The cloud would hold them off, but would, eventually, fail. Clouds such as this one were designed for comfort rather than battle, something that had never bothered him before. Actually, at any other time, Zacharel would have relished this challenge, the chance for victory. Now he experienced the tiniest shard of fear. Annabelle could be hurt. He hadn't spent these past few days seeing to her survival just to watch her fall prey to his enemy's evil.

"Show me," he commanded the cloud.

Beside him, a portion of air thickened, a multitude of colors flickering to life, blending together. He stiffened. Annabelle gasped. At least fifteen demons surrounded his home, clawing at the outer walls in an effort to get inside. They were worked into a frenzy, foaming at the mouth, desperate, their nails tipped with poison.

"They came for me," she said, toneless.

Zacharel snaked his free hand around her

waist and tugged her into the line of his body. "Hold on to me and don't let go under any circumstances."

"But I can help you fight them." Good. There'd been a layer of determination that time.

Still, he barked, "Can you fly? Or will you tumble to the earth without me?" They both knew the answer to that one.

No longer hesitating, she wrapped her arms around his neck, her fingers locked tight at his nape. Soft breasts snuggled against the pound of his heartbeat, and their lower bodies pressed together. He inhaled sharply, amazed he even noticed the sensations at such a time as this.

Focus. "That isn't good enough," he said. His hand lowered to her bottom, and he hefted her up. "Legs."

Her legs wrapped around his waist.

Their eyes met, a clash of green against that otherworldly blue — a blue currently fogged with the determination he'd heard as well as the terror he'd sensed. But she nodded, ready for battle.

Brave girl.

"At least you stopped snowing," she said.

Had he? His Deity must have heard his unspoken desire and responded, a gesture Zacharel would be sure to thank him for.

"I wish there was another way," he said. In this position, Annabelle would act as his shield. He despised that on every level, but he had no other solution. He couldn't flash her away and return — moving from one location to another with only a thought — because he couldn't flash. Only a rare few could, like the wingless Koldo.

What Zacharel *could* do was camouflage his body so that no one could see or sense him. But he couldn't camouflage Annabelle to that same degree, so that was out, too.

I need you — he projected first to Koldo because he could be the biggest help right now, then to every other member of his army. He'd never done this before, wasn't sure it would work, and cursed himself for not practicing speaking inside their minds. *Demons. My cloud. Battle.*

There was no time to await their responses, if they even knew how to reply in such a manner. "If I hand you to a man named Koldo, do not fight him. He will whisk you to safety."

"What about you?"

Excellent question. "Now," he said to the cloud, ignoring her, "I want you to leave this location. Go somewhere the demons cannot reach you, and guard the urn. I'll return to the heavens and find you."

173

Whoosh.

The cloud was gone, taking the foundation at his feet, too. Annabelle gasped, clutched him tighter. Suddenly bright morning sunlight glowed with piercing intensity. Demons surrounded him, their jagged wings flapping frantically as they struggled to understand what had just happened. Zacharel swung his sword and beheaded the one nearest him. With the flicker of the flames and the slick sound of bone detaching from bone, the others realized their prey was in sight.

They converged on him en masse. Ducking, diving and twisting, Zacharel worked his way through them. Two more bodies fell, erupting into flames as they plummeted toward the earth. Twelve remaining. They did not fight honorably, but then, he knew that about them and knew how to counteract their moves.

"I must let you go," he said to Annabelle. "Do not relax your grip."

"Got it."

When four swarmed him at the same time, swiping out, he rolled through the sky, releasing Annabelle as announced to block the two demons coming at him from the left, while using the sword to behead the two demons coming at him from the right.

Shocking him, she unhooked one leg from his waist and kicked at the demons he'd blocked, the sharp heel of her boot nailing one in the eye.

"Annabelle!"

"What? I didn't relax my grip," she said. "Not with my hands."

A demon latched on to her ankle before she could right herself, and she yelped.

Zacharel swirled his wrist back, then sliced forward, going low . . . lower . . . moving with the demon — finally destroying him. Another head tumbled through the air, black blood spraying.

"Behind you!" Annabelle shouted.

He spun quickly — but not quickly enough. Demon claws meant for his neck swiped out and connected with the side of one wing, causing a sharp lance of pain to echo through him . . . and freeze the appendage in place.

Zacharel gritted his teeth as he plunged through the daylight. Annabelle released a shrill scream of terror. Every bit of his strength and determination were needed to force the injured wing back into motion. At first, he failed to hold it steady. Finally, though, he caught an air current and jerked to a stop.

"That was close," she said, clearly battling

an urge to vomit.

Too close. "The end result is all that matters."

"What can I do to help?"

"Stay alive." No other angels were in sight. Either they were engaged in their own battles elsewhere, or he had been unsuccessful in summoning them.

"Well, you, too."

The demons found them, once again attacking from every angle. His sword blazed through the air, and because he wasn't as fast as before, another set of talons soon managed to slice through his wing.

Down he fell and this time, there was no stopping his momentum. A tendon had been severed. Annabelle's ponytail slapped at his cheeks, his lips, the inside of his mouth.

"Zacharel!" The force of the wind even managed to rip her from his embrace, her body tumbling end over end.

Cackling with glee, several demons followed her.

Zacharel thought fast. The Deity's angels could die physically because of bodily injury, yes. Impact would splatter his organs, no question, but even still he might regenerate. Annabelle was human. There was no question about whether or not she would regenerate. She would not.

He tucked his good wing into his back, and arrowed toward her. She faced the ground, away from him, her hair flying behind her. He closed the distance in a matter of seconds, withdrew throwing stars from the pockets of air where he'd stored them and nailed every demon reaching for her.

Shrieks of pain echoed as hands were detached, and one by one the beings fell away from her. Almost there . . . so close . . . contact! Zacharel wrapped his arms around her and tucked her into his chest.

Her elbows pounded at him, and her legs kicked at him. "Let me go, you sick, disgusting piece of —"

"I've got you," he said, and in that moment he knew. There was only one thing he could do to ensure she lived.

Instantly she calmed. "Zacharel?" Twisting, she wound her arms around his neck. "Thank the Lord!"

"Yes. It is I." He produced his vial containing the Water of Life. Only a single drop remained, but this was a matter of life and death. He didn't allow her to question or deny him. He simply tipped the rim over her lips so that the droplet could find its way into her mouth. "Drink."

Eyes wide, she swallowed. There. No matter what happened next, she would live. She might wish otherwise, but she would live.

CHAPTER EIGHT

This is it, the end, Annabelle thought, a delicious warmth flooding her, fizzing in her veins like champagne and completely contradicting the sense of hopelessness screaming through her mind. Wind whipped through her hair, cut at already chapped skin. And . . . and . . . oh, mercy, a sharp pain tore through her chest, her heart squeezed by a cruel fist. The warmth and fizz were forgotten. She went rigid, released a cry of pain.

"Easy now, Annabelle."

"What's wrong . . . What did you do . . . Argh!"

"The water can hurt you as it heals you."

Horrid demons, causing all of this. "But I'm not . . . injured."

"You must be. Adrenaline could have hidden whatever was wrong."

"Can you . . . land us?" Ohhhh, but she could barely speak through the agony. Those demons must have done more than scratch her.

"No. I cannot. Impact will hurt, and I will not lie, that hurt will be the worst you have ever experienced."

Won't scream, won't scream, really truly won't scream. "Any good news?"

"The hurt will not last. Soon you will feel nothing, I vow it."

"Because . . . I'll be . . . dead." *Breathe, just breathe.* But even that caused the vise grip to tighten on her heart. Sweat beaded over her skin, while her blood thickened to ice crystals. Impact would actually be a relief, she decided.

"I have ensured that you will live." Zacharel's arms were strong bands around her, offering comfort. One of his wings enveloped her, as if to offer a cushion when they landed. His other wing flapped in the breeze, ready to rip free at any moment.

She wished her heart would just go ahead and jump out of her chest. Whatever he'd fed her had to be worse than any landing and . . . Ohhhh, another wave of agony crashed through her.

Yes, this was it. The very end. After all the battles she'd survived, all the hardships, she hated that she was going out this way. *With such a bang, har-har.* She hadn't had a chance to visit her parents' graves. She hadn't destroyed the demon who'd killed them, because he had never returned for her, and trapped in the institution as she'd been, she hadn't been able to hunt him. Not that she would have known how. She hadn't gotten to tell her brother goodbye, even though he wouldn't have said a word in response.

The ground loomed ever closer. So green, so lovely, making a mockery of her forced calm. Her eyes burned, teared. Her chest constricted. Closer . . . any moment . . .

"I'm sorry," Zacharel said just before twisting, placing his back to the ground and her focus on the sky, a haze of pretty blue and white. Thick clouds, puffed in every direction. "The pain you are about to suffer, transient as it will be . . . I'm sorry," he repeated.

"Don't be. You did everything you could —"

He tensed, and she knew. Impact.

Boom! They smacked into tree after tree, jostling them one way and then the other, breath exploding from them both, mingling, until there was nothing left to exhale — Oh, wait, a harder smack than before proved her wrong, completely emptying out her lungs.

She and Zacharel rolled down, down, hitting branch after branch, not really losing momentum before they . . . *boom!* The final impact proved far more jarring, harder, harsher. But then they stopped. Just stopped.

A spiderweb of black wove through her vision. She concentrated on regaining the use of her lungs, inhaling, exhaling, too fast at first, but gradually slowing, evening out. Minutes stretched into hours, hours into eternity before she found the strength to sit up. A mistake. A tide of dizziness swept over her, turning her world upside down. She was wet, soaked actually. And oh, baby, *here* was the promised pain. A kaleidoscope of burning, aching and throbbing.

Wincing, she scanned the surrounding area.

Broken tree limbs overhead provided a perfect path for the sun, allowing hot rays to lick over her, spotlighting her. In front of her, a forest loomed. Leaves of dewy emerald brushed together, and wildflowers perfumed the air.

Beside her . . . beside her sprawled Zacharel, his eyes closed, his body motionless. Both of his wings were bent at odd angles, the robe he wore no longer white but crimson.

Blood, so much blood. *Everywhere.* All

over her — because of him. It leaked from his mouth, dripped from his ears, and where the fabric of his robe was ripped, great tides of it overflowed, reminding her of corroded water from a spout. His torso was mutilated, one of his thighs split open. His ankle, broken. The bone had sliced through his skin, the edges jagged, chips missing.

Her parents, ripped open, staring at nothing.
Her parents, lying in a congealing pool.

A hysterical laugh bubbled from her. Once again Annabelle would walk away from a gruesome scene without much damage to herself.

No. No! she thought then. She wouldn't leave Zacharel like this. Wouldn't let him die.

He's already dead, common sense piped up.

No! her stubborn core replied. She hadn't known him long, but he'd twice saved her life. He'd taken care of her. He, the man who claimed to have killed his own brother. He, the man who said he could kill *her* without hesitation. He, the man who never lied. She wouldn't fall into the trap of trying to humanize him, assigning him acceptable reasons for threatening her, but she wouldn't leave him, either. He'd done his best to protect her.

Annabelle lumbered to her knees and checked his pulse. The beat was thready, but there. There was hope!

God, if You're listening, thank You! With shaking hands, she put Zacharel back together as best she could, gagging, crying. *Just . . . stay with us a little longer. He needs help.*

"You'll heal," she told Zacharel. "You'll survive this."

Her gaze panned the surrounding forest. If she built a sled, she could drag him . . . where? She had no idea where they were. *Doesn't matter.* She would drag him until she found someone who could call for help.

"What did you do to him?"

The harsh voice slashed through the air behind her, slamming into her with so much hate and rage she fell to her hands. Blood splashed. Quickly she straightened, spun. The dizziness . . . almost too much, the spiderwebs returning and interweaving with pinpricks of light.

A beast of a man loomed a few feet away.

Trembling, she reached through the slits in her new leather pants and palmed two of the blades the cloud had given her. Good. She hadn't lost them in the fall. As she shoved her way to her feet, struggling to stay upright, she pointed both weapons at the scary-looking newcomer. "Don't come any closer. I'll make you regret it."

Ragged abrasions covered his cheeks, the edges singed, but the rest of his skin reminded her of honey sprinkled with sugar — a shocking contradiction. His eyes were black and filled with the same hate and rage she'd heard in his tone, his dark hair long and beaded, and though he wore a white robe, he wasn't an angel. He *couldn't be* an angel. No wings arched over his massive shoulders.

He glared down at her, then at Zacharel. When those bottomless eyes next landed on her, they were narrowed and crackling with orange-gold flames. Somehow, those flames were far worse than the emotions.

She blinked, and then he was standing in front of her — without ever having walked a step. Long, thick fingers wrapped around her wrists, squeezing. Still she hung on to her weapons.

"Let me go!" she demanded, trying to knee him between the legs.

He twisted, avoiding contact. "Release the blades."

And leave herself, and Zacharel, helpless? "Never!"

His clasp tightened. Even when her bones fractured and agonizing pain slicked up her arms, she maintained her hold on the hilts.

Endured worse. Gritting her teeth, she fought through the dizziness and the now-thickening spiderwebs intermingling with the ever-brightening lights, and found the strength to go for round two of Shoot His Testicles Into His Throat. He must have assumed the pain had overwhelmed her and she would submit, causing him to lower his guard, because she succeeded in connecting her knee to his groin this time.

He did not double over, but he did fling her away from him, her already abused body propelling into a tree trunk and slinking uselessly to the ground.

"Stay there." He kept her within his sights as he crouched beside Zacharel.

"No! I won't let you hurt him," she shouted, and lumbered to her feet. And . . . *Thank You, God!* She still held the daggers. Her hands were swollen and aching unbearably, but that was a small price to pay for Zacharel's protection.

Surprise lit those treacherous eyes. Because of her words, or her persistence? Whatever the reason, surprise drifted through *her* as he smoothly lifted Zacharel into his arms. Such gentleness from someone who looked more monster than man should have been impossible.

Still, she pointed one of the blades at him. "I don't know who you are or what you're doing here, but like I said, I won't let you hurt him."

"I am Koldo, and I would never hurt him."

Her knees almost buckled with relief. Koldo. She recognized the name. He might not be an angel, but he *was* Zacharel's friend. Her warrior had told her not to fight him just before commanding his cloud to vanish. "Where are you taking him? What are you going to do with him?"

"Away. Save."

That harsh voice must have jostled Zacharel's mind into activity, because his eyelids fluttered open. He struggled for freedom, saying, "The girl." He coughed, blood gurgling from his mouth.

He was still alive!

A sob of relief escaped Annabelle as she rushed forward. Only, she never reached him. Both men disappeared as if they had been nothing more than holograms suddenly switched off. She experienced a tide of panic and grief, twisting around, searching for any sign of them — and finding nothing.

This is for the best. Koldo would get Zacharel the medical treatment he needed. Without her, the demons would stay away from him and —

Strong arms looped around her and jerked her against an equally strong chest. Instinct kicked in, and she flailed, knocking her head into her captor's chin. He grunted, but his hold never slackened. Then a curtain of white fell over the forest, nearly blinding her. Next to go was the grass at her feet. For several heartrending seconds, she couldn't breathe, couldn't move, a terrible sense of nothingness washing over her.

The panic returned, stronger now, consuming, but as she opened her mouth to scream, a new world painted itself around her. A fairy tale. There was a domed ceiling comprised of light pink crystals, with a diamond-studded chandelier hanging from the center. The walls were textured in the richest of velvets, the windows smoked glass with cinched white curtains that peered into . . . she wasn't sure, could see only darkness behind the pane. The floor polished mahogany draped with several plush pastel rugs.

There was so much space, the room was divided into several parts. The sleeping area; the sitting area, where a floral-printed couch formed a half circle on one side of a square glass table, while three chairs rounded things out on the other side; and the kitchen. Fresh flowers spilled from a crystal vase in the center of the dining table, sweetly scenting the air.

As for the bedroom, the same cinched material cascading down the sides of the windows swathed the largest bed she'd ever seen.

Bed. The word echoed through her mind, a reminder of the horrors to be experienced there . . . and now she was alone with her captor.

Don't just stand there. Fight!

A surge of adrenaline giving her strength, Annabelle reached up and back, propelling her swollen fist into her captor's eye. His arms fell away from her, and she spun, intending to pop him in the throat and leave him gasping for air. She came face-to-face with Koldo, but by the time his identity registered, there was no stopping her impetus. She'd already lashed out, the blades she'd forgotten about aimed at his jugular, ready to cut into his spine.

But he must have anticipated the move, because he arced backward, out of harm's way.

Thank You again, God. Seriously. Her arms clomped heavily to her sides. "I'm sorry, didn't know, couldn't stop. Where's Zacharel?" The words spilled from her without a single pause for breath.

"Put your weapons away first," he commanded. His voice still seethed with an ingrained fury he couldn't hide, probably didn't care to hide. He was all emotion, leaving no room for anything else.

"Okay. Yes." Though she wasn't frightened of him — much — her heart thundered against her ribs as she struggled to obey. But no matter what she tried, her fingers remained petrified on the blade hilts, too swollen to move.

"Woman! Now."

"I can't," she said, the words broken. He'd already proven he would do anything to protect his friend. Like, say, throwing a strange female across a forest *after* breaking her wrists. "My hands won't cooperate."

A moan sounded from the bed, snagging her attention. The covers writhed, the pristine material suddenly reminding her of a violent snowstorm.

No, not covers, she realized. Zacharel. He lay in the center. She'd missed him because his robe was as white as the comforter, the blood somehow having washed away in the bare minutes they'd been separated. She rushed forward.

Koldo extended an arm, stopping her.

She lifted the blades, ready to strike at

190

him, despite the fact that they were on the same side, but he used his free hand to pry the weapons from her grip. Only then did he step aside. Trying not to put any weight on her palms, she crawled onto the bed, careful, so careful not to jostle the mattress.

"I'm here, and I'll guard you as long as I can," she murmured when she reached Zacharel, and to her surprise, he stilled. "But I'm not sure how long that will be," she added, more for Koldo's benefit. "The demons are drawn to me, and apparently they can find me wherever I am. Zacharel can't withstand another attack. Not like this."

His wings were still broken, and without the blood caking them, she could see that patches of his feathers were missing. His skin was chalk-white, his only color the dark bruises beneath his eyes. A large puncture decorated the center of his lower lip. The tip of a branch must have slicked straight through to his gums.

"How did I walk away without a scratch, while he looks like *this?*" she asked softly.

Koldo assumed a post at the foot of the bed. "Did you drink anything before you landed?"

She thought back, recalled how Zacharel had forced that single drop of water into her mouth, and the warmth that had spread through her body, the pain. "Yes. Not much, though."

"Not much was still enough."

Excellent point. "What *was* that stuff?"

Rather than reply to her question, Koldo changed the subject. *Must be an angel thing.* "He would not settle until I assured him you were alive. He also made me swear to keep you by his side."

But . . . but . . . why would Zacharel do such a thing? "Is there a way to speed his recovery?"

"Yes."

When Koldo offered no more, she cast him an exasperated glance. "Well? What is it? The water he gave me?" The water he'd emptied into her before tossing the vial away.

Features hardened on a battlefield no longer displayed any hint of emotion, yet still he couldn't quite hide the fire banked in his eyes. "That information is not something I will share with a human, much less a demon's consort."

"I am no such thing!"

"I will not even share the information with a demon consort Zacharel has decided to protect," he added with a frown, as if he'd just sensed something odd.

Getting answers from an angel was like rolling a boulder up a hill, she mused — a whole lot of work without much reward. "This secret something that will speed Zacharel's recovery. Can you get it? Or do you already have it?"

"Yes, I can get it. No, I do not have it."

Silence.

Make that a boulder with spikes. "Well, then, get it!"

"No."

Annnd more silence.

"Unless," he added — miracle of miracles — without any prompting from her, "you vow to keep Zacharel from the heavens for one month, *without* telling him about our bargain. The only exception would be if he were summoned for battle."

"Why do you want him kept away?" And why did Koldo assume *she* could force Zacharel to do anything? The angel wanted her to stay with him, yes. He'd also promised to teach her how to fight the demons, so, yeah, she had the stay-by-my-side locked and loaded. But that didn't mean he would do whatever she desired.

What's more, did she dare shackle herself to Zacharel for a specific length of time? As she'd said, danger currently shadowed her steps, and that danger had nearly killed him.

A good girl would leave him at the first opportunity.

Koldo braced his hands behind his back, his legs apart. A battle-ready stance she recognized, because she'd assumed the same position nearly every time she'd spied demons in the institution. "All I require from you is a yes or a no, female. Nothing more."

Her gaze swung back over Zacharel, his pain as obvious as the glint of her blades on the floor. His lips were contorted in a grimace and now veering toward the color blue. His broken fingers were gnarled over the comforter, yet too weak to twist the material. He needed Koldo's "something," whatever it was, or he would die.

Better he live with her and her danger than die without her.

"Yes," she said. *I owe Zacharel, and I always pay my debts.* At least, that was her new motto. "My answer is yes." Could she trust Koldo to keep his end of the bargain, though? Did she really have another choice?

Koldo nodded once, a stiff, rough incline of his head, causing the beads in his beard to clang together. "Very well. Now, one last question. When I leave you, what will you do to Zacharel?"

Leave her? Making her, the now-handless

wonder, the only protection Zacharel had? "How long will you be gone?"

"That I do not know."

Which could mean six hours or six days. Or even six years. "I'll take care of him as best as I can."

"The phrase 'take care of him' can have many meanings, such as kill him, save him and avenge him. Even leave him. I require you to be more specific."

Of course he did. He and Zacharel shared the trait, a desire for details while refusing to share with others. "I mean I'll tend to him, look after him. I would never purposely hurt him, and I will not leave him on his own, helpless."

He smacked his lips, as if trying to taste the truth of her claim, before he nodded. "He would hate you for calling him helpless," he said, and then he disappeared.

Hey! "Koldo? Warrior?"

Nothing, no response.

Frustration ate at her. She had no idea how long he'd be gone, where she was or what to do if demons found her before he returned. Especially since her blades had disappeared with him! *So* untrusting.

But she was used to being doubted, used to being ignored, and refused to give way to hurt feelings. So, rather than wallow, she would stand guard over Zacharel. The angel who had saved her life. The man she owed. The first person to look at her as if she were more than a murderer.

Whatever was required, she would defend him.

CHAPTER NINE

"How's my girl?"

"Good, good, I ssswear . . . if you don't mind that ssshe'sss with the angel, uh, well . . . *Zacharel.*" Fear and awe drenched the name.

Grinning, the demon high lord Unforgiveness reclined in his throne, cunningly erected from bones taken from the many angel warriors he'd killed throughout the centuries. The change in his expression caused his four-legged minion to shudder. Usually when he smiled, he was in the process of killing someone.

But then, this was almost as good. The fact that Annabelle was with Zacharel thrilled Unforgiveness to the depths of his rotting black soul. That's why he'd marked her, after all — to gain the warrior's attention.

He'd begun to wonder if the warrior would ever find her. He'd begun to regret not giving in to his desire to torture Anna-belle while he'd had the chance. Now he was glad for his restraint.

Now he could torture her *and* Zacharel.

Grin widening, Unforgiveness rubbed two blunt-tipped claws over his jaw. Every day he had to file the nails down to prevent himself from killing his prey before he was ready. Because, when the bloodlust came upon him, he lost track of his surroundings, his ambitions, and simply gorged. He forgot food tasted better if it was aged for a few months, unending terror the perfect mari-nade.

"Do you require anything more of me, sssire?" the minion asked him, still huddling there on the middle dais steps.

"Yes."

"Wh-what?"

"You will kneel before me and I will remove your head. Your stench offends me." As did the fact that he'd shown such admi-ration for Zacharel.

A sob burst from the minion's too-thin lips, but he did not deny Unforgiveness's demand. To do so would have earned him a good tormenting before his inevitable death.

"That would be . . . my pleasure, sssire."

He assumed the position.

Unforgiveness palmed his sword, swung.

The minion's head rolled down the steps. *And I never even had to stand.* He returned his sword to its rightful place against his throne arm and motioned several other minions forward. They lined the walls of the chamber, some tall, some short, but all ugly and here to serve his every twisted desire.

"You, clean the blood. You, feed the body to my army. You, bring me a morsel to eat. A good one this time, or you'll join your headless friend."

They rushed to obey. He almost wished one — or all — would defy him. That would certainly alleviate the boredom of the day. Or rather, the centuries. If only for a little while.

Unforgiveness was trapped here. Only when a human managed to summon him could he leave, and then, he could only remain on earth for the time required to complete whatever unholy task the human had summoned him for, or until the human died. Whichever came first, and to be honest — something he never was — the human usually died.

That had begun to bore him, too . . . until he'd finally stumbled upon Zacharel's mate. Oh, yes. He'd recognized what she was, and who she was meant to be with, instantly. Maybe he would tell Zacharel how . . .

maybe not. Either way, Zacharel, the warrior angel who had nothing to lose, the soldier who loved nothing and no one, had something worth fighting for.

Now the real fun would begin.

Finally Zacharel would pay for sending Unforgiveness down here.

Demon high lords were fallen angels who had welcomed evil into their hearts. Yes, Unforgiveness had welcomed the evil all on his own, but he hadn't meant to do so. How could he have known that the smallest pinch, received unintentionally, would cause more to spill inside of him until no goodness remained?

Once he'd realized what was happening, he had fought, tried to save himself. But evil was insidious, a disease that grew inside you, sometimes so slowly you had no idea it was there. Without a proper cleansing, however, it *was* there, ready to strike, and in the end, you *would* cave under its weight.

Oh, you might cry when you made your first kill, but the second, third and fourth were easier, and soon you would no longer shed any tears at all. Soon you would no longer uphold life in any form. Soon you were merely a husk of your former self.

But Zacharel had known all of this and could have saved him. *Should* have saved him. Instead, Zacharel had betrayed him.

"Your morsssel, sssire." The minion's voice blended with the sobs of the damned human female he dragged forward.

Unforgiveness blinked to focus. The female was shoved up the steps and forced to kneel between his spread legs. In her mid-twenties, with brown hair and a delicate face, she reminded him of Annabelle.

Every high lord kept a few minions at the gates of hell. When fresh meat was escorted inside, those minions fought for ownership. Down here, might equaled right. Unforgiveness craved the most bitter and hardened of the males and females, and he got them. No one challenged his minions, because no one wanted to deal with him. But every so often, he would discover a brunette beauty like this one.

Tears tracked down this one's cheeks. Her eyes were hazel, a deep green flecked with golden brown.

He captured one of the tears with his fingertip, and she flinched away from him. He expected the reaction, even enjoyed it. Once, he'd been a study of magnificence. Females had gazed upon him with wonder. Now, with his crimson scales, his blood-stained fangs, too-sharp horns and spiked tail, he was a study of horror.

"I can taste your fear already," he said.

Sobs shook her entire frame. "Please. Don't hurt me, I beg you."

She lacked Annabelle's fire and bravery. How disappointing.

But . . . just thinking his Annabelle's name filled him with excitement. How badly did Zacharel want her?

What would he do to save her?

What would he be willing to save her *from?*

The minions Unforgiveness sent her way were not allowed to rape or kill her. Unforgiveness would have the privilege. And Zacharel would have to watch it all, before at last joining her in death. Well, death of the body, for Unforgiveness would not grant Zacharel the true death: spirit, soul and body. No, he wanted the angel here, transformed into a demon high lord, his actions a film of acid on his skin, loss and failure his lifelong companions.

"Please," the human said, drawing him back into the present.

A wandering mind would get him killed. Unforgiveness curled his fingers around the female's neck and urged her face toward his. "Please what?"

"Let me go," she choked out.

His lips curled into another grin, this one slow and as dark as his soul. "Why would I do that? I must keep my strength up. And do you know how I keep my strength up, my precious?"

Tremor, tremor. "N-no."

Perhaps not, but she suspected. "Well, it will be my pleasure to show you."

CHAPTER TEN

As one day slid into a second, Annabelle remembered the joys of Zacharel's home and summoned a few weapons. A girl had to be prepared when evil monsters chased her. Sadly, nothing appeared in her hands — now shockingly healed — or anywhere else, which meant she wasn't in another cloud. Bummer. She'd already searched every corner, every piece of furniture, but had found nothing. Not even a change of clothes.

Now she patted down the walls, probing for any doorways the demons might attempt to enter, but there wasn't so much as a seam, as if the only way to enter or leave was through . . . teleporting? Was that what Koldo was doing, popping in and out as he did?

And why did the guy want Zacharel out of the heavens? she wondered for the thousandth time. Hopefully she hadn't made a fatal mistake with their exchange.

Fatal. The thought returned her attention to Zacharel. Fresh blood had soaked his robe anew, causing the material to cling to his body, the crimson obscene against the purity of the white. In the bathroom, she gathered the few remaining washrags and a small basin of water. But by the time she had the supplies situated around the injured angel, the blood had already disappeared.

How was he doing that? The phenomenon had happened several times before, and she had hoped his injuries had somehow healed. But each time before, that hope had been in vain. Gently she raised the hem of the robe, baring his legs — disappointment shot through her. He was still bruised, parts of him still twisted at odd angles. He had deep gashes everywhere, and his abdomen . . . Oh, poor Zacharel. No, his injuries hadn't healed this time, either. He was dying.

Her parents, dying . . . dead. No longer savable, gone forever.

Oh, no. She wasn't going there.

She forced herself to think about something else. Like, how, for the first time in four years, she had purpose, an attainable goal, a safety net, and if she were being completely honest with herself, a gargantuan attraction to a man. Zacharel's hypnotic

205

beauty mesmerized her. His insistence on the truth delighted her. His strength fascinated her. He had protected her, and he had intrigued her during their few conversations. He wasn't a smiler, but she suspected she'd come pretty close to amusing him a few times.

I want him to live. He was . . . She was . . . She . . .

Had fallen asleep, she realized, waking to find her chin pressed against her sternum. Exhaustion overwhelming her, she took up a post at the foot of the bed, ready to leap into action if anyone entered the room.

Where are you, Koldo? The silence in the room was broken only by the harshness of her breathing. She despised that silence — until Zacharel began to release one agonized groan after another.

She returned to his side, cooed at him, but his groans only increased in volume. He thrashed, blood soaking him, the robe and the comforter beneath him. Soon he practically floated in a pool of the stuff.

How much more could he stand to lose?

"Kill them," he gritted out. "Must kill them."

Kill the demons? Probably. They'd done this to him, after all.

"Kill them."

"Don't worry. You did. You killed them," she said softly.

She had no medical knowledge, no idea what to do to help Zacharel. Applying pressure to the wound, the one thing she *did* know to do when someone was bleeding, wouldn't help in this case. She would be applying pressure directly to . . . she gagged . . . and might do more damage.

"Kill them!"

"You did, honey. You did." Annabelle spread the faux-fur coat Zacharel had given her on the bed and stretched out beside him, tracing her fingertips over his brow. His skin burned with fever, the cold long gone. He leaned into the touch, his grimace easing the slightest bit.

"Save her."

Her — Annabelle? That, she wasn't as sure about. "You did. You saved her."

"I . . . return," a broken voice said from across the room.

She jolted in surprise, then nearly screamed in horror when she spied Koldo. Or, more accurately, what was left of Koldo.

His hands were clasped to his chest, his big fingers wrapped around something clear and thin. As he dropped to his knees, no longer able to hold his own weight, blood dripped from his now-shaved head. Gone was his robe. He was shirtless, with loose, low-hanging pants covering his legs.

Annabelle eased from the bed to race to his side. "What happened to you?"

"Make . . . him . . . drink." Koldo fell face-first to the floor, his arms extending, the clear, thin something — a vial — rolling from his now-open grip.

His back. Oh, sweet mercy, his back. There was no flesh left, just ruined muscle and fractured bone.

"Do not . . . give to . . . me." His eyes closed, as if his lids were too heavy to keep open. "Only him."

Nausea churned in her stomach. She was (somewhat) used to blood considering what she'd dealt with these past twenty-four hours, and she was totally used to violence. But this . . . so much in such a short amount of time . . . just like the past . . . rising up to consume her . . .

For a moment, she was petrified in place, memories flooding her, drowning her, *devastating* her. Somehow she found a life raft — *save Zacharel* — and tugged, tugged, tugged herself to the surface.

Make him drink, Koldo had said. Shaking, she swiped up the vial and returned to Zacharel's side. The stopper proved to be a problem, and she struggled to remove it, feeling like an idiot as she yanked and failed, yanked and failed.

"Is this the same stuff he gave me?" The same stuff that had hurt her before saving her?

"Yes," Koldo said.

Finally, Annabelle's biceps came through and the cork popped free. As unsteady as she was, she spilled several droplets down the side of her hand.

"I'm sorry, Zacharel," she whispered. Because she had no idea how much a big man like him would need, especially since he was an immortal rather than a human — would too much cause an overdose and hurt him, or would too little work too slowly? — she poured half the bottle down his throat.

A moment passed, then another, and nothing happened.

Well, what did you expect? He —

Snarled, his body bowing. He slammed his fists against the headboard, cracking the wood. Next he punched the mattress with so much force, Annabelle was bounced to the floor, more of the liquid spilling from the bottle she still held.

She scrambled to her feet, expecting to see his wounds mending, but . . . he continued to thrash, to bleed, to snarl.

White-hot fury flowed through her veins,

leaving nothing but ashes in its wake. No wonder Koldo had told her not to give him any of the liquid. It was poison! And how stupid was she to have trusted him? Well, she would —

As quickly as Zacharel had erupted, he calmed. His body sagged against the bed, and he released a soft sigh. Before her eyes, bones popped back into place. Skin wove back together, until he bore not a single bruise or scratch. Her widening gaze fell to the bottle. What *was* this stuff?

"The Water of Life." Zacharel jerked upright, scanning his surroundings, seeming to take everything in all at once. "Where is it?"

"You're healed." The words burst from her, riding the tides of her shock.

Emerald eyes landed on her, as clear as the liquid — the Water of Life? — and utterly pain free. Once again he possessed a face chiseled from dreams and honed by fantasies, lovely in a way no mortal could ever hope to be.

Her breath caught, and her blood heated with something other than fury. She wanted to shout with joy and throw herself in his arms. She wanted to dance and sing about the wonder of this mighty miracle. She wanted . . . more than she was willing to admit.

"You survived," he said.

All emotion had been wiped from his voice, offering no hint of how he felt. "I did. Because of you, so thank you. Which, I know, isn't an adequate payment. You took the brunt of the impact yourself, and all I can give you is words. I'm sorry." She was babbling, she knew she was babbling, but she couldn't stop. "If I had more, I'd give you more."

"I would like to say it was a pleasure. Yes, I would like to say that, but impact *hurt*."

She choked back a laugh. "Did you just make a joke?"

"A joke, when I spoke only the truth?" He waved his fingers at her. "The Water of Life," he repeated. "Give it to me."

"Oh. Here." She held out the bottle.

Slowly, carefully he removed the bottle from her kung fu grip. "Who gave this to you?"

"Koldo."

In his eyes she saw a flare of shock even the stoic Zacharel couldn't hide.

Uh-oh. Had the other warrior broken some kind of rule? "But I take full responsibility," she added. "I asked him to do it. Therefore, any penalty should be mine."

Koldo had more than come through for her and for Zacharel. She owed him and according to her new motto, she had to pay him back.

"Where is he?"

As much as she liked Zacharel, as much as she owed him, too, she didn't know him, not really, and wouldn't throw the other guy straight into the fire. "What do you plan to do to him?"

A muscle ticked in his jaw. "I would not harm a man who has aided me, if that is what you are hinting at."

Very well. She pointed to the warrior still unconscious on the floor. "I didn't harm him, either. He left and came back like that."

Zacharel stood, his robe falling to his feet. He replaced the bottle's stopper; a moment later, the entire thing vanished.

"How did you do that?" she couldn't help but ask. *What* had he done?

"I hid the vial in a tiny pocket of air I will now force to follow me." He bypassed her, careful not to touch her, as if she were suddenly toxic.

Message received. He wanted nothing more to do with her. *And my feelings are not hurt.* What was one more rejection, anyway? She was a freak, a murderer, a crazy girl who saw monsters, or so a thousand people had told her. So what that she'd just spent an entire day worrying over this man's health. A man who knew the truth about her. A man who'd previously protected her. Why the sudden change?

A hiss of breath as he crouched beside the injured male, glided his palm over that newly shorn scalp. "How could you let them take your hair, warrior? Why?"

Annabelle could guess the answer to the second question, but she'd given Koldo her promise never to discuss the details of their deal. So, she remained silent. What she wanted to know was why Zacharel was more upset by his friend's newfound baldness than he was by the condition of the guy's back.

Because both men were warriors to their cores? Because physical pain mattered little to them, since they'd endured so much already? Because losing something they prized, as Koldo must have prized his beaded locks, was far worse than any wound?

And yes, she knew he'd prized those locks. The intricacy of the beadwork revealed the time and attention he'd given to every strand.

"I have only known him three months, but the first thing I learned about him was his

213

love for his hair. In all his centuries, he had never cut it," Zacharel said, sadness coating the edges of his tone. "Not even a trim. I do not know why, but from what the Deity told me about him, I suspect it has something to do with his father."

So many questions skittered through her mind. "His father? So angels are born?"

"Some of the Deity's angels were . . . are born, yes, but some were created fully formed and given to him by the Most High."

"Which were you?"

"Born." He tenderly lifted Koldo into his arms. Every step careful, measured, he carried the massive beast to the bed and laid him facedown. "His hair will never grow back, you know."

"But why?"

"A sacrifice was made and accepted. If his hair could grow back, his sacrifice would have meant nothing."

And I asked him to do this. Guilt settled heavily on her shoulders, nearly drilling her to her knees. "You're sure?"

"Not entirely, no, but I know the Council. That is how they operate."

Well, then. "I'll take that to mean there's a chance his hair will grow back. Now, he told me not to give him any of the . . . water," she said, "but surely it would help him. Ease his pain."

"Drinking now would destroy him in the worst possible way, for we are not allowed to heal ourselves with the Water of Life when the wounds we received were to *obtain* that water. Other angels are even forbidden to aid in any way during the healing process."

Poor Koldo. "He's an angel?"

"Yes. He lost his wings long ago."

"And now he's lost his hair." Tears welled in her eyes. No wonder Zacharel had no desire to touch her. She was a menace, ruining the lives of all around her. Always had been.

Sighing, Zacharel trailed his fingers over that bleeding scalp. Koldo's head hadn't been shaved, she realized upon closer inspection, but ripped clean. "He will hate you if you pity him," he said. A warning for both of them?

Koldo had said something similar about Zacharel. If the two weren't careful, pride would cause them to miss out on the best kind of coddling. "No, he won't, because he'll never know. If you can get us out of here, I mean. I can't stay. I've been here so long already, and the demons . . ." Koldo wasn't in any condition to fight them now.

"Will eventually find you, and it would be

best if they did not find Koldo's secret hideout," he finished for her.

"Exactly."

"No matter how strong your draw is for the demons, they should not have found you in my cloud. Should not have come for you."

"What exactly draws them?" At the institution, he'd mentioned hatred, lying and the urge to commit violence, but she'd done her best to focus only on good things.

"What I told you before is still true," he said, as though reading her mind, "but you are a special case. Your body carries the essentia of the demon who marked you, and that essentia radiates from you."

She blinked in surprise. Such a simple answer, yet totally life changing. There was nothing she could do to stop radiating an essence she couldn't even feel. "How did he mark me?"

Zacharel stalked to the dresser and dug through the drawers, finally pulling out a robe.

Urgency bombarded her, and she barely stopped herself from gripping his shoulders and shaking him. "Tell me! He kissed me and he licked me, but I had to have come into contact with him before that because the change in my eyes happened before that, and as you once so sweetly told me, my eyes belong to a demon."

He said nothing.

She continued. "The morning of his attack, my eyes felt as if they'd been scrubbed raw and bleached. And after that, my parents . . . That first demon . . ." She cleared her throat. "I don't understand why he came. It was my birthday, and I'd just had the most amazing dream. It should have been a perfect day."

Zacharel stiffened. "Dream?"

"Yes."

"You remember it?"

"Of course. I've relived it a thousand times." She'd hoped to figure out what was wrong with it. At first, she'd loved it. But the more the scene had played through her mind, the more she'd realized something had been . . . off.

"Tell me."

"A smoking-hot Prince Charming saved me from fire-breathing dragons and asked me if I was willing to help him. I said yes. He said *I love you and want to be with you* and I said *how sweet,* and he said *will you be my woman,* and I said *yes,* and he said *then we are one.* Then I woke up in the most agonizing pain."

Zacharel ran his tongue over his teeth. "The prince was the demon, and he tricked

217

you into agreeing to his claiming."

"Uh, no. It was just a dream." A dream that had stuck with her for years . . .

"No, you only thought it was a dream. He manipulated your mind, vulnerable as it was in sleep. When he asked you to be his woman, and you agreed, you became his slave."

"But that's . . . I didn't mean . . . would never . . . They can do that to people?" she squeaked.

"If a human allows it, yes."

"But . . . how could I have known what was happening?"

"You could have, if you had been trained to distinguish the truth from the lie." When he stood in front of her, he tugged the robe over her head. "To keep you clean and warm."

The material bagged on her, draping her arms and pooling at her feet.

"Do you wish to remove the leather?" he asked.

"Yes." Since the robe shielded her body, she was able to contort this way and that to extract herself from the dirty, chafing clothing.

When she finished, she realized her skin was tingling and her cells fizzing, as though hundreds of butterflies were giving her a sponge bath. It was the strangest feeling, and she wasn't sure if the robe or Zacharel's nearness was responsible.

He lifted her hair from the collar, his fingertips brushing her nape, making her shiver. His nearness. Definitely his nearness.

He didn't jerk away, as she expected, but lingered, saying, "Soft."

Well, what do you know, she thought. He wasn't as opposed to touching her, after all. "Why did you avoid coming into contact with me before?" she asked, veering away from the subject of demons. Right now, her mind needed a break. "And don't try to say it wasn't deliberate. You basically contorted your body to maintain distance, a move I invented to establish boundaries with other patients."

"I lose track of everything important when you're near me," he grumbled.

Everything important, he'd said. Meaning, she was not. *Nice.* "Such a romantic," she muttered, slapping his hand away. "You're lucky I'm not one of those girls who burst into tears at every little insult."

"That was not an insult." He frowned, and while she knew he hadn't meant for his expression to pulse with sensuality, his lack of chill caused just that, an erotic throb inside her, where want blended with need.

"And I am not trying to romance you."

"Believe me, I know."

Frown deepening, he stepped away from her, at last ending the contact. "Do you *want* me to romance you?"

Yes. "No." *You're not very fond of men right now, remember? Not even sexy angel men.*

"Then as we were saying." Zacharel cleared his throat, and even that was steeped with his innate sensuality. "We must kill the demon who made that claim on you."

Demons again. The break was over.

"When you agreed to be his slave," he continued, "you gave him permission to do whatever he wanted with you. However, when he dies the marking will fade and the others, the weaker minions, will lose interest in you."

"So . . . the hunted must become the hunter?"

"Exactly. If we do not do this, you will never find peace."

Wait. "You said *we.*"

"Yes."

"You're willing to help me?" He'd promised to train her, yeah, but this was more than training. This was dedication to a cause that was not truly his own.

"Yes," he repeated.

Gratitude nearly overwhelmed her. "I owe

you, not the other way around. Why would you —" She pressed her lips together. If she continued along this line, she might talk him out of helping her. "Thank you. Just . . . thank you."

"You are welcome. Once you are free of the demon's essentia, you can live a long, happy life on your own. I am not saying there will never be another storm; those are simply a part of life. But you will never again experience thunder and lightning like this."

With his words, the answer to her unfinished question slid into place. *Zacharel* wanted to be free of *her*. That hurt, but she wouldn't complain. Aid was aid, no matter the reason behind it.

"I know you're going above and beyond duty already, but I need something besides assistance from you," she said, peering down at her feet. "Will you . . . well, uh, will you spend the next month with me . . . away from the heavens unless you have a battle to fight? Without asking me why?"

A pause.

A *really* long pause.

She glanced up.

Fury and pleasure blazed in Zacharel's eyes.

Why the fury? For that matter, why the

pleasure?

Doesn't matter.

"Please," she said.

"I will not ask why you want me out of the heavens. There is no need. I know the way of the angels, and I can guess. I want to know if you negotiated," he said sharply.

"Negotiated what?" she asked, going for innocence. But wait. Something she'd learned from both Zacharel and Koldo was that when you didn't want to answer a question and evasion wouldn't work, you had to make a demand of your own. "Never mind. You *will* spend the next month with me."

"Or what?" In a heartbeat he was in front of her, his hand once again wrapped around her nape. He tugged her closer, not giving her time to protest or resist.

"Or . . . uh . . . I can't even speak it, it's so terrible!"

"A falsehood. You'll do nothing, that's what. But, very well. I'll give you an answer anyway — and I will give you a month of my time." He said the words silkily, indulgence coated with cold determination in his voice. "For a price. You see, *I* know how to negotiate."

222

CHAPTER ELEVEN

I will have this woman, Zacharel thought. *If only once, I will have her. I will finally know her taste, and never again will I have to wonder.*

When Annabelle's body stood flush against his, he enfolded her with his wings, forcing her ever closer. His newly healed skin and tendons protested the movement, shooting out little aches and pains, but that didn't stop him. Nothing would.

"What's your price?" she asked softly. The sweet scent of her drifted to his nose, filled his lungs, branded him.

Your kiss. Your surrender. But did he say the words aloud? No.

He wanted to know what kind of bargain she had made with Koldo — a bargain that required her to stay with Zacharel for a month. A bargain that had provided her with the Water of Life. He also wanted to know why Koldo wanted him out of the heavens for so long.

But again, he held his silence. He liked the outcome, so he would not press Annabelle for answers she wasn't yet ready to give. Not yet, at least. Those would come; he would make sure of it.

Yes, I will have her. Despite his anticipation for the deed, however, anger coiled inside his bones. He still didn't want to want her, and he blamed her for reducing him to this . . . a man willing to forget his duty and forgo his honor simply to learn a woman's taste.

"We will discuss the terms once we reach our new location," he said more harshly than he'd intended. "The longer we stay here, the more danger my warrior faces."

She studied his features for a moment, searching for . . . what? "All right. We'll shelve our little negotiation." Reaching up, she linked her fingers behind his neck.

Always she surprised him. When he expected her to protest, she caved. When he expected her to cave, she fought him. When he expected —

— thoughts derailing . . . realigning . . . She was even closer to him now, as if they were two halves of a whole. The very idea heated his blood, making his insides burn and his skin sweat.

Zacharel.

The male voice echoed through his mind, neither a memory nor springing from his own mind. *Thane?* he asked, instantly concerned.

Yes.

You are well? And the others?

We were not attacked, but we did engage the demons chasing you.

Good. Did you leave one alive?

After the slightest hesitation, he heard, *Yes.*

As if Zacharel would protest the coming torture, when that was exactly why the demon still lived. *Find out who sent the minions. They came to steal Annabelle.*

How is she?

Well. But the only way to keep her safe is to hide her. Therefore, I will be hiding with her. Contact me when you have an answer. And, Thane, he added before the soldier ended the connection. *Check on Koldo when you have the chance.*

Why? What's wrong?

"Zacharel?" Annabelle said. "I don't mean to criticize, but you're just standing there, staring at me."

"Not you, but I need a moment," he replied, but the distraction had severed the link. He tried to open it back up, failed.

225

"Moment over."

"All right." Though she radiated confusion, she said, "So, um, again, how do you propose we leave this place?"

Concentrating on her, he said, "The same way we left the institution. My question is, will you enjoy this ride as much?"

He misted both their bodies and flew her through the ceiling, then layer after layer of stone-laden dirt. He hated leaving Koldo, but already he'd skirted the edge of acceptable by placing the warrior on the bed.

Whatever his reasons, Koldo — a warrior given to him because he'd beaten his last commander into bloody pulp — had helped him and thereby Annabelle. Zacharel hadn't thought to ever come to admire the men and women under his leadership, but he couldn't deny the fissures in his chest were expanding, making room for more than just Annabelle and desire.

They rose above the surface of grass and flowers, towering trees, and into a mid-morning sky, the sun half-hidden behind a thick shield of clouds. Birds flew in every direction, their calls shrill yet welcome.

"I'll never get used to the beauty," Annabelle gasped, awe and wonder heavy in her tone.

Yes, she was enjoying this ride as much as

the other. How would she react to other things free women could do? Things like shopping, and dancing, and dating.

"Don't you think it's beautiful?" she asked.

"I once believed it was, yes, and assumed the beauty would never wilt."

"We were born into this amazing world, Zacharel. We are meant to protect this land and its people."

"All I see is the blood of our parents, sprayed over the grass and oceans."

"They died fighting demons." Unable to recover from the extensiveness of their wounds. *"There is no greater honor than that. How many times have you said those very words to me? So why can you not focus on the purity and innocence shining at us and forget the taint of the past?"*

Neither he nor his brother had known the events that would unfold mere weeks after that conversation. Hadrenial's capture, torture, and after a year of searching, Zacharel's "rescue" of him. No longer had Hadrenial thought the world a place of splendor and glory to bask in. He'd seen the ugliness, had walked hand in hand with the evil, and he had begun to fear and hate.

"Are you okay?" Annabelle asked. "You tensed up."

For once, Zacharel wanted to lie. To give voice to the thoughts swimming in his head . . . would he also erupt? Or worse, cry? He'd told Annabelle about his brother's death, but not about his reasons for rendering that final blow. If he did, would *she* erupt and cry? Feminine tears were not something he could handle right now.

"Well? Are you?"

"Shh," he said. "I must remain focused." Truth. Otherwise he would do something he would regret.

"Shush me again, I dare you."

His lips twitched in that way he was coming to expect in her presence. He searched ahead but no demons lurked in the vicinity. Still, he should not risk taking her to a public place. Minions often followed unsuspecting humans. He should take her to a private island in the Pacific, undiscovered and untouched by humans, as planned, but . . . he changed course.

For over an hour he glided through the vast expanse of blue, going high, then low, then high again, maintaining a constant zigzag impossible for anyone to lock on to.

"Since you don't want to tell me what's wrong with you, and I can tell that you're still bothered by something," Annabelle said, "why don't you tell me why you no

228

longer believe in the beauty of the land?"

Clouds of the purest white came into view, each surrounding mountains capped with snow. Fields of green grass, and meadows rich with dewy flowers. Water so blue it seemed to hold a thousand secrets in every ripple. He no longer pictured pieces of his parents strewn across different parts of the world. He no longer imagined the horror of his brother's last days, but even so . . .

"A man's surroundings are often tainted by his memories."

Her warm sigh caressed his neck. "True. After my trial, my brother sold my parents' house, as well as everything inside it. He wanted no reminders of the horror I'd caused."

"But you did not cause that horror."

"No, but he'll never believe that." Her sadness was a live wire, crackling and dangerous.

"Words laced with faith have power, Annabelle, even negative words. If you want him to change his mind, begin to speak and act as if he has."

"What about his free will? And wouldn't a claim that he believes me be considered lying?"

"Minds can be changed — of their own free will. And no, you wouldn't be lying.

You speak it, and because words have power, your faith makes it real."

"But I don't have any faith in this matter."

"You do, but it's small. You see, faith is measurable. It builds as you think about and meditate on a spiritual truth. And do not shake your head at me. What I say is true. There are natural laws, like gravity, and there are spiritual laws, like this one. You can have what you say if you believe that you have it before you actually see that you have it. That is faith."

She thought about that for a moment. "All right, so he wants to reconnect with me."

"Good. Keep saying that. Keep thinking that. Any time a thought contrary to what you just spoke tries to enter your mind, force it to leave. One day, you'll actually believe it spirit, soul and body."

"And just like that he'll seek a relationship with me?"

"Just like that you'll release a spiritual power unlike anything you've ever known." He only wished he had applied these truths to his own life. But faith-filled confessions could take time, and if a man lacked patience, he could ruin everything.

"All right. Okay. I'll think and meditate on this stuff." She rested her head on his shoulder. So much time passed he figured she had acted on her promise and fallen asleep. Until she said, "So where are we?"

"New Zealand." At the base of one of the mountains was the entrance to Thane's cave. Most angels kept homes all over the world, because a warrior never knew where he would end up when hunting a particular demon, or when he would be injured and require rest. Like so many others, Thane had chosen a place where he was guaranteed as little human interaction as possible.

Zacharel would take her there. Later.

"I've always wanted to travel," she said.

"And now you are doing so in style."

A warm chuckle left her, a sound that threatened to overwhelm his senses with pleasure. "I can't deny that."

He bypassed the cave and sped past Whangaparaoa Bay and into Auckland. There, he landed in an abandoned alley. He hated to release his passenger, but forced himself to do so.

With a single mental command, he turned both of their robes into a shirt and pair of pants, both black.

"How did you do that?" she asked, plucking at the fabric at her waist. "And how is the material so soft?"

He wanted her fingers on him, on his skin.

Soon. "That was nothing, and I was able to do it because the robes are under my command, just like the cloud." As he spoke, he hid his wings inside an air pocket.

Expression baffled, as though she couldn't quite convince herself to believe what she was seeing — or not seeing — she reached out, paused and bit her lip. "May I?"

Her fingers on his wings . . . even better. His throat was suddenly too tight to speak, so he nodded, forced his wings to come to the edge of the pocket, so that they would be solid to her.

Contact. Buttery soft fingertips caressed the arch of one, then the other, sending electric currents racing through the rest of him. "Still there," she said, clearly awed.

For her, but only her.

She stroked him for a moment more, nearly wringing groans of pleasure from him, before she pulled away. "So what are we doing here, like this?"

He mourned the loss of her. "We are shopping for supplies. Clothes, shoes and whatever else you will need in the coming days."

Her hand fluttered over her heart. "Did you just say the word *shopping* without flinching?"

"I did. So?"

"So, that's gotta be a record. It's a world-wide fact that men hate shopping."

"How can I hate it when I've never done it?"

Her lips curled into a slow, beautiful smile. "If you weren't already an angel, I'd dub you a saint. Poor guy. You have no idea what you're in for."

Annabelle had the time of her life.

The buildings were as beautiful as the surrounding mountains, light, with lots of glass and shiny signs. The water was as blue as the sky, one blending into the other, the clouds above a replica of the sailboats below. But it was the archways and columns along the streets, and people headed in every direction, that consumed her attention.

Once, she'd taken this kind of thing for granted. For years, when she'd wanted to shop, her parents had whisked her to the mall. She had tried on outfits, and they had critiqued them. Those "critiques" had always consisted of praise.

"You've never looked more beautiful, sweetheart."

"All the boys will go crazy for you, baby."

"You've definitely inherited your mother's style, honey."

Annabelle blinked away a fresh spring of tears. When she was older, she and her friends had spent many weekends shopping for dresses and jeans and T-shirts and shoes, afterward drinking lattes, gossiping and laughing as they admired all the boys.

A wave of homesickness swept over her, followed by sorrow for what she'd missed these past few years, then determination. She was free now. She would not let what could have been — what *should* have been — taint this time with Zacharel. Look what had happened with him. He'd allowed the past to taint him, and could no longer enjoy the beauty of the land.

Besides, Zacharel hadn't done this kind of thing before. She had to be at her best so that he wouldn't decide to off himself just to end the experience, the way her friend's boyfriends had often threatened to do.

"You are not enjoying yourself?" Zacharel demanded.

"I am, I promise."

He nodded, though he did not appear convinced.

"I'll prove it!" And so began the shopping spree to end all shopping sprees. At first, as she flipped through rack after rack, she wasn't sure people could see Zacharel, even in his altered state. Then she noticed the way women stared at him, no matter their age, their mouths agape.

That's right. He's with me. She was feeling pretty good about herself, in fact . . . until she noticed the way men kept their distance from her, even salesmen. But . . . but . . . why? It wasn't like a Wanted poster hung on every wall. *Right?*

She glanced at Zacharel. He was glaring at a man a few rows over — a man now backing up, leaving the store.

O-kay, so, problem solved. But she couldn't really castigate him. He was more than a bodyguard; he was an ATM. Whenever she found something she wanted, a T-shirt, a pair of pants, boots, a purse, it didn't matter, Zacharel suddenly had cash.

"Are you miserable yet?" she asked him as he hid her purchases the same way he'd hidden his wings.

"I —"

"Hold that thought!" She had just spotted a cookie stand! She switched directions and bypassed Zacharel to eagerly bounce up and down in front of the counter, her mouth watering. "Chocolate chip," she told the gloved lady waiting to take her order. "Two of them."

Had she ever thought to do something like this again, something purely frivolous? No. And that she was . . . she could have fallen to her knees and wept. Funny that she'd fought more tears since her liberation from the institution than she had during the four years she'd spent inside.

"I do not want one," Zacharel said.

"Oh, uh, yeah, because the second one was totally for you."

He smacked his lips as he paid the bill. "Such a little liar, Annabelle."

A circumspect glance proved he wasn't angry about that. Shocker. Usually he huffed and puffed. But the heat, whatever it stemmed from, *was* still banked in his expression.

With the cookies in her hand, they resumed their journey through the shopping center. Five steps in, she had half the first cookie down. Another five and it was gone, no crumbs remaining. Now, this was living!

She nibbled on the second treat, determined to savor every bit of it. She slowed her step and forced Zacharel to keep pace beside her rather than behind her.

"You are treating that thing as if it is a great treasure," he said.

Well, yeah. Because it was. "You have something against cookies?"

"I couldn't say, as I have never had one."

Wait. What? "Never, as in never?"

"Is there another meaning for the word *never* that I don't know about?"

Ha, ha. "But that's criminal!"

"Hardly."

"But . . . why haven't you tasted one?"

"Because I choose to consume only foods that will strengthen me."

"I'm not sure you realize how ridiculous you sound. But luckily for you, Annabelle Miller is here and on the case, and she's not going to let you go another minute without knowing the perfection that is chocolate ecstasy." She stopped, pinched a piece from the edge of what remained of the second confection, and held it up to Zacharel's lips. "Open up. You're about to discover the true meaning of *delicious*."

The heat intensified, and his lips softened. He would always look like a warrior — with those muscles, how could he not? — but just then he was more of a seducer. The prince from her dream . . . only, he wasn't a wretched demon in disguise.

"You are like Eve with her apple," he said.

"Is that an insult or a compliment?"

"Both."

"Then I'm only half-offended." She traced a line of melted chocolate across his lower lip. "Open. Don't make me command you again."

He opened.

She set the piece on his tongue, but before

she could remove her fingers, he closed his lips around them and sucked. A gasp was pulled from her, all the heat she'd noticed enveloping her, spreading through her, making her quiver.

He didn't mean anything with this, she knew, and slowly withdrew from him. He had no experience, had no idea what such an action implied.

He ate the cookie and licked his lips, his gaze locked on her. Such pretty lashes, she thought, such a dynamic gaze.

Such a beautiful man.

"You're right," he said. His tone gave nothing away. "Delicious."

Trying for a flippant reply, she said, "Sucks for you that you didn't order your own," then popped the rest of the cookie in her mouth.

To her utter shock, he smiled. Smiled! Lips curving up, straight white teeth revealed, dimples out in full glory. Yes, dimples. Awareness burned and blistered, a storm inside her. He was . . . He was . . . utterly magnificent.

"I could take the morsel from you right now, just steal it from your mouth. What would you do then, brave little Annabelle?"

She swallowed before she choked. "Be grossed out?" A question when it should have been a declaration.

"Hmph," he said, his smile disappearing.

For a moment, she felt as though the sun had set, darkness reigned and light could never possibly return. "I didn't mean I would hate it if you —"

"Forget it. Come, let's finish your shopping." He grabbed her hand and urged her forward.

And by *urged* she meant dragged. "Fine. But only because you're paying," she grumbled.

"Don't worry. You'll make it up to me."

"I will? How?"

The gaze he tossed her could only be described as smoldering. "You'll see."

CHAPTER TWELVE

"Keep your head down." Zacharel tucked his wings into his back, darting down a narrow, winding tunnel. They'd been flying for what seemed forever, but he at last spotted their destination. Annabelle tightened her grip and buried her face in the hollow of his neck.

Finally, the tunnel ended, opening into a huge crystallized cavern. He flared his wings, slowing his momentum and gently setting Annabelle on the ground. Her knees shook, and for a moment, she clung to him. Then she released him and stepped away so that no part of their bodies touched. Once again he mourned the loss of her — something that caused him to grit his teeth in irritation.

He'd been obsessed with her all day. Every point of contact, every hitch in her breath, every glance she'd cast in his direction had caused the tension inside him to sharpen.

Every change in her emotions had confused him. From happy to sad to playful to morose. He'd wanted to tug her into his arms and hold her until all she felt was the happiness. But he hadn't allowed himself to do that. Every time she had laughed he'd felt his blood seethe to a hotter degree. He would not have been able to content himself with simply holding her.

And when she'd fed him the cookie? When he'd had her fingers in his mouth? He'd had to fight the urge to strip her, strip himself and finally discover why so many humans enjoyed what happened when two people were naked.

One day very soon, he would allow himself to sample her, to learn the curves of her body, and experience that kind of passion. But he would not yearn for more, would not become addicted to a woman who was both mortal and a demon's consort. He would assuage his curiosity and return to the life he knew — and liked. Wrong of him, perhaps, but this was the only option available to him.

A warrior angel could not keep a human. The brutal war between angels and demons was far too dangerous for such fragile flesh. And the war brewing between angels and the Greeks and Titans? Already he could feel the tension in the air, hear the whispers of a coming revolt. More than that, their life spans were far too different.

"What is this place?" A quiver of distress shook her as she eyed their new surroundings.

Even without looking, he knew what she saw. A rack, with shackles for someone's wrists and ankles. A bed with black sheets to hide anything that spilled. A wall of instruments he had no desire to ever use.

He could have chosen another cave that belonged to an angel like him, a male who had never before experienced desire. But he'd chosen Thane's dwelling, where he'd known these things would be, because he'd hoped to disgust and shame himself into abandoning his current path.

But no, he still wanted Annabelle. Wanted to do things to her . . .

Her eyes frosted over, nearly freezing him in place. He, who had known a cold unlike any other. "What's your price for staying with me? You said you'd tell me when we reached our new location. Well, we're here and I can't say I'm impressed."

And he never lied, did he. "You are more than 'not impressed.' You are disgusted. Yes?"

"Yes." She waved a hand toward the

arsenal before them. "Can you blame me after everything I've been through? I can guess what you want to do with me."

Her response boded ill, and he frowned. Did she find fault with the instruments — or him? "First, I would never use those things on you or ask you to use them on me. Second, I ask only that you willingly give yourself to me."

For a long while, she merely gaped at him. Then she gave him a once-over and gulped. *Then* she shook her head violently, that tumble of dark, gorgeous hair slapping at her cheeks. "If you demand my body as payment, then the sex will not be consensual, no matter how compliant I seem to be. I won't actually be giving myself to you. Rather, you'll be forcing yourself on me. Just like Fitzpervert!"

Anger burst from his bones, filling every part of him. "I am nothing like him." If Zacharel was to drown in need for her, he would be damned if he would not pull her down with him. "Do you desire me?" he demanded.

She licked her lips, gulped again. "I'm attracted to you, yes."

That eased the hottest threads of his emotion. "As I am . . . attracted to you." Attracted. Such a mild word for the cravings

243

constantly bombarding him. "So what is the problem?"

For a moment her anger far surpassed his own, blazing from her with all the heat of the sun. "I won't be forced to do anything ever again. I won't have my hands tied — literally or figuratively."

He realized his mistake and nearly cursed. He should not have brought her to a place like this, even if it suited his own purposes, and he should not have tried to push the issue. He should have allowed things to progress naturally.

But . . . lacking as he was in this area, he knew nothing about "naturally."

"I told you. I am not like the doctor. I am not like other men you have known. Why would I save you only to hurt you? But very well, if you cannot trust me, we will bargain. I told you I knew how."

That mollified her somewhat. "Very well. I'm listening."

"I will stay with you for a month," and far longer, he added silently, if he hadn't yet assuaged his curiosity. Because just then, he realized he wanted more than once. He wanted all that she had to offer. Wanted to experience everything with her. Only then would he let her go. "*If* you will vow to kiss me whenever the urge strikes you." Surely the rest would spring from there.

"But the girl . . . the one who kissed you without permission . . ."

"The situation with you is not the same. You have my permission. You have an open invitation." His tone of voice deepened, became raspier, every syllable layered with his hunger.

"Because you're attracted to me," she reiterated brokenly, toying with the ends of her hair.

"Yes."

"But what if I never want to kiss you?"

"Then you will not." But she would want to; he would make sure of it.

She looked down, then up at him, down, up. Those expressive eyes revealed a mix of trepidation and hope and . . . something white-hot. "Yes. I agree to your terms."

Agreeing had seemed like such a good idea, but now, a few hours after their bargain had been struck, Annabelle was ablaze with nervous energy. Would she have the courage to follow through? Wouldn't she?

It was all she'd been able to think about.

"You look hot," Zacharel said. He puttered around the kitchen, fixing her a sandwich.

She knew he didn't mean the word *hot* as

245

anyone else would have. "I am." The robe that had fitted itself to her body, becoming a T-shirt and pants, had returned to its shapeless form just before she and Zacharel had flown here, swathing her from neck to toes. "I could use a shower. Alone."

"A robe cleans its wearer from the inside out. Right now you are cleaner than you have ever been."

"Oh. That's cool." And that response was lame. She had to pull herself together. "I mean, I noticed its cleaning ability when you were injured." *I just didn't put two and two together.*

"Perhaps you should change into your new clothes."

"I think I will." Just not the way he probably thought.

He'd set the bags at the entrance. She dug through each one until she found what she wanted. Then, the same way she had stripped out of her leather, with the robe shielding her, she now dressed.

"Unfair," she thought she heard Zacharel mutter.

Only when her new bra and panties, T-shirt, jeans and boots were in place — and she had successfully cut through the pockets for easy access to the blades still strapped to her legs — did she finally remove the robe.

Zacharel's gaze roved over her from top to bottom — then back up again. "I approve. And now you will eat." He carried a plate to the small wooden table, sat down and motioned for her to join him.

"And we will talk," she said.

"Of course."

She'd meant to continue their bargaining, but he began to grill her for information — and she couldn't help but grill him right back. Why a cave? Why the sex toys? The answer to the first: because. The answer to the second: because.

So informative, her angel.

She shifted uncomfortably. Neither of their chairs possessed a back, and while she felt like she would fall backward every time she moved, he was perfectly at ease, the lack of slats allowing him to comfortably position his wings.

"The demon that killed your parents," he said, motioning for her to take another bite out of the most delicious sandwich she'd ever eaten. Soft, moist and bursting with sweet and spicy flavors. "What did he look like?"

"What if I said ugly, and left it at that?" Two could play the reticent game.

"I would press."

"Thought so." She chewed, swallowed, trying not to picture the beast that had haunted her nightmares all these years. With only the slightest quaver in her tone, she described the red eyes, the humanoid face and the vampire fangs. The smooth, crimson skin, the horns that protruded from his spine. The tail that had curled into a metal spike.

All the while Zacharel frowned. See? His default expression.

"That could be any number of demons, but definitely not the one who dictated which demons could and could not enter your institution. Still, we will find Burden, talk to him."

Burden. What a terrible name. "He'll be honest with you?"

"With a little persuasion, perhaps. But sometimes you can discern the truth by breaking apart the lie."

"As long as you're sure. And just so you know, I can handle danger. Don't even think about leaving me behind."

His eyes narrowed, though that failed to hide the green flames sparking to shattering life. "I could absolutely leave you behind, Annabelle, and there's nothing you could do to stop me."

"I could hate you," she seethed. "Well,

not hate you, since I now refuse to hate anyone, but I could be *very* angry with you!"

"And you think that would bother me?" Such a calmly uttered question, as if he didn't care about the answer.

But he did care, and there was no hiding that fact. Not any longer. He wanted her body, had tried to demand it as payment, and when she'd said no, he'd decided to settle for her kisses.

I don't have to be nervous about our bargain, she realized, startled, awed. Happy. He was so desperate to have her, he would take anything he could get. Even scraps.

"A little tip for you, Winged Wonder. Don't threaten the woman you want to seduce." See Annabelle take control.

He reached out, gently brushed his fingertip along her collarbone. "If it means saving your life, I'll do more than threaten you. I'll follow through. Best you realize that now, rather than crying foul later."

The touch, slight though it had been and even blocked by cotton, electrified her. See Zacharel take control away from her. "I want a man to be my equal, not my boss."

He flashed his teeth at her, his arm falling heavily to his side. "I will never be your equal. I will always be stronger, faster."

Better?

Yes, there was that, wasn't there, she thought, that shot of confidence fizzling completely. The sandwich seemed to compact inside her stomach, becoming a lead ball. "I'm not sure why you'd even want to kiss me. You make me sound like a real prize. Maybe we should just forget our bargain altogether."

He slammed a fist into the table's surface. "The bargain remains intact."

The atypical outburst astounded her, causing her eyes to widen. Must have astounded him, too, because the moment he realized just how much force he'd used, he licked his lips and added smoothly, "Otherwise, I would be allowed to desert you at any moment, would I not? And you do not want that, do you, Annabelle?"

No, because he would be able to return to the heavens. And that was the only reason she decided to capitulate. Really. "Fine. The bargain remains intact. But the more you talk, the more I dislike you. You know that, right?"

"It shall be my pleasure to remedy it. First, it is not your strength or your speed that draws me. It's your . . . everything. Your laugh, your wit, your emotions and the way they change. Your courage, your sweetness, your near obsessive delight for cookies.

Second, you are indeed a prize. You've made me want what no one else ever has. A communion of bodies."

Uh, never again would she tell this man he had no idea how to seduce a woman. His words *affected* her, deeply and inexorably. A communion of bodies. His. Hers. Theirs, as one. Just the thought caused goose bumps to break out over her skin. And there was no more nervousness. None at all. He'd just reminded her that the act was meant to be special, not shameful, between two people meant to be together.

Meant to be? *You and Zacharel?*

He flattened his hands on the table and leaned forward. "Third. The blond angel, Thane, the one you claimed to like better than me. This is his cave, and those are his tools." With a tilt of his head, he motioned to the rack that so reminded her of her hospital gurney. "Know that he will use them on you if you turn to him. *You will not turn to him.*"

Okay, that had sounded like jealousy. And the change in him, from distant and threatening to possessive and needy, was as startling as his fist to the table. She reeled, empowered all the more.

"You are right," he said, before she could reply. "Talking is doing us no good. Eat."

Well, darn. Every time she thought she'd gained the upper hand, he had to go and ruin it. "Yes, Daddy," she grumbled, and popped another piece of bread in her mouth.

That earned her a fiery glare.

As she finished off the food, she watched Zacharel through slitted lids, trying not to be obvious in her study of him. Despite his change in mood, he could have stepped from a painting, so striking was his visage. Would she ever get used to the beauty of him?

After all, his hair would always be black, his skin unwrinkled. He would never change. He would always look this way, while she would age. Ugh. She would age, wouldn't she?

The only thing different about him was his wings. They were now mostly gold with specks of white threaded through the feathers. If he was right, and he was evolving into one of the Elite, whatever that meant, he was evolving quickly.

"Just so you know," she said when she realized the silence had grown just as tense as their words. "I do not desire Thane."

He nodded, satisfied.

"So how long will we stay here?"

"No more than four days. I need to know

if demons can sense you when you're under-ground. The answer will dictate our next course of action."

Plenty of time for him to teach her a little about fighting demons. Of course, that lesson would involve physical contact, and physical contact would probably cause her hormones to go wild. She would want to kiss him, which meant, according to their bargain — which he hadn't let her terminate — she would have to kiss him.

Would she find the courage?

Stupid question, plaguing her.

What if she sucked — the bad kind of sucking? What if she turned him off kissing forever? What if she freaked out? Or, what if she liked it? What if she wanted more? What if he refused to give her more? What if he rebuked her as he'd done to that other female? That beautiful angel with the dark, curling hair? Despite the fact that he claimed to desire Annabelle.

Or, what if he wanted more than a kiss but Annabelle refused to give him more? Would he then decide she wasn't worth the effort and dump her somewhere?

No, she thought next. He wasn't a slime. He might be cold and callous, but he wasn't a liar, either. He had agreed to stay with her for a month, and so he would . . . no matter what. Would he regret that promise, though? Or would he be glad for it?

Only one way to learn the answers to all your questions . . .

Added bonus: the first time would be over, done, and the nervousness would leave her once and for all.

Well, that settled it.

"Zacharel," she said on a wispy catch of breath.

His gaze drilled into her very soul. "What are you thinking about, Annabelle?" Huskily asked, a caress to each of her senses.

Like him, she couldn't lie. Not this time, the truth already proven by the softening of her lips. "Kissing you."

His gaze immediately dropped to her lips, his pupils gobbling up his irises. "Why?"

Because you think I'm a prize. Because, when you look at me, I feel cherished rather than leered at. "I believe you'll be familiar with my answer — because."

Slowly the corners of his mouth curled up. "So what are you waiting for? You know what you must do."

CHAPTER THIRTEEN

Zacharel waited, tense, as Annabelle slowly stood and closed the distance between them. He tensed further when she at last positioned herself between his legs. Part of him screamed to stop her, to stop this. After the first tasting, there would be no going back. He would know, the knowledge a part of him. The rest of him screamed for more. For all.

The rest of him won.

His curiosity was far too great, but more than that, his need to pleasure this particular woman was too great. Her scent was the sweetest of aphrodisiacs. Her curves had been made for his hands, and his alone — as he would soon confirm. He coiled his fingers around her small, fragile hips, just as she flattened her palms on his shoulders. At the moment of contact, her heated gasp filled the space between them.

"Closer," he rasped, tugging her until they

were flush. Because he was seated, they were now eye to eye. Mouth to mouth. *Have to taste . . .*

But she didn't give him what he wanted. "If you don't like it, just tell me to stop, okay? Don't go all caveman and push me away or call me names or blame me."

"I will like it, and you will teach me what to do."

"But if you don't —"

"You're stalling." Zacharel slid a hand up the ridges of her spine and into her hair, fisting the strands and urging her to close the rest of the distance.

"You're sure?"

He pressed his lips against hers. Lips so different from his own; softer, as soft as rose petals, fuller, holding him in thrall at that very first brush. He pulled back, marveling, and then he went in again . . . marveled anew at the decadence of her . . . then again, and this time, moaning, she opened for him.

Her tongue rolled against his, bringing with it the tastes of summer: berries dipped in cream, newly blooming roses and sultry midnights.

As focused on her as he was, he was able to follow her lead. When her tongue thrust, he knew to meet it. When her tongue retreated, he knew to chase it. He relished every new experience, growling his desire for more.

Her fingers slicke'd through his hair, decadent sensations dancing over his scalp, tickling skin that had never before been touched by another's hands. "I don't know about you but I like this," she breathed, sounding surprised.

"Yes." His blood had been icy for so long, with only the occasional flash of heat to prevent him from freezing. Heat he'd only felt with her. Now that blood was molten, scorching through his veins, warming him up. Sweat beaded on his brow, between his shoulder blades, and trickled down his stomach.

Even his breath burned him, singeing his lungs and scraping at his throat. There was only one cure for the fever, and he instinctively knew what it was. He had to be closer to her, had to touch all of her. Had to *have* all of her.

"Up." A command.

When she failed to immediately obey, Zacharel cupped her bottom and lifted her, forcing her to straddle him, to settle her weight against him. And oh, sweet heavens, *yes,* that was exactly what he'd needed. Pleasure rocketed through him, a beautiful sort of torture.

She moaned into his mouth, her nails sinking into his scalp, as if to hold him in place. As if she worried he would try to get away. Never would he do such a thing. He was lost, tied only to the woman in his lap and glad for it. Except . . .

Except the new position was no longer the blessing he'd thought.

"Annabelle." He *hurt* and needed some kind of relief.

"Zacharel."

Hearing his name on her lips, uttered so breathlessly, filled him with a sense of possession. *Mine.* "Do . . . more," he pleaded.

"Okay. All right. Yes."

But she didn't, and he had to flatten his hands on her hips to stop himself from trying to caress her everywhere all at once.

"What kind of more do you want?" she whispered.

"Whatever you will give."

"I don't . . . maybe . . . rock into me."

Rock into . . . yes. As they kissed and kissed and kissed, he arched against her. Forward, back, seeking, retreating. Every point of contact wrung a groan from her and a growl from him. The pleasure blurred with pain, as unbearable as it was necessary.

How had he gone without this for so long? How had he resisted this? No wonder so many humans were willing to war with their brethren, just to have or even save the one they lusted after. This sense of connection . . . Zacharel had never before experienced its like. He wasn't just Zacharel, he was Annabelle's man and glad for it.

"Zacharel?"

Her breasts smashed against his chest, causing a brand-new ache. He had to feel her against him, skin to skin, no barriers. He released her long enough to rip his robe down the middle and jerk his arms free of the fabric, allowing what was left to mend itself and tighten around his waist. Next he ripped the cotton of Annabelle's top, causing it to gape open and her to inhale sharply.

He had ripped her bra, too, and she was beautiful. Oh, was she beautiful. He was shaking as he cupped her breasts, marveling that they could be so heavy and yet so soft. *Must . . . taste . . .*

"Wait," he thought he heard her say.

No. No waiting. He would have her *now.*

His mind fogged with more of the glorious pleasure as he dipped down and kissed one side of her, then the other. Annabelle arched her back, moving away from him, but he didn't like that, so he freed one of his hands to shackle her in place.

"Zacharel!"

"Annabelle." The fog in his mind thickened, and he failed to register the dainty hands now pushing at his shoulders, trying to dislodge him. Why had he denied himself this type of contact for so long? he wondered again. And how had he once convinced himself a single taste of this woman would be enough? He would have this, have Annabelle, at least once a day, he decided, until he'd tired of the act.

He might never tire of this.

Something sharp scraped down his cheek, once, twice, drawing blood. He released Annabelle to swat that something away, whatever it was. *Can't let it hurt her.* The moment he did, she bolted backward, tumbling from his lap. When she hopped to her feet, he jumped to his. His robe remained girded around his waist as he reached for her. But . . . just before contact, she punched him in the nose with so much force the cartilage snapped. Blood poured down his face.

He frowned, still reaching for her. *Exquisite.* "Annabelle. Kiss."

"Kiss this, you mangy rat!" She kneed him between the legs with so much force he would probably need his testicles surgically removed from his abdomen.

Pain zoomed through him, breath left him

and he hunched over. The fog in his mind cleared at last, and he looked up, confused by her violence. That's when she double tapped his cheek, and his knees gave out. He fell to the floor, bright stars winking through his line of sight . . . but not enough to block her fear-glassed eyes or the rapid rise and fall of her chest.

"Annabelle," he said, holding out his arms to prove he meant her no harm.

"No!" Mistakenly thinking he'd been trying to grab her, she went low and — actually stabbed him in the side. She had changed her clothes, but had not given up the weapons strapped to her thighs. He should have known.

"Don't ever touch me again," she spat.

He grunted, knowing she'd nicked his kidney.

She straightened, dropped the bloody knife as if it burned her. With one white-knuckled fist, she held the sides of her shirt together. With the other, she frantically rubbed the spot just above her heart. Trembling, she backed away from him. "Did you hear me? Never again!"

He had done this to her, he realized. He had reduced her to this.

Shame filled him as he stood. The cut in his side throbbed, but he paid it no heed. It would soon heal.

"Annabelle."

Her footsteps quickened, and she didn't stop her backward progress until reaching the far cavern wall. But even that wasn't enough for her. She extended an arm to ward him off.

"D-don't come any closer!" Panic coated her voice, the edges sharp enough to slice through bone. A moment later, she doubled over, a cry of pain springing from her.

Concerned, Zacharel raced toward her. She sensed him, straightened and scooted to the right, avoiding contact.

"Stop! I mean it." She swept her gaze over him, probably searching for the most vulnerable spot to punch him, and gasped. "You really do have a black heart."

He stopped as ordered, looked himself over. His chest was bare, the smudge of black just over his heart visible and larger, so much larger, now hemorrhaging into his collarbone and torso.

More of his spirit had died.

No wonder Annabelle wanted out of your embrace.

From the moment he'd realized what the smudge meant, that he finally lived with a ticking clock, that he was dying, bit by bit, he'd been okay with the end result, had even seen it as an insurance policy — but he wasn't okay with it now. If the impossible happened and he passed on before Annabelle, she would have no one to oversee her protection.

Hurriedly he righted his robe, the material weaving itself back together to shield his self-inflicted flaw. He held up his hands, palms out, a stance he prayed reassured Annabelle that he currently lacked menace. "I'm sorry that I hurt you. That was not my intention." Step by measured step, he approached her.

She shook her head viciously, hair he'd fisted only moments ago now hanging in tangles. All the while, she continued to rub at her chest. "I told you not to come any closer. Stay back!"

Just then, he would have done anything she asked — except that. If he retreated, she would never again trust him and on some deep level he did not understand, he needed her to trust him. She would build walls between them, walls he could never hope to breach, for they would be fortified by this terror and an ever-growing sense of fury. He discerned this on that same deep level, where instinct swirled with his primal need to protect her. He quickened his step, unwilling to prolong this a minute more.

The moment he reached her, she erupted, fighting him with every bit of her strength. At least she opted not to use her other blades.

Took him longer than he would have guessed, but he finally managed to capture her hands and spin her around, and though he despised the need for his next actions, he removed her torn shirt. He pinned her wrists above her with one hand and reached into an air pocket to claim the shirt he'd saved for her. The one he'd removed from its bag because it had been his favorite, a sparkling blue the same shade as her eyes.

Screaming, she bucked against him and cried, tears splashing as she shook her head. He worked the material over her head, through her arms.

All the while, he whispered into Annabelle's ear. "I will not hurt you. You are safe with me. You have nothing to fear from me."

She was too entrenched in her terror to hear him.

He would not be able to reach her this way, either, he realized. Not knowing what else to do, Zacharel flared his wings and flew her to the mouth of the cavern. Twice he nearly dropped her, so wild was her flailing, but in the end he was able to set her feet on the floor. The second he released her, she bolted into motion, sprinting through the tunnel, away from him.

Only when he rendered himself invisible did he follow after her, flying just overhead. Constantly she threw panicked glances over her shoulder, searching for him. Though she never spotted him, never sensed him, she never slowed. She ran and ran and ran, wheezing and crying. When she caught sight of the bright rays of sunlight pushing through the cave entrance, she increased her speed.

She burst into the daylight, tripped over a large rock. A mewl of pain escaped her, but she righted herself and kept going. He caught the scent of her blood and knew she'd skinned her knees.

Squawking birds took flight as she ran, and forest animals skittered away. She splashed through a puddle, then tripped again, over a tree root this time. Her palms took the brunt of the fall, abrading her flesh, and her ankle twisted, but not even that slowed her. Branches slapped at her, cutting her cheeks. Leaves stuck in her hair.

Soon she would tire. He would let her race wherever she desired until then. When she had nothing left, he would swoop in. She would have to pay attention to him as he did everything in his power to convince her of his remorse, to reassure her that nothing like this would ever happen again.

Though he wasn't exactly sure what he'd done wrong. She had enjoyed his kisses and his touch. Yes?

"Just like them," she sobbed, rubbing, rubbing, still rubbing at her chest. "Why'd he have to be just like them? I told him to slow down, but he wouldn't and now I . . . Now I . . ."

With her words, understanding dawned. After everything she had endured in the institution, he had pushed her for too much, too fast. He had destroyed her clothing, as the ones who had forced her had probably done. He had not heeded her protests, but had tried to take what he desired.

She was right — he was just like them. *Was* there a way to fix this? A way to convince her that he wasn't the monster she now considered him? In the past, when someone wronged him to such a degree, Zacharel had never been the type to forgive and forget.

She is not like you. She is softer, better.

And wasn't that ironic? He was the angel, she the human, and yet he was the one in need of pardon.

A cackle of evil laughter sounded up ahead, snaring his interest. Dread and anger

266

consumed him in a single heartbeat. Zacharel quickened his speed, moving in front of Annabelle. She had been found. But where were — then he spotted them. A horde of demons waited up ahead in trees, behind trunks and atop boulders, laughing gleefully and clearly intending to ambush her.

That quickly, they'd found her, and Zacharel would have to deal with them — but now Annabelle wouldn't trust him any more than she would trust the demons. She might even fight him as he fought them.

If he got her out of this alive, it would be a miracle.

CHAPTER FOURTEEN

"What happened to you?" Thane had only just flown himself into Koldo's underground home in Half Moon Bay when he spied the warrior laid out on the bed, his head shaved and his back slashed to ribbons.

Eyelashes crusted together with specks of blood broke apart, and dark, glassy eyes struggled to focus on him. "Water of Life" was the grumbled response.

Should have guessed. Only once had Thane beseeched the Heavenly High Council for permission to approach the river. They had demanded he first live as a mortal, among the humans, for a month. He hadn't needed to consider his answer. He had refused, and so his request had been denied. To be mortal was to be helpless, and nothing was worth that.

He crossed his arms over his chest, saying, "They took your hair." An obvious statement, but his shock was unparalleled.

"Yes."

"And you let them."

"Yes."

"Why?"

Koldo closed his eyes. "Why are you here, warrior?"

Thane wasn't surprised by the evasion. Koldo wasn't one to share his problems. None of them were. But he was surprised by the ease with which Koldo was speaking to him. Normally he couldn't get more than a brusque "yes" or "no" from the angel. "Zacharel commanded me to come."

"You just missed him. He was here with the girl."

Another surprising fact. Zacharel was *willingly* carting a human female around the world. Thane could only wonder what would happen next. "They were well?"

"Yes," Koldo said again, though this time he hesitated over the word. "He wanted her with him, within his sight. He did not like the fact that I had touched her, even innocently."

Such a long string of words. The pain must have abolished his inhibitions.

But that couldn't overshadow what he'd said. Zacharel was possessive and jealous, when he'd never displayed the slightest emotion before.

What other human emotions would their leader unleash? Especially when he lost the girl. And he would lose her. Mortals were delicate, easily crushed; angels were not.

"Where are your boys?" Koldo asked. "They're usually not far behind you."

"Bjorn is hunting Jamila. She left Zacharel's cloud a few nights ago and hasn't been seen since. Xerxes is examining the remains of a demon horde found under that very cloud."

"And you are hunting Zacharel to heed his command."

"Not exactly." He had spoken inside Zacharel's mind, as Zacharel had spoken inside his. He could do so again, could ask where Zacharel was and if he was okay or needed help, but he wouldn't. That kind of connection to anyone but Bjorn and Xerxes disturbed him as he suspected it disturbed Zacharel. "Did he say where he was going? Or what his plans were?"

"If he did, I was too busy being unconscious to notice."

Thane couldn't help himself; he grinned. Humor, from the ever-serious Koldo was as baffling as Zacharel's new obsession with the girl. And it moved Thane to do something he knew he shouldn't.

He strode to the kitchen and placed on

the counter all the items necessary for making a sandwich. He should be tracking another demon to torture. Unfortunately, the one he'd captured had not given any details, no matter what he'd done, had just stoically borne the pain. He should be alerting the other members of the army to these new developments. But he wanted to ease Koldo somehow, someway.

"You can't feed me," Koldo said from the bed.

No, he couldn't, as much as he wished otherwise. Anyone who did would be forced to bear the very pain they'd hoped to assuage — for the rest of eternity. "I'm hungry and in need of a snack. If you want what I leave behind, that's up to you." As he was learning, there was always a way around a rule.

Thane bit into the turkey-and-cheese as he strode back to the bed. He took another bite, and then another, before placing what was left of the sandwich on the nightstand. Then he returned to the kitchen and filled a glass with orange juice. He drained half the contents before the glass, too, found a new home on the nightstand.

Koldo studied the food for a long, silent moment before shifting his gaze to Thane. "I will tell you why I wanted the Water if

271

you swear never to breathe a word of what you hear."

Vows were sacred among their kind. Thane often felt as if he were a man lacking any sort of honor, that there was nothing he wouldn't do, no line he wouldn't cross, but that wasn't exactly true. He never broke his vows, and he never would. "I so swear."

A beat of stilted silence, then, "Zacharel was dying. The girl swore to keep him out of the heavens for one month if I healed him. I knew the Water was the only thing that would save him, and so I procured it for him."

He absorbed the warrior's words, trying to reason things out, failing. "Why a month?"

"I needed time to heal. Time to search . . . to act."

The potency of the warrior's relish left no doubt that the "act," whatever it was, would involve bloodshed. "Tell me."

"Your oath of secrecy extends to this?"

Meaning, he would not mention this discussion even to Bjorn or Xerxes. "It does."

Koldo gave the slightest of nods. "Everyone thinks a demon removed my wings all those years ago, and I allow them to think this because I do not want to answer any questions about the truth."

"But the truth is . . . what?" Thane asked, knowing Koldo would answer *him*. Not because he had given his vow of silence, but because the truth was a poison inside of him, a poison he was desperate to expunge.

"An angel took my wings, and I plan to kill her."

Thane had questioned why the stoic Koldo, the unflappable, unbendable warrior anyone and everyone could rely on, had been assigned to this last-chance army. He'd heard rumors about a supposed beating Koldo had rendered, but he'd never seen the male worked into any kind of temper. Now he fit a few puzzle pieces together. Whether the beating had happened or not, Koldo was a part of Zacharel's army because of the vengeful purpose in his heart.

"If Zacharel so much as suspected, he would try and stop you."

"Yes."

"And you do not think I will try and stop you?"

There was no hesitation when Koldo replied with, "No, I do not. You know the value of retaliation."

Actually, he knew the hopelessness. After his rescue from the dungeon, after his body had healed, Thane, Bjorn and Xerxes had returned. Three days and three nights were spent locked in a vicious battle for rights to that dungeon. Oh, they could have killed the demons inside, torched the place and ended things in an hour, but they hadn't wanted that. Hadn't wanted their captors to die quickly or easily.

And so they hadn't. The three of them had taken the dungeon, leaving everyone inside alive. The pain-filled screams still sometimes echoed inside Thane's mind. But he did not feel any better about the past . . . and he knew his boys did not feel better about themselves.

"You will do what you feel you must," he finally said. "I will not tell Zacharel." He paused, head tilting to the side. "Who is she, this woman who betrayed you?"

"That, I will not tell you."

"Because you think I would shield her. Interesting. I must know her. No matter, though. Here's something I'm sure you will learn about me. I love two men, and no others." There wasn't room in the small chambers of his heart for anyone else. "Your female is nothing to me."

Silence.

He sighed. "You will let me know if there is anything I can do to aid you in your quest." A demand.

"There is nothing. I must do this alone. She hides from me, and I will allow no one else to drag her from the shadows. I will be the one to unearth her."

Understood. "Very well. I will leave you to —" He trailed off as a sense of foreboding suddenly struck him, followed by a flash of images through his mind. He and Zacharel must have maintained a strong mental link, because he could feel his leader's dread and fury.

Zacharel, he said, projecting his voice into his leader's mind. So much for keeping his mental distance.

Nothing, no response.

Zacharel, what's going on?

Again no response.

Was Zacharel ignoring him? Or too injured to respond?

"I must go," he told Koldo. He would have to track the angel the old-fashioned way.

"There is trouble?"

"Worry not, for this is not something that concerns you," he evaded. He would not have the man worrying when there was nothing he could do. "I will return when I'm able."

Annabelle stood in the center of the slaughter, winded yet buzzing with adrenaline. Black blood formed multiple rivers around her. She rubbed at her chest, hoping to finally ease the burn that had begun to blaze inside the cavern, when Zacharel had . . . When he'd . . . Even now the burn increased, and she rubbed harder.

Don't think about it. Right now, demonic bodies were piled around her, the scent of rotten eggs thick in the air, pungent enough to make her gag. Yeah. She'd think about *that.* It was far more pleasant.

Zacharel had produced his sword of fire and gone to town on each of the monsters, allowing none to escape. To her surprise, he'd also placed two blades in her hands when she'd dropped her own, her last, enabling her to continue fighting.

And fight she had, the sharp metal tips slicking through jugulars, midsections and even the backs of knees, hobbling her prey for easier elimination. What she'd lacked in skill she'd made up for in creativity and determination.

"Are you injured?" Zacharel demanded, stomping across the motionless, headless bodies to reach her.

Before he could think to take back his blades, she shoved them through the slits in her pockets and into the sheaths strapped to her thighs. "I'm fine." Yes, she was cut up and bleeding, and yes, one of her ankles was twisted and throbbing, but she would hurt like this forever if it meant defeating her enemy. "You?"

He looked her over, judging the truth of her words for himself. At the same time, she looked *him* over. He was just as blood soaked as she was, with sweat trickling down his temples, his robe soaked to his skin.

"I'm well enough. Come, we must clean you up." He offered his hand to her.

To his credit, he didn't force her to link her fingers with his but waited for her to initiate contact on her own. She licked her lips, wishing there were some other way to leave this place. But he'd just uttered the only words that could have made a difference. Clean up. The blackened blood singed her skin, and already she had welts.

Expression blank, he said, "I am sorry for what I did to you, Annabelle, I truly am. I did not mean to . . . I was caught up . . . I'm sorry," he repeated.

Such sincerity from him should have surprised her, but it didn't. "I know you are," she said. And she really did, now that her mind was freed from the bondage of fear. That had been his first kiss, and he'd been caught up in the sensations, just as

277

she had been . . . until he'd ripped her top and bared her breasts, and memories of Fitzpervert and his camera of shame had flooded her. "But just so you know, I won't be wanting to kiss you again."

That part of their relationship was over. Zacharel hadn't meant to hurt her, but hurt her he had. He'd abused the very fragile trust she'd built with him. He hadn't stopped when she had wanted him to stop, and she couldn't risk something like that happening again.

Muscles ticked below eyes of green frost, a testament to a barely leashed temper. "You will change your mind."

If he ever let go of that leash . . . "No, I won't, and I won't leave with you until you accept it. And by the way, did you know you're snowing again?"

At first, he offered no reaction to her words, or her rejection. Then, with a powerful shrug of his shoulders he flared his wings, studied the feathers of one, then the feathers of the other. "I must have done something to encourage my Deity's displeasure. And I can guess what that something is."

Disappointment softened his features, making him appear as boyish as he had inside that cave, when he'd wanted her so desperately. *I will not soften.* But finally, blessedly, the burn in her chest faded.

"So that's what the snow is all about?" she said. "Why was he displeased with you in the first place?"

"I killed humans in order to kill demons. Humans worth saving, though I did not realize it at the time. People who could have been like you. I am glad I did not judge you guilty and end you without thought." Zacharel closed the rest of the gap between them, no longer content to wait for her to take his hand. His body brushed against hers, and she stumbled backward, even tripped over the limb of a fallen demon and fell to her butt. "What a shame that would have been."

She jumped to her feet, and backed up to increase the distance between them, but she never gained any ground and finally found herself pressed against a tree trunk. Her heart drummed against her ribs, but she wasn't afraid. Maybe because she knew he was no longer lost to lust, or maybe because he'd fought so tirelessly beside her, striking at anyone who'd attempted to get to her while she was distracted fighting someone else.

He'd even allowed himself to be injured, just to prevent *her* from being injured.

"What are you doing?" she asked.

Green fire lanced down at her. "You *will* kiss me again, Annabelle, because I give you my word I will not lose control a second time. I learned my lesson, and I learned it well."

"Your optimistic, faith-filled words won't work with me."

"Won't they? Do not try to tell me that you no longer desire me. I know better. I'm new at this, yes, but I'm not stupid. Your pupils are flared, your pulse is a jackhammer at the base of your neck and you liked what I was doing to you before I went too far. I can still hear your moans in my ears."

She gulped, considered lying, thought *screw it* and gave him the truth. "I did like it. You're right about that. But then I really, really *dis*liked it."

"From your tone, I can only assume you think to deny me a chance to prove myself." He leaned a fraction closer. Too close, his breath like the most decadent of caresses against her skin. "That you long to punish me. Well, I will accept punishment. For a little while."

She gulped.

"But you will trust me again, Annabelle. You will want me again, and we will be together. I will behave. You'll see."

His arrogance should have rubbed her the wrong way, but knowing he wanted her so much, that he was willing to do anything to be with her, was more an aphrodisiac than a deterrent. And if anyone possessed the strength to pull himself from the brink of satisfaction, or from anything, for that matter, it was Zacharel. From now on, he *would* control himself.

Maybe his faith-filled words *had* worked.

"I'm not sure why we want each other," she grumbled.

"Nor am I, but the fact remains that we do want each other."

"Maybe I'm just shallow. You're quite pretty."

"For now, that will do."

Infuriating man. Couldn't take an insult the way she intended. With a sigh, Annabelle wrapped her arms around his neck. "All right, I'll leave with you."

Satisfaction dominated his expression, as he anchored her against the strength of his body and shot into the air.

"Wait! My packages," she said when she realized he was not heading back to the cave.

"I do not want to risk going back and encountering more demons. We'll buy you new things."

Another shopping trip? "That kinda

sounds like a bribe."

"Whatever it takes."

She almost laughed. Almost. "Two can play that game. Expect to spend thousands — without a reward."

"As long as we buy cookies as well as clothing, I'm fine with that."

Cookies. Sneaky angel, he'd just had to go there, hadn't he, reminding her of his enjoyment, his sensual delight.

He said, "Time for your bath. Hold your breath," and swooped down, diving into a clear lake before she could demand to know why.

Icy water instantly enveloped her, colder even than his wings, making her gasp and choke and shiver. Just when she thought she could take no more, he glided out and back into the clouds.

The fact that he soared so effortlessly, despite the waterlogged state of his wings, spoke of his amazing strength. "Little more . . . warning next . . . time," she said between coughing fits.

"My apologies. How much more time would you like?"

"A hour, maybe. Possibly two." Though no amount of time could prepare her for such a frigid dipping.

"Very well. But I must admit, taking care

of a female is more difficult than even I imagined."

"Hey! I am *not* high maintenance. I'm spunky."

His gaze met hers for a protracted second. "To a man who has spent centuries seeing to only his own needs, you are indeed high maintenance, but I'm finding I do not mind maintaining you."

Chapter Fifteen

Zacharel considered his options. Demons had found Annabelle in the clouds. They'd found her in the cave. Clearly, keeping her underground wasn't the answer any more than keeping her in the heavens had been. So that left . . . what?

Knocking her out? No one had attacked her while she had slept. Or . . . wait. "How long were you in the institution before the demons found you?"

"A month, maybe."

A month. Her scent and allure must have been masked by the people surrounding her. People, then. People were not a threat but a key.

With that in mind, he flew her to a busy hotel for humans on the outskirts of New Zealand. Obtaining a room wasn't difficult. He simply misted her through the walls until spying what he wanted: an unoccupied space, with guests on either side, above and below.

"Shower. Warm up," he told her, then left to procure food and clothing. More than the impromptu bath, she'd had to deal with his declining temperature.

In the hotel's kitchen he acquired chicken and rice for her and fruit for himself, and snagged a clean uniform from the stack in back, being sure to leave enough money behind to more than cover the cost of both the food, the clothing and the room itself.

He left the uniform in the bathroom, not liking how harsh it felt against his skin. She would be scratched, and the thought did not settle well. He wished he had another robe tucked away, but he had left the extra one in the cave with her purchases. He could have flown to another location, found her something softer, but he could not bring himself to leave the hotel to acquire something better.

When she emerged on a thick cloud of steam, he saw that the clothing was too short for her. She didn't seem to mind, though, and to be honest, she looked adorable.

Without a word she placed a dagger under a pillow on the bed and one on the nightstand.

"Hungry?" he asked.

"Starved."

They ate in silence, her clean, soapy scent a live wire that connected them. Her hair was wet and slicked back into a tight ponytail, the strands like glistening ebony silk. The style left her face bare, nothing hiding those uptilted, crystalline eyes, those sharp, rose-tinted cheeks or those heart-shaped lips. Actually, *adorable* was not the right word. She was beauty personified.

What would she look like spread over the bed, her hair a spill of velvet, her eyes heavy lidded, her cheeks flushed with passion and her lips parted as she breathed him in?

"Thanks for the food," Annabelle said, at last cutting through the quiet. Her voice held traces of exhaustion, elation and . . . something else, something he couldn't identify.

"You are welcome."

Her gaze met his, steady but glassy. "So what now?"

"Now you relax. Too long has passed since you've rested."

"I managed to sleep a little in Koldo's cave, as well as during the flight here, and really, I'm not tired." The claim was disproved by her ensuing yawn. "Okay, so maybe I am. My mind's too active for any kind of rest, though."

Understandable. Or . . . on closer inspection, he could see the shadows blooming under her eyes. It wouldn't take much to quiet her mind, but perhaps she had no wish for it to be quieted. After such a trying day, nightmares were sure to plague her. He wondered if he would be the star of them.

"What do you usually do to help you relax?"

"I wish I knew. In the institution, I was given drugs."

And then forced to do whatever her doctors had wished. He could tolerate that knowledge less and less. "Climb into the bed and find something to watch. Distract yourself." That's what he'd seen many humans do throughout the years.

"Sir, yes, sir." Keeping an eye on him, she clambered onto the bed and switched on the TV, frowning, flipping channels. Eventually she gave up and pressed Off, then tossed the remote aside. "What will you do? Because I'm guessing you have something to do, or you wouldn't be pushing me to distract myself."

He must remain on alert, guard her . . . think. "I will be composing instructions for my army." Yes, that, too.

"You don't require any sleep?" She

snuggled into the covers, fluffed the pillows and peered over at him, the suspicion draining from her. Had she expected him to pounce on her?

"Some," he said, "but not much."

"Lucky. I despise the fact that I need to sleep."

Because she was made vulnerable. "I have told you that you have nothing to fear with me. You know I do not lie."

A beat of silence. A sigh. "I know."

"Do you?" he asked, peering at her intently. He now had an idea of what she would look like in bed, underneath him — and it was almost more than he could bear.

He stalked to the desk, blocking her from his peripheral vision, and sat down. The chair proved to be a mistake, the high back smashing his wings . . . that were no longer snowing, he realized. Why?

"I do," she finally said. "Really."

He could still see her out of the corner of his eye. Soft, warm, inviting. "Good." Up he stood and stalked to the room's only window, gazing through the gap in the curtains.

The setting sun cast pink, purple and blue rays over the horizon. Below that, he saw arcing trees, lush, green grass and a colorful spread of flowers. He'd been here once before. Had thought to fly past, but had stopped to watch the wedding taking place in the gardens.

Two people, pledging to love each other for the rest of their lives, in sickness and in health. Had Annabelle ever dreamed of doing so? With her high school boyfriend, perhaps? Zacharel pressed his tongue to the roof of his mouth.

"So . . . you lead an entire army of angels," she said through another yawn.

"Yes. There are three factions of the Deity's angels. The Elite Seven, who were created rather than born, the warriors and the joy-bringers."

"You're a warrior."

"Yes, but as I told you, I believe I am evolving into one of the Elite." He wondered if the metamorphosis would stop if he failed to continue to please his Deity.

Yes. Yes, it probably would. Most likely, he would not be given the title of Elite until the end of his year of service — if he survived.

Annabelle's brow wrinkled with confusion. "How can you be given such a title if you were born?"

"One of the Seven was recently killed, and someone must take his place, whether born or created." Once Zacharel had considered himself a wise choice. Now? Not so much.

"So you guys, what?" Annabelle asked. "Get together and march into battle, slaying demons?"

"Basically, yes. I receive my orders from the Deity, summon my army, and the soldiers come to my cloud. I relay the orders to them, and off we fly."

"But you're not the only army who does this, right?"

"Right. There are many angelic armies under the Deity's command. Most guard and patrol a certain city, and are sent into a full-fledged battle twice a month. Mine has not been assigned to a particular location, but travels the world. We aid humans, fight demon hordes, and anything else we are told."

He wasn't sure what he'd do when he and his soldiers were given their next mission. The thought of leaving Annabelle alone hollowed him out. Not that she would be helpless. The ferocious way she fought had astonished — and impressed — him.

"During the interim," he added, "we are to heal if need be, to train, to hunt individual demons or, if necessary, to aid other armies who request backup."

"Why are you and your men given more tasks than the other armies? Because you guys are stronger and more likely to win?"

Or because they had less to lose, he mused. "You would have to ask my Deity. He has not yet revealed the answer to me."

She released her hair from the ponytail, and combed her fingers through the strands. He shouldn't have noticed, but he'd angled his body toward her, seeking her unbidden. "Maybe I will," she said. "So how do you find the demons you hunt individually?"

"We can follow their trails of evil and destruction, but most times, as with you, our Deity points us in the right direction."

"Why didn't he send an army to the institution sooner?"

"He did. Many times. But soon after the demons were slain, others found you."

"Wow. I was being helped all along and had no idea. I'd always assumed I was on my own, that I could count on no one but myself."

"The Most High, and thereby the Deity, always desires to help you humans."

"I love knowing that. It's comforting. But you know, even though others were sent, you were the first angel to ever visit me."

And he would never be gladder for anything. He hoped she was, too.

The covers rustled as she rolled to her side, and oh, sweet heaven, he would have given anything to join her. "Several times, the word *consort* has been mentioned but no one has told me exactly what that means. I can guess, but since you're being so accommodating and informative, and since you owe me big-time, will you finally spell things out for me? Please."

He turned to her fully. Her hands rested under her cheek and the length of her hair draped over her arm. His desire for her thickened.

No, he could not bear this.

You will act the gentleman. "You are not above manipulation, I see."

"Not even a little."

He cut off his smile before it could form.

"A girl's gotta use whatever weapons she can."

And he would enjoy the use of those weapons, he thought. "Being a consort is the equivalent of wearing a ring when you marry another human. It means you belong to your partner . . . that you carry his name."

She bolted to a sitting position. Those eyes of ice darkened for the first time, fury a starburst of color. "I belong to no one!"

"Not ever?"

"Not ever."

All amusement lost, he popped his jaw. "Understand something, Annabelle. While we have our . . . agreement, you do, in fact, belong to me. You will not be with another man. I will not share." He waited, but she offered no response. "I will now hear you concur."

She leaned back, propping her weight on her elbows to have a better shot of him. "I'm too busy reeling."

If she willingly gave herself to another man . . . No. She wouldn't. She was to be his, and only his. End of story.

"I'll pretend like you aren't a caveman," she said. "And I'll promise not to be with another man . . . as long as you'll promise not to be with another woman."

That she demanded his fidelity after everything that had happened delighted him. "So promised. And that is one of the reasons we must find and kill this high lord who thinks to claim you." *He will not have what is mine.*

"Do you know where he is?"

"No, but I will just as soon as I find out *who* he is."

"You will. *We* will."

He liked her faith in him. "I'm curious as to why he deserted you after marking you." Zacharel would not have done so. Could not fathom anyone *wanting* to do so. "Can you remember anything else about him?

Something you have yet to tell me?"

She fell back against the pillows, her eyes squeezed closed as though to block images inside her mind. "I've told you everything. He came, he conquered, he vanished."

"And he didn't try to take you with him?"

"No."

"Astounding." Zacharel's gaze slipped over her, trying to see past the covers to the succulent curves that rested underneath. *Do not go there. She is tired, stressed, and it is far too soon.*

He hopped to his feet and stalked to the bathroom. There, he drew a hot bath, making sure to pour some of the hotel's bath soap into the water. Wildflower-scented steam soon curled through the air. She'd already taken a shower, but humans enjoyed baths for more than cleaning themselves, yes? He placed a towel next to the tub and nodded, satisfied everything was in order.

In the room, he was careful not to look too closely at Annabelle. He would mentally strip her, would imagine her luxuriating inside the bath, and then he would pounce, giving life to her earlier worry.

"The bath is ready for you."

Covers rustled. "For *me?*"

"Of course. I certainly do not want to smell like flowers."

"My skin is probably going to peel off me after all this water, but a bath is simply irresistible considering I haven't had one in four years!" She was on her feet and racing past him in a snap. The door closed and locked behind her. He remained where he was, torturing himself as sounds of falling clothing, splashing water and moans of pleasure blended.

If he'd wanted her before, he *really* wanted her now. He wanted her naked and wet and pliant and eager. How long before her desire for him returned? How long before she trusted him again? Oh, she trusted him on some level, or she wouldn't be here with him. But sex, as he was learning, required more.

When at last she emerged, she was more delectably fragrant than before and dressed in the uniform.

"Thank you so much," she breathed, flinging herself back on the bed. She twisted around to face him, her skin dewy and flushed, alive with health. The otherworldly blue of her eyes glistened like melting ice in the summer sun, an image made all the stronger because of her new morning-meadow scent. "I had no idea how much I needed that."

Beneath the hunger for her was a satisfaction that his actions had brought her to this point: relaxed, refreshed and delighted.

"Have you been standing there the whole time?" she asked.

A stiff nod.

"But I was in there for over an hour."

He knew. He'd done nothing but count the seconds. There were three thousand, six hundred seconds in an hour, and she'd spent three thousand, seven hundred and four seconds in there.

She paused, nibbling on her bottom lip as he'd noticed she was prone to do. It was an action that betrayed a sense of nervousness. He couldn't help but stare. He wanted his own lips on her, soothing whatever wounds she caused.

"Are you thinking about kissing me?" she asked.

"I am, yes," he said.

She gulped. "I can't believe I'm even contemplating this, after I told myself — and you! — that I never would. But you're being such a sweetheart that I can't seem to help myself."

Every muscle in his body tensed. "You mean . . . ?"

"Yeah. I mean. I have a question for you first."

"Ask." Anything.

"Will you let me . . . well, tie you up?"

His blood, already heating, went molten. "If you wish, but you should know that no chains can hold me. I would be bound simply to ease your mind."

"Well, it's not really easing to know you could bust free!" A moment later, her shoulders slumped against the mound of pillows. "I wouldn't be able to do it, anyway."

He barely managed to cut off his roar of denial. "Kiss me?"

"No, bind you."

"Because you hated being bound yourself." A statement, not a question. He was learning her.

"Exactly." There was an eternity of silence before she gave a soft sigh. "But okay, all right. We can try the kissing thing again. But I'm in charge," she rushed out. "You have to do what I tell you, when I tell you."

Elation sprang through the fissure still growing in his chest, followed quickly by determination. He would get this right. He *had* to get this right. She wouldn't give him another chance. "I will not disappoint you."

A tremor moved through her.

A tremor of apprehension? Though every cell he possessed screamed to close the distance between them, he rocked back on his heels, staying in place, giving her time to come to grips with what would soon happen. "What convinced you?"

Her gaze lowered and she whispered, "The bath. I was reclining in the tub, loving the warmth of the water, but all I could think about was the fact that I was alone. I imagined what it would be like if you were in there with me, washing my hair, rubbing my shoulders. Just . . . I don't know, holding me close."

The fantasy was admitted with so much longing he could restrain himself no longer.

Zacharel approached the bed. She watched him, licked her lips, flattened her hands on the bed, then on her stomach, then on the bed again, as if she couldn't decide which was best. He placed one knee on the mattress, leaned forward. Her breathing quickened. *Slow and easy.* He crawled over her, gently clasped her by the waist and rolled them both, flaring his wings as he placed *her* on top of *him.* She gasped at the swiftness of his motions, but she didn't bolt away. However, she did sit up, refusing to recline against him.

He lay there, waiting, thinking she would relax. Her eyes were closed, the long length of her lashes casting spiky shadows over her cheeks. With every second that passed, however, she tensed a little more.

"Annabelle."

"Yes."

"Look at me," he said.

Those lids squeezed tight. "No."

"Annabelle. Please."

"*Now* you say please?"

"Annabelle."

"My eyes," she whispered. "You hate the taint of them."

He belonged in the depths of hell for saying such a thing. "They are lovely."

"But you said —"

"A mistake. Difficult as it is to imagine, I make them, too."

"All right." A pause, then her lids parted, and those beautiful blues were peering at him.

"Thank you."

At last she settled against him, and he felt her mouth curl into a grin. "Welcome."

"I'm going to put my arms around you," he said. When she offered no protest, he fit action to word.

A delicate sigh left her. "So . . . what are we doing?"

"Taking a moment to enjoy each other." He traced his fingers along the ridges of her spine. "At least, I am. Are you?"

"Yes. I — Your heart is pounding," she

said, sounding surprised. Her ear rested directly over the pounding beat.

"Only you have that effect on me."

"Well, we're even, then."

Minutes passed, perhaps hours. Every new second was a rapturous torture. He breathed her in, happily drowning in her heat, and he vowed to stay like this all night if that was what she preferred — but to his delight she began to move against him, urging him to do . . . something. The tips of her fingers traced the ridge of his navel.

"Zacharel?"

He released her to reach up and grab the headboard. "I will not let go." Not this time, no matter how badly he wanted to touch her. "You will control everything, just as you wished."

Still she hesitated.

"I mean it. Even if I break the bed apart, I will not let go of this railing. Not until you tell me otherwise."

"You are so on your A game right now." She lifted to her knees, straddled his waist and settled against him. The exquisite pleasure-pain of the sensation had him sucking in a breath.

If only he could will his robe away . . .

Down, down she leaned.

"Kiss," she said. Her mouth claimed his,

her tongue sliding past his teeth to duel with his tongue. And oh, the sweetness of her taste intoxicated him far more than anything else.

For a long while, she alternated between kissing him and pausing to look at him, as if judging his control. Whatever she saw in his expression always managed to reassure her, because she would dive back in for another helping.

He wasn't sure how he managed to hide the force of his arousal from her. He felt like a rubber band pulled too tight, ready to snap at any moment. What could he do to propel her to that point? Move against her, as she had moved against him?

He shifted slightly, brushing against her — but that wasn't nearly enough, and merely fueled his desire all the more. But . . . a groan escaped her, and then, oh, finally, blessedly *then,* she stopped taking time to look at him, stopped searching his face, and gave him a kiss that seared his soul, her mind seemingly as lost as his was.

Her fingers tangled in his hair, angling his head for deeper, better contact. On and on this new, hotter kiss continued, until they were biting at each other, moaning and groaning and saying incoherent things. He wanted more, so much more, and his

301

muscles bunched and knotted from the strain of holding back.

Then she began to rock against him, her entire body rubbing, rubbing, rubbing against his. He was desperate to get closer to her, as close as a man could be with a woman. Wanted it, needed it so badly.

"Zacharel, I want . . . I need . . ."

Exactly want he wanted and needed, he prayed. "Anything. Name it, and I will give it to you."

"Roll to your side."

He obeyed in an instant, so that they were face-to-face, body-to-body. His every exhalation blended with her every inhalation, mixing their breath, making them one, even in so small a way.

"Your hands . . . on me," she commanded. "But only if you want to. I mean, we can stop if you'd —"

"No stopping," he rushed out, then forced himself to say more slowly, "I want. I do. More than anything. But I'm not in a hurry." On some level — probably. "I'll go nice and easy." He would force himself.

"Okay, yes. Please. Slow."

He released only one hand from captivity to lift the hem of her shirt. Her skin was a mesmerizing bronze, and his a lighter gold; it was such a delicious contrast, inflaming

the spark of his desire to yet another fever-
ish degree.

"You are so beautiful, Annabelle."

"Really?"

Yes, oh, yes. "Your mind . . ."

"Is on you, only you. Or were you trying
to tell me how beautiful my mind is?" she
asked with a little giggle.

A pleasant blend of relief and satisfaction
soared through him. He had made her
laugh, in bed. "What do you want me to
do?"

"What are *you* wanting to do?" she
breathed.

Strip himself, strip her, touch, taste,
consume, learn, know, nothing held back —
things she wasn't ready for. *Steady.*

"I will put my hands on you, as you
demanded." He cupped her breast, paused,
waiting for her reaction. She moaned at the
pleasure, thrilling him. His hand began to
burn, burn so deliciously, hotter than the
rest of him as he kneaded her.

Another moan left her.

Yessss. More.

"Your skin is like fire," she said on a moan.

"Bad?"

"Wonderful."

He tightened his grip on her breast, allowed his fingers to trace over the little pink

bead in the center again and again.

Until she gasped out, "Zacharel, I can handle the next step. Promise."

Taking her at her word, he bent his head, lower, lower still, but when his lips hovered directly over her, he paused, again waiting. Though she panted and mewled, she never turned from him, or tried to shove him away.

Steady. His tongue flicked out on an exploratory mission. Such sweet, sweet contact nearly undid him. Having the warmth of her skin on his tongue . . . the taste of her in his mouth . . . was there anything greater?

"I'm here with you," she promised.

He allowed his tongue to play, tracing from one side of her to the other and then back again. Something he learned in the ensuing minutes: the more he played with her, the more broken entreaties he earned from her. Each one pleased him, driving his own need higher still. He wasn't sure how much more he could take.

Very carefully, he dragged his hands along the plane of her stomach and untied her pants. Her cries of approval did not cease, so he allowed his fingers to tunnel down . . . down . . . She wasn't wearing any panties.

"Wait," she said brokenly, her legs squeezing together.

He froze.

Cheeks rosy, she asked, "Are you . . . Do you know . . . what to expect?"

She wasn't expressing concern for what was happening, but concern for his mind-set. "I do."

"And you're okay with that?"

"Sweetheart, I am more than okay with that."

A pause. "You called me sweetheart," she whispered. Gradually her legs parted. "I like that."

Then I will do it again. He continued his journey and oh, she was perfect. So utterly perfect. She had liked his kisses and caresses — and she liked what he was doing now, if the short puffs of her breath were any indication.

For a long while he simply learned her, and her reactions taught him what she liked best. He loved when she strained against him, loved when she mumbled inarticulately. Loved knowing he was causing such a strong reaction in her.

"You are the most decadent creature ever created, sweetheart," he said. He withdrew his hands from her, hands that were still burning in a way he'd never experienced, and she cried out in distress. "I'm here," he assured her, "and I'm not going anywhere. I just want to lift you, just want to be able to go deeper."

He placed a pillow under her hips and returned to what he'd been doing. Soon she was gasping, rolling her hips toward him, touching him as intimately as he was touching her . . . driving him wild . . . making him hunger for what he didn't understand. . . .

. . . hunger so desperately . . .

He was in pain, but he couldn't stop this. *Need more, have to have more.*

The same fog he'd experienced before was trying to roll in, to consume him, but he resisted. Yes, his blood had heated, becoming fire, singeing him all the way to the bone. Yes, his teeth were gnashed together and his muscles knotted more painfully than ever. But *he* was master of his body, not desire. He would make this special for Annabelle. He would not ruin it.

At least, that's what he told himself — before she lifted his robe and took his length in hand and he nearly jolted off the bed. She stroked him up and down. He loved it. He hated it. He needed more, more, more, but couldn't withstand any more. Would die, surely.

The faster she moved her hand on him, the faster he moved his fingers in her. It was . . . it was . . .

Happening. Something was happening to him.

As she cried out, arching her body against him, utter pleasure overshadowed every bit of his pain, starting in the middle of his spine and arrowing up and down, affecting every inch of him. His hips bowed toward her, and his own hoarse cry filled the room.

All he could do was hold on to Annabelle, pray she never let go of him and die a thousand little deaths, each one making him rise up again, a different man, someone stronger and better, weaker and worse. Because in those moments of absolute, utter vulnerability, where nothing seemed to matter but the female who had given him such divine bliss, he realized he was already addicted to what she made him feel.

Give her up?

No. Never.

CHAPTER SIXTEEN

Annabelle had never before spent an entire
night in a man's arms, had never thought
to, since Heath had always had to jump out
the window of her bedroom so that her
parents wouldn't catch him. But last night,
she had remained snuggled into Zacharel's
side. Warm and strong, he held her, soothing her back to sleep when bad dreams
dared to intrude.

She woke well rested, drug free and ready
for whatever came. Or so she thought. By
the time she'd brushed her teeth and showered, she had to face Zacharel and nerves
nearly got the better of her.

The things he'd done to her . . . He was a
man who had given her more pleasure than
anyone else ever had, burning away the ter-
rors of the past, leaving new, amazing
memories to sigh over for years to come.
She wanted that again. But . . . did he?

Probably not, she thought when she

emerged from the bathroom once again wearing the maid's uniform, because he did not look happy to see her. Although, if she were honest, his unhappy look pretty much matched all his other looks. Except for his smile, when those gorgeous dimples made an appearance.

I really want to see those dimples again.

He stood in front of the bed, his white robe pristine, unwrinkled, and his muscled arms crossed over his chest. He smelled of morning sky and sunshine, his hair brushed to a glossy shine.

"What's got you in such an irritated mood? No demons attacked us last night," she said, going for bravado rather than timid insecurity. "And notice I used the word *irritated* and not *irritating,* even though that's what I was thinking."

"I am not in a mood," he replied. "Perhaps I am just overcome by my first sexual experience."

Oh . . . well. Okay, then. Blood rushed into her cheeks, heating her skin. "You sure didn't seem like a beginner," she admitted.

"Thank you. Also," he continued blithely, "I am content. I was right. You are harder to find when other humans surround you, which means I now know how to protect you."

"Subject change accepted," she muttered.

"That was not my intention." He frowned, his emerald gaze moving just over her shoulder, as if someone had intruded.

She twisted, looking, but found nothing out of the ordinary. When she turned back, he was frowning at her.

"Your glow is more pronounced," he said, "and the cause is not the lamp. I left my mark on your skin. My essentia."

Heart drumming in her chest, she held an arm up to the light, turned it left, then right. "I don't see anything."

"You have glowed since the first day I met you, but the fact that the glow is now more pronounced tells me it was and is not natural."

"I wasn't touched by another angel, if that's what you're implying."

"I'm not. No two essentias are the same, and you definitely carry mine. I wonder . . . could you have been born with mine, meant for me and only me? I have never heard of such a thing happening, of a mark appearing before a claiming, but . . . anything is possible, I suppose." As he spoke, he shook out his wings. "I will check . . ."

She lost track of his words, her mind ensnared by the beauty of those wings . . . so strong, so majestic, so wonderfully gold.

"I have already given you permission to touch my wings, Annabelle."

Now he sounded irritated. "I know."

"Then why are your hands fisted at your sides, rather than on me?"

"Because you look so enthused by the idea."

He opened his mouth, snapped it closed. "Sarcasm?"

"Good call."

His put-upon sigh echoed between them.

Her fingers uncurled and stroked over the arch of those golden wings. They were as hard as iron and ridged — until you encountered the feathers. Oh, baby, those feathers were softer than goose down. She caressed the tips, marveling when one of the longer ones loosened and fell into her palm.

Zacharel latched on to her wrist, but didn't toss her hand away or claim the golden feather as his property. All hint of amusement gone, he said, "Look at me, Annabelle."

A wave of trepidation swept over her as she obeyed. Had she done something wrong?

"You may never do this with another angel. Do you understand?"

Her brow furrowed with her confusion. "Is it against the rules?" But . . . sex wasn't.

Obviously. So touching shouldn't have been, either.

"Those who have not experienced sexual desire do not like to be handled in any way, especially by humans. Those who *have* experienced desire will view your attention as a request for a bedding."

And thereby ruin whatever good mood she'd managed to attain. "I won't touch anyone but you, I promise."

There was a heavy beat of silence. "That man, Dr. Fitzherbert, touched you without permission. In the ways I touched you last night?"

Just like that, a dark, sticky cloud tried to envelop her. Her shoulders curled in as every emotion she'd experienced inside the institution barraged her. Fear, shame, hatred, guilt, helplessness, sorrow, grief. But as quickly as they hit, they vanished. She absolutely refused to dwell on them, and shot each one with a mental bullet, killing it dead. Those things acted like a dinner bell for demons, and she refused to supply a buffet.

"Yes," she said.

"Perhaps it is time he reaps what he has sown," Zacharel said.

"Meaning . . . what?"

"I will force something terrible on *him*."

Rather than thrill her, the vow worried her. She wanted Fitzpervert out of a position of authority and unable to hurt anyone else, but she wanted Zacharel safe far more. She'd brought enough trouble to his door already.

"Is that your job?" she asked, though she already knew the answer.

"No." A grumble.

"Then you'll get into big-time trouble for doing it. And don't try to deny it. I distinctly remember you telling me that you weren't allowed to harm humans."

"Some actions are worth the trouble they bring."

Doubtful! "I get doing all the damage you can to demons. They're pure evil, they'll never feel remorse for the terrible things they do and they'll never change, will always try to hurt people. But harming a human isn't necessary. That would make you no better than, well, Fitzpervert. He hurt me just because he could." Fire flashed in his eyes, but still she persisted. "One day I'll do what's needed to let the world know what a monster Fitzpervert is, I promise. But I'll do it the right way. So, I want you to tell me you'll let this go, Zacharel . . . whatever your last name is. Do you even have a last name?"

"Come," he said, ignoring her boast, her

313

demand *and* her question. He released her wrist, only to snake his arm around her waist and draw her closer.

"Zacharel Come. That's a terrible last name. I feel sorry for your wife, if you ever decide to marry."

His lips twitched, and she thought, *I performed that little miracle. I made him kinda sorta smile.*

"We have much to do today, Annabelle."

"So what? I told you. I'm not leaving until you've done a take back."

He slid his hand up her back to toy with the ends of her hair. Then, "Give me time to think, at least," he said. "I will not lie to you, which means you must allow me time to consider all my options."

Sound logic. Also irritating and irrefutable. "Very well." But she would prevail, and that was that, she thought, tying the end of the feather to the top of her corset. The gold gleamed prettily against the blue of the scrubs.

Zacharel's eyes flared with a different kind of heat than before.

Anger? "What things do we have to do?" she asked. If he was mad, he was mad. He could deal.

"First, we shop." His voice practically dripped with ice crystals.

O-kay, he was clearly more than out of sorts with her. What kept causing these split-second changes in him? Annabelle stepped away from him and crossed her arms over her middle. "I have another condition to my departure," she said, tying the blade sheaths at her ankles. "You have to tell me what's bothering you." *Commanding a warrior angel, Miller? I'd like to see you follow this one through.*

"I don't have to do your bidding, Annabelle."

Once before he'd pointed out the differences in their abilities. He ruled by might and the power of the sword. She was a spunky little scrapper who talked a big game. He could force her to leave with him, and there would be nothing she could do to stop him.

But last night he'd given her the right to question — and defy — him. "You will," she said with all the determination she felt.

He flashed his teeth in a scowl and eased onto the edge of the bed. He rested his palms on his thighs. To stop himself from shaking her? "You will not like what I have to say."

Dread knotted her stomach. "Say it anyway. I'm a big girl. I can take it." Maybe.

No. No, she couldn't. He looked far too serious.

"You expect leniency from me now, but I cannot give it to you. We must track a demon high lord, and my attention cannot be divided. Yet even now, as I hold myself back from you, all I can think about is how soft you will feel if I embrace you, how much I enjoyed your cries in my ears and how easy it would be to strip and take you here and now."

Oh . . . my. "Zacharel, I love hearing that." Was weak-kneed because of it.

"Truly?" His gaze met hers, and she saw the fire banked there. "Because you will not be dealing with your lover this day, but your leader. When I issue an order, I will expect you to obey it without question."

"Hello. I will absolutely —" Wait. On the surface, what he asked seemed reasonable. Only when she dug deeper was she able to discern that how they interacted today would determine how they interacted from now on. There would always be another demon to hunt. And, with her . . . consort out there, she would always be in danger.

Not that they'd always be together.

Anyway. If she acted the obedient little soldier today, Zacharel would always expect her to be an obedient little soldier. Perhaps even in bed. They would never be equals.

"Okay, listen up," she said. "For four years I was told what to do, what to wear, what to eat, what medications to take, when to leave my room and when to stay in my room. If ever I disobeyed, I was disciplined harshly and *then* I was forced to do what I'd first been told. I will not have that kind of relationship with you. I would rather have no relationship at all."

"You see. This is what I suspected would happen." His knuckles leeched of color, and she suspected he was pressing into his thigh muscles with so much force he would have bruises for days, the swiftness of his healing no match for the extent of the damage. "If one of my men dared defy me, I would —"

"What? Beat him?" she finished for him. "Well, I'm not one of your men."

"Beat him, yes. I have done that. I have done worse. And you want to be one of my men. You asked me to train you."

"And so far you haven't taught me a single thing."

Silence, heavy and oppressive.

"Very well. Let's remedy that." He was on his feet an instant later, his arms snaking around her and lifting her off her own feet. She experienced that strange sense of weightlessness as he whisked her through

317

wall after wall and into the garden outside.

Without any preamble, he dropped her on her butt. Air gusted from her lips, her brain rattling against her skull. People milled along pebbled paths, she noted, but they paid her and Zacharel no attention.

"Having an audience doesn't change how I'll treat you," she grumbled softly. "If anything, you've earned yourself a full-on feminine assault."

"They cannot see or hear us," he said.

They couldn't? "Hey, you," she shouted, looking around. No one so much as twitched. Wow, they really couldn't.

"By the way, if I wasn't clear, I think you're a turd," she mumbled, jumping to her feet.

"You wanted to train, and so we will train." As he spoke, his robe was transformed into a pair of loose black pants. No shirt. "But first . . ."

His sun-kissed skin darkened . . . darkened . . . taking on a crimson hue. Horns sprouted from his shoulders, his wings morphed into something hideous, a thin membrane wetted with blood, and a tail grew between his legs, a metal spike at its end.

A scream ripped from Annabelle's throat. She withdrew the blades from their sheaths, and acting on instinct, lunged toward the creature straight from the depths of her nightmares, slashing at him. Horror, betrayal and shock blasted through her, turning her blood into toxic sludge. This thing was a demon, and he'd tricked her. All this time he'd tricked her, even gotten her into bed.

"You disgust me!" she shouted as she went for his throat.

Easily he latched on to her wrists, spun her and pinned her against the hard length of his body. "Calm down and think, Annabelle."

Despite his grotesque appearance, his voice was the same, was Zacharel's, and the knowledge caused some of her panic to flee.

"You still feel safe with me," he continued. "You feel no hum of evil. I haven't changed; I've simply changed your perception of me."

Still she fought him, desperate to free herself.

He maintained a steady grip. "Calm down," he repeated. "Think. You've seen me change my clothes in a blink. You've seen me change the color of my wings just as quickly. It is I, Zacharel, the man who held you in my arms, who kissed and touched you."

The rest of her panic fled, and realization

at last dawned. Her movements slowed . . . stilled . . . and she drew in a deep breath . . . exhaled. . . .

When the demons came, they exuded a rotten scent and a sticky film of evil she couldn't quite scour from her skin. With Zacharel, there was only that sky-rich fragrance and the warm caress of male flesh. "Why did you . . . change your . . . appearance?" Her mind might recognize the truth, but her body was still catching up, breath rasping from her lungs.

"I cannot train you to watch for a tail if I do not have a tail. And do you recall the time I told you it's possible to overcome fear with action, that how you act is more important than what you feel? I want you to learn to act against a demon even if your heart is pounding and your knees knocking together."

Okay. Okay, she could do this. "You can let go of me now. I'll behave."

"Why start now?" He pushed her enough to make her stumble. She twisted around, facing him, keeping the daggers at her sides. His eyes were still a mesmerizing green, and helped anchor her in reality rather than sinking into the past as that metal-spiked tail clanged back and forth, back and forth.

Her gaze lowered and she watched the

thing slither along the ground, unable to help herself. "Did you just make a funny, Zacharel?"

"You tell me."

Suddenly the tail struck out, winding around her ankle and jerking, but somehow *not* cutting into her skin. She fell, hard, and glared up at him.

"You should have jumped up immediately and tossed one of your daggers at me," he said casually. "I could attack you right now, and you would have no defense."

Uh, she could stab him — because she still had her daggers. He hadn't been smart enough to take them away, so there. "Well, for starters, you didn't tell me that I had permission to spill your guts."

"And a demon will tell you such a thing? Give you such a warning?"

An excellent point. Embarrassed by her weakness and stupidity, she lumbered to her feet and grumbled, "So this is how you teach? Through trial and error?"

"You would not like my other method. Now. This time, when you see that I'm coming at you, act first."

Got it. She waited, watching as his tail swished . . . swished . . . and launched toward her. As instructed, she jumped up, causing the spike to dance through the air.

But he had expected her to do so and the tail changed direction, darting back toward her to again wind around her ankles and send her to her bottom.

Dang it! "Just so you know, I'm usually better. The fact that I'm alive should convince you of that."

"No, the fact that you're alive convinces me the demons weren't actually trying to kill you. And just so you know, twice now *I've* killed you," he said. "In battle, demons will always go for the dirty move. They will strike you from behind, kick you while you're down, hit you where it hurts most."

"Okay." Up she stood. "All demons can suck it, so the next time you come at me, you're gonna get it."

"Good." He offered no more warning than that, striking at her, his tail swiping, missing, swiping again, missing again.

With that final jump, she angled just enough to land on his tail, earning a yelp of pain from him. Grinning, she said, "Even though you're a horrible teacher, I think I'm gonna like this lesson."

His lips curled in the barest hint of a smile, a dimple there and gone, before he arced one of those beastly wings at her. Jumping up would do no good this time. The stupid appendage was too wide. She did the only thing she could. She spun low, swiping out with her dagger and cutting through the tissue.

He hissed out a breath and jerked the wing back into his side. Blood dripped down golden feathers — feathers soon replaced by black tissue as he fortified his image. For a moment, Annabelle worried she'd gone too far.

Then Zacharel nodded with satisfaction. "Excellent. I'm not such a horrible teacher, after all."

"Actually, my instincts got you stabbed, not your majestic tutelage."

Another hint of a smile. "I will endeavor to do better."

"You mean I'm the first to complain?"

"No. But yours is one of two complaints I'm willing to heed."

What a sweet thing to say. *But that's not going to stop me from hurting him during the next round.* "And the other came from . . . ?"

"My brother."

So far, every time he'd mentioned his brother he'd shut down soon afterward. After last night, she hoped he would trust her with details about what had happened. "The brother you . . . killed?" She wanted to know more about him, this man she had welcomed into her bed.

"Yes." He said no more, but the sadness in his tone said enough.

At least he hadn't changed the subject. "Why did you do it?" Before, she'd speculated that it had been an accident. Now that she knew him better, she had big-time doubts. Zacharel was not someone prone to accidents. He was too guarded, too careful. He would have had a reason.

The ice shuttered back over his emerald gaze. "He was better off."

Clearly that marked the end of the conversation. But . . . now she wondered if the brother had been sick. That's usually what *better off* implied. Poor Zacharel. "Well, I'm so sorry for your loss."

Before the last word left her mouth, he was on her, his clawed hands shoving her down but not cutting her. Surprised, she flailed as she fell, loosening her hold on one of the daggers.

Between one blink and the next, his weight was pinning her in place, his hand manacling her arms above her head, rendering the weapon she did have useless. Argh! She bucked once, twice, but couldn't dislodge him.

"If I were truly a demon," he said with the same coldness she'd glimpsed in his eyes, "what would you do to escape me right now?"

"Bite you when you lean down." As she'd had to do in the institution time after time.

"And risk swallowing tainted demon blood?"

Rocks filled her stomach, their edges sharp. "What happens when you swallow tainted demon blood?"

"You sicken."

His tone implied *you could die.* Trying not to panic, she thought back over the past four years. The only times she'd gotten sick were due to overdoses of the drugs the staff had forced on her. So, she must not have swallowed any of the blood. Right?

"Pay attention to me." He gripped her shoulders and shook her. "To free yourself, you are to stab one of my horns."

"Okay, but not all demons have horns."

"And I will show you how to fight the hornless next time. Today, you learn how to deal with horns."

In other words, concentrate on the here and now.

"But you're holding my hands captive."

"And you cannot somehow trick me into loosening my grip?

Well, yeah. Him, she could. But someone else? "Let's say I manage it. Wouldn't the dagger just lodge there, leaving me without any kind of weapon?" Teeth were no longer an option — ever.

"Yes, and that's the point. The hard outer shell protects a soft, vulnerable center. If you cut into the nerves properly, you can paralyze the demon for several seconds, sometimes even minutes."

Now, there was a tip she could use.

"All right. Let's test this theory of yours."

Just as she geared up to trick him into loosening his grip, three enormous shadows fell over them and Zacharel leapt off her. Thinking the demons had found her, she scrambled to her feet. Rather than a misshapen enemy horde, however, she saw the blond warrior from the institution — Thane. He appeared and landed at her left, white wings threaded with gold outstretched.

At her right appeared a robed warrior with hair and scarred skin the same shade of white. The only color he possessed was in the red eyes even now glaring at her.

Directly in front of her was the biggest male alive — possibly ever created — his skin the most luscious shade of gold she'd ever seen, his eyes a rainbow of brilliant colors.

"We've been searching for you, Zacharel," Thane said. "We tried to reach you mentally, but you failed to respond."

Interesting that he recognized Zacharel, even in this form. Interesting, too, that he had called her angel by his name rather than Majesty, as he'd done at the institution.

"I had closed myself to receiving."

Like switching off a phone?

"Shall we change our visage, as well, and join the party?" Thane looked over Zacharel's demon skin and frowned. "You're bleeding." He turned to his companions. "He's bleeding."

"She cut him," the rainbow-eyed guy said, his incredulity unmatched. "Her blade still drips."

The scarred guy took a menacing step toward her.

She braced her legs apart, ready to greet him. "You want to taste my blade, too? 'Cause I'll let you if you try and challenge me."

Zacharel moved in front of her. In a blink, the demon visage was gone, his dark hair, sun-kissed skin and robe returned. "No one touches the girl. Ever. Anyone does, and he will die."

"Yeah," she said, jumping in front of him — only to be pushed back. "He'll die." Would no one ever look at her and think *she's innocent?*

327

All three men gaped first at Zacharel, then at her. Then one by one they nodded. And if she wasn't mistaken, they cast each other sly, amused glances. That amusement baffled her.

"Two shockers in one day," Thane said. "First, concern for my commander. Second, watching a tiny fluff of nothing act as his protector. Are you ashamed, Zacharel?"

Zacharel tossed her a *this is your fault* glare. She shrugged, not sorry in the least.

"Well, now that we know Zacharel is so well guarded," the rainbow-eyed warrior said in a sneering tone, "we have business to attend to." Any lingering amusement vanished. "We thought you'd like to know that the demons that attacked your cloud were sent by Burden and we now have his location."

Zacharel reached back and clasped Annabelle's hand, as if he needed to assure himself she was there and she was well.

The one with red eyes perused Annabelle up and down before dismissing her. "He's at the Black Veil. We tracked him down, but did not have an opportunity to fight him. He let us know that he has Jamila, then he demanded 'the weak and vulnerable Annabelle' in trade — and don't try to gainsay me, female," he added without looking her way. "You are."

"Am not," she grumbled. She so was, when compared to these creatures.

To Zacharel, he continued with a clenched jaw, "He also said that if you go with an angel escort, he will behead Jamila. If you refuse to go, he will behead Jamila."

Annabelle translated: in essence, Zacharel was screwed.

CHAPTER SEVENTEEN

The Black Veil was a human nightclub located in the pulsing heart of Savannah, Georgia. Zacharel had hunted many demons along these sultry midnight streets, and wasn't surprised Burden had made a home there, or that he'd possessed the body of the human who owned the club, just to feed off the turmoil of the patrons.

Intensely hot this time of year, Savannah's humidity was so thick it left a film on one's skin — even angel skin. Had it not been for Annabelle, Zacharel would have asked the Deity for the return of the snow.

He was not in his customary robe, but wore a black mesh tank, black leather pants and scuffed combat boots. To add to the look, he'd spiked his hair down the center — a Mohawk, the humans called the style — and rimmed his eyelids with kohl. Tattoos now sleeved both of his arms, and once again his wings were hidden from human eyes. All necessary changes.

To garner the aid of the only men who could slip inside such a club and act as his backup without Burden's knowledge, he'd had to vow to dress like this and let the whole world see him. It was utterly ridiculous. If there'd been any other way, he would have hurt the men — the children! — in ways they could not imagine for even daring to suggest such a thing.

Annabelle alternately marveled at the change in him and at the luminosity of the full moon. Other humans gave him a wide berth, nearly flattening themselves against building walls to widen the distance between them.

Annabelle danced around him, grinning. "Can I just say what a bad boy you are right now?"

"Of course you can. You just did."

"No, I mean — Oh, never mind, you spoiled it." Her lips dipped into a pout.

A pout he wanted to kiss away. He might look all "bad boy," but she looked . . . edible. Her hair curled down her back in wanton blue-black ringlets. He'd dressed her in a tight black-and-white-checkered gown with bows at the top and ruffles at the bottom, so that no one would question their association. The hem fell just below her knees, showcasing smooth, bare legs and strappy red heels. She looked like a Goth seventies housewife, ready to await her husband with a spiked drink.

Besides, the more innocent she appeared, the more Burden would underestimate her. And yes, that meant Zacharel was operating under the assumption that Burden and Annabelle would fight, despite the fact that Zacharel would have given up all of his limbs to prevent the two from breathing the same air.

Above all, he wanted her safe. Was *desperate* to keep her safe.

For a man who'd felt nothing for centuries, Zacharel suddenly felt as if he was drowning in emotion, and not just the desperation. He felt worry for Annabelle's safety. He felt an intense desire to at last experience everything she had to give before it was too late. He felt concern for Jamila's safety. Felt guilt over the way he'd treated her. And as irrational as it was, he felt anger that she had allowed herself to be captured.

She had been under Burden's control for *days*. A lot could be done to an angel, a female, in that amount of time.

Earlier, he'd attempted to project his voice into her mind, but she'd never responded. His Deity, however, had.

I am displeased. She is your charge, your responsibility. You will handle this.

He would. But . . . he should have left Annabelle behind, he thought. He still could. It wasn't too late.

But if he did, she would hate him. Hadn't she told him she would rather die than be locked away? And to leave her behind, he would have to lock her away. He couldn't do that to her. Not even he was that cold.

Besides, what if that was what Burden wanted? To have Annabelle left alone, unprotected, so that he could snag her? But no, that couldn't be right. The high lord couldn't know what the human had come to mean to him. He would assume the coming interaction was business as usual, that Zacharel would care more for his angel than the human. Therefore, if Zacharel arrived without her, he would be proclaiming to one and all that she meant more to him than his duty, his vengeance and his army. She would become more of a target than she already was. Then again, they would find out anyway.

The fact that Annabelle was currently covered in Zacharel's essentia would proclaim to one and all that he had been with her. But only that, he thought next. Not what she meant to him.

Very well, then. He was decided. She would stay with him.

"You remember everything I told you?" he asked. "How to behave?"

"After the way you drilled everything into my head? Stay beside you, don't talk, don't lose focus, don't, don't, don't. No, I've forgotten," she said flippantly. "What I don't know is the plan."

She trusted him to rescue Jamila without trading her, and that would have to be enough. He could not risk telling her the rest. "Do you have any questions for me? Other than ones about the plan?"

"Well, yeah. Now that you know where this Burden guy is, why can't you just swoop in and fight him, while your secret friends — and I'm still waiting for you to tell me about them — then save Jamila?"

The warriors he'd enlisted were part of "the rest." He might not tell her about them even when the battle was over and the smoke cleared. "Burden, coward that he is, has possessed the body of a human. I am limited in the things I can do to him."

"What if he attacks you?"

"I still will not harm him." Much.

"But that's not fair!"

"A similarity between our worlds. Nothing ever seems to be." But all things, no matter how terrible, could be worked to his good, Zacharel was coming to learn. "Though we will not be able to destroy the human, he will not walk away unscathed. Dancing with a demon brings only suffering — that is a spiritual law, and he will learn the truth of that tonight."

"Fine. But we're sure this Burden guy isn't the one who killed my parents, even though he's the one who ordered the other demons to hurt me?"

"Yes. There are ranks among the demons, and Burden is not of high enough rank to manifest in the presence of humans."

"Okay, so answer me this. How did Burden possess the human?"

"The human welcomed him inside, giving him entrance one way or another."

"Like . . . a dream?"

"Sometimes. Sometimes a demon will watch a human, waiting for the perfect time to strike. If one does not appear, the demon will try to create an opening. He will whisper into the human's ear. *Tell this lie . . . say that cruel thing . . . do this hateful thing . . . do that savage thing.* If the human fails to rebuke the demon, the demon's hold will grow stronger, finally allowing the creature to crawl inside his mind."

"But how do you rebuke a demon? How

are we to *know* we're supposed to rebuke a demon?"

"Trust me, there is a way and I will teach you. But not now." She needed faith she did not yet possess. Faith that would not spring from words alone. She would need time they didn't have, time to hear a divine lesson with not just her ears but with all of her being. Were he to try and teach her despite that, she would become frightened, and that would make everything worse.

"Why don't the demons possess your Deity's angels? You guys seem to have as many faults as we do," she grumbled.

"They torment us, too. Never doubt that."

He pressed his shoulder into hers, maneuvering her into a darkened alley. The odor of urine and brine wafted through the air. He could have flown straight to the club's door, but he wanted Burden to know he was on his way. The demon's spies would spot him — in fact, he'd seen three minions in the past five minutes, peeking from around the corners of buildings before crawling up the sides and scampering away.

"Well, well, what do we have here?" A human teenager stepped from the shadows. He was in the process of zipping his pants, and Zacharel could guess he'd been using one of the buildings as a toilet. He reeked of alcohol and cigarettes. "A hot little Chinese babe and a nuisance who better run if he wants to continue breathing."

"I'm not Chinese," Annabelle snapped.

"Whatever. You're hot, and that's all that matters." Two other teens stepped from the shadows and lined up beside him.

None were demon possessed, but all three were stupid. Zacharel was double their size, but because they had weapons — two had knives, he discerned, the silver tips gleaming in the moonlight, and one, the leader, had a gun — they considered themselves invincible.

"What've you got on under that dress, huh?"

"Be a good girl and give us a peek."

Oh, yes. They were stupid.

Zacharel felt the pulse of Annabelle's fear before she beat it back, determination taking its place.

"You are making me angry," he said, "and you do not want to make me angry."

All three boys snickered.

"Why? Because you'll turn into a hulking green beast?" one taunted.

More snickers abounded.

"Why don't you beat it, before we beat you?" the leader said.

Another added, "You can have your girl

back when we're done with her," before laughing. "Promise."

"Oh, you shouldn't have said that," Annabelle said far more calmly than he would have guessed possible. To him, she added, "Teach them a little, tiny lesson, Zacharel. Please."

"Whatever you desire." Zacharel tugged Annabelle in front of him and wrapped his arms around her to protect her from what was about to happen. He unleashed his wings from the pocket of air and in seconds was able to create a mighty wind. Each boy soon found himself facedown on the dirty ground.

They struggled to rise, but the wind pinned them in place. He could have snapped their necks before they'd ever realized he'd moved. He could have ripped open their chests and spilled their guts. In fact, he just might. He could always revive them before death staked its claim, saving himself from a whipping — or worse.

He flapped his wings harder, faster, and the wind increased in velocity, the whistle of it masking the ensuing cries of pain. The pressure was building, Zacharel knew, about to crack bone and splatter organs.

But murdering a human isn't necessary. That would make you no better than, well,

Fitzpervert. He hurt me just because he could. Annabelle's words came back to haunt him. *Why don't the demons possess your Deity's angels? You guys seem to have as many faults as we do.*

No. He would not do this. He would not destroy these boys just because he could, and he would not give way to the urge to commit violent acts. That would be a fault.

Annabelle wrapped her fingers around his wrists and squeezed. "Okay, enough. You'll get in trouble, and I kinda need you tonight. And really, your well-being is more important than giving these boys what they deserve."

"Was already stopping," he admitted, stilling his wings and easing the pressure.

The boys remained on the ground, sobbing.

"Do you have anything to say to her?" he demanded.

"I'm sorry, man. Real sorry." Snot ran down the speaker's nose.

"Won't do it again, swear."

"Please, just let us go. I'll pay you. I've got money."

"Enough!" Zacharel forced the boys to their feet. First they flinched, then they wobbled. "You will march straight to the nearest police station and confess your crimes. Fail to do so, and I will come back for you."

As much as Annabelle had doubted him lately, he halfway expected the boys to do the same. However, they reacted to the ring of truth the way he was used to, their eyes glazing over, their heads nodding. No need to flash the visage of a hulking green beast, then.

"Why are you still here?" he snarled. "Go!"

They raced away from him.

Annabelle patted him on the shoulder. "Good job, Z. Really impressive work there."

"Sarcasm?"

"Not this time, Winged Wonder."

He faced her and grinned. "Thank you."

"Welcome."

This woman managed to amuse him no matter the situation, and that, more than anything, revealed the depths of his attraction to her. And he wasn't afraid of such an admission, not this time. He was becoming used to his feelings for her.

"You know, you're pretty when you smile," she said, patting the side of his cheek.

"Fierce, woman. I am fierce."

"If you say so."

He dragged her the rest of the way through

the alley, pleased when she offered no protest. At the end, he turned right, hustled down another alley then turned left, and no one else tried to stop him. Finally the entrance to the club came into view.

Two demon-possessed bouncers stood sentry, a line of humans winding down the street and hoping to get in. Hard rock pumped through the seam in the doors, though there was an underlying beat of sensuality. One he might not have recognized before Annabelle. Now he knew how smoothly two bodies could move to such a rhythm, grinding when they met before parting, already eager for more.

The males gulped when they spotted him and quickly moved aside, allowing Zacharel to stride past without incident. He shouldered the doors apart.

"Baby's got street cred," Annabelle muttered, whatever that meant, as someone in the crowd shouted, "Hey! How'd they get in so easily when —" The doors whooshed closed, cutting off the rest of the complaint.

A waitress glided past, a tray of drinks in her hand. Males and females writhed together on the dance floor, just as he'd imagined, mouths seeking, hands roaming. Atop the shoulders of several of the men and women were minions. Most were small, monkeylike creatures, with dark brown fur and long swinging tails.

"Can you see the demons sitting on their shoulders, whispering into their ears?" he asked Annabelle. "Influencing their thoughts and actions, trying to create a stronghold?"

"Where?"

"There."

"N-no."

And she did not like that she couldn't, he surmised. "My guess is that you can only see demons of a certain rank and higher."

"Should we, I don't know, fight them? And what's a stronghold?"

"Us? No. That is up to the humans. And a stronghold is what I was talking about outside, a permanent place in the life of a mortal, inside the mortal's mind, where whatever wickedness the demon is pandering consumes every thought, every action."

"Is this like the rebuking thing? They have to be taught how to fight what they cannot see?"

"Yes. They must learn the spiritual truths and laws and act accordingly."

Beyond the dancers were the tables. Empty glasses and beer bottles were scattered everywhere. His gaze cut through the sultriness of the dark to see money exchanged for drugs, prostitutes studying their nails as their breasts were fondled, but he found no sign of his helpers.

"Hey, man, you got a light?" a male voice said.

Zacharel jolted to attention. The male stood in front of him, a cigarette balanced between his lips.

He stood as tall as Zacharel, with hair so thick and luxurious any woman would covet it. The mass was a symphony of colors, shades of flax interspaced with caramel, chocolate and coffee. His eyes were a deep, fathomless blue, and his hauntingly lovely face something out of a catalog — or the heavens — and completely at odds with his warrior's body.

Finally.

Annabelle gasped as if she had just spotted something precious, and Zacharel could only gnash his teeth in irritation.

"Cigarettes kill," was all Zacharel told the man. *Can't punch him. Really can't punch him. Especially since I asked him to come here.*

"So do a lot of things," he grumbled. He tugged out the cigarette, dropped the butt, his gaze raking over Annabelle, assessing. "Pretty female. She yours?"

"Yes." Zacharel's tone shouted *so back off.*

Paris, keeper of the demon of Promiscuity, grinned slowly and with a satisfaction that only increased Zacharel's irritation. "She mute?"

"No." Though she certainly seemed that way. Her mouth was hanging open, but no sound was emerging.

A husky laugh slipped from Paris, and Zacharel could only marvel at the change in him. A few months ago, there'd been no one more miserable than this male. But then, the right woman could bring any man back to life, couldn't she?

"Try not to take offense. She can't help herself." Whistling under his breath, Paris strolled away.

"You have something to say about everything," Zacharel said to Annabelle, "and yet you are struck speechless in front of *him?*"

"It's his scent . . ." she replied unabashedly, watching Paris's muscled back until he disappeared in the crowd. "I've never smelled anything like it. Chocolate and coconut and champagne, and utterly mouthwatering."

"He is possessed by the demon of Promiscuity," Zacharel blurted out.

"What! No way."

"Yes way."

"Possessed," she echoed hollowly.

Good. She would never again gaze at Paris

344

in such a longing manner. Petty of him? Maybe. Did he care? No. "Most of the people here are demonically influenced, as I told you, but a few are actually possessed. Burden employs them — the demons, I mean, and pays them to tempt any of the Black Veil's patrons who are not yet so evilly inclined."

Her fingers tightened around his, and he knew she hoped to take strength from him. "So what are we supposed to do now?"

"Now we wait."

Thankfully, they didn't have to wait long. A female parted the masses on the dance floor, then slowly strolled toward Zacharel. One of the most beautiful women he'd ever seen, she had a silky fall of pale hair, skin a light dusting of rose and eyes as golden as the moonlight outside.

Large breasts were barely concealed in a red leather dress, patches of material cut from the sides to reveal perfectly flared hips. The dress's hem stopped just below her bottom, making it clear there were no panties to shield the apex of those mile-long legs.

Beautiful, yes. But also one of the demon possessed.

He could sense the human soul banging at the doors of her mind, desperate to escape the demon's hold. It had been a recent possession, then. Within a few days, most likely.

She stopped in front of him, but her gaze focused squarely on Annabelle. "There's my sweet little geisha. How I've missed you."

"What did you just call me?" Annabelle gasped out.

The human male, Fitzherbert, had said those exact words to her, Zacharel recalled. *Sweet little geisha.* Zacharel did not believe in coincidences. The demon now possessing the woman in front of her must once have possessed someone at the institution. Not Fitzherbert — Zacharel would have sensed it — but someone who spent a great deal of time inside the building. A patient, most likely, which made sense. Minions who'd created a stronghold inside a human mind could convince their hosts to do almost anything. Burden would have wanted one with easy access to Annabelle, watching, listening, probably even encouraging others to hurt her, then reporting back.

Glossy pink lips curled in a seductive smile. "Did you miss me, too, little geisha? I could take pictures of myself and give them to you. That way, whenever we part, you can look at them and think of me."

For some reason, the comment enraged Annabelle. She grabbed — and launched —

two of her daggers. Both were soon embedded in the other woman's chest.

"I'd like a picture of you just like this," Annabelle snarled. "Thoughts?"

The female let out a shriek of shock and pain . . . then unleashed a stream of black curses, ending with, "I'll straight-up *murder* you!"

Some of the dancers noticed the violence and screamed, running for the door. Others just kept bumping and grinding.

"You will do no such thing," Zacharel said.

The woman gritted her teeth and removed the now-dripping blades with a sharp jerk. "Control your pet, angel."

"Unlike you, demon, I do not stoop to controlling humans." And if his Deity thought to reprove Annabelle, he would stand in the gap and bear the punishment for her.

Funny that he had complained about just such a thing only a few days ago. Even funnier that he was more than willing — happy — to now do so.

"Sorry about that," Annabelle muttered. "Rage got the better of me."

He clasped her hand, squeezed. "Because of the demonic charge in the air, that will be easier to do. Guard your emotions."

"Enough!" the demon shouted. Her eyes

narrowed . . . eyes now glowing a bright, bright red. Clearly she did not appreciate being ignored. "This way." With that she turned and led them through the club, pausing to look smugly over her shoulder. "But do not expect Burden to be as welcoming as I was."

CHAPTER EIGHTEEN

Annabelle struggled to maintain a calm facade during the entire journey to the main office. The three of them pounded up a winding flight of stairs and through the smoky haze of the VIP lounge. She managed to hold her head high, even when people stopped what they were doing — having sex, snorting coke, torquing veins — to glare at her and Zacharel. Demons had to be resting on their shoulders, as Zacharel had said, but she couldn't see them.

When at last their trio stepped inside a seeming paradise, her struggle for composure jumped to the next level. Everything looked so normal, yet deep down she knew it was oh, so wrong. The room was spacious, with white walls and a white shag carpet interspersed with black, creating hypnotizing squares. Bookshelves lined the wall behind a desk shaped like a half-moon. A chandelier hung overhead, positioned in the center of a three-tiered ceiling.

Nice, right? But behind the desk sat a beautiful golden-haired man in his mid-thirties, the high back of his leather chair rising several inches above his head, Dr. Evil style. He was far too thin, like, sickly thin, but his pose was all about the casual, his elbows resting on the chair arms, his fingers steepled over his mouth. Still, he couldn't hide his air of cruelty.

Who was he? The last line of security before they reached the demon?

His eyes were a darker shade of blue than Annabelle's own, and dulled, his lashes brown yet tipped in gold. The shadow of a beard scruffed his jaw. He wore a navy blue pinstriped suit and smelled of money, musk and pungent alcohol.

The two armed guards behind him wore muscle tanks and leather pants, their expressions expectant. No doubt they were the type to shoot first and ask questions later.

The beautiful blond girl from the club, the one Annabelle had stabbed, plopped into a couch beside the door, mumbling about the best ways to torture pesky humans as she patched herself up.

"Hello, Burden," Zacharel said.

Burden. *This* was Burden? The demon-possessed man who had ordered all those other demons to attack her inside the institution? *I shouldn't have wasted my last two knives on the girl.*

Dr. Evil's smile became all the more welcoming — and all the more sinister.

"Ah, Zacharel," Burden said. "I'm so pleased you received my invitation."

"I will see Jamila now," her angel replied, pleasantries clearly over.

"Your manners . . . for shame." Burden's voice was all satisfaction and potent desires. "Business first? How rude. May we offer you a drink? A whore? A hit?"

Silence.

"No? And what about you, my dear?" His navy gaze moved to Annabelle, slithered over her body and mentally removed her clothing. "Would you like anything?"

Zacharel stiffened as she said, "I'd love something. For starters, I'll take your head on the floor, detached from your body. After that, we can talk about my next demand." So he'd told her to keep her mouth shut and her hands to herself while they were here and she had failed at both. So what?

You're already a target. Do not make yourself more of one, he'd said.

That would have been great advice . . . when dealing with anyone but a demon. She could not come off as weak. Demons pounced on weakness, exploiting it. But she *would* rein herself in from now, she vowed. Zacharel had a plan; she knew he did. He and the other three angels had stood in front of each other, silent, for half an hour, their facial expressions changing every few minutes. Somehow, someway, they had been communicating with each other. Not that anyone had explained anything to her when they'd finished.

Burden's chuckle echoed through the office, cold and slick. "Your thirst for blood does my heart proud, Annabelle. But I wonder . . . are you hiding any more weapons?" Another once-over ensued. "Oh, yes, I think you are."

She wasn't, but so wished she was.

He motioned to one of the guards, and it was obviously an order to frisk her.

Zacharel moved in the blink of an eye, a sword of fire in his hand, and poised at the demon's throat. "No one touches her."

The guards made no move to stop him. Either they were too afraid of him, or they had their own orders to obey.

Burden shifted in his seat, but any discomfort he felt was quickly masked with an air of superiority. "If you strike at me, my people know to kill Jamila."

"I would be no kind of leader if I protected

one of my charges above another. So I repeat, no one touches the girl. Ever."

That's my man.

"Very well. No one will touch her while you're here," Burden allowed, evidently not the least bit upset that his authority had been questioned.

"Agreed."

Wait. What?

Zacharel's sword vanished.

The demon's grin returned. "Because I'm so generous, I'll allow your woman to keep her weapons."

"That's sweet of you," Annabelle said, acting as if she did, in fact, have a few surprises tucked away. *Now it's time for you to zip it, Miller, and let Zachie do his thing. Remember?*

Burden ignored her, but said to Zacharel with a bit more edge to his tone, "She'll find I'm not as easy to hurt as the beautiful Driana." He nodded briefly toward the woman still nursing her wounds on the couch.

"This conversation grows tiresome." Zacharel flexed his fingers at his side, before curling his hands into fists. "Let's move on."

Burden lifted a pen from his desk and twirled the thing one way, then the other. "Impatient as ever, I see. To be honest —" he chuckled at his own words "— I'm a little surprised you came. You had to know I wouldn't keep my end of the bargain to return Jamila to you."

Zacharel eyed him impassively. "That goes without saying."

Wait. He'd known they were walking into a trap? Then what the heck were they doing here?

"So why are you here, angel?" Burden asked.

"I will tell you. *After* I see proof that Jamila still lives."

Burden flinched at the layer of truth in Zacharel's voice. "Some things never change, I suppose. It's comforting to know you're as suspicious as you are impatient."

"And you, in turn, are as untrustworthy as you are repulsive."

The demon inclined his head in acknowledgment, as if he'd just received a compliment. "Thank you. But why don't I liven things up and do the unexpected? I'll give you your proof," he said, "*after* I have your word that no other warrior angels are here or even nearby."

He had guards all over the club, and probably cameras, too. He should already know the answer.

"Why should he believe you this time when you've already admitted to lying?"

Annabelle demanded.

Burden laughed. "Smart girl. But he believes me because he can taste the truth of my words."

Zacharel ran his tongue over his teeth. "I can. And I agree to your terms. My angels are not here."

"Someone else's angels?"

"No. I am the only angel you will be dealing with."

Burden pursed his lips, pondered the situation then nodded. "This is somewhat disappointing. I expected the mighty Zacharel to put up some kind of fight, at the very least. Now I have to wonder why you are so agreeable about this. You knew you could not save Jamila. You knew you were bringing the human into the danger zone."

"And you know that according to the bargain just struck I'm not required to give you that information."

"True, but I had to try. I'm sure you understand." The demon leaned forward and propped his elbows on the desk. "Here is what's about to happen. I will show you your precious angel, as I agreed. Then, you will either walk out of my club without bloodshed or you will stay and watch as my men and I enjoy the human."

Annabelle's heart skipped a treacherous

beat. *Zacharel will not walk away. He will not leave you or let these men hurt you. More than that,* you *will not let these men hurt you.*

Zacharel smiled, but it was a cruel one, full of frost, cut with a promise to deliver pain. "You truly think you and your men, or even an army of men, could take me?"

"Maybe, maybe not, but your Jamila will die while we fight."

Zacharel shrugged, seemingly unconcerned. "Show me what you promised to show me."

Only Annabelle's determination to see this through held her in place as panic threatened to overwhelm her. She trusted Zacharel. Right? But so cold was he right now, the snow could have been falling from his wings. *Just remember, he told everyone to leave you alone, and that has to count for something.*

Burden tapped a few keys on the state-of-the-art computer on his desk, then paused. His eyes glazed with satisfaction. "Are you sure you want to see this?"

If Zacharel felt any foreboding at the demon's smug tone, he hid it well. "Yes."

He swiveled the monitor around.

Annabelle's knees nearly gave out. The image on the screen . . . Oh, mercy, the image. Jamila was bound to a bed, her stomach

356

pressed into the blood-and-feather-laden mattress, her back a mess of torn muscle and mutilated flesh.

She was alive, as Burden had promised, but someone had cut off her wings.

"She's a screamer, this one," Burden said, his relish palpable. He turned the screen back around and reclined in his seat. "I think I'll let her heal, and when her wings grow back, remove them a second time. And a third."

Oh, no. No, no. No! Annabelle had been there and done the whole subjected and forced thing. She wouldn't allow the same to happen to Zacharel's charge. "You'll pay for this," she said. "Where is she? Tell us. Now!"

Ignoring her, the demon addressed Zacharel. "Always a pleasure doing business with you, Zacharel, but I believe the terms of our deal are now met and concluded. You have seen proof that the angel still lives, and in exchange you have gifted me with this delightful young human. I'll keep my end of the bargain, again, and not touch her until you're out of the building. And if you're a good boy and leave without incident, I'll be the one to have her today. If not, I'll allow every man inside the club to have her." He motioned to Driana, who still sat on the

357

couch. "Show him out."

"Me?" the demon-possessed female said. "But I'm —"

"Show. Him. Out." Though spoken calmly, there was no doubt Burden would hurt her if she dared question him again.

"Yes, sir" was the cowed response.

"Go with them," he told the guards. "If he tries anything or speaks to anyone, kill him."

But Zacharel remained in place. "Why let me go without trying to harm me, at the very least?"

Wait, wait, *wait.* He wasn't going to say anything about leaving her behind? Wasn't going to protest, even a little? *Probably just part of his plan. Any second now, he'll erupt into a sword-wielding hero and* Burden *would be the one to cower.*

"Don't get me wrong. I would enjoy killing you, then killing your sweet little Jamila, but there would be a trial and who has the time? This way, there's nothing you can do but remember your failure."

Zacharel stood still for one heartbeat, then another, silent, stiff. Annabelle waited for him to act, to finally show the slimeball there were consequences for acting this way. Except . . . he turned on his heel and walked away.

He'll spin around and attack. Just watch.

Driana opened the door. The guards went first, filing out to await Zacharel in the hall.

Zacharel followed on their heels.

Annabelle's panic beat at the gates of her mind, desperate to escape.

"Zacharel," she said in a weak, trembling voice.

His shoulders stiffened, but he never turned around. He was actually leaving her? Impossible.

"Zacharel!" she snarled.

He paused. His head turned, giving her a view of his profile. He said nothing.

Driana sauntered up behind him. "I'll take good care of you, green eyes. Promise."

Don't do this, Annabelle silently screamed, but he gave no notice. But . . . but . . .

Driana faced her, grinned and waved goodbye. The door shut with a sickening click.

The gates in Annabelle's mind swung wide-open, panic spilling through her. He'd done it. He'd lured her here under false pretenses. He'd handed her over to the enemy — to men who would try to destroy her — choosing Jamila's safety over Annabelle's, despite his pretty words to Burden about valuing all his "charges" equally. He'd tricked her. Used her.

Nothing you can do about that. Not now.

Now she had to find a way out of this.

Burden chuckled. "And then there were two. What think you of that, little girl?"

Annabelle met his gaze with all the bravado she could muster. "I think it's time to finish this. You and me, right here, right now, winner take all."

He rubbed a too-long pinky nail between his teeth before he said, "I see now why you've garnered so much interest. I find I admire your courage, foolish as it is . . . and I know I will enjoy breaking you. Which I'll do, before I escort you to your new master."

"Ohhh, a new master. Scary. Why don't you keep me instead?" she suggested. "You can give me a tour of the club." *I can knee you in the balls and run.* "We'll get to know each other better and . . . who knows what else."

"Darling, it's impossible to trick me. I'm —"

The door split down the middle. Suddenly wings wrapped around her, shielding her view of the room. "I'm here," Zacharel said. "I just had to get the guards outside the office."

Oh, sweet mercy! Zacharel had never intended to leave her alone, she realized, had always had her best interests at heart.

She should be ashamed of herself for assuming otherwise, but at the moment she was simply too grateful.

"I thought —" Her words were cut off as gunfire erupted. The horrible clang of metal against metal — and then metal popping through flesh and into bone. Grunts and groans sounded. Shock and confusion blasted through her, holding her immobile. War had broken out, but all Annabelle could do was stand there, clutching the collar of Zacharel's robe.

Robe? Yep, she realized. The street clothes had melted away, returning to a flowing drape of material. "Friends of yours?" she asked.

"Yes. Their timing leaves something to be desired. They should have burst into the office much earlier," he added more loudly.

"Hey!" someone said. "We got up here as fast as we could."

"Then you need more training," Zacharel growled.

Annabelle gave him a shake. "What can I do to help?" She owed him. Because really, this had all happened because of her. She didn't want anyone else hurt on her account.

A pause as Zacharel panned the room. "There is no need for you to do anything.

361

Burden is already contained."

"True that. We're all done, big guy. You're welcome, by the way," said a husky voice she recognized.

A voice she would never forget, because it shivered through her with unnatural force. Of course, the scents of champagne and chocolate drifted to her nose, confirming her suspicions.

The man possessed by the demon of Promiscuity was here.

Annabelle would have assumed a defensive position — or maybe offensive — but Zacharel held her steady.

"You're not done until you clean up the mess," he announced harshly.

Wait. They were working together?

Do not assume the worst. Not this time.

Grumbles, then, "Whatever you say, angel cake," a woman said. "Dibs on telling others what to clean!"

"Kaia," a man groaned. "You are *such* a brat."

"You're only jealous you didn't think of it first."

"True."

Different sounds soon filled Annabelle's ears. Something being dragged. A body? A trash bag being opened. Heavy things falling inside, landing. Mumbles of complaint.

She blocked each one. "Why didn't you tell me your plan?"

"Because demons can taste fear."

"And he needed to taste mine to believe you," she finished for him.

"Not necessarily. Even though you are learning to look past such emotions, I needed your reactions to be honest." At long last, Zacharel's wings lowered.

Annabelle spun. Smears of blood covered the walls and floor, though she could tell someone had tried to wipe them away. Other than that, there was no sign that a battle had taken place. Four bloodstained male warriors and the three females stood in the center of the room, each studying her with avid interest.

She would have studied them right back, but then she caught sight of Burden, still at his desk, his cheek pressed into the surface and a blade poised at the center of his neck, between two ridges of spine.

A horribly scarred man held that blade with a steady hand. "What do you want me to do with him, angel?"

"My men will come and collect him. We have questions, and he has answers."

"You said your men were not here," Burden gritted out.

Zacharel smiled the cruelest of his grins.

"And they are not. Yet. I told you I brought no angels with me, and unlike you, I'm a man of my word. But I didn't make any promises about demons, did I? Allow me to introduce you to the Lords of the Underworld."

CHAPTER NINETEEN

Thane, Xerxes and Bjorn strode into the office, but they didn't say a word, and they didn't stay. They collected Burden and took off. Everyone watched, silent.

As their footsteps echoed, Zacharel introduced Annabelle to the group who'd saved the day. Most were demon possessed, yet clearly Zacharel knew them, liked them — and wouldn't let her hurt them. Lucien carried Death. Strider carried Defeat. Amun carried Secrets and, of course, Paris, the guy who'd needed a light for his cigarette, carried Promiscuity.

The best she could do was incline her head to acknowledge she'd heard their names. Demons were demons, no matter how you sliced it. She wanted nothing to do with them.

The women weren't possessed, but they seemed just as dangerous — if not more so. Kaia was a redheaded Harpy, whatever that meant. Anya was a gorgeous blonde stunner and the supposed goddess of Anarchy, and Haidee was . . . undoubtedly something, though no one would say what.

Haidee's tanned skin glowed with health and vitality, a rosy blush stained her cheeks and a smile brightened her face. She rocked pink highlights in her hair, her arms were sleeved with tattoos, and she wore an adorable Hello Kitty dress. Zacharel refused to so much as glance in her direction, had barely even acknowledged her, yet Annabelle battled the urge to walk over there and hug her.

Why?

Better question: Harpies, goddesses, human-looking girls of mysterious origin — what else was out there? What else was Annabelle ignorant about?

A glint of silver caught her attention and Annabelle bent down to pick up . . . a dagger. Sweet! The battle was over, yeah, but better safe than sorry, considering what surrounded her.

"You're glaring at my friends, and now you're armed. Why are you glaring at my friends, human . . . girl . . . person?" The redhead stepped into Annabelle's personal space, claiming her notice by rising on her tiptoes to pat her on the top of her head.

"Never mind, I can guess. You think that because they're possessed, they're pure evil. Well, news flash, china doll. The demons are evil, but the guys who house them are marshmallows. I'm the real nightmare here."

At five feet nine, Annabelle towered over the girl. She lifted her gaze to Zacharel, who stood as unyielding as an iron fence, silently asking if he would get into trouble if she knocked Kaia around. Did no one know the difference between Chinese and Japanese?

He gave a negative shake of his head. "Never mess with a Harpy."

"I still have no idea what a Harpy is," Annabelle pointed out.

"A death machine, that's what," Kaia said.

"But . . ."

"No buts, Annabelle." Zacharel looked to the redhead. "And, Kaia. Behave."

"Fine. But only because you somehow turned this black as night day into a bright shining light, so I'm gonna do you a solid and obey. Want to know how you did that, huh, huh? Good, I'll tell you." She barely paused to pop a bubble with her gum. "You used to give Lysander crap about dating my darling sister, but look at you now. You're pulling a Paris and dating a Hunter, aren't you, and they're the worst of the worst!"

Pulling a Paris? A hunter?

Zacharel must have sensed Annabelle's confusion. "The Hunters are fanatical slayers of the paranormal. They will do anything, even destroy an entire city of innocents, to meet their goals."

"I am *not* a Hunter," she snapped.

"That's what they all say, honey."

Zacharel released a long-suffering breath. To Kaia, he said, "Annabelle hasn't yet learned that a man is not the same as the demon tormenting him, that a man can fight the evil and win, and that too many people believe in acting on what they feel and see rather than believing that they can have more, do better, like the Lords. And I can't blame her. I have only recently learned this lesson myself."

So the Lords had fought against the evil of their demons and won? Such a victory must have come at a terrible price, she thought, remembering the number of battles she'd fought and lost. Respect for them bloomed, and she forced her grip to ease on the dagger — only to realize Kaia had wrapped her hand around her wrist, claws sinking past skin, probably even into bone. Scalding heat radiated from her.

"You're too hot," Annabelle gritted out. Hotter than Zacharel's hands sometimes were.

The tiny female smiled unabashedly. "I know, right! But my twin sister is way hotter, I promise."

Twin? There were two of them?

"Kaia," Zacharel began, as Annabelle said, "Let go of me, tiny tot. Now."

"Tiny tot. Cute. But what's the magic word?"

"Kaia!" Zacharel and Strider said in unison.

"Nope. That's not it."

Annabelle blurted out a rough, "I'll kick you in your lady balls if you don't."

"Bingo!" One by one, Kaia pried her nails loose, leaving little red welts on Annabelle's skin.

"I think you're the weirdest person I've ever met," Annabelle groused.

"And you're the sweetest. So tell me," Kaia said, and popped another bubble. "Is Zacharel a good lover? Because I've got big money on the answer being no. Yeah, he has big hands, and he really knows what to do with them on a battlefield, but have you ever tried to banter with him? Dude is clueless. I figure the same cluelessness extends to the mattress mambo."

"Uh . . ." Suddenly everyone in the room was staring at her. Including Zacharel. "He's, uh, great?" Never had she been more uncomfortable.

"Oh, man." Kaia's shoulders slumped.

Strider, the demon keeper of Defeat, whooped and fist-pumped the air. "Told you, baby doll. *I told you.*"

Kaia spun, piercing him with a glare. "The fact that you won a bet about another man's sexuality isn't something to brag about, you idiot."

He blew her a kiss. "You're sexy when you're a sore loser."

She brightened, fluffed her hair. "Of course I am, but I challenge you to prove it."

"With pleasure." The two just kind of leapt at each other, kissing as if the other's mouth held a lifesaving supply of oxygen.

Does anyone else find this bizarre? Apparently not. A rapid-fire conversation ensued between the rest of the males.

Zacharel: "The club?"

The scarred warrior, Death: "Cleaned out."

Zacharel: "The humans?"

The beautiful Promiscuity: "Unharmed, as requested."

Zacharel: "Demons and the demon possessed?"

The goddess of Anarchy joined in, pumping her fist toward the ceiling as Strider had done. "I killed them dead!"

Zacharel: "What?"

Anya, pouting: "Fine. I only killed them dead in my mind. I had Lucien lock them up, as you commanded. Happy now?"

The big, black warrior with dark eyes said something through sign language before throwing his arm around the pink-haired babe. Amun and Haidee were dating . . . or whatever it was called when two not-quite humans hooked up?

Zacharel gripped Annabelle's shoulders and forced her to face him. When she met his gaze, the rest of the room ceased to exist. There was only her angel and his emerald eyes. He said, "I'm leaving you here, with the warriors and their women. They will not hurt you, and you will not hurt them."

First she experienced another wave of panic — *he's leaving you again!* — then anger — *you don't need him, you can take care of yourself!* — then determination. Who better to teach her about the different kinds of demons than demons themselves? Wasn't that why Zacharel had morphed into one during their first sparring lesson? Although . . . could she really believe anything these people told her?

"Fine, whatever," she said, trying for a

lighthearted tone. "So where are you going?"

He ignored the question. "Vow it."

She sighed. "I won't hurt your friends —
unless they attack me. I vow it. Now, where
are you going?"

"Below. I will not leave the club without
you, and no one in this room will attack
you," he said loudly, so that everyone could
hear. "They will keep you safe, putting their
lives at risk if necessary. Even if they do not
trust you. Won't they?"

Silence.

"Won't they?" he shouted.

Wow. She'd never heard him raise his
voice like that.

Murmurs of agreement echoed.

"Just so you know, I'm trustworthy," she
grumbled.

"Are you?" He gave her a little shake. "It's
too bad you wouldn't say the same about
me. You thought I meant to trade you and
desert you here. You actually thought I
would let Burden and his men hurt you to
save another angel."

Anger radiated from him, shaming her.
"Isn't that what you wanted me to think?"

"Yes, but you didn't have to do it."

"Well. Hmm. Maybe I didn't. I mean, I
don't actually recall ever saying anything

about the stupid plan you refused to share with me until too late."

"You thought it. There's no denying that."

Being with a man incapable of telling a lie — a whole lot of awesome. Being with a man who could taste when *you* lied — sucked the big one. "I'm sorry, okay? I've never had someone protect me before. This is new to me."

He got in her face, his warm breath mingling with hers. "Are you truly sorry for your wrongful beliefs, or are you merely sorry I deduced the truth? Think about that while we're apart. And when next you see me, apologize again and mean it." With that, he strode from the room, Amun and Haidee following behind him.

Annabelle studied the remaining occupants. Immediately they all spun innocently away, some even whistling under their breath, others checking their cuticles.

This was gonna be fun.

And yes, that was sarcasm at its finest.

I deserve this, Zacharel thought darkly. He so deserved a woman who would give him as much trouble and grief as he had given his Deity. But his new army was supposed to teach him this lesson, not his lover.

And she was his lover, despite the fact that

they had yet to consummate their relationship. He would tolerate nothing less. But oh, how he missed the days of ignorant bliss, when he hadn't known the pleasure to be found in a soft, warm body. When he had not known the driving force of anger.

Yes, anger.

Anger was like fear, and he did not have to act on it. He could ignore it. *Had* ignored it, for the most part. But the fissure inside his chest was close to bursting. Annabelle had doubted his integrity, and he had wanted so badly to spank her. Perhaps scream at her. Instead, he had cringed at the very idea of hurting her feelings and making her cry, and so he had done nothing.

"I've got a little piece of advice for you." Haidee kept pace beside him. Once a Hunter and a keeper of Hate, she now carried a pinch of Hadrenial's love, all because of Zacharel's split-second decision to save her.

A mistake, perhaps. Looking at her now *hurt.* But he'd wanted her to live, her loss too much for Amun to bear, the warrior's grief reminding Zacharel of his own after Hadrenial's demise, and "sharing the love," as the humans like to say, had been the only way.

"I have no need of your advice," he said.

They pounded down the VIP stairs and into the main part of the club, where Thane, Xerxes and Bjorn waited with Axel.

Axel, another of Zacharel's warriors. "I hear it's party time," he said with his usual irreverent grin.

"Only if you consider the torture of another a party."

"Uh, isn't that the classic definition?"

Until Jamila was found, this man would be her replacement. Perhaps not the wisest choice, Zacharel thought now.

Concentrate. Burden was pinned to the wall with daggers. A wad of fabric had been stuffed inside his mouth, but his watchful gaze spoke for him. He hated Zacharel, and would have given anything to kill him.

Soon, Burden would want to die himself. Demons could not be killed if they possessed a human, but one of the pitfalls was that they could be easily bound, and they could feel pain. Lots and lots of pain.

"Just a sec," Haidee said, stepping in front of Zacharel to claim his attention. "I've decided to give you my amazing advice anyway, because I owe you one. And before you decide to doubt me no matter what I say, I'll tell you that Amun read your Annabelle's mind."

Amun, the keeper of Secrets. He could speak, but didn't, because all the secrets he'd unearthed over the centuries would spill from his lips unbidden.

"You did not harm Annabelle's mind?" he demanded. Amun could do more than read minds; he could steal memories, ripping them out of their hosts.

The warrior shook his head — then flipped him off. No need for an interpreter. He did not like that Zacharel had questioned his honor.

"Tell me whatever you wish, Haidee, but make it quick." Zacharel glared down at her.

Ever gentle, she cupped his cheeks. "I can read Amun's mind, which means I know what he knows, and what he knows is that your woman needs to be one of the most important things in your life. Above your job, definitely. Her brother turned his back on her, and her boyfriend dumped her. She hasn't experienced unconditional love in so long, you'll crush her if you keep her without committing to her."

"I *have* committed to her," he protested. After what they'd done in bed, he'd more than committed. He'd decided to keep her. "Besides that, her spirit is strong. No one could crush —" *I could,* he realized. Annabelle had trusted him at her most vulnerable — until he'd walked away — something she would not have done if some part of her heart were not engaged. She was falling for him, just as he was falling for her.

If he wasn't careful with her, he would hurt her worse than she'd ever been hurt, commitment or not.

"I will consider your words."

"Good. You don't, and I'll hook her up with Kane. Or Torin. I like her, and both men need a good woman to —"

Zacharel snapped his teeth at her before stalking across the dance floor to his men and his prey.

I see the Lords came through for you, Thane said inside his head.

"There's no need to hide our words now," he replied aloud. "Amun can hear what we think."

Horror descended over Thane's, Xerxes' and Bjorn's expressions. Axel wiggled his brows at Amun and said, "Like what you hear? I'm thinking special thoughts just for you."

Amun frowned.

Before war could erupt, Zacharel said, "Amun will not pry, and as long as you keep your minds blank, he will hear nothing from you."

Amun nodded to support his claim.

After a long pause, three of the men nodded in return, though they merely gave a stiff bow of their heads. Axel blew Haidee a kiss.

Wonderful. "Now, then. Let's do what we came to do." Zacharel reached out and removed the fabric from Burden's mouth.

"You look just like him, you know," the demon said without preamble, smug, so smug. "I wonder . . . would you scream just like him?"

Do not take the bait. "Who?" he found himself asking, despite the fact that he knew the answer. Surely the demon would not dare to go there.

"Who else?"

His brother. Burden had dared, suggesting he had been there when Hadrenial was tortured. *You knew better than to engage a demon in such a way.* And now, all he could think about was the fact that it *was* possible. Hadrenial had never voiced the names of his tormentors.

Fury fanned to new life in his chest. How easy it would be to sink a blade into that vulnerable human throat. The body would die, Burden would be freed, captured and returned to hell — or killed. Maybe that's what Burden wanted, though. To prick at Zacharel until he reacted violently, allowing the demon to take his secrets with him.

He looked to Amun. His ability to uncover the truth was one of the reasons Zacharel had specifically requested the warrior's presence here. Oh, Zacharel could taste a lie, but this way, he wouldn't have to bother with an interrogation, wouldn't have to risk upsetting the Deity. Amun could simply dig inside the demon's mind and find his secrets.

His thoughts are a jumbled mess, Amun signed. *A mix of the human's and his own.*

"I need to know where he's keeping Jamila, a soldier of mine. I also need to know who he's working for," Zacharel said. "Someone told him to hunt and torture Annabelle, and I want to know who that someone is."

He's been thinking about the angel, Jamila, quite a bit. I'm sorry to be the one to tell you this, angel, but she's already dead.

Though he tasted the truth, Zacharel fought it. *Ten minutes ago, he showed us video feed of her. Alive.*

The feed was recorded earlier. Amun patted him on the shoulder. *I'm truly sorry, but they've already killed her. Her injuries were just too severe to recover from.*

For a moment, his heart felt like a hammer against his ribs rather than the organ responsible for his life. He tried to comfort himself with knowledge that Jamila's suffering was over, but that didn't help. She was dead, gone, because *he* had failed to protect her.

The shame and guilt he felt . . . they were worse than having bullets in his chest, skin, muscle and bone ravaged. The Deity would penalize him, of course, and he would accept without protest. Whatever was meted out, he deserved.

I will probe his mind about the other, his leader, Amun signed, *but it might take me some time.*

Time was the only thing Zacharel didn't have. Frustration joined the collage of emotions clawing at him. "Do whatever it takes — anything short of death. And when you find out, have Lucien track me down."

"Meanwhile," Haidee said, stepping forward. Beads of ice welled from her pores, turning her into a living sculpture. "I'll be helping my man out, don't you worry."

"Wh-what is she?" Burden stuttered with sudden horror.

"She's exactly what you deserve," Zacharel gritted out. Haidee could freeze a demon to its core, and for beings who lived among the flames of hell, that was not a pleasant sensation. Burden's screams would echo for days to come.

Or not.

When he opened his mouth to release his first, Haidee traced her fingertip across the edges of his lips. The ice spread from one ear to the other, silencing him. Any other time, Zacharel would have stayed to watch. This time, he dismissed his men and said to Amun, "If ever you or your brothers wish to be free of your demons, come and see me. I've learned how I can help."

With that, he strode away to collect his woman.

There was one more place they could go for answers.

CHAPTER TWENTY

Thane and his boys spent the rest of the day searching for Jamila's spirit, and when that proved unfruitful, hunting for the prison where her body had been kept, determined to burn it to the ground. But Burden had hidden it well, for they found no sign of the building in the heavens or on earth.

The need to save what was left of her rode Thane hard, as did fury and a feeling of helplessness. Every minute spent in a demon's *care* damaged your spirit, soul and body, and he hated that Jamila had died without a single ray of hope.

He hadn't worked with her long, but he had liked her, and had admired her strength. Had she lived to be freed, the experience would have changed her and not for the better, but he could find no solace in that.

Zacharel blamed the high lord pulling Burden's strings, and was on his way to speak with someone who might know exactly who that high lord was. For now, there was nothing else Thane could do. He needed a distraction.

He needed a new lover.

He prowled The Downfall's main room. He saw warriors and joy-bringers mingling, drinking and laughing. Not everything was fun and games, though. In shadowed corners, vampires drank from willing victims. A few Harpies occupied spots at the bar. A Phoenix shifter who resembled the one he'd already had gyrated on the dance floor, even crooked her finger at him, but he ignored her. His Phoenix hadn't recovered from their passions yet, and he would have her rather than one of her kin. If he took another, he would not be allowed to touch the first, no matter how much he paid.

The Phoenix were *that* possessive — and that selfish with others of their race — so until she was ready for him, he would try another type of creature.

Several other females summoned him over, but he ignored them, too. Tonight he wanted someone who would overwhelm his senses and make him forget his failures of the day. He wanted something different from the others he'd had.

He found that someone locked in a conversation with a male siren. Thane closed the distance and simply towered beside their table, waiting to be noticed. Only took a few seconds for the male to glance up.

"Excuse — Oh, Thane," the siren said, his voice as lovely as a symphony. "Is something wrong?"

He crossed his arms over his chest. "She's taken for the evening. You may find someone else."

"But —" Again the siren caught himself. He glanced behind Thane to the guards leaving their posts at the walls to flank his sides. Even if the male knew Thane could not kill him without consequences, the same could not be said about the guards.

"You're right. I will."

The chair squeaked over the tiled floor as the siren straightened and moved away, careful not to brush against Thane.

Thane easily slid into place.

Cario, a woman of questionable origins who had frequented his club quite often lately, glared over at him. Thane kept tabs on all the regulars.

"I liked him," she said.

When she had always left the club on her own? "He never stood a chance with you and you know it."

Rather than melt under the charm of his

voice, she scowled at him. "You can't know that."

"I know that you'll like me better."

"There's no way you can know that, either."

"Wait. I'm sorry I wasn't clearer. That wasn't a suggestion, but a command."

Finally, the reaction he had craved. Slowly she grinned. She leaned back in her chair and crossed her arms over her chest, the position a mimic of his earlier one. "Why would I like a man who refers to me as a woman of questionable origins?"

"I did not refer to you as such."

"Not out loud, no, but in your mind."

Thane frowned. The only being who should be able to read his mind was Zacharel, because Zacharel was his commanding officer. And then, of course, the keeper of Secrets, Amun — something Thane still did not like. But a female? Never!

He could walk away, he supposed. *Should* walk away. Two mind readers was two too many in a lifetime, never mind a single day. But he stayed. No one else had caught his interest.

Cario wasn't beautiful in the classic sense. She wasn't beautiful in any sense, really, but she was strong, with chin-length platinum hair, hard features and leanly cut muscle. He would enjoy watching her submit.

"I cannot guess your race," he finally said. "You appear human, yet you have the demeanor of a Harpy. Therefore, your origins are indeed questionable."

Her smile melted into a frown. "You angels and your honesty. It's beyond annoying."

"And yet you will never have to wonder if I truly mean what I say." He signaled the bartender for another drink for her. A shot of ambrosia-laced vodka, by the scent of it. The sloshing glass arrived a few minutes later.

She downed the contents and slammed the glass on the tabletop between them. "Mmm, that's good stuff."

"Only the best for my lovers."

"I'm not your lover."

"But you could be."

She rolled her eyes.

"Do you want to know what else is good, Cario, woman of questionable origins?"

One dark brow arched, the expression somehow softening her features. "If you say your penis, I'll barf."

He shrugged, and tried not to smile. "Then I will not say it."

"Well, I won't take you on, just so you

know. Not you, and not any of your friends. Your tastes are legendary, and not at all similar to mine."

"You would —"

"Like it if I tried it, blah blah blah, but the answer is still no. But here's a question for you." Her head tilted to the side as she lost herself in thought. "If I said yes, that I'd be with one of you, who would you pick? Yourself or one of your friends? Perhaps the right answer will change my mind."

He immediately excluded himself from the running. He might need the distraction, but his boys needed it more and he always, *always,* placed their needs above his own.

When they had parted upon reaching the club, Bjorn had sported red-rimmed eyes and lines of strain around his mouth. He could use a release. Xerxes had abstained from sex last night, and though he might not like the touching involved, he still needed the contact. And of the two, Bjorn had an easier time picking — and winning — a female.

"So Xerxes it is. Very well, I accept. I will be with him," Cario said with a nod, and there was a gleam in her eyes. One of intrigue and anticipation, and he thought perhaps she had desired the angel all along and that was the reason she had come here so often.

As happy as he was with her supposed change of heart, he gritted his molars. "I would appreciate it if you stayed out of my head."

"That's nice," she replied, and he knew she had no plans to stop.

Well, then, if he couldn't keep her out perhaps he could make her regret listening. *Why do you want Xerxes? Did you see him from afar and fall in love with him? Is that why you've come here so often? Is that why you've never gone home with another male? Surely you realize how hopeless such a love —*

"Shut up," she snapped. "I don't love him."

"You must feel something. You certainly signed up for the sex fast enough." He meant no disrespect, was merely pointing out another truth, as well as expressing his curiosity. Besides, he was as easy as she was and had no room to judge.

"I won't talk about him."

"Will you try and hurt him?"

"No. Never."

Truth. In one fluid motion he stood and held out his hand. "Let's go, then." He would take her to Xerxes, then he and Bjorn would drink themselves into a stupor.

Cario hesitated only a minute before twining their fingers. He tugged her to her feet and ushered her out of the room, up the stairs, past guard after guard and into his personal hallway, where luxury blended with comfort.

"I've never been up here," she said, her tone giving nothing away.

"Nor will you ever be again."

"A one-time thing, huh?"

For her? "Yes." A mind reader would be tolerated only long enough for climax to be achieved.

Xerxes, like Thane himself, had had the softer emotions beaten out of him. And an ongoing relationship between two hardened beings like Xerxes and Cario could never work. The two would kill each other. Although . . . if one of the hardened were shattered . . .

Look at Zacharel. Once as cold as ice, he now burned white-hot, placing his Annabelle's well-being above his own.

The entrance to Thane's room opened, the sensors recognizing his identity. Bjorn must have watched him on the wall of monitors, because the warrior stood at the ready with two drinks in hand.

"Where's Xerxes?" Thane asked, accepting one of the glasses and draining the contents.

Bjorn's gaze slid over Cario, and he nodded his approval. "Checking on his charge."

"I'll handle McCadden and send Xerxes to you." He gave the female a gentle push toward Bjorn and stepped into the hall, shutting the door behind him. Down the hall he stalked. Xerxes' door was closed, but heated voices trickled out.

"— lock me up. I'm sick of it!"

The voice was unfamiliar to him, which meant the speaker was McCadden.

"Your feelings matter little. I was not told to make you happy. I was told to keep you safe and out of trouble."

"Well, *I* told *you*. I'll leave the Lords of the Underworld alone. I'll stay away from my goddess."

"She isn't *your* goddess," Xerxes shouted.

"She is! I fell for her. I crave her, and I know she craves me."

"And that is exactly the reason you will stay here, in this room."

A black curse was hurled, and then the sounds of struggling bodies erupted. Oh, no, no, no. McCadden would pay for daring to challenge Xerxes. And if the warrior vomited after this . . .

Jaw clenched, Thane pushed open the doors — these opened automatically only for Xerxes — but stopped short when he

390

saw the outcome of the brawl.

Xerxes had McCadden pinned, one hand at the guy's neck, the other holding his wrists above his head. The warrior was breathing heavily, peering into McCadden's eyes with determination.

"Do you yield?"

"Never."

"Foolish."

"No, just proving a point. Now get off me," McCadden snapped. "Now!"

Xerxes jumped off the man with a low growl. He tangled a hand through his hair — but he didn't vomit. "What point were you trying to prove?"

"That you can't force me to do anything."

"I can and did. I will."

"If you think so, then you are as deluded as you claim I am about my goddess."

Thane wasn't sure how Xerxes could tolerate the other's touch when all others bothered him. "May I interrupt?" he asked.

Xerxes whipped around to face him, red suffusing his cheeks. "I'll beat him into submission if I must," he muttered.

"Whatever." McCadden walked away and slammed a bedroom door behind him.

Thane arched a brow, but mentioned nothing about the fallen's defiance. "I found you a woman, my friend."

Xerxes cast his gaze to his feet, hiding whatever emotion had sprung in those crimson eyes. "Not tonight. I'm too tired."

"But —"

"No. I can't. I just can't."

Something was going on with him. Something more than usual. "I will give her to Bjorn, then."

A terse nod from the warrior.

He should leave. Thane knew he should leave, but he couldn't bring himself to abandon his best friend. How tormented Xerxes appeared. There had to be something he could say to help. "I could use some company. Will you join me?"

"I — Yes." He threw a glance over his shoulder to McCadden's door. "All right."

He'd cut himself off before speaking a refusal. Xerxes loved him too much to deny him. Thane knew his friend would have preferred to stay here, trying to garner a vow to behave from the fallen angel, but he wasn't sure that was wise. The two would fight again, and as on edge as Xerxes was, he might do something he would regret. Like murder the first person he'd . . . not *befriended,* that wasn't the word. Maybe . . . *tolerated,* since his torture.

"I love you, you know," he told the warrior halfway down the hall. "No matter what, I love you."

"As I love you."

When Thane reentered his bedroom, he was surprised to find Cario and Bjorn standing across from each other, silent and glaring daggers.

From one heated scene to another. Well, he'd certainly gotten the distraction he'd craved, hadn't he. "Something wrong?" Thane asked.

Both tossed him a scowl, but only Cario answered. "No. Nothing. Just enjoying . . . your friend's . . . wit." Her gaze snagged on Xerxes. She licked her lips, shifted from one foot to the other. "Hello," she said, voice now a shimmering whisper.

His friend gave no reaction.

The acrid taste of her lie claimed Thane's attention. She had enjoyed nothing. Grimacing, he strode to the wet bar and filled three glasses with single malt. He downed his and took his friends theirs, knowing they hated the foul flavor of lies as much as he did. They accepted gratefully.

"I cannot be with this creature," Bjorn said, his disgust clear.

"You were never on the menu," she replied tartly, gaze still on Xerxes. As tough as she'd looked down at the bar, she now resembled an eager little girl at Christmas, ready to open her presents.

"What a blessed day this has turned out to be, then," Bjorn said drily.

"I've eaten little boys like you for breakfast. Believe me, you do not want to mess with me."

Bjorn was quick to snap back, "Actually, there's nothing else I'd rather do than mess with you. And I doubt you've eaten them so much as feasted on their rotting carcasses."

She lost her eagerness. Actually appeared insulted. "I do not feast on the dead."

"You sure about that?"

Her elbow whipped back, then slammed forward. If Bjorn had not possessed amazing reflexes, she would have broken his nose. As it was, he was able to catch her fist midair, preventing any damage.

"Such a weakling," Bjorn said with more of that disgust. Disgust now laced with smug superiority.

"Is that so?" She knocked her forehead into his, and this time he couldn't stop her. A grunt left him as he released her. He swayed on his feet.

Anger rose inside of Thane. "You do not hurt my friends, female. Ever. You told me you would not, and I heard the truth in your claim."

Her nose went into the air. "I must have lied."

No. He would have sensed it. But it was apparent she had changed her mind. "You will leave now," Thane said. As if that had still been in question. She was lucky she was still alive. "I'll escort you out."

"Escort me out like so much garbage? I don't think so." She spun on her heel and pegged him with the fierceness of her frown. "I'll show myself out."

"Feel free." He moved aside.

She cast Xerxes another glance, as if she expected him to do or say something. The warrior did not. Finally, she stomped past Thane, past Xerxes — careful not to touch him. The door slammed closed behind her.

How many doors would he be forced to replace before this night ended?

He kept his gaze on the monitors, ensuring she did indeed leave the club. A quick call, and he added her name to the list of people never allowed to return.

"Is there anything I can do for you?" he heard Xerxes ask Bjorn.

"No." The single word sounded as if it had been pushed through a cavern of broken glass.

"My apologies for the poor selection," Thane said. "If you would like someone else, I can —"

"No!" they said in unison.

Fair enough. "What did she say to you after I left?" he asked.

Bjorn massaged the back of his neck. "She's a mind reader."

Xerxes' eyes widened as he stepped backward, toward the door, as though he meant to hunt her down and slay her for such an ability.

"I know," Thane said. "I figured that was a price worth paying for an hour of her time. Besides, she would not get much from us. Merely sexual thoughts."

Rainbow eyes glowing with otherworldly rage, Bjorn snapped, "She mentioned what had happened to us. She knew every detail."

"Impossible." Only the three of them knew the worst of the particulars, and there was no way she could have unearthed so much buried so deeply even with weeks of constant contact.

"Nevertheless. She did."

Should have killed her. Thane picked up his phone a second time and told the vampire at the other end, "I have changed my mind. If the woman named Cario ever returns, don't turn her away. Detain her." He slammed the receiver back into its cradle and struggled for calm. "What shall we do for the rest of the night?" They hadn't spent a night without at least one of them being with a female in years, but now more than ever, he was desperate for a distraction.

"I want to discuss ways to rescue Jamila's body so we can give her a proper goodbye," Xerxes said.

Shoulder's slumped, Bjorn muttered, "If there's anything left of her."

"We won't know until we find her," Thane said. "We must search every demon hideout possible."

"But we'll be putting our own lives at risk for a dead woman," Bjorn was quick to add. Searching a hideout was how they'd been captured all those years ago.

"Some lives. In all the ways that count, we're already dead," Xerxes replied softly.

CHAPTER TWENTY-ONE

Annabelle paced the length of the newest hotel room while Zacharel reclined lazily on the bed. After she'd apologized (and meant it), he'd flown them all over the globe. Days had passed, almost every moment spent in flight as he ensured no demons followed them, and he deserved a rest. But to remain unaffected while she freaked out? So not cool.

"We're in Denver," she said. "Minutes away from my brother's house." They'd gone there first, but no one had been home. A blessing or a curse, she wasn't sure.

"Yes."

Of course that's all he had to say, the jerk. Why wasn't he telling her this would be okay, that her brother would welcome her with open arms and she would leave happier than when she'd arrived?

"I'm going to see him, talk to him." And question him about the days before her parents' murder. Cold fingers of dread crawled the length of her spine. Could she do it? Did she have the courage? She could face demons, no problem. But her brother?

The last few sentences in his final letter played through her mind.

I never want to speak to you again. You took away the only people I loved, and I will never forgive you for that. For all I care, you can rot in hell.

"He won't help us," she added, her tone hollowed out.

"He will. Now I will hear you say so."

I will not sigh. "Is this the faith thing?"

"Yes."

"Fine. He will." She glanced over at her angel and just . . . stopped moving. He utterly took her breath away. Dark hair disheveled, green eyes alight with need.

Need. He has need. Of . . . me?

A decadent fire consumed her in seconds, burning her up. She remembered how cool his touch had once been, then how hot, and oh, sweet mercy, she wanted to feel that change again . . .

"I'm going to keep our bargain," she blurted out.

His chest stilled, as if she'd taken *his* breath away, and his hands flattened on the comforter. "I cannot stop you."

Wait. "You want to stop me?" she practically shouted.

"No. But I think you are currently over-dressed."

A laugh bubbled up. Sneaky, teasing angel. "Well, then, let me see what I can do about that." Trembling, she reached down, fisted the lapels of the hotel robe she'd donned after taking a shower and slipped the material from her shoulders. Hair cascaded into place, tickling her bare skin, and his body went taut.

"The rest, sweetheart." A hum of arousal rose from him, luring her, always luring her. "Remove the rest."

He wanted her naked, she realized. Vulnerable. His to do with as he pleased. Just then, she was utterly okay with that.

She hooked her fingers into the edges of her panties she'd bought in the gift shop, hesitated only a moment then pushed the tiny scrap down her legs. A conscious effort was required to straighten and hold her arms at her sides rather than hiding her curves. She was okay, but she was also nervous about his reaction.

"You are so beautiful, Annabelle. A work of art." Slowly Zacharel rose to his haunches, wings stretching out behind him. He removed his robe and crawled to the edge of the bed.

Oh, baby. *He* was the work of art. Every inch of his body was cut by hard muscle and potent sinew. Skin stroked by the sun glowed with crushed diamond luminosity. But . . . the smudge of black on his chest, just above his heart, had spread, little rivers winding out of it in several different directions.

It wasn't a tattoo, couldn't be.

"Zacharel," she said, concern for him overshadowing her desire.

"You and you alone have nothing to fear from me."

He'd misunderstood her concern. "Zacharel . . ."

"Come here, sweetheart. Please."

Sweetheart. How could she resist such an endearment? And the *please?* Yeah. Utterly helpless. They could discuss the smudge later.

Much later.

A step closer to him . . . Another . . . She paused. "I know this will be your first time. I don't want you to worry if —"

"We will not have sex," he said, the force of his determination a hard brush against her skin. "Not today."

"But . . . why?" *And was that whiny tone hers?*

401

"When we are finally together, you will not fear me in any way."

"But I'm not . . . I wasn't —"

He waved his hand through the air even then crackling with tension. "I have considered this a lot. I have never done anything with a woman, but now I will do everything with you. And in the doing, we will build up to the sex."

Uh, just what did "everything" encompass?

Okay, so, maybe she *was* a little scared. But that wasn't going to stop her.

"I want you, Annabelle," he said in a silky tone.

"I want you, too." An achy whisper.

"Then come the rest of the way."

Another step, and another . . . until he was able to wrap his wings around her and urge her the rest of the way. The feathers tickled her in the most delicious way, softer than silk, more decadent than fur.

As if he couldn't help himself, he pressed his lips to hers, feeding her a soft, decadent kiss of comfort she would never forget.

"I like this," he said.

"Yes."

"I think I will like the rest even better."

Her heartbeat quickened. "Let's find out."

"If you're sure . . ."

"I am."

Zacharel guided her backward and rolled her over, then positioned himself between her legs.

In the ensuing hours . . . days . . . maybe weeks . . . he explored every inch of her, slowly, diligently. He learned her. Nothing was taboo, nothing was wrong. All she could do was cry out at the incredible pleasure. He was hesitant at first, careful with his hands, his caresses soft. But that soon changed, his grip becoming stronger as he kneaded her breasts . . . as he explored lower.

He used his fingers . . . and she realized she could do something more than cry out at the pleasure. She could writhe. She could claw at his back, drawing blood.

"Sorry," she managed to gasp.

"I'm not." Such a guttural tone. Earth-shattering. "Do it again."

She wanted . . . she needed . . . him, only him, but he'd stilled, she realized. Had ended all contact. He was on his knees, peering down at her . . . and licking his lips.

"Zacharel?"

He leaned down, and oh, it was like he'd started all over again because he was once again learning her body — only this time he was using his mouth. He kissed every inch of her, managing to wring one orgasm after another from her, until she was begging him to stop.

He stopped, all right — to reposition himself, pinning her to the bed with his weight.

"No words . . . Cannot tell you . . . *Loved.*" A rumble of need sprang from deep inside him as he next devoured her mouth, slanting his head this way and that to taste her from every possible angle. Her pleasure expanded, the fire in her burning hotter. Her entire world became focused on the man so devoted to her body.

"Anna . . . touch me. Your turn."

Anna. He'd shortened her name, made it into an endearment, a curse and a prayer. A command. A command she heeded. As slowly and as intently as he'd learned her body, she now learned his. And because nothing had been taboo for him, nothing was taboo for her.

With her every touch, every lick, he moaned his encouragement. His strength delighted her. The smooth texture of his skin tantalized her. He had zero body hair. He was beautiful and perfect and every brush of her fingers against him, every glide of her mouth against him was a revelation. This was the way sex was supposed to be, never mind that they weren't going that far. This was exactly what he'd talked about. A union of bodies.

Finally, when he could stand no more, he fisted her hair to guide her mouth back to his.

She stretched out beside him, gave him one kiss, two, then peered down at him. As lost to passion as he was, he was no longer the refined, polished angel she was used to dealing with. He was tousled. He was tense. He was snipping and snarling and rubbing against her.

"Want you to feel the pleasure again," he gritted.

"I'm so close, but I want you to feel . . . need you to feel it, too."

"I will. I do." He moved his hand between her legs, his fingers hot, and she was instantly *there,* stars winking behind her eyes, her lungs no longer working.

She lost track of everything, even Zacharel, floating away, returning, only to leave and float some more. But he must have gotten there, too, so tightly had she been squeezing him, because his roar of satisfaction brought her back to the bed.

She pried her eyelids apart, that roar still ringing in her ears. Her lungs had started working at least, but her breaths emerged too shallowly. Her body was trembling, a delicious lethargy curling through her.

Somehow she found the strength to lift her head and peer down at Zacharel. He lay beside her, his cheeks flushed, his eyelids at half-mast. His lips were swollen from being bitten, and his chest was rising and falling with the swiftness of his breaths. He, too, was trembling.

"Anna . . . lie here. . . ." He patted the black spot just over his heart.

"That is a command I will obey without question," she said, draping herself over him.

Sweaty skin fused to sweaty skin, and their hearts beat in unison, too fast, too hard, yet a rhythm that comforted her.

"That, I liked," he said.

"Which part?" she teased.

"Every part. By the time our month away from the heavens is over, I will know your body better than my own. There will be nothing I haven't done to you, nothing we haven't tried."

By the time our month away from the heavens is over, he'd said, and she instantly sobered. This relationship wasn't permanent for him. She'd known that since the beginning; he'd made no secret of it. And even she had considered all the reasons they were better off apart. But . . .

Yeah. But.

She'd come to want more.

"Did I scare you with my words?" he asked, mistaking her reaction. He traced his fingers over the ridges of her spine.

"No." And that was the truth. He'd hurt her, cutting her deep in her soul, but he hadn't scared her. Well, she had him now. That would have to be enough. And when the time came to separate, *she* would be the one to walk away. Too many people had left her, and she wasn't going to watch another do so.

Not ever again.

CHAPTER TWENTY-TWO

Zacharel had never experienced anything as consuming as being with Annabelle. No matter what they did, as long as they were together, touching, seeking, he was swept up, undone. Remade.

Afterward, apprehension would attempt to overtake him.

She made him feel too much. He wanted her too desperately. A relationship could never work, not permanently as he craved — as he *would* have for as long as possible.

When his month on earth was over, he would ask her to move into his cloud. She would say yes. He would accept no other answer.

"So, what now?" she asked him around a yawn.

"We sleep."

"Nope. Sorry, but I already knew the answer and that wasn't it. Now we talk. I want to know more about you."

Such soft, smooth skin she had. Her light, floral scent cast a silken net around him, the gossamer threads somehow stronger than anything he'd ever before encountered. "Such as?"

"Well, here's what I already know. You were born rather than created. You had a twin brother, but for some reason you won't explain, you had to kill him."

He waited for her to continue.

She sighed. "Okay, so you aren't ready to take my hint and talk about him yet. What else do I know? Oh, yeah. You have a black spot growing on your chest, and it concerns me. You lead an army of angels, and I think you're just now discovering how much you respect your own men."

"First, do not be concerned with the spot. Second, what makes you think I respect my men?"

"Nice try. Like I wouldn't notice you didn't say the spot was nothing for me to be worried about, only that I wasn't to be concerned. I'm on to your tricks, buddy."

"That will not change my response."

"*Anyway.* From the day at the institution to the day those three angels found us in New Zealand, your entire demeanor and tone have changed with them. Well, changed *slightly.* But with you, slight is major."

Very observant, his Annabelle. "Yes, I do respect my men. When I needed them most, they came through for me. I was told they were unfit for the heavens, that they were too violent, too irreverent to handle their duties, but I no longer believe that is so. They have each suffered in some way, and they have dealt with their pain the only way they know how." As he had.

"I'm with you. I've only met a few of the guys, and granted, they all looked pretty dangerous, but there was something remarkable about them. Something worth fighting for."

He liked that she defended those under his charge. "What else do you know about me?"

"Only one other thing. That you're friends with a group of demon-possessed warriors."

"And you want to know more?" He weighed everything she'd said she knew about him against everything she'd hinted that she wanted to know. "What do you want to know first? The difference between the born and created angels, or how my association with the demon possessed came to be?"

Another sigh left her, this one warm and sweet and ripe with understanding. She understood that he had struck his brother

410

completely from the conversation, yet she didn't push. "The difference between the born and the created, please."

He should not share his secrets. And to willingly, happily do so when so much danger surrounded them? Even worse. But he wanted to share all that he was, so that in turn, she would share all that *she* was.

Haidee's earlier words suddenly played through his mind. *Your woman needs to be one of the most important things in your life. Above your job, definitely. Her brother turned his back on her, and her boyfriend dumped her. She hasn't experienced unconditional love in so long, you'll crush her if you keep her without committing to her.*

As he'd told Haidee, he was committed. He just wasn't sure how to show Annabelle how important she was to him. He *had* to place his army first. He *had* to place his duty first.

"Uh, Zachie?"

How bad was it that he'd even grown to like the shortened version of his name, as long as it sprang from this woman's lips? "The born are only part of the Deity's troops and must be protected the first decade of their lives," he said. "They are weak, and must be taught to eat, to walk, to fly."

"Look at me, Zacharel! Look how high I'm flying!"

"You're doing so well, Hadrenial. I'm proud of you."

"Like humans," Annabelle said, "minus the flying, of course."

"Yes." He toyed with a lock of her hair. "The created were strong from the moment they first blinked open their eyes, but they never quite learned to understand the humans they were meant to safeguard. But that is why both the born and the created are useful. They excel in different areas, one picking up the other's slack."

"Who created them?"

"The Most High."

Despite his status, Zacharel had never come to understand or sympathize with the humans. He had grown out of his weakness, but the humans had never seemed to do so. They had reminded him of grains of sand — there, but easily lost in the masses and forgotten.

What about the human in your arms? She is not weak, and you will never forget her.

No, she wasn't, and no, he wouldn't.

The warmth of her breath caressed his chest. "I'm trying to imagine little Zacharel. Were you allowed to play games as a child?"

"No. Hadrenial and I had duties, even

412

then. When we weren't training, we acted as messengers and scouts, and sometimes even served as escorts for human spirits to their eternal home."

Hadrenial had hated that part of their life.

"Look how her loved ones cry over her loss. I can't bear to see so much pain."

"They will see each other again. One day."

"Will they? What if one goes to heaven, and the other to hell?"

"We will not be to blame. They will."

"Surely there's something we can do to help them, to make sure."

Zacharel had wanted to take over the duty of escorting the spirits completely, but he hadn't allowed himself to do so. He'd hoped his brother would eventually become desensitized to it, that he would no longer feel the tenderness that had shadowed every aspect of his life.

He was wrong.

"I'm so sorry," Annabelle said, drawing him back to the present.

He tensed, afraid he had accidentally spoken the long-ago conversation aloud. "Why?"

"You were deprived. Every child, even an angel warrior-in-training, deserves to relax and have fun." A warm chuckle left her. "My brother and I used to play hide-and-seek in the house, and one time I hid a little too well. He looked for me for over an hour, and ultimately I fell asleep. He asked my parents for help, and the way they tell it, they tore the house up searching for me. When they couldn't find me, either, they called the cops, thinking I'd been kidnapped."

The joy in her voice . . . *I want to make her feel that way.* "Where were you?"

"In the dryer, snuggled up with the still-warm towels." Another chuckle, sparkling like champagne. "Maybe one day you and I can play. We'll —" She stopped, just stopped.

Assuming something was wrong, Zacharel held out his hand, preparing to summon his sword of fire while at the same time scanning the room. No demon jumped from the shadows or misted through the walls, and he relaxed.

"Never mind," she said. "So anyway, how'd you become friends with those demon-possessed men?"

She'd stopped herself because she'd wanted to speak of the future, their future, but had thought better of it.

"You will stay with me, Annabelle," he said.

"For now," she replied.

"Far longer."

"I know. For our month."

That sounded like the beginning of a brush-off speech. "You are planning to leave me afterward?" he ground out.

"Well, yeah. And why are you suddenly so cranky? My plan should make you happy."

"I am not happy."

"But you said you wanted to part after our month on earth."

"I said no such thing. You will stay with me and that's final."

"Actually, no, I —"

He spoke over her. "Now I will tell you my story." He didn't pause, didn't give *her* a chance to talk over *him.* "One of the warriors was being tormented by hundreds of demon minions. Because of that, he was inadvertently poisoning those around him. I was part of another army at the time, and we were sent in to save him, or kill him if we couldn't. His friends . . . protested. I had never before interacted with their kind, and soon realized they'd fought their demons, were still fighting the demons every day, somehow braver, better, more honorable than others I'd encountered. They would never allow the evil to dominate their lives."

"Well, you're brave and honorable, too,

Zacharel."

He did not taste a lie. She truly thought so. "Then why would you wish to leave me?"

"Because" was all the stubborn woman would say.

Because she did not know the truth about him?

He had never spoken of the events that had led to Hadrenial's death. Not to another angel, not even to his Deity. But he would tell Annabelle, he decided. He would tell her everything. She would finally know, and they could build some kind of future from there.

"My brother was abducted. We were together, escorting a spirit to the heavens when a horde of demons attacked us. I fought them, and I thought Hadrenial managed to whisk the spirit to safety. But . . ." He swallowed a mouthful of bitter regret. "Though the spirit made it to the heavens, Hadrenial did not. He had simply disappeared."

She traced a heart over the smudge on his chest. "Not knowing what happened must have been torturous."

"Yes. I searched. For an entire year I searched, yet there was never a sign of him. I interrogated every demon I could, and always they denied knowledge of him. But then, one day, I came home and he was there. Just . . . there, tied to my bed. He was a mere shell of himself, for his captors had starved and beaten him. Worse, they had pitted his morals against his need to survive. For every scrap of food, every day without a fist in his face or gut, he had to do something reprehensible, like hurt a human they threw into the cell with him."

Warm liquid dripped onto his chest, and he knew tears were sliding down Annabelle's cheeks. "I'm so sorry," she said again.

"I am not the one who was forced to endure such misery."

"But you *were* miserable."

"Not like my brother."

"Pain is pain." She kissed the center of the heart she'd traced. "Did you remain celibate all of these years because of what he endured? He found no pleasure in life, and so you wouldn't, either?"

"No. Of course . . . not," he said, catching himself there at the end. He had never thought about it that way, but stated so bluntly, he found it hard to deny. "I do not know."

"When I was first arrested and taken to the institution, I didn't fight back when other patients harassed me. I didn't argue with my doctors, and I took every pill

417

handed to me. I wanted to be numb, but more than that, I had seen how much my parents suffered and knew I had failed them in every way, so I felt like I deserved whatever bad things happened to me."

"You were a child. What more could you have done?"

"Like you were a child when your twin was taken?"

His jaw clenched painfully. She was trying to absolve him of his own wrongdoing. While he liked that she tried, there was a difference in their stories. She had fought for her parents' lives; he had taken his brother's.

"Hadrenial begged me to kill him. I couldn't do it, though. Not at first. I loved him with all that I was, and I finally had him back. I thought he would heal, and physically he did. But he was determined to die and kept hurting himself in the worst of ways. Kept hurting others in an attempt to force them to act against him. I knew one day he would succeed and if that happened, his spirit would be cast into hell. I would never again see him."

"So you finally did it." Her voice was layered with sadness.

"Yes. I killed him to save him."

He expected disgust. He expected horror.

Instead, Annabelle calmly asked, "And also ensured you would one day be together?"

"No," he croaked. "He did not wish to live, even in the afterlife. I ensured he experienced the true death. I poisoned his spirit."

"I don't understand."

"Like humans, we are spirits, the source of life. We have a soul, or the embodiment of our logic and emotions — and we live in a body."

"So . . . what is the spirit if it's not the same as the soul?"

"The soul is the middleman, so to speak, intertwined with both the spirit and the body. Without the spirit, the body could not survive, for the spirit is the outlet, where the electricity awaits, the soul is the plug, and the body is that which is propelled into action. Make sense?"

"Yes."

"For a true death, you must destroy all three. I poured water from the River of Death down his throat, killing both spirit and soul, and then burned his body." And yet, some small part of Zacharel still hoped for the best, imagining that Hadrenial had not truly died even then, but that his spirit had passed into the Most High's kingdom, where he awaited Zacharel's death so they could be reunited one day.

"I'm sorry, Zacharel. The agony of such a choice . . . the pain of such a loss . . ."

If he said any more, he would break down. He sensed it, grief churning deep in his gut, ready to spill out. "Sleep now, Annabelle." He kissed the top of her head. "Tomorrow you must face *your* brother."

By morning, holding Annabelle in his arms had sharpened Zacharel's newfound need into a deadly edge. She had tossed and turned, rubbing her body against his, tracing her hands all over him.

He had done nothing about it. And he wouldn't, not until he had her pledge to remain with him.

While she showered — and he fought the urge to join her — he summoned Thane and commanded the warrior to procure for her a pink T-shirt and a pair of jeans, as well as new undergarments. Also in pink. Zacharel wanted to see her in the feminine color, and so he would. It was as simple as that.

To his utter bafflement, Thane already had the desired clothing in one of his air pockets. As Zacharel removed the tags, he wondered if the items had been meant for the man's lovers.

"Do you have an extra set?" Just in case.

"Of course." Thane handed him the clothing, and Zacharel placed the extra in an air pocket.

"She'll need these, too, I'm sure," Thane said, handing him two bejeweled blades.

He claimed them, saying, "Wait here." Leaving Thane on the balcony, he deposited the first set of clothing in the bathroom, the air thick and misty and smelling of floral shampoo. Even sweeter, Annabelle was singing off-key.

"Loves like a hurricane, something, something, something, bending beneath the weight, something, something, mercy."

She did not know all the words, he realized, and had to fight a grin. Adorable. But what struck him deepest was that she sounded . . . happy.

He left before she caught him listening — and enjoying — and returned to the balcony. The door was still open, the chill of dawn seeping inside.

Thane stood on the edge of the railing, at the ready.

"Your next mission is food for her," Zacharel said.

"I'm her servant now?"

"No. You are mine."

A pause. "Why am I not offended by this?" the warrior murmured. "Why am I actually enjoying myself?" White wings threaded with gold exploded into motion, and Thane disappeared in the air. He wasn't gone long, ten minutes at the most, yet he returned carrying a sack overflowing with breads, cheeses and fruits.

"Thank you."

A gleam of surprise in Thane's sapphire eyes, followed by a respectful incline of his head. "Anytime. I think."

Zacharel rattled off an address. "Make sure the owner is home. If he's not, wait for him. Once you have verified his presence and I have taken your place, you are free for the rest of the day."

Another thank-you, and Thane again disappeared.

And just as Annabelle emerged from the bathroom fifteen minutes later, *He is home* whispered through his head.

He meant to acknowledge the words, and would have, if he hadn't been struck dumb. He could only stare at Annabelle. The steam formed a cloud around her, creating a dream haze. She had dried her hair, the mass hanging down her arms, straight as a board. Pink cotton clung to lush breasts. *I've had my mouth on those.* The jeans kissed her legs with erotic abandon. He wasn't sure how he felt about the fact that Thane had nailed her sizes.

She looked so young and fresh, so . . . innocent. "You like?" she asked.

"More than like. You are beautiful."

"I can't take full credit. It's the pink."

"It's the woman."

Slowly she grinned. "Someone is on his best behavior today." She glanced at the table piled high with the food, then back at him. "I'm too nervous to eat."

"You must keep your strength up. I will tolerate no excuses."

"Sir, yes, sir," she said with a sassy salute. "And by the way, I take back my *best behavior* comment."

"There can be no take backs."

"Can, too."

He supposed, now that he'd licked every inch of her, the nature of their relationship would never be the same. She'd tried to warn him; she would never take his orders, and he would just have to like it.

As long as he had her, he would like it.

She picked at the food for half an hour before he grabbed her hand and a banana and led her outside, using an air pocket to shield her from prying eyes. By the time they reached her brother's home, she'd managed to choke down half the fruit. Not good enough, but it would have to do.

He caught a glimpse of Thane, who was in the process of flying away, when he landed on the porch. Though Zacharel wanted to whisk inside the home, Annabelle insisted they knock and wait for an invitation to enter. Manners. Such a novelty. But Zacharel suspected the brother would not open the door to her, and for that reason, he made sure only *his* face was noticeable through the windows and peephole by keeping Annabelle hidden.

"Maybe we should go," Annabelle said, rubbing at the center of her chest.

She did that every time she was nervous. Or scared. Why? "He will not hurt you. I will not let him."

Her crystalline gaze was grave. "There are a thousand different ways to hurt someone, Zacharel."

That, he knew well. "There are also a thousand different ways to heal. Trust me in this. Your faith is out there. You said you expect a relationship with your brother to bloom, and you are even beginning to believe it, whether you realize it or not. That's why you're here. So, even when it doesn't look like it's going your way, continue to believe. If you do not give up, you will see results."

As he rapped his knuckles against the

424

wood, his robe became a plain white T-shirt and a pair of loose-fitting drawstring pants. He waited one minute, two, then knocked again. When that failed to gain results, he rang the doorbell over and over again. He knew Brax Miller was inside; Thane would not have let him leave.

Finally a voice snapped, "I'm coming, jeez." Footsteps pounded, and in the next blink hinges were squeaking and a tall, leanly muscled male in his mid-twenties was opening the door.

Brax possessed the same blue-black hair as Annabelle, only his was cut short and shaggy. He had uptilted eyes of gold rather than crystalline blue. The eyes Annabelle had once had, Zacharel would bet.

"Yeah?" the man said. He was shirtless, his jeans hastily tugged on and gaping around his waist.

Beside him, Annabelle sucked in a breath. Not that the human heard. He couldn't sense her in any way. "You are Brax Miller." A man who had inherited a lot of money after his parents' death. Money he would blow through entirely within the next year, according to the report Thane had brought him all those days ago — the one detailing Annabelle's life, as well as her remaining family's.

"So?" His jaw held the faintest trace of a beard, and his eyes were red-rimmed, lines of tension branching from them. Not from lack of sleep, either. The scent of alcohol and . . . Zacharel sniffed . . . heroin seeped from his pores. Wonderful. He was a drug addict, his memory probably tainted.

Didn't matter. Zacharel had to try. "So you will let me in, and we will discuss your sister."

A terrible stillness came over the man. His reaction to the ring of truth in Zacharel's tone, perhaps. Next, a terrible mix of emotion detonated inside those golden eyes, and he snarled, "I don't have a sister!" He attempted to slam the door in Zacharel's face, but Zacharel shoved his foot between the door and its frame.

"We gave your way a try," he said to Annabelle. "Now it's time for my way." He flattened his palm on Brax's chest and pushed. Just a little push, but the man flew backward and slammed into the foyer wall.

Zacharel shouldered through the door, kicking the thing shut after dragging Annabelle in with him. As the addict jumped to his feet, intending to launch himself into an attack, Zacharel removed the air hiding Annabelle from view.

Brax caught himself, stumbled forward,

then back. For a moment, he could only stutter over the words *Annabelle* and *institution* and *here.*

"Surprise. I'm out," she said, unmistakably dejected.

"Believe," Zacharel snapped at her.

She gulped, nodded. "And I'm happy to see you. One day, you'll be happy to see me."

Her brother gathered his wits, squared his shoulders. "What are you doing here? Your escape has been all over the news, but I didn't think you'd be stupid enough to come to *me.*"

In a blink, Zacharel had a hand wrapped around Brax's throat and his body pinned against the wall, his legs dangling. Until her faith was made manifest, he would have to ensure Brax behaved himself. "You will watch the way you speak to her, or you will suffer."

A soft hand on his shoulder, a beseeching voice in his ear. "Zacharel. Let him down, please. Despite everything, I love him the way you love Hadrenial. I don't want to see him hurt."

Golden eyes widened, bulged, really, as Zacharel increased the pressure. "Just a little longer. He disrespected you."

"Think about what he's been through,

though. He saw the bodies in our garage, he saw the blood. Then he had to relive it when the police showed him pictures of the crime scene. He thinks I'm responsible."

Brax's lips were turning blue. Still Zacharel held on.

"All right, how about this?" she said. "We have questions and he might have answers. Remember? And if you kill him, my faith won't have a chance to change things."

"Oh, very well." Zacharel opened his fingers, causing the man to collapse onto the tiled floor.

"I won't . . . help you . . . escape," Brax said between gasps for air.

Her chin lifted, making her the picture of stubbornness he remembered from so early in their relationship. "I don't need your help."

Brax released a bitter laugh, and climbed to his feet. "Are you here to again tell me that monsters slaughtered Mom and Dad, then?"

Her chin lifted higher. "Not monsters, plural. Monster, singular. But, no. All I want to know is what you did the few days leading up to their murder. Anything unusual, like visiting a psychic or playing with a Ouija board?"

He scowled at her. "I don't care what your

friend does to me. You're crazier than I suspected if you think I'll talk to you about this."

"You were warned," Zacharel said before Annabelle had time to react. He smiled, but it was not the kind smile Annabelle could wring from him. It was the cruelest of all. His wings flared from his back as he grabbed Brax by the waist. "You don't care what I do to you? Well, let's see if I can change your mind."

CHAPTER TWENTY-THREE

Between one blink and the next, Zacharel and Brax vanished.

Annabelle waited, and waited, but neither male reappeared. Worry ate at her, because she knew they'd be back, eventually — she just didn't know if her brother would be dead or alive, and she wanted him alive. He *would* crave a relationship with her, as Zacharel had promised. He just would.

She'd missed him so much. Despite his current feelings toward her, he was still her big brother, the one who had rubbed the top of her head with his knuckles until she cried about the burn, the one who had tickled her until she'd laughed so hard she'd actually peed a little, and the one who had hugged her anytime someone had hurt her feelings.

Today, at her first glance at him, she'd wanted to cry. Not from homesickness, though she'd experienced that in full force, but from sadness. After all this time, it seemed the happy-go-lucky boy had grown into a tormented man.

He was two years older than Annabelle, and she'd always looked up to him, admired him. In high school, all the girls had wanted to date him, and all the boys had wanted to be him. He'd never been without plans, everyone hoping to hang out with him. On multiple occasions, he'd gotten into trouble for sneaking out. Twice he'd wrecked his car. Then he'd gone to college and seemed to calm down, get serious.

Now . . . He was like a shell of his former self.

Annabelle wandered through the house, a rustic two-story made of natural stone and timber, with a breathtaking view of the mountains from the backyard. First thing she noticed was the fact that he was a slob. Clothes, empty food wrappers and beer bottles littered the floor and tabletop surfaces. He owned very few knickknacks, and had zero pictures of her or their parents.

No, wait. He had a picture of their parents, resting facedown on the nightstand beside his queen-size bed. Why facedown? And oh, seeing her parents smiling up at her when she righted the frame caused her chest to constrict and tears to well in her eyes.

What do you want to be when you grow up, Annabelle?

Her mother's soft voice whispered through her mind.

She closed her eyes, imagined equally soft fingers smoothing hair from her face, then tucking the wayward strands behind her ear. *I can't decide. I want to travel the world. I want to help people. I want to wear beautiful gowns, and eat amazing food and host the best parties.*

A warm laugh caressed the air between them. *That's a lot of wants. I'm thinking . . . a flight attendant who marries a prince?*

Annabelle swallowed back her sobs and forced herself to walk away. The master bathroom was open, and she stepped inside only to stop short. An empty syringe, a spoon, a lighter, a rubber band, plastic bag with several small, brown-colored balls of . . . a drug, for sure, but which drug, she didn't know.

She thought back to Brax, standing at the door. He hadn't worn a shirt. Had he sported track marks? She . . . couldn't recall. She'd been too busy sprinting from one emotion to another. From elated to guilty to nostalgic to angry to guilty all over again to regret and finally to the sadness that had nearly brought her to tears.

432

Maybe he wasn't a user. Maybe he had a roommate and —

But no. With those red-rimmed eyes, those hollowed cheeks and sallow skin, he was the drug user, track marks or not, roommate or not. No wonder he'd turned the photo of their parents down. He hadn't wanted them to see what he was doing in here. Her shoulders slumped, the weight of responsibility settling heavily. He'd probably started using to escape the pain of all that he'd lost.

"Darling, I'm home," a female called from below.

Darling? For a moment the weight lifted. How bad could his drug habit be if a woman was willing to put up with it? Then a horrible stillness came over Annabelle. She recognized that voice. But . . . from where?

She'd heard it recently, she was sure.

"Darling? Didn't you hear me?"

Realization slammed into her. Driana, from the club. Demon possessed. Evil. Breath froze in Annabelle's lungs, crystallizing, cutting at her. A weapon. She needed a weapon. She had the new blades Zacharel had given her, but last time knives had failed her. Frantically she searched the bathroom and bedroom for something better . . . and finally found a gun under a pillow.

She'd never fired a gun before, wasn't even sure the thing was loaded, but maybe the threat of being shot would be enough to send Driana running. Bracing her legs apart, Annabelle raised her arms, aiming the gun's barrel at the open space in the doorway.

"Brax?" Footsteps echoed, getting closer and closer. "Darling, answer me. I know you're here. Unless you're dead?" A cackling laugh. "How sad that would be."

A few seconds later, Driana rounded the corner and entered the room. The beautiful blonde spotted Annabelle and gasped, stilled. Her eyelids slitted, but not before Annabelle caught a glimpse of satisfaction and triumph. "Well, well. You decided to join us."

Annabelle's aim remained steady as she ran her gaze over her opponent. Gone was the slutty dress. Now Driana wore a conservative business suit in charcoal-gray, the jacket and pants fitted to her sultry curves. If she was stitched up and bandaged, Annabelle couldn't tell. "You're dating my brother?" she demanded.

"Dating." A grin as Driana opened her purse and withdrew a tube of lipstick she traced over her mouth. *Smack, smack.* "No. I prefer the term 'debauching.' But, fine, whatever. Call it what you will. It's all the same to me."

"Might want to guard your words. I'm the one with the gun."

"Well, go ahead. Pull the trigger. Hurt me, kill me. Bring the cops in." Driana dropped the tube back into the purse. "They're out there, you know, watching this house, waiting for you to contact your brother. One shot and they'll think you're here to finish the job you started four years ago, the complete annihilation of your entire family."

Do not react. You came here for answers, so get your answers. "Why did you target my brother?"

"Target someone? Me? I would never —"

"You so would, demon, and I won't listen to your lies."

A pause. Another grin. "I forget that you know the truth — that you know what I am, and I don't have to pretend. Driana had been with him for over a year before I arrived, but he'd never proposed, you see, and I helped her realize she just needed a little something extra to convince him of his eternal love. She was more than happy to let me aid her."

"Why would you go after them? They've done nothing to you."

"You humans. So many questions, when the answer doesn't ever really matter. I was asked to monitor your brother's contact with you, to ensure he always hates you and you have nowhere to run, and, well, I jumped at the chance. Now, I grow tired of this. Let's liven things up, shall we?" Driana pulled a small gun from the purse and fired before Annabelle realized what was happening.

Boom! Boom!

A sharp sting in both her shoulders, jerking her backward, to her knees. There was a gush of warmth down her torso. Her arms fell to her side, too heavy to hold up, but somehow she maintained her grip on the gun. All she had to do was lift it and squeeze the trigger, and this would be over.

"Don't worry," Driana said. "Neither was a kill shot. But the cops should have heard them, should be leaping from their car right now and racing inside any second."

Lift . . . lift . . . inch by agonizing inch . . . breathing through the pain. "Thank you, demon, because now a third and fourth shot won't matter." Finally Annabelle had the gun in the air. Praying her aim would be sufficient, she hammered at the trigger.

Boom! Boom!

Driana reacted as she had, jerking backward. Blood sprayed across the hallway walls, her throat torn open, now a gaping mass of crimson and meat. Her head lolled to the side, her gaze fixing somewhere behind Annabelle.

Dead, she was dead.

Annabelle hadn't meant . . . Had only hoped to . . . *What had she done?* Pure evil had stolen her parents from her, and now she'd stolen this girl from someone else — from Brax.

A green-and-black mist began to rise from her body, a monster quickly taking shape. It had ruby-colored eyes, a skeletal face and stooped shoulders, and it hissed at Annabelle, baring fangs dripping with thick, yellow liquid.

If she'd had the strength, she would have screamed. Below, the front door crashed open. Male voices shouted instructions at each other and warnings for whoever had the gun. Footsteps slapped against the floor. Another hiss, and the demon shot through the ceiling, out of view.

Annabelle dropped the weapon, and labored to her feet, searching for a way out. Dizzying sickness consumed her, hazing her surroundings.

Zacharel appeared in front of her, his features tight with concern. He may not have been here, but he must have been close by. Must have heard the shots, too. His arms slid underneath her, and in seconds, they had cleared the house and were in the air.

She rested her cheek on his strong shoulder and closed her eyes. "My brother?"

"Is alive. I should not have left you alone. I am sorry. So sorry."

"I killed her."

"I know."

"Her demon got away."

"I know that, too." He eased her down onto something cold and flat. A bed, she realized, blinking open her eyes. She was in a motel room, her brother seated on the bed across from hers.

Though her vision clouded more with every second that passed, she could see that his eyes were swollen from tears, his cheeks were scratched and bleeding, and he was shaking uncontrollably. She tried to sit up, but Zacharel held her down.

"What happened to him?" she managed to get out.

"I showed him that monsters do, in fact, exist."

"And the b-bastard dropped me o-out of the s-sky," Brax said through his shudders. "T-twice."

Zacharel ripped her soaked T-shirt from

her body with a single tug of his hands, then slid her bra straps aside more gently. How they'd managed to remain intact, she might never know.

"You'll notice I caught him twice, too." With barely a breath, her angel added, "The bullets went all the way through."

That was a good thing, she hoped.

Brax rubbed at his shoulders, as if in sympathy. "Wh-who shot you?"

"Your girlfriend," she said, a wave of cold blasting her, beginning where the wounds originated, then spreading through the rest of her, making her shiver, keeping her awake.

"Driana?"

"Do you have another girlfriend?" Zacharel snapped. A long while passed in silence while he stared down at her, his eyes bright with determination.

"But she would never . . . She's . . ." Shock increased Brax's trembling. "Is she okay?"

Don't tell him. Stay silent. "I'm sorry, but she's dead." He deserved to know. "I shot her."

He peered at her with growing horror. "What kind of monster are you? Wait. I remember. You're the Butcher of Colorado."

Zacharel was at the other bed, backhanding Brax and nearly dislocating his jaw before Annabelle could blink. "Your woman was demon possessed and tried to kill your sister. Annabelle was protecting herself."

A fresh bout of tears streaked down Brax's cheeks. "N-no. I refuse to b-believe that. She couldn't have been demon possessed, she just couldn't! She hasn't been herself lately, but . . . but . . ." The force of his sobs had him curling into himself. And finally, blessedly, the ring of truth struck his core and he accepted what Zacharel had said. "I'm . . . sorry, Annabelle. If she had been herself, she would never have tried to hurt you."

"Don't worry about it," she said as Zacharel returned to her side.

"Are you okay?" Brax asked.

"I'll be fine," she said. She hoped. She ached, oh, did she ache, her muscles throbbing, her bones creaking, but she kept her features relaxed. "I've healed from worse, right, Zacharel?"

The angel nodded. "I'll make sure you heal this time, too." Jaw clenched, he withdrew a clear vial from the air. The Water of Life. "Open."

"No, I —"

With one hand under her neck, lifting her head, and the other tipping the vial back, he

440

ensured a droplet hit her tongue before she could finish her protest. Cool, crisp, the clean flavor slid down her throat, into her stomach, and torpedoed through the rest of her. As new cells were created, as muscle and tissue wove back together, her pain magnified, chill replaced by heat.

But then, a few minutes later — an eternity, surely — strength replaced her weakness, and most of the pain dulled, leaving her in a breathless heap atop the bed.

No, not true. Her pain hadn't dulled but had simply relocated. Her chest, just above her heart, began to burn, burn unbearably, and only getting worse.

"What's wrong with her now?" Brax asked.

A frowning Zacharel ignored him, saying to Annabelle, "You are still hurting?"

"Yes." She rubbed at her chest, reminded herself to breathe in, breathe out and concentrate on something besides her body. But that was easier said than done, because oh, no, no, no, she felt as if she were actually on fire from the inside out. "Help," she squeaked.

Strong hands pinned her arms against the mattress before smoothing over her chest. Zacharel rubbed gentle circles at first, creating friction, then increased the fervency of his strokes. "Breathe, sweetheart. Breathe."

"Trying."

"In. Out. In. Go get some ice," he shouted.

"Can't."

"Not you. You continue breathing. Out. In. Good girl."

She must have blacked out at some point, because the next thing she knew, she lay in a cool puddle of water, her chest on the road to normal. She was able to breathe easily and without prompting.

"Better?"

"Yes, thank you, but listen up." She ran her fingers over her sternum, the skin frozen and wet. "I don't want any more of that water. I would have eventually healed from the gunshot on my own, and I can't tolerate that burning again."

"Your pain has now eased completely. I do not consider that a waste."

"Well, you aren't the one who just got back from hell."

"You are alive, aren't you?"

She blinked at him, incredulous. "You're arguing with me *now?*"

"What should I be doing?"

"Fawning, you turd."

He flashed the quickest of grins. "Chalk it up to a rookie mistake." He pulled a T-shirt out of the air, and helped her dress. He motioned to her brother. "Tell her what you told me."

Her gaze strayed to Brax. He watched her and Zacharel with horror, as if only then realizing how close they were. His shivers had slowed, at least. "You healed." He snapped his fingers. "Just like that."

"Tell her." A harsh command that would meet with harsh reprisal if ignored a second time.

"After you tell me why you didn't heal Driana."

Zacharel's hands curled into fists. "The water cannot bring back the dead. Now talk."

Brax gulped. "I came home for your birthday. You, Mom and Dad went to dinner and the movies to celebrate a little early because you were going to be with friends on the actual day, and I said I wasn't feeling well. While you were out, a friend of mine from high school came over. He brought a book and . . . a joint with him. I hadn't gotten high in so long, and I felt like total crap, so . . ."

Dread settled in the pit of her stomach. "What's the name of the book?"

"I don't remember."

"What kind of book was it?"

"Some kind of, uh . . . spell book."

Her gaze darted to Zacharel. He'd tried to tell her something had welcomed the demon into her life. She hadn't believed him, and hadn't really thought the answer would lie with her brother.

Zacharel nodded, telling her without words the book was indeed the reason.

"Why weren't you killed?" she demanded. "Why wouldn't you wake up the morning of the . . . of the . . . I screamed for you, I shook you, but you never even opened your eyes."

"I was passed out from the grass. I just . . . I'm sorry, Annabelle. I really am."

"Why wasn't he killed?" she asked Zacharel.

"A demon rarely kills his summoner right away. They want a host to possess, so that they can remain on earth. But I'm betting your brother was not possessed because you were spotted, you were desired, and the need to mark you distracted the demon. Your parents got in his way. After that, I'm not sure why you were left."

Deep breath in . . . out . . . Here were the reasons for her parents' murder finally laid bare. But there was no comfort with the answers. No sense of closure.

Zacharel glared at Brax. "Do you yet realize that *you* are responsible for your sister's circumstances? *Your actions* killed your parents, not hers, yet you allowed Annabelle to suffer for your crime. You abandoned her when she needed you most. You."

Brax gave a violent shake of his head. "I — I didn't. Or if I did, I didn't know. I promise you I didn't know. You have to believe me."

The way he had believed her when she had spoken those very words to him?

Your prints are all over the knife, Annabelle! Yours. Only yours. No one else's. Do you really think we're that stupid? Do you really think anyone will believe a monster did this terrible thing? Oh, a monster did it, all right, but that monster is you.

Of course her prints had been all over a knife. She'd grabbed one just in case the monster came back.

"You don't remember anything else about that day?" she asked, pushing the ugly memory to the back of her mind. "A dream, maybe, where someone seemingly wonderful asked you something terrible?"

"No. I'm sorry," he said, tears streaming down his cheeks. "I'm so sorry."

Unable to deny him, she offered him a soft smile of forgiveness. "It's okay. We'll get through this." He was the only family she had.

He closed his eyes as if her forgiveness was too much for him to bear.

"What do we do now?" she asked, gaze settling on Zacharel. She gasped, did a double take. "Your wings."

"What —" He flared out one, then the other. A curse exploded from him.

Snow once again fell from the tips of the feathers.

CHAPTER TWENTY-FOUR

His Deity was displeased with him. Again, Zacharel thought. For once, however, he knew why beyond any doubt, without being told. He had assumed responsibility for Annabelle, and she had then killed a human, demon possessed or not.

Not that Zacharel blamed her for her actions. He would rather suffer the Deity's displeasure than lose her, and he would have lost her had she not reacted and protected herself. The blame rested on his shoulders, and his alone. He had trained her a bit in the art of fighting demons, but he had not prepared her for a situation such as this.

"The police will wish to speak with you," he told her brother. "Tell them what we have discussed and you'll find yourself locked away as Annabelle was."

A thousand emotions crossed the boy's face. And he was a boy, no matter how much older he was than Annabelle. He lacked her courage, and her fire. "You're leaving me? But the monsters . . ."

"We're leaving him?" Annabelle echoed.

"Yes. You are the draw, not him, which means you are in constant danger. And *that* means you will place your brother in danger if you stay with him. Once you leave him, he should be fine."

"Should be?" she demanded, and he knew that wasn't good enough for her.

"Will be," he amended. He would send one of his soldiers to secretly guard Brax. "I'll make certain of it."

The siblings peered at each other, silent, neither sure what to do or say next. Brax certainly didn't deserve a sister like Annabelle, but Zacharel was still envious of him and this moment. He would have given anything to see Hadrenial again.

"Well, then." Annabelle cleared her throat. "Take care of yourself, Brax."

"You, too. And, uh, Annabelle?"

A warm breeze suddenly wafted through Zacharel's mind, the first sign of the Deity's coming summons. He stiffened, losing track of the siblings and their stilted goodbye.

Zacharel, my soldier. A voice that was at once soothing and commanding echoed inside his head. *I have need of your services.*

You will gather your army and stop the demons attempting to infiltrate my temple. As this battle will take place in the heavens, I will not have to worry about collateral damage, will I.

Not a question. Definitely a dig about his past performance. Also an order from his Deity, as well as his next assignment.

For however long he was needed, he would not be searching for Jamila's tormentors, would not be protecting Annabelle, but fighting demons. He'd feared such a moment, and now that fear ate at him with razored teeth.

But wasn't that always the way? Whatever a man feared, he received. A spiritual law as binding as all the others.

"Zacharel?"

He pulled himself out of his mind. Both Annabelle and her brother were staring at him, blinking with confusion.

"Come," he said. "We must go."

"Uh, Zacharel? What just happened? You were flickering in and out, as if you were here but not here."

"That's because I *was* here but not here. Part of me was with my Deity in his temple in the heavens. That temple is being attacked, and I have been charged with its safekeeping."

Color drained from her cheeks.

"Do not worry. I will leave the moment the temple is safe, and we will return to earth." Not just because of Annabelle's bargain, but because he would be desperate to whisk her to safety.

"I —" Her mouth floundered open and closed. "Thank you."

"You are welcome. Now come."

With a final wave to her brother, she closed the distance to Zacharel and wrapped her arms around his neck. He misted both of their bodies and flew her straight into the afternoon sky. Brax's shout of, "Take care of yourself, Anna," followed them, and Annabelle had to blink away a sudden tear.

The sun was hidden behind gloomy storm clouds, the heavens a blanket of darkening velvet. Higher and higher they ascended, until the only spots of color stemmed from angels, the off-duty warriors darting one way, joy-bringers darting the other, all determined to complete a task.

"So many," Annabelle gasped.

He maneuvered her through the masses, twisting and rolling and finally reaching a clear patch of air. "Cloud!" he shouted. "Return to me."

Five seconds passed . . . ten . . . twenty, but his home eventually appeared around him. However, the misty walls were no longer a soft baby-blue; they were black, as slick as oil, as though weeping the essence of evil. His stomach twisted. He hadn't expected this, hadn't known it was possible. A cloud had never changed so drastically and so quickly.

"What happened?" Annabelle said.

"I don't know. It's dying, perhaps." The demons that attacked must have poisoned it somehow. "My bedroom. Show me."

His bed appeared, as did his nightstand. He reached inside the pocket of air and withdrew — Relief nearly buckled his knees. The urn was safe.

"Follow me to the temple, and remain within my sight," he commanded the cloud. "Guard her, give her anything she requests, and when I return, I will end your suffering." A pang inside his chest. Of remorse? This home had been his only . . . friend for a very long time.

Annabelle clutched at his robe. "Let me help you."

He hardened his heart against her; he had to. "You have no wings, and carrying you will hinder me."

"But surely I can —"

"You are helping me by staying here and protecting my greatest treasure."

"Bedroom furniture?" she asked drily.

"Inside that urn is all that I have left of my brother." Before she could ask questions he wasn't prepared to answer, he meshed his lips against hers, his tongue plumbing the depths of her warm, wet mouth, stealing a last taste before the coming battle.

By the time he lifted his head, he wanted only to stay with her. But from the very beginning he'd known the temptation for more was the danger of her. He caressed a fingertip along her cheekbone, whispered, "Perhaps the urn isn't my *greatest* treasure," and left her.

Annabelle's first thought: *Did he just imply what I think he just implied?*

Her second: *The little woman stays home, while the big strong tough guy goes to war.*

Would their relationship always work this way?

She studied the urn she was to protect. Clear liquid swirled inside, thicker than the Water of Life, with violet beads glittering throughout. Angel ashes?

Whatever it was, she would protect the stuff, as she'd been asked to do, and hopefully her debt to Zacharel would be paid. He had reunited her with her brother, convinced Brax of the truth, and though the relationship was anything but smooth, it was no longer hate-filled, either. The possibility for more, for better, was there.

To the urn, she said, "I need a change of clothes and a cool, new weapon. Also, wings would be nice." The last was said on a wistful sigh. "Your brother has done a marvelous job of protecting me and providing for me, but I'd love to show him I can protect and provide for myself, too, you know."

"Very well," said an eerie, laughing voice — one that did not come from the urn. A second later, the cloud shook so violently, she had to grip a bedpost to remain standing.

"What's going on? Who's there?" No one had appeared; she was still alone.

The moment the shaking stopped, she looked around to assess the damage. Everything appeared the same — until she looked down at herself. Her T-shirt and jeans had been replaced by . . . What the heck? A sexy devil costume?

She now wore a short red dress, with patches of material cut out of the waist, just like Driana's, the hem stopping just below the curve of her butt. A padded forked tail uncurled to her feet. Five-inch stilettos encased her feet. Red fishnets stretched to midthigh, garters hooking them to . . .

matching red panties. Great. Also, her blades were gone.

"Is this supposed to be funny?" she demanded. "You better tell me who you are and where you are. *Now*."

More laughter, more shaking, and then a rusty pitchfork with glass shards hooked to each of the prongs appeared on top of the bed. "Can't forget the rest of what you wanted."

Her weapon, she realized, the one she'd requested. Wait. Was *the cloud* able to speak now? "What am I supposed to do with —"

Another round of laughter interrupted her. The shaking started up again, more intense than before. Her mind whirled with possibilities. She'd asked for a change of clothes and gotten *this*. She'd asked for a new weapon and gotten *that*. Dread became a noose around her neck. She'd asked for wings and would get . . . what?

When the laughter at last quieted and the shaking stilled, a sharp pain lanced up her spine. But that was it. A pain there and gone, and for a long while, nothing else happened. She began to relax.

"Cloud," she said. "I've changed my mind about the clothes, the weapon and the wings. Okay?"

"Sorry, naughty girl, but I'm not the cloud

— and there can be no take backs. Just give it a moment. You might like it."

As if on cue, warmth burgeoned between her shoulder blades. At first, it was actually comforting. But that warmth heated . . . and heated . . . until it was blistering, surely crackling with actual flames.

"Stop this," she demanded. "Whatever you're doing, stop."

Hotter and hotter . . . sweat beading over her skin, breath emerging shallow and fast. But okay. She could handle this. She could — The flesh between her shoulder blades ripped open and blood gushed down her back, something sharp slicing through muscle.

Her knees gave out, and she collapsed. "Stop! Please."

"Why would I stop now? I've been waiting for you, knew you would return."

The voice came from across the room this time, and she managed to lift her head enough to see a grinning demon step from the oozing black wall. Not the cloud, after all.

Stay calm. Don't let him feed off your emotions.

Fighting the pain, dizzy, she lumbered to her feet and grabbed the pitchfork. "How'd you . . . hide from . . . Zacharel?"

"Your angel is not all-powerful, and he cannot see all things. I followed the cloud after our attack, and laid siege." The creature was tall, though thin, with scales as smooth and shiny as black ice. His eyes were red, not the pretty ruby of so many of his brethren, but edged with rust. "The cloud is now mine. Mine to control . . . to pervert however I wish."

"A cloud . . . can't give a human . . . wings."

"Well, you are more than human, aren't you, naughty girl? You belong to a demon."

Calm . . . "I belong to myself." Drawing on every ounce of strength in her being, she jabbed the tip of the pitchfork at him.

He hunched his body and twisted out of the way, rendering her attack ineffective. Flashing his too-sharp teeth, he said, "No need to play rough. I'm not going to hurt you . . . much."

Again she jabbed the pitchfork at him. This time he wasn't fast enough. Contact. The prongs sank deep into his thighbone, the long handle vibrating from the force. Only, he was not the one to scream and drop to his knees as agony overwhelmed him. She was. The muscles in her leg . . . torn to shreds, surely.

His chuckle rebounded from the walls.

"Do you really think I'm stupid enough to give you a weapon that could harm me?"

"Yes," she gasped out. "I really do."

He took no insult. "The beauty of the pitchfork is that the one who wields it feels the injuries it causes. Tell me if this hurts." He jerked the prongs from his thigh.

Another scream left her, a black mist fogging her line of vision. Not because of *her* thigh — though yeah, that was beyond awful — but because of her chest. Whenever she received an injury somewhere else, razors seemed to scrape at the burn there, as if Zacharel had just poured his water down her throat.

"Well?" the demon asked.

"Endured . . . worse."

"If only I was not forbidden to taste you." He closed the distance between them and crouched in front of her, his vile scent overwhelming her senses. "My master has Zacharel's other female, did you know that?" He opened his palm, revealing a curling lock of dark hair. "The pretty angel."

"He has what remains of her body, you mean."

"No. She lives."

"You lie."

"Do I? Can you really take that chance?"

No. No, she couldn't. A conscious effort

was needed to keep the urgency out of her tone, to hold herself still. "Just who is your master, huh, that he can do what even Zacharel could not, and bring someone back from the dead?"

"I am not to tell you. I am to introduce you to him. And if you ask him nicely, I bet he'll let the female go. Or not. Mostly not. But that doesn't mean you can't try."

His master had to be the high lord who had stabbed her parents, the demon who had marked her, tainted her . . . ruined her. How she'd dreamed of facing him.

So yes, she was tempted to give in and go. But would she allow this creature to leave this cloud alive? No. Never. She might not have her blades, and the pitchfork might be a no go, but she had her fists and she knew how to use them.

The demon's rusty gaze flicked to the nightstand. "We will be bringing Zacharel's brother with us, of course." He clapped, happy with the way things had turned out. "I'm not sure which will hurt him most. The death of his woman or the loss of all that remains of his cherished sibling." He straightened, reached toward the urn. "Let's find out."

Though she felt as if she were ready to burst apart at the seams, Annabelle struck.

CHAPTER TWENTY-FIVE

Zacharel and Thane hovered over the Deity's temple, watching as hundreds of winged demon minions raced through the night-darkening sky, slowing only when they reached the rivers winding around the structure. Those rivers flowed to the edges of the cloud, cascading over the sides in breathtaking, star-framed waterfalls.

Most of the demons successfully fought the currents and managed to crawl through the gardens to the alabaster steps, past the ivy-rich columns to the towering double doors leading inside. But the doors they couldn't breach, no matter how much force they used as they slashed, banged and kicked.

For a moment, Zacharel was taken back to the night he'd met Annabelle. The demons had mindlessly attacked then, too, all in an effort to reach her. But she was not inside, so . . . what could they possibly want this time?

"They've never attacked our Deity like this," Zacharel said. His wings were heavier than usual, the snow continuing to fall. "Why now? For what purpose?"

"I can only assume they are following orders," Thane said.

"Yes, but whose?"

"Not Burden's, that much we know. He's out of commission."

"The one pulling his strings maybe?"

"Maybe."

"Who else would sacrifice an entire horde on a suicide mission? And again, for what purpose?"

"Only one way to find out."

Yes. Interrogation.

"I don't like this." He traced his tongue over his teeth, observed his own cloud — a horrifying black stain in that expanse of deep blue — for a long, silent moment.

Even though Annabelle was inside, the demons did not attempt to infiltrate the cloud. Oh, they would cast longing glances its way, even move toward it, but all would catch themselves and return to the desecration of the temple.

Thane sighed. "Let's say the minions are here simply to distract us. Let's say another horde is somewhere else, waiting until we are engaged in battle to act. We still cannot walk away from this. We have the Deity's orders and we must abide by them."

Zacharel worried two fingers against his jaw. "You're right. We do. But that doesn't mean the whole of my army is needed for this."

He pictured half of his troops and projected his voice into their minds. *Patrol the heavens nearby, looking for anything suspicious, any type of demonic disturbance.* If they were surprised by the new method of communication, they hid it well. This was easier, quicker, and he only wished he'd done it before now.

He received one *Yes, sir!* after another.

On my signal, he projected to the other half, *we attack.*

To Thane, he added, "You, Xerxes and Bjorn will escort three demons to Koldo. Alive." Koldo wasn't well enough to fight, but he *was* out of his sick bed. "Find out what you can from them. I'll join you when the temple has been fully cleansed."

Thane slapped him on the shoulder. This was the first time they'd touched outside of training. "Consider it done." With that, the angel left Zacharel to gather his friends.

He shot another glance at his cloud — he just couldn't help himself. Still no demons

461

attempted to enter. What was Annabelle doing? Fuming over his desertion of her? Worrying after his health?

You are a warrior. Act like one. He blanked his mind, raised his hand and created his sword of fire. In a blink, his soldiers had their swords raised, as well. No one broke rank, acting before the signal was given. That was new, too.

Zacharel's war cry blasted through the heavens. "Now!"

The angels swooped down, Zacharel included. The demons froze in place, most quaking, but none leaving. He hacked his way through them, black blood spraying over the pure alabaster and mother-of-pearl facade of the temple, heads rolling down, down, his opponents dying with . . . smiles, he realized, as if they knew a secret he did not.

Again he looked to his cloud, but still the demons stayed away from it. Perhaps he should check on Annabelle. She —

A heavy weight slammed into him, flipping him end over end. He lost his hold on the sword, and it vanished. He crashed into the bottom step, air shoving from his lungs. No, not shoving. Seeping out. The organs had been punctured — because a pair of horns had embedded in his chest. A paralyzing poison was sprayed directly into his body.

Distraction killed. He knew that. Oh, but he knew that, and now he would pay. His muscles spasmed as he commanded his arms to punch and his legs to kick, but the limbs did not obey. The demon jerked free, laughed gleefully and shouted for his friends. Soon, minions swarmed Zacharel, biting at him, clawing at him, and there was nothing he could do to stop them.

Are you still at the temple? he projected to Thane.

Nearby. A rasping reply, indicating the swiftness of the warrior's motions as he spoke.

I'm at the bottom of the steps. Help . . . me. He'd never had to request aid before, and that he had to here and now . . . it was humiliating.

An eternity seemed to pass before grunts and groans of pain sounded around him. Teeth were ripped out of him, horns were severed, and one by one the demons began to collapse around him.

"Don't worry. I've been where you are." Thane remained poised beside him, slaying any minion who dared approach. "The toxin should wear off in a few minutes."

Zacharel could only lie there, feeling as

though he'd been thrown into the fires of hell. At least he could still see his cloud . . . a cloud that now had three spots of color in the center. Dark, blooming . . . red?

Red. Blood. Annabelle's blood.

A demon fell from the center, shooting toward the earth like arrows.

The cloud, he mentally shouted at Thane. *My cloud. Inside. Annabelle. Help her!*

Thane didn't stick around to ask questions, but darted up. Instantly, the minions who'd been waiting on the sidelines, too afraid to attack with the warrior there, swarmed Zacharel. He nearly bit his tongue in half, so forcefully did he strain. He wasn't surprised when his shoulder bone popped from its socket. But did he manage to free himself from the taint of the poison? No.

His face was clawed. His chest was slashed. His legs were sliced. The demons were too happy, too distracted to notice when his muscles finally began to twitch back to life. First his fingers wagged, then his toes, then finally, the toxin dissipated completely. He popped his shoulder back into place and surged into motion. Roaring, he created another sword of fire and swung in a circle, cutting through everyone who clustered around him. Heads flew, and bodies collapsed.

He spread his wings and bolted into the air. Almost there . . . "Annabelle!" When he attempted to enter the cloud, he ricocheted backward, bones vibrating from impact.

Thane flew around from the other side. "There's some kind of block. I can't get through without killing your home."

"I'm sorry," Zacharel told the cloud as he swung his sword through the blackened ooze. This was not the merciful death he'd imagined, but it was a death nonetheless. He had to reach Annabelle. Instantly a doorway was created, the edges sizzling, the fire growing, spreading. Zacharel leveled out and zipped to his bedroom.

Horror filled him. Blood dripped from the walls, covered the bed and the nightstand, and even formed little pools all over the floor — but there was no body. *No urn.*

Thane approached his side. "She is stronger than she appears. Whatever happened, she will recover."

"Yes." Would she, though? A vicious battle had clearly taken place here. "Annabelle," he shouted.

No response.

Doing his best not to panic, he searched room after room as the cloud continued to burn from the outside in, soon to vanish forever, but found no sign of her. She had simply disappeared. "She's not here. How can she not be here?"

"Could she have . . . fallen?" Sympathy laced Thane's voice.

No. *No!* Zacharel arrowed out of the cloud and toward land, Thane right behind him.

I watched a demon leave the cloud, he projected. *That demon could have taken her with him, and I simply missed her.*

If that was the case, she would have fought the demon the entire way down, willing to die rather than be captured and imprisoned. If somehow the demon had managed to maintain his hold on her, she would be hurt, and hurt terribly, but Zacharel would rather she hurt than die.

Hurt he could save. Dead he could not.

Now, however, he had an answer to his earlier suspicion. The demons had attacked the temple for a reason, only he had not guessed they'd desired his distraction and Annabelle's solitude. Furious with the demons, with himself, he straightened far too close to the earth's surface, nearly shredding his wings as they slowed his momentum. The landing jolted his entire body, causing him to stumble forward.

The first thing he noticed was the demon carcass in pieces on the ground. A fresh kill, the blood liquid, without clots, and not from impact but from claws. Two demons fighting against each other? For rights to Annabelle, perhaps. Zacharel looked around through narrowed eyes, searching for any sign of her. Miles of forest in every direction, the animals and insects unnaturally quiet.

To the left, moonlight reflected off of something. Something of Annabelle's? He raced over, leaving a trail of ice in his wake, and picked up — his brother's urn. It was empty.

The glass shattered in his hand.

"What is it?" Thane asked as he landed.

Zacharel bent down, patted the ground. Dry. His twin's essence had not spilled here. It could have spilled inside the cloud, and if that was the case, it was gone forever, rendered nothing but ash. Destroyed by his hand just as Hadrenial himself had been. Or one of Annabelle's attackers could have emptied it out on the way down. But Zacharel didn't scent —

Wait. Yes, he did. He scented his brother: the morning sky, dew drops and a hint of the tropics. Someone had absorbed his essentia.

Another breath and Zacharel realized the scent was fading. Whoever carried Hadrenial's essentia was running away. Annabelle?

Or a demon? Or both?

"Zacharel?" Thane asked.

"Go. Help your boys interrogate the demons," he said to Thane. If he had to destroy the world to save Annabelle, he would, but he would not allow his soldier to be blamed in any way.

Without waiting for a reply, he raced forward, telling himself not to allow any more fear or fury. Not now, not later. Already his chest was on fire, surely bleeding, the fissures he'd once felt now full-blown wounds as the emotions poured through him.

Branches slapped at his cheeks, ripped at his robe. Jagged rocks sliced into his bare feet — the demons must have removed his shoes. Along the way, he bypassed two more demons, one dead, the other in the process of dying. He didn't stop, but created another sword and slashed in half the body of the living.

At the edge of the forest was an electric fence. Annabelle, a human, would not have made it over the spiked top, yet whoever carried the essentia of his twin *had.* He was chasing a demon, then. Only question now was whether or not that demon was dragging Annabelle with him.

The primal instincts that had driven him

to seek Annabelle for pleasure sharpened into something dark and deadly. The fury utterly consumed him, no holding it back, budding into the most destructive force he'd ever experienced. He flared his wings, intending to fly up and over, but his gaze snared on a speck of something dark on the metal links.

Blood. Red, not black. Fresh. Saturated with *Annabelle's* scent.

Well, then. No other questions remained. She *was* out there, and she needed him. Whatever he had to do, he would save her. Even at the expense of his own life.

CHAPTER TWENTY-SIX

Annabelle struggled to breathe. Her throat was horribly swollen, the airways already partially blocked. What little oxygen she managed to draw in only exacerbated the problem.

Demons dropped from the sky, homing in on her like heat-seeking missiles. No matter where she hid — inside bushes, the tops of trees, holes in the ground — they found her as if she had a neon sign pulsing above her head. *Here. She's here.*

She had more injuries than she could count, and the wings . . . those hideous wings that had grown into misshapen branches with bulbous membranes rather than feathers completely unbalanced her. Didn't help that a dead demon corpse was slung over her shoulder, slowing her down. But she couldn't move on without him.

"Hey, what you doing? Massster callsss."

Annabelle jolted as the speaker came into

view. On a limb just above her, a half man, half snake demon, like the one Zacharel had killed the night they'd met, followed her, his tail winding and unwinding as he slinked forward.

The demons kept doing this, talking to her as if she was one of them. But then, maybe she was. Scales had replaced her skin, claws had replaced her nails, and she had no idea what had happened to her face, could only feel the grotesque differences in the shape of her bones.

The transformation had happened as she'd fought the demon in the cloud, each change coiling from the burn in her chest, a burn that had spread, worsening as her fear had deepened, sharpening as her anger had grown. She'd tried to calm herself, even after she'd managed to win the battle, but by the time she'd made the connection between her body and her negative emotions, it had been too late.

"Come. And why you carry dead anyway?" He reached for her. "To eat? I help eat."

"Don't you dare come near me!" she shouted, the world going dark for only a second. Less than a second, really.

But when she refocused, fresh blood covered her shaky hands, dripped from her gasping mouth. The vile taste of it even

471

coated her tongue. And the snake . . . his body was in pieces and scattered at her feet.

She hunched over and vomited. This, too, kept happening. Demons approached and she momentarily blacked out, only to find them dead when she resurfaced. *I don't just look like a demon, I'm becoming one.*

What would happen if Zacharel found her like this? Would he reject her? Kill her? Or would she black out and kill *him?*

A sob lodged in her throat as she hefted her burden back on her shoulder. *I can't be one of them. There's another explanation, surely.*

A thick tree root tangled with her foot, and her foot lost, propelling her face-first into the dirt and twig-laden ground. Stars winked through her vision on impact, but somehow, she maintained firm hold of her burden.

She scrambled up. The demon's headless torso slammed against her back, pressing against new tendons and bending her wings, making her cry out. She wasn't sure —

Something else, something harder, slammed into her from behind. Her feet were swept out from underneath her and she smashed into the dirt. This time, she did lose her hold and the demon shot forward, flipping end over end before smacking into a tree.

Before Annabelle could react or right herself, equally hard fingers were daggering into her scalp, jerking her up, twisting her around. Fierce emerald eyes peered down at her, Zacharel's face so overcome with rage his features were actually altered. His cheekbones appeared sharper, his lips thinner. Even his body seemed bigger, his muscles straining the fabric of his robe.

"Zacharel, please. Let me go before I —"

"Be silent." He backhanded her, and if he hadn't been holding on to her dress with his other hand, she would have smacked into another tree. "You do not speak unless I tell you. Understand?"

A thousand other stars winked through her vision. He shook her, and she cried out.

"What did you do with the human girl?" He got in her face, placing them nose to nose. "I know you did something, for you smell of her."

Stay calm. "I — I am her. I'm Annabelle." Her jaw was already swollen, the two parts refusing to work properly. Could he understand her? "I'm Annabelle."

His eyes slitted dangerously. "You are not."

Oh, yes. He could understand. He simply did not believe.

His grip lifted to her neck, and he hauled her off her feet, her legs dangling. He kept her suspended like that for several heart-stopping moments. All the while she kicked at him. He was going to kill her. Here, now, he would choke the life out of her, thinking she was a demon. And he wouldn't be pleasant about it, wouldn't make it easier for her.

"Taste . . ." she managed to gurgle out. *Taste the truth.*

A twig snapped a few feet behind him. He dropped her as he spun. As she gasped for breath, she crab-walked backward. If she could stand, she could run. If she could run, she could hide until she figured out a way to get through to him. But her legs failed her, the muscles like two-ton boulders.

She watched as Zacharel produced his sword of fire and struck, burning through a bush. A sharp cry was released — and then cut off abruptly. The scent of charred leaves and rotten fish filled the air, wafting on a sudden, frigid breeze. A *thump,* a demon head rolling, followed by another *thump* as the body fell forward.

He spun to face her, the sword still in his hand. One step, two, he approached her.

"Zacharel. D-don't. Me. Annabelle. Taste. Truth."

Still he approached.

Annabelle blinked, darkness closing in around her. "Please . . . taste . . ."

"I will never taste a demon."

"Words . . . taste . . . words . . ." She met his gaze as long as she could, waiting, hoping . . . slipping into darkness.

Zacharel watched as the female demon stood on suddenly steady feet. Between one blink and the next, her eyes went from ice-blue to blazing crimson, the silky length of her blue-black hair lifting from her scalp as if she'd just been struck by lightning. Nails elongated into daggerlike claws, and —

Ice-blue eyes. Like Annabelle.

Blue-black hair. Like Annabelle.

It's me, Annabelle.

He stilled, his study of the creature intensifying. She wore a red dress similar to the one Driana had worn at the club. The material was ripped, gaping and bloodstained. Dark green scales covered her body — a body shape his hands knew intimately. Her shoulders were stooped, with monstrous wings stretching from around her back, the ends twisted into sharp little knots and points.

Taste the truth.

Demons were liars and tricksters, but when he smacked his lips, it wasn't a lie or a trick that he tasted. He savored the sweet taste of truth.

The being in front of him *was* Annabelle.

How had this happened? And oh, Deity, what had he done? Thrown her. Hit her. Choked her. Zacharel released his grip on the sword, the flames instantly dying away. Shame unfurled inside him, dropping him to his knees.

No wonder he could smell Annabelle on her. She truly was Annabelle. And he had hurt her. Hurt her terribly. He would never be able to forgive himself.

He remained in place as she closed the distance between them. "I am sorry, so sorry, Annabelle." Would he never take proper care of her? Would he always bring her pain?

Her head tilted to the side, as if she heard him, understood him, but the crimson in her eyes brightened, as if she cared not about his apology. And in the ensuing minutes, she proved that very thing. Her claws slashed at him, her little fists beat at him. She twirled with a skill she had not previously possessed, cutting at him with the tips of her wings.

Not once did he attempt to stop her. He deserved this. He deserved this and so much more, and if she wanted to take his head, he would give her his head. *I'm worse than any demon.*

Finally, though, she jumped away from him and stopped, just stopped and blinked.

"Annabelle?"

She wavered, closed her eyes. A moment passed before she was able to refocus, but when she did, he realized her irises had returned to that startling shade of ice-blue.

"Annabelle!" He leapt to his feet.

"Zacharel?" At least, he thought she'd said his name. The word was jumbled, nearly inaudible.

"I'm here." Steps slow and measured, he approached her. He didn't want to rattle her.

As though a strong wind had just slammed into her, she teetered over, fell.

He whipped into motion, catching her before she hit and easing her down. "I'm so sorry, love. I didn't know it was you."

Tears filled her eyes, spilled down her cheeks. "Zacharel," she repeated in that same broken tone.

"Yes, love. I'm here."

A gurgle of panic left her. Was she scared of him now?

She squeezed her eyelids tightly shut. "Did I . . . kill you?"

Her poor mind couldn't distinguish between reality and nightmare. "No, love." He caressed a fingertip along her bruised jaw. Hadrenial had pleaded for death. Annabelle had pleaded for life. Look what he'd done to them both. *Hate myself.*

How many hours, days, weeks had he agonized over his decision to do what his brother asked and strike the killing blow? And afterward, when the decision had been made and the action done, how hard had he cried? So hard he'd broken nearly all of his ribs. So hard he'd vomited blood. But even then, he hadn't wanted to die himself. He'd wanted to live and avenge. Now, he would have welcomed a killing blow.

"You didn't kill me. I live."

She coughed, a trickle of blood sliding from the corner of her mouth. When she settled, she whispered, as though ashamed, "Something's . . . wrong . . . me."

His voice remained low, gentle. "I know, love, but we'll find a way to fix you."

"Demon . . . in cloud . . . he waited, tried to take brother . . . I —"

"Shh. Don't worry about that right now."

Still she persisted. "Didn't let . . . Fought."

"I know, love, I know, so tell me what happened later, all right? Right now, I want you to drift off to sleep. All right? I will protect you, I swear it."

"No! Listen!" she said with a sudden burst of strength. "You can't leave the demon behind. . . ." Her body sagged, the strength gone as quickly as it had arrived. "Have to take him . . . with you . . ." Muscles going limp. "His body . . . please."

Understanding at last dawned. The slain demon must now carry Hadrenial's essentia. And she had been carting that heavy weight around, trying to escape, fighting for her life, because she had vowed to protect Zacharel's greatest treasure.

"I won't leave him behind, love. Sleep now," he said again. In sleep, she would not feel the pain. She would heal.

She had better heal.

"Thank you," she said on a sigh, her head lolling to the side, but her eyes blinked open, as if she didn't trust him enough to do as he'd asked.

Thank you, she'd said.

Thank. You.

Two words that would forever haunt him. He did not deserve her thanks, and he was certain he would not receive it again when she awoke and came to her senses.

Not knowing what else to do, he pinched her carotid, stopping the flow of oxygen to her brain, forcing her to pass out. A mercy, and yet his shame nearly suffocated him.

So badly he wanted to pour what remained of the Water of Life down her throat. Anything to save her. But he couldn't. He wasn't sure what had been done to her, and he was too afraid the liquid would act as poison to her, as it did with other demons.

She's not a demon! instinct shouted.

He tenderly laid her on the ground, then rushed to strap the dead demon to his back. When he returned to Annabelle, he gathered her close to his chest and stood, careful not to damage her wings further. Her weight barely registered, she was such a slight thing.

Slow and easy, he flew to his former leader's cloud and demanded entrance. As he waited, Annabelle began to shiver. Her body temperature was too low — because she'd lost too much blood?

The cloud opened to him, and he glided inside. To his despair, Lysander was not the one to greet him. Instead it was Bianka, Lysander's female, a Harpy with an affinity for trouble and wickedness.

Chewing gum, she looked him and Annabelle over, twirling a strand of her long black hair around her finger. "About time you brought me a cloud-warming gift, but did you have to pick one of the ugliest demons I've ever seen?"

"That was *so* rude, insulting the warrior's present like that," another female said. Kaia, Bianka's twin sister, strode over, a half-empty bottle of Boone's Farm in her hand. In Burden's office, what seemed forever ago, she had been dressed for war. Now she was wearing an angel robe and all about relaxation. "Besides, I've seen way uglier."

"Enough," he growled. Witnessing the twin sisters and their us-against-the-world rapport used to fascinate, reminding him of what he could have had with his brother. Just now, only Annabelle mattered.

The girls looked at each other and giggled, and it was then he knew. They were drunk.

"Why don't you put it over there," Bianka said, pointing to someplace behind her, and then beside her and then in front of her, "next to the demon-skin rug I'll probably give you for Christmas. Or under the table. Or better yet, on the porch where it might be accidentally on purpose kicked to the earth."

How did his leader stand her? "Where is Lysander?"

She flashed her fangs at him, suddenly irritated. "Someone, and I won't mention your name, Zach, abandoned his post at the Deity's temple, which meant my man had to step in and save the day. So I decided to have a girls' night."

Another crime Zacharel would be forced to answer for, but that was not a current concern. "My woman needs tending. If you will show me to a bedroom —"

"Told you Big Z had the hots for someone," Kaia burst out.

"And I told you to stuff it. Guaranteed he misspoke just now." Bianka anchored her hands on her hips. "Tell my sister you don't have the hots for a woman. Or a demon. Or anything with a pulse."

"She is not a demon," he shouted, the intensity of his anger shaking the cloud.

The black-haired Harpy cringed and clutched her ears. "Uh, do you want to pipe down before I rip out your tongue and slap you with it? Word on the street is, there's such a thing as an inside voice. I'm skeptical, but do me a favor and give it a try."

He forced his voice to gentle. "Annabelle is human. My human. She needs help. Now."

"Let's back this word train up. A puzzle piece just slid into place inside my magnificent brain. *That's* Annabelle?" Kaia stepped forward, clearly intending to brush Annabelle's hair out of the way and study her face.

He snapped his teeth at her. While he

lacked fangs, he did not lack menace. "No touching."

Kaia acted as if she hadn't heard him and did exactly as she wanted. Typical of the Harpies. "Okay, wow. It is. What happened to her?"

"I'm not sure." *But I will find out, and I will fix it as promised.* "Bedroom. Now. Please," he added, hoping against hope that would work. With Harpies, you had a fifty-fifty chance of getting what you wanted — or dying.

"You better do it, B," Kaia said with a sigh. "You know how Lysander gets all wussed-out when you so much as scrape a knee? Well, Zach here is worse with his little princess. Maybe 'cause she's human and so inferior. Although I think we can scratch the word *human* from her list of descriptions."

"She is not inferior," he roared. "And she *is* human."

Bianka studied him for several long, silent minutes. "You're right, Kye. Zach is worse. So, all right, come on, angel. This way." She skipped down a hallway.

He trailed after her, leaving a line of snow in his wake.

"Hey, Zach," Kaia called. There was a pause, the sound of gushing liquid and then a few gulps. She must be drinking straight from the bottle. "You do realize you've got a headless demon strapped to your back, right?"

"Of course. I put him there."

Bianka stopped and waved her hand through the baby-blue mist beside her, a doorway appearing.

Zacharel brushed past her and stepped inside.

A large bed waited in the center, perfect for warrior angels with above-average wing-spans, and now perfect for humans with demon wings. He tenderly placed Annabelle on the mattress, smoothed the hair from her face and drew the covers over her body. "We won't stay long. Demons sense her, wherever she is, and attack."

"Kye and I just happen to be in need of a good fight. Stay as long as you want."

That was the thing with the Harpies. They might irritate him, but they always had his back. Even better, they were amazingly skilled warriors. Still, tossing Bianka and Kaia into a dangerous situation — while they were drunk — was a guaranteed way of earning the ire of Lysander and every Lord of the Underworld.

"Thank you, but we'll be gone within the hour."

"Dude, you are so missing out on the best nunchuck skills ever, but whatever. I offered, and that's all I can do — before I pretend you never spoke and do exactly what I want." He heard footsteps, a grumbled "Save some wine for me, you hussy!" then only the rasp of Annabelle's breathing.

He removed the demon from his back, the body flopping lifelessly to the floor. The disgusting creature must have opened the urn and touched what it contained inside, the essentia instantly absorbing into his skin.

Zacharel misted his hand, reached inside the creature's chest and — yes, felt the warm flood of his brother's essentia against his palm, the fizz of something more than blood, seeking him, wanting out of the demon's shell.

For a moment, Zacharel was transported back to the night he'd done this to his brother. Just as before, he held tight, and when he pulled his hand free, something thick and clear coated his skin. Something . . . what was left of his brother. *Will not react.*

Before a single drop could absorb into *his* body, he commanded the cloud to produce an urn. He scraped the rim from fingertip to elbow, until every bead had fallen into the container. After sealing the lid, he shoved the urn into a hidden pocket of air. Angels and demons alike would be drawn to it, but he would never again make anyone else responsible for its safeguarding.

Zacharel turned his attention to Annabelle. He cleaned her up, bandaged her wounds and dressed her in a warm, fur-lined robe. All the while, emotions threatened to overwhelm him. More of the shame, more of the fury, helplessness and hopelessness. He couldn't imagine what had been done to her, to turn her into this. Even when a demon possessed a human's body, the appearance of that human was never altered.

Annabelle was a demon's consort — in theory, not in truth, he thought as a wave of possessive heat moved through him — but she would have transformed four years ago, at the moment of her marking, if the act was destined to change her. So . . . what did that leave? Not that he minded her appearance. She had been beautiful before, but she was equally beautiful now. She was simply his Annabelle. But she would be bothered, and he could not bear that.

Zacharel eased beside her and traced his thumb along her scaled cheekbone. A soft sigh left her as she leaned into his touch.

She might do the opposite when she awoke, and turn away from him. She would remember what he'd done to her, how he'd hurt her. She would probably run from him.

He swallowed back a roar of denial. If she wanted to run from him, he would have to let her. He could never atone for what he'd done to her. Never. But he could follow and protect her for the rest of his days. If that meant giving up his place in the heavens, so be it.

She would have to be an important part of his life, Haidee had said.

She was. Far more important than his job, his home.

Unable to stop himself, he touched her now, while he could, and the more he stroked her, the more — sweet Deity, the faster her wound began to heal and her scales began to diminish, until only bronzed skin remained. The wings withered, finally disappearing from view.

His human Annabelle was back. How, why, he didn't know, but he offered up a prayer of thanks, anyway, something he hadn't done in centuries.

A rustle of clothing sounded behind him, and he spun, drawing his sword.

Lucien, the Lord of the Underworld possessed by Death, held up his hands, palms out. Black hair shagged over his forehead, and his lips curved down, a thick, jagged scar bisecting one corner. "Whoa there, angel. I come bearing news." Fatigue dripped from each of the words.

Zacharel released the sword, barely registering when it vanished. Urgency battered him. "Tell me."

"Amun finished digging through Burden's secrets. The high lord you're looking for, the one who claimed Annabelle, is named Unforgiveness."

Unforgiveness. The name echoed through his mind. Finally, an answer and yet, relief was not forthcoming. "I have never fought him." Had heard of him, yes. Who hadn't? The baddest of the bad, the worst of the worst. Zacharel had hunted him the few times he'd heard the demon had been summoned by a human, but always Unforgiveness managed to hide before his arrival.

"Thank you," he said to Lucien, already relaying the information to Thane.

We managed to capture three more minions, Thane said inside his mind. *We'll find out what they know about this Unforgiveness.*

Lucien inclined his head in acknowledgment. "You're welcome. And now I hope we're even and never have to work together again." With that, the warrior disappeared.

Zacharel bundled Annabelle in the blanket from the bed and lifted her into his arms. More than not wanting to draw the demons to Bianka's cloud, he did not want Annabelle waking up and lashing out at anyone but him.

Oh, Annabelle. Will you ever be able to forgive me, when I'm not sure I can forgive myself?

CHAPTER TWENTY-SEVEN

Annabelle awoke with a jolt, jerking upright. She was panting, sweat running down her chest and back in rivulets. The most terrible dream had plagued her. She had become a demon, had raced through a forest and had fought Zacharel.

Zacharel.

With his name came a burst of dread she couldn't explain, but knew she was supposed to tamp down. *Dangerous,* she thought.

What was? The emotion? Or Zacharel?

Her gaze darted around. She was in another hotel room, alone. *I should run. I have to run.* She didn't question the thought, just threw her legs over the side of the bed. Before she could unfold to a stand, Zacharel appeared in front of her, his expression unreadable.

The dread spiked.

Stay calm. You have to stay calm. Confused, unsure, she froze. "What are you doing?" she asked.

With a pained moan he dropped to his knees, and suddenly she *could* read his expression. Agonized, ashamed, regretful, horrified . . . Just then he was a broken man, the pieces scattered in too many directions to ever find and glue back together.

"I . . . I . . . Zacharel?"

"I'm sorry, Annabelle. So sorry."

In the next instant, the truth hit her with the force of a baseball bat. What she remembered wasn't a dream. She *had* turned into a demon. She *had* raced through the forest. She *had* fought Zacharel.

Eyes wide, she held out her arms, but a robe blocked her view of herself. She only dared to breathe again when she rolled back the sleeves and saw the light brown of her skin.

Winding her arms around her back proved more difficult, but she had to know, had to — no wings! Thank the Lord! Her back was smooth where it should be smooth and ridged where it should be ridged.

Zacharel watched her without uttering a word. Still on his knees, humbled before her.

Her arms fell heavily to her sides. "You hit me," she stated flatly. Gone was the dread, but in its place was a bone-deep disappointment.

His head bowed, his chin hitting his sternum. "I know."

"And you didn't know who I was."

"No. I did not."

He wasn't even trying to defend himself. He could have told her that type of change in a human was unheard of, something he'd thought impossible. He could have reminded her of her reaction to him, when he had morphed into a demon.

"Why did I transform? How did you turn me back to normal?"

Not once did he glance up. "Tell me what happened in the cloud first. Then I will tell you everything I know, or even suspect. I will hide no detail from you."

"Very well."

He listened as she spoke, and every so often, he nodded. By the end, his shoulders were slumped as if a heavy weight rested atop them.

"Clouds can do many things," Zacharel said, "but they cannot change a human into a demon. The demon lied about that part. Nor would a minion have had the power to do such a thing."

"But then how could I have changed if it wasn't the cloud or the demon?" Dread shot through her, soon chilling every part of her. "Does that mean I'm no longer a human, and my outside was just catching up with my insides?"

"Possibly. I think, when you were marked, more was done to you than either of us realized. I think the demon replaced a piece of your spirit."

No, surely not. She would have known. Right? "How is that possible?"

"He would have reached inside your body with a spiritual hand, and, like a blade can remove a limb, taken what he wanted. Probably just a small portion, no bigger than a dime. He would then have replaced that piece with one of his own, exchanging the two, bonding you far more than a married couple . . . melding you."

White-hot fury exploded through her, completely overshadowing the dread, and she found herself beating at Zacharel's shoulders. "*For the last time,* I'm not married to the demon who murdered my parents! I'm not! And I'm not melded, either!"

He never lifted a hand in defense. "If that was indeed done to you, your life is linked to his. As long as he lives, you live. As long as you live, he lives. I had not considered that possibility before, but it is clear to me now."

Questions rained through her mind, her actions slowing . . . stopping. "But . . . but . . . Why send other demons after me? If I died, he would have died."

"Remember when Thane mentioned something blocked him and others from taking you physically? I believe that same something prevented them from rendering a killing blow, as well."

"But I . . . I just can't be melded to him." And of course, the burn in her chest fired up as it always did when her . . . negative emotions . . . got the better of her.

That's right! The burn had played a part in the change, and her emotions had played a part in the burn.

She told Zacharel, and he nodded, saying, "That makes sense. The only question now is why the demon did it. Without your knowing consent, and the dream would not have provided that consent, he violated one of the highest heavenly laws. Free will."

Her heart skipped a tortured beat. Something in his tone . . . "And you're an enforcer of those laws, right?" That's what he'd told her during their first meeting, she was sure. And *that* could only mean . . .

"No," she thought she screamed, but the word emerged as a whisper. "No."

"Yes," he confirmed.

"So you will be the one to carry out his sentence?"

A nod this time, rather than a verbal response.

Another heartbeat was missed because she suspected the answer. "And that sentence is?"

There was a long, tense pause. He looked up, he looked down, then left and right, as if he wanted to be anywhere else. Finally, she heard, "Death."

Every fiber of her being rebelled at the thought of her own. By upholding the law, Zacharel would be killing the demon, yes — but he would also be killing Annabelle. "How would this . . . merging —" she gagged "— cause me to change into a demon four years after the fact?"

"I've seen the way the Lords of the Underworld come to physically resemble their demons when their own negative emotions overtake them. It's just as you described. They lose control of their humanity, all reasoning abolished. The demon inside the cloud knew what had happened to you all those years ago, so he knew how to elicit the response he wanted."

"I agree, I do. I mean, the emotion thing was my idea. But I don't understand how four horror-filled years could have passed without a single change, and then all of a sudden, boom."

"You are forgetting that you were drugged for all of those four years, and those drugs were meant to suppress the depths of your emotions. Even when you began to feel things strongly again, the drugs were likely lingering in your system and diluting the full extent of your feelings."

"But I've been over the withdrawals for a while," she said, clinging to a hope that they were wrong.

"You've also been injured or recovering. Weakened."

Yes, there was that. "But what about the Water of Life?"

"It healed the human part of you, but aggravated the demon part, and it, too, would have slowed your transformation."

And she'd certainly been aggravated the two times he'd fed her the stuff, hadn't she.

Hope withered. Her chin quivered, and her eyes welled with tears she refused to shed. She was part demon. The truth whispered through her. *She was part demon.* It was a scream of outrage and helplessness this time.

Calm, you have to calm. "Will I change again?" she croaked, though she already knew the answer. Could already feel the burn sprouting in her chest.

"With extreme negative emotion . . . yes, I think you will."

"Can the demon piece be removed from me? Replaced with something else?" Another spark of hope formed . . .

"No. Too much time has passed."

. . . and was destroyed.

I won't cry. I won't.

"The demon you carried through the forest, he had absorbed my brother's essentia. There was a piece of me in there, too. But I did not die when the demon died because nothing had taken root. And I was able to remove everything from the body without any resistance because that essentia recognized me. What's in you *has* taken root and *would* resist. It would not recognize me, nor want any part of me."

She heard his unspoken words. If he tried to free her, she would suffer and probably die anyway. "I don't care about the pain or even dying. Get the demon out of me." Now!

"You might not care about dying, but I do," he said simply. "I will not do that to you. Ever. Do not ask it of me."

Only took a moment to understand his vehemence. He still suffered over doing the same to his brother, and could withstand no more. So no, she couldn't, wouldn't ask it of him. "Wh-what should I do, then?"

"I will find the high lord. I will lock him away." Zacharel rested his head in her lap, his arms wrapping around her waist. His body began to shake. "I am sorry for this, Annabelle. So very sorry."

She felt something wet and warm saturate the fabric of her robe, and frowned. Tears? No. No, this strong, proud warrior could not be crying. "You would lock him away rather than kill him, despite your law and your orders?"

"For you, I will do anything." He looked up at her, lashes spiky and eyes glassed. He *was* crying. "And I give you my vow, here and now, Annabelle, that I will not kill you. I will not allow another angel to kill you."

And he would probably be killed for his own crimes in the process. "Don't do that."

He rushed on. "Somehow, someway, I *will* find the demon who did this to you. I *will* lock him away." His grip tightened on her. "I will do everything in my power to safeguard you always. And if you cannot bear to look upon me, I will do so in secret."

"No, I —"

"I finally comprehend what the Deity was trying to teach me," he said, cutting her off, "what I failed to realize all these centuries. I thought I had learned, but still I would have done what I felt needed doing."

"What are you saying?"

"Collateral damage. The people I have killed and allowed to be killed were demon possessed or cavorting with demons, and I thought their murders justified. But what if they were like you? Innocent? What if it was not just them I hurt in the end, but the people who loved them and still had hope for their salvation? What if there *was* hope for their salvation? Actually, there *is* always hope. I know that now."

His hold on her tightened as his tears fell in earnest. "I am sorry, Anna. Not because you know my sin but because it caused you so much pain."

Seeing him so torn up soothed her in a way nothing else could have. He cared about her. He felt remorse. Glory, he *felt*.

Sighing, she sifted her fingers through the silk of his hair. The fact that he had as much reason to hate demons as she did, yet he wasn't rejecting her now that he knew she was . . . she was . . . She couldn't think the words again. The truth would have to be dealt with, but that would come later. For now, she just wanted to bask in this moment and in the man who loved her.

And he did. He loved her. He might not

realize it, having denied his emotions for so long, but she was certain of it — just as she was certain that she loved him, too. He had saved and protected her. He had seen the best in her, and was helping her do the same. He allowed no one to disrespect her, and wanted only the best for her. He would never leave her, and she would never leave him.

Yes, he was a difficult man, a complex man, and he wasn't used to the emotions he was now experiencing, or even softness. But he gave both to her, and she would give both right back to him.

He was a part of her now, more so than . . . than . . . Anyway. He was a beautiful part, a welcome part, strong and courageous and fun to tease. He was tender and gentle, yet hard when she needed him to be.

She cooed at him until he quieted, and though she regretted the need to do it, she finally extracted herself from his hold. He offered no protest, kept his head down, once again refusing to face her.

"I'll be right back, okay? Don't go any-where." She raced into the bathroom before he could reply.

As swiftly as possible, she took care of business, brushed her teeth and removed her robe. She was naked underneath, and utterly scrubbed clean. So clean, in fact, she sparkled. However the angel robe worked, she was grateful.

Now, for Zacharel. He needed her, and she needed him. They both needed to forget what had happened, what would happen, if only for a little while.

The hinges on the door squeaked as she emerged from the bathroom. Cool air kissed her bare skin, spreading goose bumps along her arms and legs.

Zacharel sat at the edge of the bed, his elbows propped on his knees, his head bent. His wings were spread out, a wealth of gold now without any hint of white. Or snow, she realized. Once again, he'd stopped snowing.

"According to our bargain, I'm supposed to kiss you anytime the urge hits me, and you're supposed to accept. Right?"

His gaze snapped up. He'd dried his face, but he couldn't mask the glassiness of those emerald eyes. "Annabelle," he said on a rumbling breath, looking her over. "After everything that's happened, you cannot mean —"

"I do." Slowly she walked to him. When she stood between his legs, she placed her hands on his shoulders. His muscles were knotted. His gaze moved to hers, as if he couldn't trust himself to continue peering at the rest of her.

"I want to be with you," she said. She frowned as a thought hit her. "Unless you're not allowed to be with a woman melded to a —" Her lips pressed together in a thin line. She didn't want to think the words, and she didn't want to say them. "It's okay if you can't. I'll just —"

In a rush of motion, Zacharel had his arms around her, and her feet kicked out from under her. She tumbled forward, and he positioned her in his lap. For balance, she had to straddle his thighs.

"You are mine," he rasped. "Only ever mine. I accept all that you are, and we *can* be together."

Relief poured through her, a beautiful waterfall. "I'll make you so happy you said that, Winged Wonder." Very gently, she pressed her lips into his, a soft melding, a gentle exploration.

"You forgive me?"

"There's nothing to forgive."

"Thank you, Anna. Thank you. And I know, the words are not enough. I will *show* you how I feel. Let me show you."

She opened her mouth, and he rolled his tongue against her. His decadent flavor instantly consumed her; he was the finest aged wine, strawberries dipped in the richest chocolate, and as fresh as a newly sprung river.

The kiss remained tender and sweet — until he reclined on the mattress and his hands began to roam. The intimate contact ignited embers of sensation throughout her entire body. Their tongues dueled with more force, their lips pressed with more fervor, and they drank and drank and drank of each other.

He laved her breasts, explored her belly, kissed every inch of her legs until she was writhing. Until *he* was writhing. Until they were both desperate. Then he turned her over and laved her upper back, explored her lower back, and once again kissed every inch of her legs.

When she could stand no more, the pleasure too much, she pulled his robe from him and urged him to lie down on his back — and she took over. *She* laved and explored and kissed *him*. And oh, the taste of his skin . . . It was as rapturous as his kiss. The sweetest of candies, drugging, addictive . . . and she knew she would crave this for the rest of her life.

"Anna, I need . . ."

"More, always more." Was that slurred voice hers?

"Yes."

Yes. A word filled with hope. "Take it, then."

He cupped under her arms, drew her up, parallel to his strong length, and rolled her over. He settled over her, pinned her.

"I want to take, as you said, but I need another kiss first." He lowered his head and she lifted hers, and then their tongues were thrusting together.

Gentle . . . firm . . . hard . . . wild . . . The kiss spun out of control. He kneaded her breasts and thrummed her nipples, his skin was like a living flame. A heat so different than what burned inside of her. A heat that would seep all the way to her bones, torching the memory of the demon.

"Another," he said, his mouth taking and giving, demanding and surrendering. Her nails scraped along the ridges of his spine, between his wings, and her hips arched as she sought closer, deeper contact. She was utterly consumed by this man, and all the happier for it.

"I love seeing you like this," he admitted.

"Underneath you?"

"All mine." He moved a hand between their bodies, between her legs. And oh, had he learned how to play her. He knew when to sink in slowly and when to increase his speed. He knew when she needed more . . . and more . . . "I can't get enough of you."

"Zacharel," she said on a wispy catch of breath. "Please. All, everything."

He stilled, a droplet of sweat winding down his temple. "You are never to beg me for anything, Anna."

"Then you have to . . . I need . . ." She bit her lip and rubbed against him. *"Please."*

He cupped her jaw and forced her to stare into his eyes. "Me, you need me."

"Yes." Always.

He rubbed the tips of their noses together and said, "Will you let me have you?"

"All, everything," she repeated.

"Everything? Truly? Because I told myself I would not take you until I had your pledge to remain with me. Now, I do not deserve such a pledge."

"Probably not, but I still give it." She'd just realized how much she loved him. Like she would really let him go. Yes, she'd once thought to leave him before he could leave her, but that was living in fear, and fear was as much a prison as the institution had been . . . and so much worse. "Can you pledge the same?"

He peered down at her with utter joy. "I can. I will. You are my first, last and only lover, Annabelle Miller. I will never take another."

"Oh, Zacharel." Had more beautiful words ever been spoken? "You are my last and only lover, too."

"Now I make you mine." Inch by decadent inch, he sank inside her, claiming her, branding her. When at last he was all the way in, he stilled, strain branching from the corners of his eyes. "I am . . . How could . . . *Love this*."

"Hmmm," she purred. "Yes."

"You belong to me," he said.

"To you."

"No other."

"No other," she agreed.

His lips found hers, their tongues meeting in a tangled clash. His hands rediscovered her breasts, kneading.

"You feel so good."

"Yes, but . . ."

"More?"

"Please."

"Like this?" He moved slowly at first.

"Yes, please, yes, exactly like that."

He moved faster. Faster still. Finally, all she could do was wrap her legs around his waist and hold on. He chanted her name over and over, a prayer, a curse, a *mooooan* he couldn't quite contain. She groaned with her pleasure. Every moment, every movement, was perfect, utterly soul changing.

"Anna . . . I'm going to . . . have to . . ."

"Give me everything."

A roar left him, his entire body bowing. He hit her as deep as he could possibly go, so wonderfully deep, and yet she still arched up and tried to take him deeper. As he shuddered with completion, satisfaction found her and she cried out, holding him tight . . . holding on forever.

Even minutes later, when he fell upon her, heavy and lax, she refused to let go. When he rolled, he took her with him and she ended up sprawled on his chest.

"I have no words, Anna," he said softly.

"Good." She didn't, either. All she knew was that she would never be the same. This would forever change her.

This would forever change *him.*

He placed a reverent kiss on her temple. "Perhaps I do have two words . . . Thank you."

A soft laugh left her. Perhaps a little change was a good thing.

CHAPTER TWENTY-EIGHT

Zacharel made love to Annabelle all through the night. He could not get enough of her. Would *never* get enough of her or the pleasure she gave him. He loved her breasts, so perfectly lush and perfectly tipped. He loved her stomach, a soft hollow with a tempting navel. He loved her legs, their smooth expanse of wicked delights.

He loved everything in between.

He loved the sounds she made, the way she moved, the softness and sweetness and the passion he experienced with her. He loved what she did to him, hugging him, kissing him, making him feel as if he were the most precious thing on earth.

But what he loved most was being inside her, one with her. A part of her. Twined around her, their breath mingling. Yes, the physical sensations that came with that part had delighted him, but the mental . . . the emotional . . . were even better.

Love. He was the one who had never known its true meaning, he realized. It was not just a pretty word. Genuine love was a gift. Special. Necessary. A lesson his brother had tried to teach him, but one he had ignored. Until now.

Now . . . as Annabelle glowed with Zacharel's essentia, a subtle light that seeped from her pores, as if the sun was living just under her skin. He loved that, too.

Mine, he thought. *She is mine. I will not share her.*

"If you can bear to take a break, you insatiable beast, there's something I want to do," she said, climbing from the bed for an endless, abhorrent moment.

She grabbed a pen from the desk before putting him out of his misery and straddling his hips. He propped his back against the pillows as satisfaction of a different sort consumed him. They were together, no matter what their bodies were doing. Something else he loved.

"By the way, this isn't a hint for more," she said. "Not this time."

"Tease." How she thrilled him, every aspect of her. A fall of blue-black hair around her shoulders, cheeks flushed and dewy. Ice-blue eyes sparkling, lips swollen from his kisses.

"Why did you need the pen?" he asked.

"We'll get to that. First, you gotta tell me. Am I going to get in trouble for debauching you?" she asked, then chewed on the end of that pen as she waited for his answer.

A terrible habit, he thought, gently tugging the thing from between her teeth. "Are you sure you debauched me? Because I'm not convinced. Perhaps you should try again."

The warmth of her laughter filled the room, enchanting him. He wanted her to laugh like that at least a hundred times a day.

"*Such* a guy thing to say, but no more attempted debauchings tonight. I have to save *something* for tomorrow."

That she planned to spend another day with him, that she had just given him something to look forward to, that she truly had forgiven him . . . If he'd been standing, he would have dropped to his knees, once again humbling himself before her, thankful and grateful. Now he smiled. A genuine smile of delight.

She reached out and traced a fingertip along the curve of his lips. "I love when you smile like this." Her fingertip moved to his cheek, to the dimple Hadrenial used to flash him. "You're . . . Actually, there are no words for what you are. *Beautiful* isn't adequate, and *exquisite* barely scratches the surface."

Appearance had never meant anything to him. Until now. "Thank you?"

Another laugh bubbled from her, her skin and her face glowing with health and life and vitality. *She* was the one who defied description. "Yes, that was a compliment. Now, then. The trouble thing."

"No, you will not get into trouble. Remember, the Deity's angels have a different purpose than the Most High's, and are therefore governed by the same set of rules as the humans. Yes, my race was created by the Most High, and given to the Deity, but we are more like you. Not that you will ever hear any of us admit it."

"Well, all right, then. The pen. I want to play a game with you." She placed the tip just over his chest, frowned then looked up at him. "Wait. Another question, or a demand really. Tell me about the black spot. It's bigger than last time — and last time it was big!"

His gaze flicked to the spot in question. Yes, the black was already several inches larger than it had been two days ago. "When my brother died, I saved his essentia. His love."

"His spirit," she said. "Or soul?"

"Love is an emotion, yes, but it's also a power. So I took from his spirit. I took out a piece of mine, as well, so that some part of us would always be together. That removal killed this part of me —" he tapped the spot "— because I did not replace it."

A dread-filled moment passed as she absorbed his words. "Why is it spreading? And don't try to redirect me, or shut me down or tell me not to worry like you did last time. I will play a card you don't want me to play, because yes, I can be devious like that, and then we'll both feel bad."

He would not have her feeling bad. "The growth was slow but steady until my Deity punished me with the snow for daring to ignore his orders. Afterward, the growth was fast and steady."

"You didn't answer my question." She crossed her arms over her chest. "*Why* the growth?"

"It is . . . death."

Her jaw dropped, but she snapped it shut. "Put back the piece you removed. Right now! That should stop the spread of death."

"I cannot. What's in the urn is a combination of Hadrenial and me. I cannot separate the two. They have already bonded." Like the demon had bonded to her, he thought, his hands curling into fists.

Her chin went into the air, and he knew her stubborn side was kicking in. "Well, think of it this way. I'm not asking you to separate the two. I'm telling you to use the combination."

Oh, yes. Stubborn. "I failed to save his life. I even rendered the deathblow. I do not deserve to live off him."

"You gave him what he wanted. You ended his torment. You deserve —"

"Annabelle —"

"Zacharel. You are far better than you give yourself credit for. How many times have you saved me? What would I have done without you? What will happen to me if you . . . if you . . . I can't even say the word! Do this. Please."

How could he deny her anything? "I . . . will think about it," he said, and he would, but deep down he knew that he would not change his mind. If he did as she wanted, he would forever carry a piece of his brother. Him, a man utterly unworthy of such a blessing.

"Thank you."

Guilt rose, but he shoved it aside. "Now, will you show me why you have the pen?" he asked, changing the subject.

"My pleasure," she said with a smile only

half the wattage of the others. "Have you ever played tic-tac-toe?"

"I've never played anything."

"Well, then, prepare to be dominated. I'm a master. I win against myself every time we play."

He snorted.

Hand steady, she began to write on him, treating his chest as if it was a sheet of paper and drawing what seemed to be hundreds of tic-tac-toe boards. He was X's, she was O's, and they tied every game.

Well, they tied until she used his nipple as the center O, lancing sensation to a groin he'd expected to be dead for days. He moaned, and that caused her to laugh, and of course, that laughter distracted him. She finally won.

By the time they finished, he was marked up from neck to toe, and so was she. Although he hadn't drawn boards on her — he'd written his name. And suddenly he understood the appeal of tattoos. He liked his name inked into her flesh and suspected he would like having hers inked into his.

Annabelle formed a circle with her fingers, looking at him through the center as though she was a scientist and her hands a lens. "I want to take a picture of you just . . . like . . . this. You're —" Her eyes darkened to a haunted navy blue, and her hands fell heavily to her sides.

Each of his muscles petrified, but he fought through and cupped the side of her cheek. "What's wrong?"

"He removed my clothes and took photos of me." Her gaze practically seared a hole in Zacharel's chest.

"Who?" he whispered fiercely, but he already knew the answer. The knowledge that a man had forced his attentions on this lovely woman had irritated him before, even angered and offended him, but now, after everything he and Annabelle had shared, after having his own hands on her, after having her hands on him and learning the beauty of such contact, he was beyond enraged.

"Dr. Fitzpervert. He did more than take pictures. He touched me, too." Shame coated her voice, dripping, dripping, coating his skin with a layer of the same black oil that had covered his cloud.

"Where did he touch you? Tell me everything, Annabelle."

In a blink of time, Zacharel felt as though he was breathing fire, his body burning up with fever. While Annabelle was strapped to a gurney and drugged, the human responsible for her care had squeezed and licked her, and touched her in places he shouldn't. And that the horror of a human had kept reminders of these violations, that he most likely found joy in them . . .

"I'm sorry that was done to you." Sorry he hadn't found her sooner.

At last she looked up, and the same fire inside him swirled in her eyes. "When I'm stronger, I'm going back."

She was strong enough now, but Zacharel caught the fright in her voice, a piece of her past she had not yet overcome, and knew some part of her expected the doctor to drug her and lock her back up, making her helpless all over again.

Silent, Zacharel rose from the bed and dressed. He tugged Annabelle to her feet, helped her dress in the new set of clothes Thane had left at the door, pulled a robe over the clothes, and drew her into his embrace. Still without saying a word, he flew her out of the building and across the night sky, cool air whipping against them. She remained quiet, too. No doubt she knew where he was taking her.

Thane's report about Annabelle's life had listed every address of every person she'd come into contact with. The closer they came to Colorado, the colder the air became, and even with the fur lining in her robe, Annabelle was soon trembling.

"We don't have time for this now," she said.

The doctor's one-story home came into view. "We'll make time." Zacharel should have made time before this, in fact. "There is a time for mercy and a time for fighting back."

He flew inside, landed and let her go. He wanted to hold on to her, and he also wanted to inflict maximum damage on her tormentor, but this wasn't about him and his wants, he realized then. This was about Annabelle's needs. Torturing Fitzherbert would make Zacharel feel better, certainly, but what would that gain Annabelle? Merely a fleeting sense of satisfaction.

He strode through the home, Annabelle at his heels.

"What are you going to do?" she asked softly.

"Me? Nothing," he replied in his normal tone. This was her war, and her long-awaited victory. He noticed the neatness, the simplicity. Fitzherbert enjoyed comfort over luxury, yet favored aesthetics over practicality. An odd combination. "Unless you desire something of me."

"Shh! What if he's here?"

"He is. I can hear him breathing. But he

cannot sense us." Yet.

She relaxed, but only slightly.

The lights were out, but Zacharel's gaze cut through the shadows without any problems. He found the bedroom and positioned himself at the end of the queen-size bed. Fitzherbert was a lump in the center, snoring peacefully.

Beside him, Annabelle tensed.

"He is divorced with two children," Zacharel said. "Teenagers. They live with their mother, so he is alone."

"Do you think I should . . . kill him?"

If she did, Zacharel would be blamed. As with the demon-possessed Driana, he wasn't concerned by her actions. He would gladly bear the consequences. "Will that bring you peace?"

A moment of silence. A sag of her shoulders. "No. For the rest of my life I would remember what I did to him, rather than what he did to me. I will have killed a human the way a demon killed my parents."

"I will kill him if that is what you desire, and I promise you, I can make his pain last. Or, if you prefer, I can end him quickly. I would be satisfied either way."

Another round of silence as she wrung her hands together. "No. I won't let you go down for something like this."

Then he would never, ever tell her that her actions were as his own.

"Will you . . . I don't know, wake him up and hold him still?"

There was no need for her to ask twice. With only a thought, Zacharel allowed their presence to manifest. He spread his wings and rose, hovering over Fitzherbert, grabbing him and tossing him into the wall. Plaster cracked and dust plumed around him. In a flash, Zacharel closed the distance, latched on to the doctor's neck and lifted him off his feet, pinning him to the wall.

Impact had woken Fitzherbert up, and now the man struggled for freedom.

Annabelle switched on a light, and when the human saw who held him — and who watched him — he stilled, his skin turning a putrid shade of green. His jaw dropped, a bit of spittle rolling from the corner of his mouth.

"Tell her where the photos are," Zacharel demanded, loosening his hold just enough to allow the man to speak.

The green deepened. "I d-don't know what you're — Okay, okay, I know," he rushed out when Zacharel tightened his hold. "They're deleted. Of course. I swear."

A foul taste suddenly coated Zacharel's tongue. "A lie. And I do not like liars, Dr.

Fitzherbert." He tightened his grip, making it more of a vise than before, and felt the man's bones begin to crack.

You aren't to kill him, remember?

"He wouldn't risk having them developed," Annabelle said with only the slightest tremor in her voice. "I bet they're still in his phone. Or maybe on his computer."

Fitzherbert burst into motion, clawing at Zacharel's arms.

"I bet you're right," Zacharel said.

Paler by the second, Annabelle picked up the cell phone resting on the nightstand. She pressed a few buttons, frowned. "I was wrong about the phone. There are no photos saved in here."

The doctor relaxed. "Told you," he squeaked out.

"You mentioned a computer. Check the one in his office. Two rooms down."

The flailing renewed.

Annabelle left the room, her footsteps fading. Zacharel released Fitzherbert, the disgusting man slamming into the ground, wheezing for air. Before he could scramble away, Zacharel crouched down and placed his knee in the man's chest.

"You aren't going anywhere. You hurt my female."

The human held up his hands, palms out,

all innocence. "I don't know who you are, but I do know she's a killer. Violently insane. I'm her doctor. I would never —"

Zacharel backhanded him, breaking his jaw and ensuring silence. "I told you. I do not like liars. You hurt her, and one way or another you will suffer for that."

Wide eyes filled with horror, the doctor wilted on the floor. He knew. He knew he had reached the end of the line.

"I have encountered males like you before. You are weak, but you like to pretend you are strong. That's why you pick victims who cannot fight back." He arched a brow. "I wonder, does your wife know what a vile coward you are? Is that why she left you? Do your children know?" Zacharel got in his face. "Do not worry. If they don't, they soon will."

Annabelle stomped into the room, tears tracking down her face, her chin trembling. "You sick pervert! You . . . you . . . monster!" A screeching catapult, she launched herself at Fitzherbert, punching him, kicking at him.

Zacharel stepped out of the way, and waited for her to finish. Already her skin was patched with demon scales, her nails sharpened into claws. She'd removed the robe, and he could see that the back of her shirt was ripped, the jagged edges of wings trying to emerge.

Eventually the last of her energy drained. She threw herself away from the now-bloody man and sobbed.

"Tell me," Zacharel commanded softly.

After a few gasping breaths, she managed to get out, "The pictures were on his computer. They were also loaded into a digital frame, along with those of other women he's abused. They flash as he works."

"Did you delete them?"

"No. I wanted to, almost did, but . . . I want to take him and the evidence of what he's done to the police. I want him to pay for what he's done the right way."

Fitzherbert's struggles renewed, his panic nearly tangible.

"And so he shall."

Though it took some convincing — in the form of Zacharel's fists — Fitzherbert eventually dialed 911 himself and confessed his crimes. That done, Zacharel gagged him, stripped him and staked him to his own front lawn to await his arrest. His neighbors came out to watch. The fact that nobody attempted to intervene told him that Annabelle wasn't the only one who loathed the good doctor.

Annabelle was fully demon by the time

the policemen arrived, so Zacharel kept her hidden from prying eyes, not only with his abilities, but also by tucking her into his side and covering her with his wings.

At first she struggled against him. "D-don't touch me when I'm like this. I can't bear it."

A lie. She could bear it; she also needed the contact as much as he did. He'd hurt her while she was in this form, and so she assumed he found her ugly, repulsive even. He needed to prove otherwise.

"Come closer to me." He forced her to tuck herself into the line of his body. "I want to show you something."

Her claws embedded in his chest, and she released a dejected breath. "Let me guess. The end of a dagger?"

A lance of self-directed anger, no longer contained near his heart, but shooting through his entire body. "I told you I would never again hurt you, and I meant it."

Silence.

"You're right." She sighed. "I'm sorry. I'll go wherever you want me to go."

"Good girl. And as you once told me, I'll make you so happy you said that."

CHAPTER TWENTY-NINE

Screams of pain and pleas for mercy roused Koldo from his nap. He sat up, the scabs on his back splitting, fresh blood flowing. To his left, Thane, Bjorn and Xerxes exuded relish as they interrogated three demons chained to his wall. The scent of rot and diseased blood saturated the air.

He experienced a rush of disappointment and even anger. His home was ruined now. The home he'd spent centuries building, hiding and decorating. The only place he could fully relax, unwind. The luxurious prison he'd meant to keep the angel who had removed his wings. But that plan had been blown the moment he'd brought Zacharel and the human girl here, so . . . if he blamed anyone, he had to blame himself.

He rubbed at his scalp and the patches of stubble that remained. He was bald now. Would probably be bald forever, the mirror image of his father's people.

"Learn anything?" he asked no one in particular.

Thane paused in the removal of his victim's claws only long enough to say, "Their orders came from the high lord Unforgiveness."

Unforgiveness. A true nightmare Koldo had never had the pleasure of fighting — but had wanted to fight many times over. The demon caused more trouble than any of his kind. "And those orders were?"

"We're still working on that part."

Koldo swept his gaze over the minions. Bigger than the little ones that latched themselves to humans, but no less dangerous, they were broken, cut and bleeding, hunched over, fighting for breath, even crying. Had any humans been here, they would have felt sorry for the creatures. Perhaps even pleaded for mercy, too. Koldo felt no such sympathy. How could he? He knew what these beings were capable of, knew the destruction they had rained would continue if they were freed.

To consider a demon redeemable was a fatal mistake.

His legs shook as he stood. Shook more as he walked over to Thane, who sat on a stool in front of his minion, and patted the man on the shoulder, careful not to brush against his wings.

The warrior with the sweetly curling hair and the wicked, heavenly eyes glanced up, frowned. "Do you desire a turn?"

There was a hitch in his voice, and Koldo knew Thane fought the need to rebuke him for daring to touch him without permission. But this was Koldo's home, and Thane was here without permission of his own. "No. I want you to let the minion go. Alive."

Thane leapt to his feet, the stool skittering back. His boys did the same, flanking his side in seconds. They formed a wall of muscle and might, a support system no one else would ever be able to breach. "You must still burn with fever to even suggest such a thing. It will only possess, rape and murder."

How little these men thought of him. But unlike Zacharel, he would not embrace his ability to speak in the minds of his fellow soldiers and convince them otherwise. That was an invasion, plain and simple, and he didn't trust the men to only listen to his words and never attempt to search through his mind, his memories.

He barreled between Thane and Bjorn and gripped the minion by the throat, forcing the male to look up, into his eyes. One crimson orb was missing, blood trekking down a bony cheek.

"Only one of the three demons here will walk away," he announced.

Behind him, the angels hissed with outrage. But they didn't contradict him, and he was grateful for that, at least.

"I have a message for your high lord. Will you be the one to deliver it?"

The minion brightened instantly. "Yes, yes, of course. Would be my pleasure to serve you in this way."

A lie, most surely.

"No, no. I'll deliver it," the minion beside him said. "Let me."

"No, me," the third rushed out. "I'll do anything. Anything!"

Koldo kept his gaze on the one he held. "I do not believe you. And that is why I'm keeping a piece of you here. If you want that piece back, you'll have to come and get it with proof of your actions." That said, Koldo ripped off the creature's right arm.

A scream of agony, jagged at the edges. The spurt of black blood.

He tossed the appendage to the floor. As greedy and selfish as demons were, they could not bear for anyone else to have what belonged to them.

"I'll go," was the panted reply. "I'll go and return. Swear."

Truth or lie? Other angels would have been able to tell, but because of his father, Koldo could not. "When you see him, tell Unforgiveness that his cowardly hiding will not save him from our wrath."

Koldo removed the chains.

In a blink, the demon bolted up and through the side wall, disappearing from view, laughing gleefully.

"What now?" Thane asked, angry.

"Now," Koldo replied, "I follow him to the high lord. I have a lock on his spiritual trail." An ability he hadn't wanted the demon to know about, hence the pretense that he expected proof. "Once I discover where Unforgiveness and his horde are staying, I can lead Zacharel straight to him. In the meantime, kill these two. They are no longer needed and now possess information they shouldn't."

Amid the demons' protests and the warriors' grunts of approval, Koldo hid himself in a pocket of air, knowing that not even the angels could sense him any longer, and followed the trail the fleeing demon had left for him. He saw sparks of pink — relief. Fetid green and slick black, like diseased oil leaking from a car — the need to hurt someone mixed with fear.

The minion surprised him, doing as Koldo

had commanded and going straight to the high lord. Through layers of dirt and rock, through long, winding tunnels, and into hell, a land of fire, ash and utter doom. Prairies and hills were scorched, charred to nothing. Ash curled through the air, creating a choking breeze. The intensity of the heat licked at him, causing his skin to sweat and welt. Screams of agony assaulted his ears, followed quickly by eerie laughter.

Angels were not allowed to enter without permission. Hell was not their realm, nor was it under their control, subject to their rules. But again, Koldo was not just any angel. His father had — No, he would not think about the man and why, exactly, he could pass between heaven and hell. He would then think about his mother.

Koldo caught sight of the minion, zipping along a bone-laden bridge. Water did not flow beneath, but blood, so much blood. Spikes anchored one side of that bridge to the other, a soul writhing in the center of each. At the end was a palace of gloom and torment, comprised only of human skulls. Thousands of empty eye sockets seemed to watch him.

As he entered, the fine hairs at the back of his neck rose to attention. Would the Deity grant Zacharel permission to come here?

Or would Zacharel have to fall first? Whenever an angel fell, his wings were permanently removed and his weak, vulnerable body cast here. If that happened, Zacharel would not stand a chance.

Perhaps I can end things here and now. It wasn't wise for a lone warrior to take on a horde, especially when that lone warrior was injured, but if there was a chance . . .

Koldo found the minion in the throne room. Up the dais steps his gaze went, landing on the giant lounging across the throne's arms. The minion bowed.

This had to be Unforgiveness.

The bones of his face were exaggerated, his forehead too wide and bulging. His teeth were sharpened into fangs, and his skin a smooth expanse of crimson. Wings knotted and ridged curved from around his back and scraped at his thighs, as well as the throne. A long, thin tail rested in his lap, his fingers toying with the metal spike at the end.

"— said he would give my arm back to me if I delivered proof I told you his message."

"Did he, now?"

"Oh, yes. Will you give me proof?"

Unforgiveness motioned one of the many demons behind his throne. The male came forward — and beheaded the one-armed minion.

The spectators chortled.

Unforgiveness held up a hand for silence. "The day I have been waiting for has finally arrived. The battle has truly begun."

Koldo looked around, cataloging the details. There were over two hundred demons in this room alone. No telling how many others the high lord commanded. No, he could not take on this army all by his lonesome. Not in this condition.

There were several columns scattered throughout, each with a human spirit chained in front.

Spirits were corporeal here, and therefore subject to the laws of the realm's nature. Blood dripped from each unconscious person.

They weren't dead, he knew that much. When a spirit was killed, it withered away — only to reanimate a few days later, still trapped in this pitted, fiery realm of pain.

Koldo wished he could help, and that was one of the main reasons angels were never allowed here. They wanted to help, but couldn't, and the guilt would stay with them forevermore. Koldo forced himself to look away from the bodies. But not before he caught a glimpse of . . . Surely not . . . That couldn't be . . . He stalked to the only column on the dais.

It was.

Jamila's dark hair hung in tangles and mostly concealed her face. She was cut and bruised from head to toe, soaked in blood, her wings gone, but she was alive, her chest rising, falling, rising. But . . .

She had died. Hadn't she? Or had that, too, been a trick?

Her eyes were closed, her breath more of a wheeze than anything. Death waited for her even now, ready to sink past her skin and consume her at any moment.

"Well, well." Unforgiveness breathed deeply, as if he savored something sweet. The creature pushed to his feet. Everyone in the room quieted. "I smell you, angel. I know you're here."

Every soldier in the demon's army tensed, readying for combat.

Out of habit, Koldo nearly created a sword of fire. *Steady. He can't know where you are.* But those crimson eyes were locked on him, as though observing his every move.

"We've killed her, you know. Over and over again we've killed your female only to revive her before it was too late."

Steady. Responding would verify his presence and reveal his location, even though

Unforgiveness already seemed to know where he was, and that would be a mistake. The creature might sense him, but he couldn't see him. This was a trick, and if he appeared, the other demons would see him, too.

"You are Koldo, yes?"

He pressed his lips together, barely managing to cut off his angry response.

Unforgiveness walked a step closer, stilled. "No need to confirm. You are. I've studied Zacharel's new army at length. Why else do you think I sent so many minions to earth? Some were to fight, but some were to watch and report back. You, Koldo, are the only member who can flash. You are the only one with the ability to follow a demon into hell."

Koldo ground his teeth together.

"Oh, yes, I know all about you, just as I knew you would be the one to find your way down here, hoping for answers. I have to admit, I'm glad I was right." Unforgiveness motioned to another demon, the one standing directly behind his throne. "Bring her."

Happy footsteps clomped away, leaving an awful silence in their wake. And when the minion returned a short while later, he was dragging a struggling angel behind him.

Koldo's angel. The one he had searched for . . . the one he wanted to kill more than he wanted to live. Shock and fury became a toxic poison in his blood.

"Ah, I sense my little welcoming gift is not in vain. You've been tracking her, yes?" Unforgiveness asked.

At his sides, his hands fisted. She was just as he remembered. Beautiful in the cruelest of ways, for she looked as innocent and sweet as a woman could, and yet she had the blackest of hearts hidden beneath. Her hair was as long and as dark as his, though hers was woven with streaks of gold. Her eyes . . . such a pretty shade of lavender. A smattering of freckles around her nose, the only flaws in her pale-as-cream skin.

Yes. His mother was indeed beautiful.

So badly he wanted to close the distance, grab her and disappear. But she was chained to the demon, and Koldo would have to take them both. The demon could kill her on the way home, and Koldo wouldn't be able to stop him.

"I'll bargain with you," Unforgiveness said smoothly. "You'll do what I tell you, and in return, I'll give you the two female angels. This one and Jamila. If you decide to defy me, I'll kill the pair here and now and ensure neither can be brought back."

The minion forced the angel to her knees. Koldo peered at her, but she kept her gaze on his feet. Did she have any idea the things he planned to do to her?

He looked back at Jamila. Her eyes were now open, dulled, but filled with hope and regret. Her mouth opened and closed, as if she had something to say but couldn't quite get the words out. Or maybe she feared she would cry out and beg.

"Listen carefully, warrior." Unforgiveness outlined what he wanted Koldo to do, leaving no detail to chance. "You have one day to make this happen. One day. Not enough time to plan anything on your own, but just enough time to do what I desire. After that, I kill the females. And do not think you can swoop in with more soldiers and save them. Those soldiers would have to enter through the gate, and my spies would alert me. Do not think to sneak back in yourself, for I would sense you. Do not think to warn Zacharel, for you will now be traveling with my minion. Ditch the minion, and the females die."

Lead settled inside Koldo's stomach as each of his options was systematically ripped away.

"You see, I've thought of everything." Once again Unforgiveness was grinning. "Do we have a deal or not?"

CHAPTER THIRTY

Zacharel snuggled Annabelle close. Finally her human form was returning. But then, he'd done much to calm her down, flying her to the stars, as close as he could get her without allowing the atmosphere to freeze her, caressing her arms, her belly, kissing the curve of her neck. When she trembled at the beauty of both, he changed direction and took her to a beach to watch the sunrise and bask in the warmth, still caressing her, still kissing her.

During the first hour, she was withdrawn. During the second, she was stiff as a board. Through it all, she was quiet. He'd gotten used to the way she spoke her mind. He missed that, and wanted it back.

Now they were inside another hotel room, lying on the bed, simply breathing each other in. He'd live in rented rooms if necessary, anything to keep her safe and happy This one was bigger than any of the others, cleaner, nicer.

"Sweetheart," he said.

"Yes."

Finally, a word from her.

"You know I desire you, whatever your form."

"I . . . Yes."

"Do you remember when I told you that I wanted to do everything with you?"

Another yes, though this one was barely a whisper.

"That hasn't changed. I will. Starting now."

Her eyes flared with shock. "But we've already done everything! And you really want me? *Now?*"

She did not know, after all. "Now. And always."

His determined assurance gave her pause. "But I'm . . . hideous."

Patches of demon scales still remained, yes. "You are lovely no matter your outward appearance, and some things need to be repeated." Proving that had been the point of tonight's excursion, and it was clearly time to step up his efforts.

"How can you say I'm lovely? You hate demons as much as I do."

"You are not a demon." He stood, tugging her to her feet beside him, then forced her to spin, placing her back against his chest. He walked her to the wall, pressed her close. Her trembling gasp was more about the heat radiating from him than the chill of the plaster, he suspected.

He slid his hands down her sides, her hips, and latched onto her wrists. He lifted her arms and flattened her palms over her head.

"Leave them there." A command, and when he released her, she obeyed.

He stripped her, then caressed her until she was mewling uncontrollably, until the curve of her spine was pliant, until she was trying to mold herself against him. Eventually her head fell to his shoulder, allowing his breath to fan over her. The heat she threw off . . . far more than his own and exactly what he needed, driving him to passion as only she could.

Against her ear, he whispered, "Did you like being with me?"

"Yes." Said on a broken moan. "I did."

"And you want me again."

"Oh, yes."

He traced each of her ribs before dabbling at her navel. "I told you that you would never have to beg me for anything, but I've changed my mind. Before I take you, you'll beg me, Anna. You'll beg me and you'll scream and you'll beg some more." He needed to know her desire was as potent as his own.

Throughout the centuries, he'd witnessed every sexual act imaginable, each performed for different reasons. Lust, domination, curiosity, humiliation, degradation, calculation, revenge, hope, the desire to have children, the desire to cause pain. Love he'd always sought to deny.

But that's what he wanted with Annabelle. Love. He wanted a giving and taking, a shared experience.

"Zaaachaaarel," she said in a sing-song voice.

"That's a good start." He could smell the sweetness of her arousal, a fragrance that stroked him from the inside, heating him up, making him burn hotter, so much hotter.

"What if I refuse to beg?"

"You won't."

For a long while, he taunted them both, stroking her everywhere but where she needed him most. Her fingers curled on the wall. *Bang, bang.* She pounded those little fists, desperate for relief. But did she beg? No.

Finally she began to talk, telling him all the things she wanted him to do to her . . . all the things *she* wanted to do to *him*. . . .

. . . touch him . . .

. . . stroke him . . .

. . . liiick him . . .

By the time she quieted, his nerves were so sensitized, he could barely stand. Definitely couldn't stand still. He rubbed against her, again and again, the friction ecstasy . . . misery. He imagined her hands on him, all over him. He imagined her mouth on him, all over him.

He craved.

"Those things you will do to me." He barely registered the fire, ice and sheer grit in his voice. "Next time."

She turned her head, giving him a peek at her profile. The most adorable of pouts tugged at the corners of her lips. "And now?"

"Now I continue my quest to make you beg." He chuckled as her pout deepened. "You didn't think I'd forgotten, did you?"

He got serious, no longer content to tease her. He worked her until she was alternately gasping and moaning, playing with her breasts, stroking where she needed him most, until her hands were off the wall and in his hair, her nails scouring his scalp. Oh, how she clung to him in the most decadent of ways. She purred. She moaned. She writhed. And all the while he continued to rub against her, desperate to fill her.

"Please," she finally begged. "I give. Please, please, please!"

"I will never say no to you."

She threw a little grin over her shoulder, her eyes as bright with humor as they were hot with arousal. "Good, because now I want *you* to beg *me.*"

He did not hesitate. "Please, please, please, Annabelle." At last he lifted his robe, positioned himself, and slid inside the glorious sheath she provided. "Please."

"Zacharel," she said on a moan. "Faster. Please."

"Or . . ." He went slower — before stopping altogether. His legs were trembling, threatening to give out at any moment, but he would savor every second of this, would be so careful with his woman.

"Zacharel."

He inched back into motion. . . .

. . . a little faster . . .

"Please."

Still a little faster . . . The pleasure was cut with agony, but he loved it, loved every sensation . . . faster . . . faster. . . .

Her fists again banged into the wall as she shattered. He was right there with her, shouting her name, branding her with all that he was.

Long minutes later, when they had both calmed, he picked her up and carried her to the shower. She didn't speak a word as he cleaned her, then himself. No remnants of the demon form remained, and he was glad. She was composed and sated.

And . . . he hadn't once kissed her, he realized suddenly.

Zacharel looked her over. Soaking-wet hair was plastered to her head, cheeks and shoulders. Ice-blue eyes watched him, droplets clinging at the ends of her lashes. Her cheeks were flushed to a rosy pink, her lips swollen and teeth-marked. She must have chewed them. Her body was reddened where he'd kneaded her, and shaky, so beautifully shaky with satisfaction.

He cupped her jaw. Forever he simply stood there, continuing to peer at her, allowing her to study him and hiding nothing from her. He wondered if she saw the same loveliness he saw in her, if she saw the reverence and the hunger he felt for her. If she saw the hope for something more. For all. She must have, for she reflected everything back at him.

For so long, he'd had nothing — and she had somehow become his everything.

Without explaining himself, he fused their lips together. He wanted the kiss to talk for him, to prepare her for his next confession. Their tongues met, rolled together, dueled, a kiss not meant to arouse but to give.

When finally he lifted his head, he stared down at her and gave voice to action. "I love you, Annabelle."

She was more than his other half; she was the best part of him.

"I know."

That was it? That was all? "Tell me how you knew this." When he himself hadn't known until today, this moment. *And then tell me you love me back!*

Her expression was so soft, so radiant. "It's the way you are with me. You're not like that with anyone else. And let's not forget my earlier appearance and the fact that you didn't stab me."

He waited, but she said no more. Her fingers toyed with the ends of his hair, winding the strands into ringlets. "What am I like with you?" Some men could give their love and expect nothing in return. Zacharel wasn't one of them. He expected everything. Would demand it.

"Softer, sweeter. A protector." She chuckled warmly. "Insatiable."

He adored the way her voice dipped so huskily at the end. "How am I with others?"

"Harsh, matter-of-fact, demanding. A tyrant."

"Good. I must be that way with my men. I am all that stands between them and banishment from the heavens."

"How?"

"My fate is their fate, for the Deity tied me to them as punishment. Though I no longer see it as such," he said.

"I'm not sure how I feel about that."

"Do not worry. I will whip them into shape. Perhaps literally. But in the end, they are mine to guard, just as you are mine. The loss of their wings, their immortality, would haunt me. They are good men."

"You love them, too," she said.

He was far from ready to entertain such a notion, but he admired and respected them greatly. "What about you? Do you love me?" Subtly hinting hadn't worked; perhaps outright asking would.

Frowning, she said, "Do you want me to love you?"

"Yes." She must. Otherwise he would . . . what?

"Will you know if I lie?"

"Yes. But you will not be lying!"

Slowly her frown changed into a smile. "Goodness, but you are *so* easy to tease."

"Annabelle," he growled.

"Oh, all right. I love you," she said. "I love you with all my heart." The first had been grudgingly offered, but the second . . . adoration had dripped from her voice.

Satisfaction was a sublime avalanche inside him, falling into every part of him, overwhelming him. "You will stay with me always."

Her somber air returned, and this time, he would bet it was real. "Of course. I won't break my pledge, but we'll have to find a way to contain the high lord who wants me. Otherwise, demons will chase me for the rest of my life, and you'll be in constant danger."

"Some things are worth *any* amount of danger."

"Zacharel," a hard male voice said from beyond the shower stall. "Something's happened."

Annabelle yelped.

Instantly Zacharel's satisfaction dried up, replaced by fury. With himself, not Koldo. How could he not have heard his soldier enter the bathroom? "Step into the other room. Now."

No response. No opening and closing of the door, either. But the warrior was no longer there.

Zacharel jerked the towel from the rack at

the back of the stall and wrapped the material around Annabelle, unconcerned by the fact that the water would soon soak it.

"Stay here," he told her, then exited to deal with the latest disaster. And he knew it was a disaster. Nothing else would have brought his warrior here.

CHAPTER THIRTY-ONE

Annabelle heard muffled male voices as she searched the bathroom for something to wear. What she found was two washrags and another towel. Not exactly appropriate attire for a meeting with angels. But if she had to pretend dishrag was the latest style, she would. She wouldn't remain in here like a shameful secret.

Zacharel must have sensed her growing frustration and determination, because he opened the door, peeked inside, winked and tossed in a robe before once again disappearing.

She sighed dreamily, still reeling from what she and Zacharel had done and admitted to each other. Oh, she'd already realized he'd fallen in love with her, but there was something so magnificent about hearing the words. Of knowing, beyond any doubt, that she, Annabelle Miller, had tamed such an exquisite animal. An ice-cold warrior that possessed a streak of carnality that, once unleashed, would never again be caged.

Shaking, she tugged the white material over her body and exited the bathroom.

"— have found Unforgiveness," Koldo was saying.

Her gaze immediately sought Zacharel. He, too, wore a robe. Lamplight gilded his exposed skin, her angel now a golden statue of perfection and might.

Zacharel watched her rather than his soldier and motioned her over. But apparently standing at his side wasn't close enough, because he wound his arm around her waist and tugged her so close they practically melded together.

When neither man seemed inclined to restart the conversation, she decided to do it herself. "So where is Unforgiveness and what's the game plan?"

A beat of tense silence, then, "Hell," Koldo announced. "He is in hell, and he claims he will release you from his bond if Zacharel agrees to fall."

Ice thickened Annabelle's blood, scraping against her veins, stinging. "No way. Just no way." He would lose his immortality. He would lose his ability to see — and fight — demons. But they wouldn't lose their ability to see and fight him. "He's not falling." To

Zacharel, she added, "You're not falling. Why would the demon want you to fall, anyway?"

"I'll be easier to kill, less a thorn in his side. But you do not get to decide this for me, Annabelle."

"You'd be the stupidest man ever to live if you agreed to this. He's lying. You know he's lying. He'll never willingly release me." That was just a guess on her part, but one thing she knew: demons were incapable of telling the truth.

"For a chance to free you, I would do anything."

"No!" The fact that Zacharel would even consider falling upset her. Any other girl probably would have jumped with joy, because such a sacrifice proved beyond words that her man loved her. But Annabelle wasn't any girl, and she knew everything falling would entail. Not just Zacharel's ruination, but his men's, too.

He would never be able to forgive himself. He'd already lost his brother, and the fact that he'd been the one to render the final blow was a constant dagger inside his chest, eternally chafing, never allowing him to heal.

"We're wasting time," she said. "I want you to go to your Deity — and not fall!"

"So what would you have me do?"

"Ask him to do something, I don't know, powerful. Mighty."

He shook his head, dark hair dancing at his temples. "I am due punishment, not aid. Besides, all he can do is grant me permission to enter hell, and that will do us no good."

"Punishment?" Her heart skipped a beat. "Why?"

His hold on her tightened, his way of saying, *Not now, woman. Later.* In answer, she pinched his hand. Her way of saying, *I won't let this go, angel.*

She twisted, cupped his cheeks and forced him to peer down at her. "Remember what we talked about?" she asked, letting the words *locking Unforgiveness away* remain unsaid. "Why it's so important to go that route? So talk to your Deity, okay? Please. He gave you an army, a promotion. Angry with you or not, there's got to be something more he can do."

He opened his mouth — to protest, she knew.

"If you don't, someone else might find and defeat Unforgiveness." If that happened, she would die, and Zacharel would blame himself.

Indecision played through his eyes, now a

stormy jade. She was manipulating him, and she knew it, but she didn't know what else to do. She would rather he fought Unforgiveness than lose everything.

"I don't want to leave you," he said.

"Please, Zacharel. Do this for me. For us. Koldo will stay with me."

He massaged the back of his neck. "Very well. I will talk to the Deity, but I cannot promise a favorable outcome." His gaze slid to the tall, strong warrior beside them. "Stay here. Guard her. I won't be gone long."

Yes!

Koldo nodded.

"I love you," Zacharel said, and kissed her.

"I love you, too. So much."

He paused for a moment, as though he couldn't bear to leave her, then flared his wings and leapt through the air, through the ceiling, disappearing from view.

"Do you hope I will kill you while he's gone?" Koldo asked. "Is that why you sent Zacharel away? You are bound to Unforgiveness, and by dying, you will kill the demon and save Zacharel in every sense of the word."

"I hadn't been, no."

"Why not?"

"Because Zacharel would blame himself — and you."

"There are ways to ensure he never knows what happened."

"Are you threatening me?"

A shrug of those wide shoulders.

To save Zacharel from falling, she would do just about anything. Even die. Zacharel would blame himself no matter what Koldo said, and he would mourn her, but he would live a long life. All in all, that seemed like a fair trade. He would continue to lead his men. Eventually he would meet another woman — Annabelle disliked her already — and rediscover love, heal.

"How did you know I was bound to the demon, anyway?" she asked. She'd only just figured it out herself, and she'd told no one. Nor had Zacharel.

He ignored her question. "Just so you know, a simple stabbing will not kill you, female."

"Hey, no one said anything about stabbing!" she said with a frown. But if she did this, how would she go?

"But you are willing to sacrifice yourself for Zacharel?"

"Of course."

"Even fight Unforgiveness?"

"Especially that. Why do you want to know?"

Again, he ignored her question. "Even if

Unforgiveness will hurt you before he kills you, yes?"

"Yes, but I could totally win, you know."

"No, you could not."

She flexed her biceps. "Do you see these things? I so could."

"You could not win with those. It would take something else. Something I am not sure you possess. So why are you willing to risk yourself?" he asked, head tilting to the side. "I do not understand."

Easy. "I love Zacharel, and I want to protect him from harm — even harm he would bring himself. I don't know if he told you about his brother . . . ?"

A sharp cut of his head in negation. "He did not tell me, but we all know of Hadrenial's death."

But did any of them know exactly *how* Hadrenial had died? If not, she wouldn't be the one to tell, so she settled with, "The loss nearly ruined him, and he still struggles with feelings of responsibility and remorse. If he falls, his army — *you* — will be forced to fall with him, and he won't be able to live with that."

A hard frown greeted her words. "No. He would have told us."

This she would have to tell, because it was the only way to make Koldo understand.

"He was given charge over you, and his fate will be yours. All of yours."

"How do you know this?" Anger pulsed from him, as sharp as a blade.

"He told me, and you know he doesn't ever lie."

A moment passed in silence. He nodded, as if he'd just made a decision. "You are very brave, Annabelle." It was the first time he'd ever used her name, and that he'd laced his tone with such respect nearly floored her. "Perhaps you do possess the extra something."

In the corner of the room, she spied movement, glanced up and nearly screamed. A serpe was coiled in the far corner of the ceiling, watching.

Fight-or-flight kicked in — and fight won. She braced her legs apart and fisted her hands, ready.

But all the demon did was hiss at her, then at Koldo, and slither away.

"Wait here. I shall return, and you shall have what you desire," Koldo said — and vanished.

CHAPTER THIRTY-TWO

Zacharel was surprised by the ease with which he was granted an audience with the Deity, especially considering the recent turmoil in the heavens. Usually, even angels who had been summoned here had to wait.

The day of punishment had arrived.

He'd known his recent actions would get him in trouble and he hadn't cared. Still didn't. Annabelle had become the most important part of his life, and he would endure the worst of the worst for her.

At least most of the damage done to the temple had been cleaned away, the grass and flowers tended, the rivers purified. Blood no longer decorated the walls or steps. Lysander's army formed a gate around the edge of the perimeter, stopping anyone who approached.

All but him, that is. He sailed through with only a nod of affirmation. He landed on the last step, striding forward without a hitch. To his surprise, Lysander met him at the huge, arching doors and entered alongside him. With his pale hair, dark eyes and wings of the most magnificent gold, Lysander was the standard most angels were measured against. Beauty personified, once cut from the same emotionless cloth as Zacharel.

"You were expected," his friend said, voice echoing through the foyer. The domed ceiling was not painted to resemble the night sky, but actually revealed it. Stars twinkled from their black velvet perches, so close stardust danced through the air like diamonds.

He tried not to let the announcement rattle him. Gaze on a thick column comprised of shimmery crystals, smoothed and polished to reflect all the colors of the rainbow, he said, "I'm . . . sorry I left you to defend the temple."

Lysander slapped his shoulder. "When your woman has need of you, nothing else matters. This I know well."

He could only hope the Deity felt the same way. They rounded several corners and finally came to another set of doors. The large, arching entrance was guarded, for it led straight into the throne room.

"Any advice?" he asked.

"You are a good leader, with sharp instincts," Lysander said. "Trust yourself, and you'll come out of this just fine."

The two angel guards, bigger and taller than most, threw open the double doors and Zacharel strode past without his friend. The room was emptied out, no guards, no orchestra, no decorations, only a solid gold throne on top of the dais.

Upon that throne sat the Deity, and as usual his appearance amazed Zacharel. He looked as innocent and frail as an aged human, with deeply lined skin, silver hair and shaky hands.

Zacharel bowed his head and dropped to his knees, his wings tucked into his sides. Of all the meetings he'd had here, this was the most important, yet he had no idea how to begin.

"I am surprised you came without a summons." The unassuming voice was soft and gentle.

And yet you expected me, anyway. "I need your help."

"And you expect me to give it?"

"I know I've done wrong, but I will not apologize." He would never offer a token apology again. Like Annabelle, he would stand for what he believed in and never back down. "I did what I had to do to protect my woman, and I would do it all over again."

Eyes of the deepest black swirled, oil glistening in the sun. "Did I hear you correctly? You'll do *anything* to protect a human?"

He nodded. "My human."

Trembling fingers tapped against a weathered chin. "You say that now, but I wonder. . . . You thought you would come here, state your case, ask for what you desire, and that would be that. Well, once upon a time, I would have allowed such a thing. But no longer. I cannot baby you forever."

Baby? "I am a warrior," he said, squaring his shoulders. "I know I am due several whippings first, and I willingly accept them."

"You are due, yes. You took responsibility of Annabelle, and yet you allowed harm to come to her on more than one occasion. You even caused her harm yourself. Then you sat back as *she* harmed others."

"Yes. And I accept whatever you decide to do, but I ask that you help me, too."

A pause.

Such a thick silence.

Then, "You desire my help with Annabelle even though she is a demon's consort?"

"She is not a demon's consort," he gritted out. "She is mine."

Unperturbed, the Deity continued on, "And you wish for me to help you challenge the demon who thinks to take her from you."

"A demon who has harmed many humans in his quest to reach her."

Another bout of silence, just as thick but now so heavy Zacharel's shoulders drooped under the weight.

"Much has changed for you since we last spoke," the Deity said.

"Yes," he repeated. His heart drummed erratically.

"Tell me, Zacharel, what you have learned."

This, he did not have to think about. "I have learned the value of human life. I have learned the value of love and commitment. I have learned to place another's needs before my own."

"Have you truly?"

"Yes."

"Let's find out, shall we. Tell me, Zacharel. Would you sacrifice yourself for your Annabelle?"

So casually asked, but with the Deity, there was always a purpose. "I would." No question.

"Would you sacrifice something dearer even than that? Would you sacrifice your brother's life to save her?"

He frowned. "My brother has no life to give. He is dead."

"No. He lives."

Zacharel . . . had no response to that. Like the angels, the Deity would not lie. That meant . . . That couldn't mean . . . Could *only* mean . . .

"True death is not what you think, angel. A spirit cannot die."

"But the Water of Death —"

"Is not what you think, either. Your brother is alive. He survived."

Hope filled him. Joy filled him. So fervently had he prayed for something like this. "More than the water, I also burned his body."

"And his body was put back together."

Hadrenial was alive!

They could be together, he thought. They could fly together. Talk and laugh. His brother could meet Annabelle, and they could be a family. They *would* be a family.

"I ask again," the Deity said. "If both Annabelle and your twin stood before you now, if you could only save one life, whose life would you choose?"

In a single heartbeat, his hope withered. His joy fled. "Why would you ask me to make such a choice? As punishment for my

crimes?" he asked, stomach twisting painfully.

"You have hurt several humans though
you knew better. You saved a human at the
risk of your own life. You are due both a
punishment and a reward."

A punishment and a reward. He could
have his brother, or he could have Annabelle, but not both. Hadrenial, the most
beloved of the angels, so pure of heart, so
caring and kind, Zacharel had been
humbled. Or Annabelle, who was just as
caring and kind. Hadrenial, whom he had
missed with all of his heart. Annabelle,
whom he craved with the whole of his body.
Hadrenial, whose life was cut short by torment and tragedy. Annabelle, who challenged and confounded him at every turn.

"And if I cannot choose?"

"Then I will choose for you, for there cannot be life without death, or action without
consequence. This you know."

His hands fisted. "What of me? Take my
life, and allow the pair of them to live."

"When no such choice was given to the
humans you allowed to be slain?"

A question that was really a statement.
There would be no changing the Deity's
mind. There never was. "May I see him?"
he asked. "Will you tell me how you saved

him? I removed his love."

"There is more to man than a single element, Zacharel. You took his goodness . . . but left what was festering."

"I left nothing."

"You left Unforgiveness."

Was he implying . . . No. No! Yet even hearing the word was a blow to the gut. "Where is he?"

A light appeared in front of Zacharel, growing brighter . . . brighter still . . . until he worried he would be blind for the rest of eternity. "Look, and see. Your brother and your woman."

Annabelle spent five minutes alone. That was it. Just five. She had no idea her entire world would change before the sixth ticked past — when Koldo reappeared in the hotel room.

A grinning demon stood at his side.

"Unforgiveness," Koldo said, shoving him in her direction.

Instinct caused her to scramble backward. She reached back and grabbed . . . a lamp, she realized when the "weapon" was in front of her, the cord jerked out of the socket. Her knives were on the nightstand, and the nightstand was far from her reach.

"What are you doing, Koldo?" she demanded. "What's going on?"

"Hello, Annabelle," the creature said. "Don't you remember me?"

"I wasn't talking to you, demon. Koldo?"

"He cannot leave this room, but then, neither can you," Koldo said. "I made sure of it."

"At my request," the demon said, his grin widening.

"I brought you to her, as you demanded, but I will not bring Zacharel here."

"That is not —"

"Your plan, no. Do not think you will be able to leave on your own. My cloud now surrounds the outside of this room and it will ensure you remain."

A low growl erupted. "What game are you playing? One word from me, and the females in my charge will be savaged. Do you hear me? Savaged!"

"That's a lie. They'll be rescued before that happens. And by the way, you didn't think of everything," Koldo replied easily. "I did. Annabelle, he's all yours." And with that, he vanished, leaving Annabelle a second time.

A moment passed before she was able to orient herself, to look past her fear and her confusion and the sudden burn in her chest. When she finally realized who — and what

— she faced, she released a shrill scream. "You!"

Here he was, her parents' killer, except he was even bigger than she remembered him. Taller, far more muscled, but still with that barbarian's face and a vampire's fangs. Horns on his shoulders, dripping poison, she was sure, and a tail swishing between his legs.

"Do not worry, mate of mine. I won't make you suffer just yet. I'll play with you first. The fun stuff will begin when Zacharel swoops in to the rescue. And he will. Koldo will not be able to stop him."

"I'm not your mate." A violent tremor threatened to rock her off her feet, the burn in her chest intensifying. *Steady. Calm. Can't let emotions get the better of you.* "So you're Unforgiveness, the coward who sends his minions to fight for him, huh." *Better.*

His fangs elongated as he said, "You'll pay for that, and so will Zacharel. Where is he, by the way? Not far, I hope." He looped around her, much as Zacharel had once done, studying every inch of her. A hungry predator who'd just spotted prey.

She turned with him, never letting him have her back. "He's busy doing something important." Subtext: *you're not.* "This is between you and me." *And I will come out*

564

ahead. I have to.

"This was never between you and me. I waited centuries to strike at Zacharel, and wasn't sure I'd ever have the chance. Then your worthless druggie of a brother summoned me into your home and I scented you. Imagine my surprise. I knew instantly who you were to me . . . who you'd be to Zacharel, and so I exchanged a portion of your spirit with mine, then sent others to torment you until his notice was gained. I'm a very patient male, you know." His tail swiped out, intending to knock her ankles together and her body to the ground.

Because of Zacharel's tutelage, she expected the action and jumped up, throwing the lamp at him, slashing his cheek before shattering on the floor.

He stilled, rubbed the now black spot. "That wasn't very nice."

"Neither was your lie. There's no way you could know what I would come to mean to Zacharel."

A wide grin bloomed. "Isn't there?" There was just enough venom in his voice to drill through her doubt.

"No." Still he circled her, again and again. She wanted to leap at him, to attack and get this party started, but she had to work her way to the nightstand first.

"What if I told you that I was Zacharel's brother? His twin? His other half?"

One inch . . . two . . . "You'd have a better chance of convincing me that you're Santa Claus." Even though his claim solved the mystery of the essentia — why Zacharel had seemed to touch her before ever having met her.

That tail whipped out a second time, faster, harder. "Perhaps I am. I so love leaving little presents behind . . . like the bodies I left for you, all those years ago. Your parents, yes? Killing them was *so* amazingly sweet."

Might vomit. But at least she managed to gain another inch.

"I could have left them alone, you know, but I wanted you trapped in one location. I knew you would be blamed and locked away, ready to be rescued by a beautiful dark-haired angel. And so you were."

Might sob. "What do you gain from all of this?"

"Vengeance. Zacharel killed the man I used to be. I woke up in hell, forced to live with the very beings responsible for my torment."

"No," she repeated. "You lie!" That tail came at her once, twice, but she managed to jump both times. Zacharel had done the same to her, so she knew to leap backward, out of the way of a third strike.

She saved herself from injury, but she also put herself farther away from her blades. Dang it. There had to be another way. The burn —

The burn! She could have more than hands. She could have claws. And if she could have claws, she could have fangs, wings and horns of her own. All weapons of destruction.

She might have a chance of winning.

Part of her wanted to stop trying to subdue her fear and anger and simply unleash them. Fine, more than a part of her. But she wouldn't do it. She would not fight evil with evil. That wasn't who she was or who she wanted to be.

I can do this. I can. She launched herself into the demon's body.

He hit the ground and rolled, smashing her, but her hands were free and she rammed her fist into his throat. He rolled again, placing her on top, but he didn't leave her there. He grabbed her by the wrist and tossed her over his shoulder. She hit the far wall, plaster raining around her, pain shooting through her.

Not out yet. Up she jumped and raced toward him. He met her in the middle. She bit at him. She sliced at him with her nails. She swiped up pieces that had broken off the lamp and cut at him. She kicked at him. She fought with every ounce of strength she possessed — more than she'd ever before exhibited. All the while, he was a snarling animal, with no rules to hinder him, no hesitation to lessen the damage he caused. No considering a better path. And yet, still she managed to give as good as she got.

A few times, he tried to kiss her and once even succeeded. He touched her in private places simply to taunt her. Each time, she managed to maintain her cool, causing him to explode in anger.

Those explosions actually aided her. He forgot to block her punches, too focused on getting his hands around her neck to choke her.

"Look at you," he taunted, circling her now.

"Check a mirror," she taunted back.

She was bleeding, bleeding some more, and she was hurting, but he was bleeding just as profusely and had to be hurting just as badly.

"Just give up! Zacharel's brought me nothing but pain and suffering, and I will do the same to him. I will not allow you to stop me."

She wouldn't, couldn't, give in. "If you really are his twin —" *can't be, he can't be* "— then you asked him to kill you. Commanded it."

"He did not have to heed me!"

"What did you expect him to do? You kept trying to kill yourself."

"He could have tried harder to save me. He could have found a way to reach me in the darkness."

For a moment, only a moment, she caught a glimpse of the man he used to be: tormented, pain-filled, ruined. He was a darker version of Zacharel.

This really was Hadrenial, she realized. Zacharel's twin. He'd turned his back on his angel heritage and become a demon.

Even still, how could she kill the man Zacharel had missed so deeply for so long? Even one as evil as this? Zacharel would never be able to forgive her.

Forgive her.

Unforgiveness.

She caught the irony and laughed without humor. An argument took place in her mind, common sense warring with her love for Zacharel.

You have to do this. It's the only way. Besides, you'll be dead, too, so you won't witness Zacharel's reaction.

Yeah, but she would die knowing she had caused the man she loved unequivocal, eternal pain.

If you don't do it, Unforgiveness will continue to hurt Zacharel, you, and countless other families. Zacharel is a good man. He will forgive.

From the corner of her eye, she saw that Koldo had returned. He was just as cut up and broken as she was, and he was not alone. Thane stood beside him, bleeding like everyone else. Koldo vanished and Thane remained in place.

He created a sword of fire with one hand and stepped forward. Stopped, frowned. He patted at the air with the other, as if there was a barrier in front of him.

"Thane!" she said.

He met her gaze — and his eyes widened. He banged his fist against . . . nothing, his mouth moving, but she could not hear what he was saying.

Unforgiveness swooped in, going for her neck. Teeth met skin, every muscle in her body suddenly vibrating with unimaginable pain. She punched at his temple, but failed to dislodge him. Warmth cascaded down her chest as his swallows became haphazard. Weakness stole through her, insidious and undeniable.

"Thane," she cried, even though she knew he couldn't hear her, either. He continued to bang at the air.

On my own. But that was okay. She was ready to die and take this demon with her, because she knew that was the easiest solution, but she knew the demon wouldn't kill her like this. He only wanted to weaken her.

Time to teach him better. She forced herself to relax into his dark embrace, letting her arm fall away from his shoulder, landing on his thigh — and she sliced into his femoral artery with her claws.

She wouldn't weaken.

Roaring, he propelled away from her. Dizziness claimed her as she lumbered to her feet. She approached him.

He did his best to remain out of reach. "Zacharel!" he shouted, turning . . . turning. Flames sprayed from the tips of his claws, creating a circle of fire around the two of them. "If you don't enter this room I'll burn her to death in it, I swear."

"He can't hear you," she said. "It's just you and me." She saw that Xerxes and Bjorn now joined Thane, and though Koldo kept popping in and out, he was once again missing in action.

"Show yourself, Zacharel! I want you to experience all that was done to me. I want you to wallow in the knowledge that you failed someone else. That you failed the woman you love. I want you to suffer and suffer and suffer."

Smoke curled around her, twining up her legs, into her nose, making her cough.

I'm sorry, Zacharel, she thought, spying a piece of the lamp at her feet. *I have to do this.*

"Zacharel!" he shouted, and she swooped up the shard and launched at him.

She sliced through his throat, blood welling, dripping, pooling on the floor. He collapsed to his knees, clutching the wound, gasping for breath. But when she went in for the killing blow, he grabbed hold of her wrist and jerked her down beside him, laughing all over again.

"As if you could win against one such as me." As he spoke, he scraped a horn against her neck, pricking the skin. Not deeply, but enough to burn.

Her body began to twitch, finally cooling until . . . she could feel nothing. Neither hot nor cold, pleasure nor pain. More than that, she could no longer move.

A self-satisfied Unforgiveness loomed over her, the flames licking all around them. "All this time I played with you, hoping he'd come. If he will not, if he continues to refuse, I'll take you here and now and end you anyway. Let him find you violated, with your tormentor dead beside you."

I haven't lost yet, she tried to project with her eyes. *I will pull through.*

"Zacharel!" he shouted again, head thrown back, spine arched. "Have you no desire to save your female? This is your last chance."

Koldo stepped inside the fiery circle. "I do. I have a desire."

"How did you open the shield?" Thane demanded, rushing in behind him.

"Easy. The shield is my cloud," Koldo said, holding out his arm to stop the warrior's progress.

"Annabelle —"

"Not yet."

Unforgiveness's tail lashed out and slashed Koldo across the cheek. "Where's Zacharel? Bring him here. Now."

"He is in the heavens. He is not coming."

A dark play of emotions passed over the demon's face. "Very well. This ends now. But I won't let you capture me and save her." His tail jerked backward and poised at Annabelle's throat, cutting into one of the puncture wounds. "If you want her to live, you'll let me leave with her."

Finish him, Koldo. Please.

Blood dripped down Koldo's cheek. "No, you will not be leaving. I will be killing you. And I know that by killing you I am killing her, but that is the sacrifice she was willing to make. I will have to be content with the knowledge that I saved the world from your evil."

"Do this, and the angels will die."

"Impossible. They have already been saved."

"How — It doesn't matter." The barb dug ever deeper as Unforgiveness ground out, "Zacharel will not want me dead."

"What we want is not always what we need."

Koldo held out his hand, created a sword of fire and struck, removing the demon's head — just as his tail sliced through her neck.

Instantly black cascaded through her mind. She floated . . . floated away . . . floated into nothingness. For a fleeting moment, she thought she could hear Zacharel's screaming.

CHAPTER THIRTY-THREE

"Nooooo!" Zacharel's scream echoed through the Deity's throne room.

He had tried to escape, and he had failed. He had beat at the double doors to no avail. He'd been forced to watch his woman combat his brother. The revelation of the monster his brother had become had nearly destroyed him, but his fear for Annabelle's safety had proved stronger and had kept him fighting for his freedom. Still he'd failed, and ultimately he'd been forced to watch as one fought for the good of those she loved while the other fought for revenge, as they bled and Hadrenial cursed. Forced to watch as they both died.

Once again, he'd watched his brother's head roll away from his body. Only this time it was worse, because Zacharel's woman died alongside him.

"No!" He clawed at the walls, and suddenly he was clawing at air, the throne room

575

gone and the hotel room in its place. He stood in the center of the charred circle, the smoke cleared and two dead bodies at his feet.

Annabelle's robe was ripped to shreds, her neck gaping open.

Koldo stumbled out of the circle as if he'd been pushed, and maybe he had. He tried to get back in, but couldn't. He and Thane, Bjorn and Xerxes tried to beat at an invisible wall to no avail.

Zacharel fell to his knees, tears gliding down his cheeks. "Can one still be saved?"

"Yes." Though the Deity was not there, his voice echoed through the enclosure. "All you must do is choose."

"How can you do this to me? How can you ask me to choose between the only two people I have ever loved? And for someone else's sin! Are you really so cruel?"

"Cruel? What you have not yet learned is that the deaths you cause hurt me in ways you will never understand, and I'm glad that you will not. Such a burden you would not be able to bear. So, am I cruel for giving you a choice rather than leaving you with nothing?"

Yes, he wanted to scream. But he knew it was a lie. "I'm sorry," he said. "So sorry.

Take me instead. I willingly give my life for theirs."

"Were I to do that, the two people you so love would know nothing but torment. They would fight for the rest of eternity."

His shoulders slumped, all that was left of his hope withering, dying. How could he do this thing?

His Deity continued, "You think I know nothing of love, but the truth is, *you* are only just discovering what love really is. Your brother will gladly take all that you've learned and destroy you with it. He will bring great harm to your men. The men you took responsibility for. The men who need you now more than ever. And yet I offer him to you, knowing how much *I* will lose if you accept."

Zacharel's mouth opened, closed. He was caught up in a storm, every emotion he'd ever suppressed surging up to drown him.

Still the Deity was not done. "You want to speak with your brother, I know. You want to ask him why he did these things. You want to beg his forgiveness for what you did to him and for what he suffered. You want to hear him lash out at you, to rant and rail, and give you what you believe you deserve. You want closure. You want him to have the life *he* once deserved."

"Yes." *I want to hug him. I want to fly beside him and watch his features light. I want to hear him laugh with joy rather than cruelty.*

"You can have all of that. Simply take what is in the urn and place it inside Hadrenial's body. Eventually, he will heal from his wounds, yes, even the beheading, and you will have all that you desire. Though it will take time, he will be restored to the man he used to be, before he became the demon Unforgiveness."

The urn appeared at Zacharel's side. "And if I do that, what will happen to Annabelle?"

"Her spirit will journey on."

So be it. Two bodies, motionless before him, spilling over him. Chilling with every second that passed. His beautiful Annabelle, the only pleasure he had ever known. His brother, the man he had betrayed and now owed. He saw his men, still outside the circle, still banging at walls they couldn't see.

They wanted to help him.

They couldn't help him.

He reached inside the urn, the liquid warm, swirling up to greet him. He lifted his arm to the light. Life and death, resting in his palm right now.

He twisted to face the bodies. Whatever happened, he knew the Deity would not allow him to choose and then miraculously bring the other to life, as well. Sacrifice was sacrifice, and like Koldo's hair, it would mean nothing if it was easily replaced. Besides, what was in the urn was enough to save one, but not two.

"I have made my decision." And it had not really been a decision so much as saying goodbye to someone he loved. Zacharel placed his hand over Annabelle's heart. Something else he'd learned since meeting her: you could not allow guilt and shame to make your choices for you. Only love should drive a man, and he loved this woman like no other.

Annabelle was a part of him, his future, and if he must live, he knew he could not do so without her.

The liquid spilled over her, soon absorbing into her skin . . . her soul . . . her spirit. Color washed over her too-pale skin, and her wounds began to heal, her flesh to weave together.

"I'm sorry, Hadrenial," he whispered. He'd said those same words before, so many times, countless times. He'd hurt then as he hurt now. He didn't care what his brother had become. He loved Hadrenial still, and always would.

Too, he would always remember the boy

Hadrenial had been. Would never forget the bond they had shared.

"What will happen to him?" he asked the Deity.

"You will be pleased to know a part of him will live on through your Annabelle. Not through the piece of his demon self, for that piece has died, but through the essence of his love. And because you mixed something of yourself in there, she will be bound to you, now and always, your life for hers. She need only give you a piece of herself to complete the joining and stop the spread of your spiritual death."

"Thank you," he found himself saying. "For this chance with her, I thank you."

"She was always meant to be yours. The question I needed answered was whether or not you could appreciate the gift."

"I can. I do."

"I know."

Breathing deeply, Annabelle jerked upright. As she patted her neck, her chest, perhaps searching for her fatal injury, her gaze searched the room. "What happened?" she croaked. "Why am I alive?"

"I had a choice, and I chose you. I will always choose you."

"Zacharel?" Tears welling in her eyes, she threw herself into his arms. "I have the worst news! I fought your brother. He was alive. I . . . He . . . I'm so sorry. I killed him. There was no other way, and —"

"I know." He pulled back and righted her robe, shielding her breasts from view, then crushed her back into his chest. She clutched at him, and she cried, and all the while he shook. How close he'd come to losing her . . . how much he'd now gained. He cared not for who saw him in this weak moment.

"Oh, Zacharel. I have so much to tell you."

"There's nothing I do not already know, love. Unforgiveness is, was, my brother."

Her breath was a trembling rasp as she disengaged from his embrace to frown at him. "How did you know that?"

"I was forced to watch the fight. I tried to reach you, would have done anything to reach you. I am sorry I did not." He cupped her cheeks, so glad to feel the warmth flooding them. "I'm so very sorry for all you were forced to endure."

"Don't you dare go into a shame spiral. You have nothing to be sorry for."

"At least *try* to hold a grudge." He placed a soft kiss on her lips. "You'll make me feel better."

The kindest of smiles flashed up at him. "I think that's the first lie you've ever told.

So, uh, how am I healed?"

"I gave you the love my brother once carried."

The smile slowly faded. "Your greatest treasure. You shouldn't have —"

"*You* are my greatest treasure, Annabelle. Never doubt that."

Her eyes filled with another stream of tears. "How can you say that? I helped kill him."

He wiped away a tear with the pad of his thumb. "No matter what happened, I killed him, then and now. Never doubt that, either." He would never have the closure he craved, but that was okay. That was life. He had Annabelle, and that was all that mattered. "I love you."

"I love you, too. And thank you. You're my treasure, too."

"Good, because you now have a choice to make. You may meld to me, merging your life span with mine."

A gleam of hope in those blue — no, blue no longer, he realized. Watery eyes of gold peered up at him, a shade more precious than any he'd ever seen. "Or?"

"Or nothing. That is your only choice."

She pressed a kiss into his lips, as soft and gentle as his had been. "I thought you said you knew how to bargain, but right now I'm just too happy to instruct you on the proper way. You've got yourself a wife. Or a consort. Or a mate. Or whatever you want to call me!"

"You have been my wife since the beginning, I think. That very first day, you taught me how to feel. You saw me at my worst, and helped make me better. What we do next will be a much stronger bond."

Cheers erupted around them, and he turned. His entire army now filled the room. Thane and Koldo must have summoned the rest of his men.

Thane dropped to his knee, head bowed.

Koldo did the same.

Bjorn and Xerxes, too, then Axel, and then, one by one, the others joined, until the twenty members of his army were showing their respect.

Zacharel pushed to his feet and helped Annabelle to hers. She pressed into his side, her head resting on his shoulder.

"Don't you dare think about busting on Koldo," she said. "He might have tricked me into . . . uh, I mean, he saved the day. And he and the troublesome trio saved Jamila, I think."

Part of him wanted to throttle the man for daring to place Annabelle in such a dangerous position, but the other part of him recognized the desperate bid for victory. "Is this true?"

Koldo nodded, remained silent.

"He saved another angel, too, I think," Annabelle added.

The warrior did not nod this time, nor did he maintain his silence. "She is no one else's concern. I will see to her."

Something about his tone . . . a hardness, a coldness Zacharel had once possessed. Like him, like Hadrenial, Koldo would end up on a path to destruction if he wasn't careful.

His gaze swept over the sea of angelic bodies, white-and-gold wings, hair a kaleidoscope of colors, from the blackest of jets to the lightest of snows. All of these warriors were as he had once been. Adrift, lost. They needed a leader.

More of a leader than he had been.

From this moment on, he would be that leader. With Annabelle at his side, he could be anything, do anything.

"Rise," he said, and they obeyed. "We are not like other armies, and so I will no longer treat you as such. We teeter on the edge of banishment, and I will allow none of you to fall. You are mine. Changes are coming, and I hope that you like them, but I won't be bothered if you do not."

Silence.

"You have all sensed the war brewing in the heavens. The greatest war we've ever known — and we've known plenty. When it will finally break, I'm not sure. I only know what has been whispered. The Deity's angels will be fighting the Titans and Greeks — more and more have escaped from their immortal prison. All of this will happen despite the fact that a new queen sits on the Titan throne and she is on our side. Or maybe *because* she is on our side.

"As for now, go home. Rest. Tomorrow I upend your entire world."

Thane, Bjorn and Xerxes shared an uneasy look before flying out of the room. Koldo scowled. Then every member of the army was gone, and Zacharel was alone with Annabelle.

He misted her into another room, one that was clean. "You, I upend now." He backed her into the bed.

Her knees hit and she fell to the mattress with a gasp and a chuckle. Blue-black hair spread around her shoulders. Her robe gaped open, revealing one of his favorite parts of her.

"So naughty, my angel," she said. "And look! Your wings are solid gold now. And there's no snow!"

He looked at the left, then the right. "I am now one of the Elite." One knee on the mattress, two, he straddled her thighs. "That will be celebrated — later. Right now we have a melding to begin."

She was a sensual feast for his eyes. He was so mesmerized, he missed the movement of her hands. She latched on to his shoulders and pushed him down, placing herself on top.

Her grin was languid. "We'll get to the melding. After you've begged." A vow.

A vow she made good on. Her hands roamed over him, stripping him, stroking him, and all too soon he was begging, unable to help himself.

Just before she collapsed over him, wings of white burst from between her shoulder blades.

She sat back up, gasping, and looked the wings over. "What the . . . I don't . . . How did that . . ."

A genuine laugh shook him to his very depths. "When you held the demon essentia, your negative emotions brought forth the demon appearance. You now hold an angelic essentia, and so your positive emotions bring forth this appearance. Now, enough distractions. I want you again, Anna."

"Well, it *is* my turn to beg . . ."

Hours later, when they were both sated, she snuggled in his arms, resplendent and his, all his. This was the life he'd never dared dream for himself. One he would cherish forever, because he knew how close he'd come to losing it.

"So about this melding," she said with a yawn. The wings had vanished, but they would be back.

"You had first to pledge your life to mine, and you did — when I made *you* beg. I took care of the rest."

"Took care of — so we're melded?"

"Now and forever. As soon as I knew you were willing, and while you were distracted, I took a little piece of your spirit. It can be painful, and I did not want you hurting." Not ever again.

"My sweet prince." She kissed the beat of his heart. "Hey, your black spot is gone!"

"You saved me."

"I guess that means you owe me. Which brings me to the second order of business, then. I want to help you fight demons."

"I never doubted it."

"Really? You'll let me, without pouting like a baby?"

"First, I never pout. I ponder, and probably quite sexily. Second, as you've told me, you have already spent too much of your life in a cage. I will not put you in another." But that did not mean he would sit back and let some demon harm her. Zacharel would do his utmost to guard her during every battle. Besides, when one of them died, the other would follow. He would never have to be without her.

"I think that's the sweetest thing you've ever said to me."

"I am a sweet man."

She laughed with carefree abandon, and he loved the sound, was determined to make her laugh like that every day for the rest of their eternity.

"What's so funny?" he teased. "I *am* a sweet man."

"And what's this sweet man's plan for his army, hmm? What changes are you about to rain down on their heads?"

"Discipline, dominance and consequences. Of course."

Another laugh. "You're right. *Sooo* sweet."

"No, but then, my sweetness is reserved for you. Only, ever for you."